THE CRANE WAR

THE METAFRAME WAR: BOOK 5

Graeme Rodaughan

Published by System Zero Productions Pty Ltd, 2019

Trade Paperback ISBN-13: 978-0-9945952-9-4

EPUB Edition ISBN-13: 978-0-6487843-3-3

Cover art by Huw Jones

For Linda, for her unfailing love and support that always leaves me in awe.

I would like to thank a number of people who have assisted with my progress as an author, including Alex, Tim, Lisa, Lena, Marie, Eldon, Michael, Christopher, Perry, Nick, Andrew, Laura, Daniel, Ginger, Jody, and the regular crew of Beta and ARC readers at the Castle Dracula group and my many friends and followers on Goodreads. You have all contributed more than you know to my craft and your support and encouragement are invaluable for this journey.

Books by Graeme Rodaughan

The Metaframe War Series

A Subtle Agency
A Traitor's War
The Dragon's Den
The Day Guard
The Crane War
The Key of Ahknaton

Omnibus Volumes

A Subtle Agency Omnibus (includes A Subtle Agency, A Traitor's War, and The Dragon's Den)

Forthcoming Books in the Metaframe War series

The Metaframe Adept

Dramatis Personae

The Ancients

Ahknaton, Ruler of the Southern Realm, High Priest of the Temple of Thoth. Master Architect. Ramp Master.
Hakron, Second prince of the Southern Realm. Master Scribe. Ramp Master. Ahknaton's brother
Mekra, Princess, Ahknaton's wife.

The Vampire Dominion

Cornelius Crane, King of the Vampire Dominion
Chloe Armitage, General, The Americas, ex Order of Thoth and Crane's chief enforcer
Haras Mosule, General, Middle East, ex Red Empire warrior of the 3rd rank
Dieter Franz, General, Western Europe
Clayton Maze, General, Africa
Shen Zhen, General, East Asia
Frederic Hoffman, Senior Squad Leader, praetorians

The Exiles

Arthur Slayne, (Exiled) Master Strategist, Force Leader, Weapons Grandmaster, Speed Talent
Dwayne Washington, Order Helper

The Mirovar Force Team

Francis Mirovar, Force Leader, Weapons Master
Jay Creeley, Operative, Weapons Master
Peter Lamb, Operative, Armorer, Strength Talent
Chiara Romano, Operative, Combat Surgeon
Anton Slayne, Order novice
Li Wu, Order novice, Weapons Master

The Blake Force Team

Justin Blake, Force Leader (South West) Weapons Master, Strength talent. Former student of Gang Wu
Samuel (Coleridge) Taylor, Operative, Weapons Master

Taylor Feury, Operative, Weapons Master
Patrick Wichowski, Operative, Loremaster
Tim Leung, Operative, Netmaster
Max Guerra, Operative, Netmaster
Red Cevarre, Operative, Combat Surgeon

The Red Empire

Shabbah al Ahmar, aka 'The Red Ghost,' aka Dalien Morte. Head of the Red Empire
Al Ghurab, aka 'The Raven,' Operative inserted into the Order of Thoth
Thueban Kabir, aka 'The Great Serpent,' aka 'Taipan,' Weapons Grandmaster, warrior of the 3rd rank
Tamsah al Ramil, aka 'The Sand Crocodile,' Fist team leader, warrior of the 2nd rank

Shadowstone

James Haley, Chloe Armitage's aide de comp
Louise Wesson, Head of Operations, United States
Gareth Nightingale, Operative, Jerusalem
Architect, AI specialist, East Coast Hub
Siobhan Ulysses, Operative, Panopticon Fortress
Regina Cormack, Commander, Panopticon Fortress
Max Hendrickson, Corporal, Squad Leader, Day Guard

Other Players

Akimitsu, Mekrarian vampire

Gullette, Chameleon, Call of Command

Hana Tanaka, Scientist
Sakura Tanaka, Hana's older sister, member of the Clan of Red Shadows

Ottaviano de Borja, Cardinal, Vatican

Prologue

"The great god Set plotted in secret against the other gods. His plan was uncovered by the wise Thoth, but too late, for the trap was sprung and all were lost from this world." – Ancient papyrus carbon dated prior to the beginning of the first kingdom of Egypt

"After half a lifetime of research I have still not unlocked the mysteries of the Divine Engine of Thoth, except to say that it is as old as time itself and rests as a lever on the fulcrum of reality. An adept with full mastery of the Engine could push on that lever to reshape the universe to their will." – Isaac Newton's secret journal

"I learned of the Metaframe in my later years. I was deeply shocked by the initial implications that in some sense the laws of physics were mutable, but further research demonstrated that the fundamental laws were as persistent as time itself. More to the point, the Metaframe is a navigational device between alternate realities. While the laws of physics stand still, reality is a mutable construct subject to anyone who can access the Metaframe in full." – Deathbed declaration of Albert Einstein

"This is not our original universe." – Nikola Tesla – Collected Speculations and Notes

– Unpublished documents from within Cornelius Crane's secret library

* * *

"The secret and true purpose of the Basilica is to provide a hiding place for the Key of Ahknaton. The fate of the Key was entrusted to my ancestor and this will be its place of eternal rest." – Whispered by Michelangelo.

* * *

Beneath St Peter's Basilica, Vatican City, Sunday Night, January, 1978.

Nineteen workers had already died over the last month. Their bodies carted off in secret by devoutly loyal Swiss guards and disposed of by faithful Mafiosi. Their deaths had been various and unique, but once one of Michelangelo's traps caught the men, the ingenious machines ended their lives with extreme agony and utter violence.

The most recent had died in a caustic pool. The report had detailed that the man's lungs had bled in violent freshets through his mouth as he drowned. Cardinal Ottaviano de Borja wondered which was worse, the caustic pit, or the moving wall that flattened a screaming man into oblivion, or his personal favorite – the five giant hooks on black chains that drew and quartered one hapless fellow. Rigor mortis froze his death scream upon his face before the cardinal's workers recovered his separated body parts and shipped them away for disposal.

The others all died hideous deaths: flayed alive, pressed through a net, drowned in putrefying fluids, disemboweled, gassed with an unknown substance that caused the flesh to boil, skewered, incinerated, vertically and horizontally bisected, or poisoned with a raving, suicidal mania – the last causing the victim to bludgeon himself to death with his own hammer while shouting mad oaths about demonic possession.

The old master had not yet managed to rig a trap that would freeze someone to death, but Ottaviano believed there was still time to discover such a device. Perhaps devils had whispered deadly inspiration into Michelangelo's ears, inspiring him to create the lethal maze beneath the famous basilica. But why create such an enigma? Why fill it with deadly traps? What was the prize hidden here? For surely there was something of utmost value sequestered within the heart of Michelangelo's secret labyrinth.

A secret Ottaviano kept perfectly. Not even his holiness, the Pope, knew what was happening deep beneath Saint Peter's Basilica.

Ottaviano wrinkled his nose, lifting a perfumed red-silk handkerchief to his face. Sweat carved rivulets and tributaries through the thick grime coating the hairy arms and legs of the nearest workers. The cloying odor of their labors filled the air of the subterranean maze. His personal assistant, Umberto Rossi, lifted an electric lantern high above his broad shoulders. Its sharp, white light illuminated the men straining on ropes and pulleys, hauling a giant flagstone up from the floor, revealing another space beneath them.

The workmen secured the ropes, the massive flagstone resting ten feet above the gap in the floor. The cardinal stared into the black depths. Rossi took a step closer, his lamp cutting a swathe through the gloom. The broad flagstone wobbled above the pit, held in place by thick ropes. Avid curiosity filled Ottaviano. What new deadly trap awaited the next man to descend? He grinned, and pushed Rossi in the middle of the back, hard enough to make him take a step forward, but not hard enough to send him into the shadows below.

Rossi jerked backward from the edge and whirled around, a dark look flitting ever so briefly across his peasant's face. He quickly regained control and asked quietly, "Your Eminence?"

"Send in the next man," Ottaviano commanded.

"There are no more volunteers."

"Then you will have to suffice."

Rossi's dark eyes hardened. He nodded once and turned to examine the entrance into the lower tunnel. The laborers backed away, clearing a space around the young priest and the shadowed opening in the floor. They raised more electric lanterns to aid his examination. He knelt next to the entranceway in the floor, directing the light from his lantern into the space below him.

"What do you see?" the cardinal demanded.

"It's a room … a small room. There is a single door. Wait … I can see something … written." Rossi dropped feet first over the side, disappearing from view.

Ottaviano advanced to the edge of the gap in the floor. There was a door of dark wood, bound in iron on the left-side wall. Rossi was examining an inscription on the front of the door.

Ottaviano peered at the gilded letters, his eyes narrowing with effort to read them himself. Rossi's broad shoulders partially shielded the letters. He called down to the priest, "What does it say? Quickly now."

Rossi turned his head back over his left shoulder and said firmly, "Cave magnum malum."

A thrill of excitement ran up Ottaviano's spine. *Beware great evil.* Surely, Michelangelo's prize resided behind this doorway. He snorted derisively. "Beware great evil." The laborers surrounding the hole all took a step backward, many crossing themselves or making some other sign of superstitious fear.

Ottaviano despised their terror, but of course – that was the difference between lesser men and himself – they needed him to tell them what to fear. *Beware great evil.* Well, of course, but define evil? Was death not evil? Had the original sin of Adam and Eve not introduced mortality into the world? Was its opposite, the absence of death, the persistence of youthful immortality not the epitome of good? If immortality was not good, then why were angels immortal? Why was God immortal? Jesus Christ had conquered death. Jesus Christ was immortal. Clearly, the goal of a good Christian life was to imitate the son of God and conquer death by becoming immortal.

Ottaviano had been little more than a boy when these thoughts had come to him while studying the Bible. He had not shared them with the feeble minds of his fellow students or the foolishly pious old priest who taught the class. The idea had possessed him, but its seeming impossibility had defeated him – then he'd discovered within the secret libraries of the Vatican that vampires were real.

Immortality – it was possible. He hungered for it like nothing else in his life. The endless nameless whores, the cocaine, the heroin, the children he'd consumed in frenzies of lust, the raging violence he'd meted out in well-hidden dungeons in Rome, along with the years of repeated attempts to satisfy his many and varied carnal appetites paled before his need to live forever.

What need would he have of redemption from a long-dead god-child when he could live forever.

He would not grow old, hairless, wrinkled, and *limp*. He'd not risen through the ranks of the church faster than anyone on record for nothing. With great position came great power, but the church could not satisfy a man of his vigorous and overarching ambitions.

It was time to send a message to his patron. The vampire who'd guided him into his position of secular power. With Michelangelo's prize as his payment, immortality would be his.

"Get a rope," he ordered the laborers. "Get Father Rossi out of there."

It was time to send the most important message of his mortal life. Before the night had ended, he'd never witness another dawn.

It was a small price to pay to live forever.

***

The Key of Ahknaton lay within Arthur Slayne's reach.

Arthur's spy inserted into the cardinal's personal staff had notified him of the discovery of the last vault less than an hour before. 'Cave magnum malum,' was the surviving clue from Michelangelo's secret notebook that signified the resting place of the Key of Ahknaton. He'd rushed to Saint Peter's Basilica. Father Rossi had guided him to the vault, and now kept watch back in the labyrinth.

There was no time to waste. His opponents had undoubtedly twinned Rossi's message with another to the cardinal's patron. A still unknown vampire, but Arthur suspected the only vampire who would come for the stone would be Cornelius Crane – the king of the Vampire Dominion. The only real question was how much time did he have left before the vampires arrived? Crane would not come by himself. At the very least, a squad of his praetorian guards, or possibly his chief enforcer, Chloe Armitage would attend him.

Father Rossi had forewarned Arthur. He could only assume Crane's agents had alerted his chief opponent. It was a foregone conclusion Crane would have done exactly as Arthur had, and prepositioned himself and his forces nearby for a swift move once his agents revealed the location of the Key of Ahknaton.

He squatted on his haunches next to a lone electric lantern, hesitating, his left hand hovering a foot away from the polished black obsidian stone. The Key rested on a three-foot-tall marble pillar in the middle of a rectangular room twenty feet wide and twice as long. A single bright-white flame floated an inch above it. The stone's starry surface writhing dreamlike beneath an enchanted white tongue of fire.

Clearly, Arthur mused, Michelangelo had kept the full extent of his sorcerous powers secret from everyone.

Apart from its color and intensity, the flame appeared identical to one found atop a lit votive candle. However, it flickered and danced without any means of support. Each febrile movement casting uncanny shadows as dark as outer space on the polished marble walls arching thirty feet above his head. The eldritch shadows dragged at the edges of Arthur's vision, inspiring a possessive desire to turn his head and search for what was hiding within their black hearts. Was something lurking there, a hidden intelligence, or was the fell light of the flickering ivory flame simply a doorway to paranoia and madness?

Arthur focused his mind against the lure of the shadows and studied the flame, his eyes narrowing and his lips pressing into a thin line. Was it an illusion? A trick of the mind to fool the unwary? He wished it was, but knew he couldn't be that lucky. No, the sorcerous flame was all too real, and was without doubt, Michelangelo's final, most powerful, and subtle ward guarding the Key of Ahknaton. Watching the flame intently, he brought his left hand in from the side. He stilled his mind to silence, preparing to Ramp instantly on the first sign of danger. At a distance of three inches, the flame leaned toward his hand, as if attracted to his open palm by an invisible magnetism.

Arthur froze, the flame leaning avidly toward his naked flesh. He watched it for three long seconds, a cool sensation growing in the palm of his hand until icy tendrils prickled his skin. He drew his hand away and rubbed at the three-day growth of dark beard on his chin.

The flame returned to its former position above the Key and continued to defy the known laws of physics.

He stepped away from the pillar and paced through the still, dry air of the vault. He needed to think this through. Michelangelo had engineered every trap in the maze for cold, calculated lethality. This final ward wouldn't be any different. If he failed here, the next person to enter this final vault would step over his lifeless corpse and pick up the Key of Ahknaton without risk. That would almost certainly be the cardinal and he'd most likely hand it to Crane.

Arthur whispered to himself, "Minimal useful information. No time to find out more. Sometimes you've just got to smack the shit out of something." He strode to the far end of the chamber, drawing his katana from the scabbard strapped to his right shoulder. He flourished the blade, the black pearl in the handle gleaming with life in the enchanted candle light.

He fell into deep silence, the Ramp flowered within, and he blurred forward toward the front of the vault. He swung the Black Dragon through a wide arc, the flat tip of the blade connecting with the stone.

A human figure stepped into the open vault doorway.

The Key of Ahknaton speared toward the open doorway like a bullet. The white flame following the stone like a faithful guardian. Shadows advancing in its wake like a dark shroud from the depths of hell, momentarily overwhelming Arthur's electric lantern.

The stone struck the cardinal just below the sternum, disappearing through his scarlet cassock in a spray of blood, his face freezing with shock. The cold-white flame reached him a moment later, blossoming with a sibilant hiss into a pillar around his body.

The stricken prince of the church shrieked, his voice rising in pitch and volume as the white flame inhabited every particle of his body. He danced like a demented puppet controlled by a drunken idiot, staggering across the threshold into the vault in a shambling mess of flailing limbs. The cardinal lurched forward, the white flame, as cold as the infinite depths of space, sucking all heat out of the room.

Waves of frigid air rolled off the flame-encased figure, forcing Arthur to retreat. He shivered, the hairs on his skin rising to attention, backing away as the cardinal staggered forward. Shadows pursued by the engorged flame leaping away to the far corners of the chamber.

The cardinal jerked his way into the vault. The man's face twisted in an agonized parody of a human being. His eyes bulging. His flesh driven white as snow by the sorcerous cold. Blood dropped in thick congealed blobs from ears, nose and mouth. He shrieked again and again. Great singular gasps punctuating his wild screams. His utter desperation to survive driving his flesh beyond all limits of suffering. His eyes swelled to the size of golf balls, bursting like over-ripe grapes, leaving dark crimson holes in his face. His hair sloughed off in waves, shattering as it struck the floor. His tongue, rigid, and frozen solid, protruded through his gaping mouth. His jaw spasmed and clenched, shattering the tongue, sending shards of red flesh and white tooth enamel flying.

All about the cardinal, a nimbus of white flame rose and swirled above his head, rising higher and higher to lick at the peaked ceiling thirty feet above.

Arthur covered his face with his left arm, the searing cold forcing him back to the rear of the vault as the cardinal shambled on creaking, bone-snapping steps toward the central pillar.

Compelled by the mystic flame, the prince of the Church advanced toward the short, central pillar. Each step truncated his height, flesh turning to dust with each tortured yard. His feet long gone; he lurched forward on stumps. Cardinal Ottaviano de Borja reached the pillar and collapsed around it. His final despairing shriek silenced mid-breath as he dissolved into a pile of gray ash. His final remains settling in a dusty heap surrounding the base of the stout pillar.

The Key of Ahknaton reposed once more upon the flat top of the marble pillar. A single thunderous note peeled throughout the chamber. Whatever magic warded the Key was now over. The Key sat, an ancient, alien thing, its skin writhing with captured starlight. Arthur dropped his arm, his gaze flashing across the chamber.

The Key was unguarded, ready for him to take it.

Movement dragged his gaze away from the Key. A tall lithe woman with long dark free-flowing hair, stepped gracefully across the threshold into the vault. She wore a close-fitting black jumpsuit. A lightweight black leather coat draped her shoulders and swirled around her knees. The gore-soaked blade in her hands was instantly recognizable – the Red Dragon.

Armitage!

Cornelius Crane emerged from the shadows in the sunken antechamber. He was wearing a dark suit beneath a black leather trench coat. He momentarily doffed a dark-gray fedora hat and ducked to clear the low entrance of the doorway. He strode into the vault, his gaze arresting on the Key for a brief moment before flicking upward to lock upon Arthur at the opposite end of the chamber.

Arthur snapped the Black Dragon into guard position above his left shoulder. The naked blade gleaming majestically in the electric lantern light. Against either of these opponents he'd have taken his chances, but against both together? He tightened his eyes for a moment, the only way he was going to escape this vault alive was by finding a way through the two most dangerous vampires in existence. He summoned the wild Ramp into veiled existence, able to unleash its coiled power in an instant. The wild Ramp rode strong emotions, welling forth from a place deep within. Blue fire suffused his nerves and muscles. A dry smile curled the edges of his mouth, his gaze watchful and alert.

Crane drew his weapon. The long bastard sword clearing the scabbard at his waist with a sibilant hiss. He held it with his right hand, the dusky blade slanting down across his body from right to left. The length and heft of the weapon a perfect match for his vampiric speed and strength. His brown eyes widened in avid interest, he smiled and said, "Mr. Slayne, I presume. You have answered the last question posed by Michelangelo in his secret notes – what is the final ward guarding the Key of Ahknaton?" he nodded once. "Such assistance should not go unrewarded. Yes, I think a quick rather than a slow death will do."

Armitage flicked her sword, fresh gore painting the nearest wall in a thin red ribbon. The blade vanished before reappearing in guard position above her left shoulder. A slight smile graced her sensual lips. Her vivid blue eyes studied Arthur, her gaze as relentless and cold as an advancing glacier.

Crane raised his right eyebrow; it was all the signal Armitage needed.

Three things happened at once.

Crane swapped his sword to his left hand, the smoky-gray blade angled point first at Arthur. He blurred toward the pillar, his right arm outstretched, his long fingers grasping for the Key of Ahknaton.

Armitage leaped, wall running to Arthur's left. She shifted the Red Dragon to her left hand. The gleaming blade arcing down like a silvery thunderbolt.

Arthur had a single reckless chance to win the Key and his life. He drew the wild Ramp to fruition, cobalt fire racing along his limbs. He blurred toward Crane. Taking advantage of the polished marble floor, he leaned back, sliding feet first toward Crane's boots. With his right hand held high, he feinted toward Crane's blade with the Black Dragon.

The vampire king leaped into the air to avoid Arthur's attack.

Sliding beneath Crane's leap, Arthur swept the Black Dragon back against Armitage's savage strike. His katana met the Red Dragon with a ringing blow, blade scraping against blade without sparks, neither weapon able to consume its sibling's edge.

Armitage passed behind him, her sword deflecting away.

Above him, Crane fell toward him, his great blade slashing down.

Arthur's right foot spun in a wide arc across the floor. Pivoting on his other foot, his left hand rose up, sweeping across the top of the marble pillar. His head swiveled; Crane was closest, Armitage advanced upon him from behind. He snapped the Black Dragon up again, grinding the meteoric-iron blade against the vampire king's descending sword.

The blades met, scraping against each other without sparks. Crane's blade was the equal of his own. The tips of Arthur's outstretched fingers brushed the Key – sending it spinning away. The momentum of his right-foot kick curled him upright on his left foot. Pushing forward in a single movement, his left-hand closing into a fist on empty air, he sprinted toward the open doorway.

A pair of thuds reverberated behind him; Crane's boots landing on the polished stone.

Armitage advanced through the vault in a whisper of displaced air.

Arthur instinctively jerked to the right, a thrown blade slashing past him. The Red Dragon embedded itself to the hilt in the dark wood of the vault door; a thunderous crack of violated oak echoing throughout the maze.

Blurring through the doorway, he flung his left hand out, slamming the heavy door shut behind him. The silvery blade of the trapped katana, a gleaming dragon's tooth protruding into the sunken antechamber. He leaped, landing in the upper tunnel. He severed a pair of thick ropes. The Black Dragon, flashing in the soft light of the lanterns. The giant flagstone crashed back into the floor with a reverberating thud. It was wide and heavy; it'd taken a dozen strong men with ropes and pulleys five minutes to lift it ten feet off the floor.

It would slow the vampires by a matter of seconds.

Seconds, Arthur hoped would be enough for him to escape. He ran for his life, reaching the streets beyond the boundaries of Vatican City a couple of minutes later. He pulled to a halt in a darkened alleyway, his sword drawn, peering into the street lamp lit gloom behind him. His eyes searched the rooftops for the slightest movement but only still shadows and gloomy outlines greeted him.

He took a deep breath and sighed. Father Rossi was dead, his gutted corpse passed in the maze as he'd made his escape, another member of the Order of Thoth lost to Armitage's blade. Arthur's eyes narrowed with disgust. He'd escaped with his life, but he'd lost the Key of Ahknaton to the vampires. The bitter ashes of defeat and failure choked his throat – he could barely draw breath into his lungs.

Slamming his sword into its scabbard, he turned away, disappearing like a wraith into the shadows.

* * *

"Wisdom is borne on two vessels; one is joy and the other is sadness. Both must be honored or both will be lost." – Gang Wu

* * *

Boston, April 26th, Eighteen years before the present, 23:12

Arthur Slayne stood on a parapet overlooking the Massachusetts General Hospital.

The tang of a late spring shower filled the night air. A Nokia mobile phone began ringing a couple of yards behind him. He crossed his arms over his chest and frowned down at the multi-story obstetrics wing across the street. The black clouds decided at that moment to begin their next shower and light drops began to wet his dark, unruly hair.

Gang Wu spoke behind him, "Arthur, it's William – you have a grandson, they've named him Anton after Anna's father."

Arthur sighed with relief, Anna's labor had been long and hard. She'd insisted on a natural birth, trusting in her Ramp genetics to ease the process, but there had been difficulties and the birth had dragged through the afternoon and into the night.

Arthur, Gang Wu, Jonathan Thunder-Axe, and the recently married Francis and Juliette Mirovar had kept watch from the top of the building across the street. Anna and William Slayne had hidden within Boston for a year under the aliases of Anna and William Smith. The five people watching from above, like guardian angels or flesh and blood gargoyles, were the only ones who knew the truth.

A truth the Order of Thoth must never discover. It wasn't enough for Ramin Kain to frame him for the murder of his friends, George Madison and Mary Creeley, to see him exiled from the Order, to corrupt an institution he revered. No, Kain had come after his family. He'd given their location to the vampires, and they had barely managed to survive an attack by an overwhelming force.

The vampires hadn't counted on Francis Mirovar, Gang Wu and himself visiting his children that night. It had been bloody mayhem, but the extra forces had ensured the survival of all instead of the death of William and Anna. It was dangerous to be a Slayne, and the current leadership of the Order would stop at nothing to eliminate everyone associated with his name.

Arthur's assembled friends had helped him move Heaven and Earth to keep Anna and William safe by hiding them. His new grandson would probably never know the Ramp, the abilities would skip a generation while the corruption of the Order of Thoth burnt itself out, or destroyed the Order altogether. He would provide for the following generation. He would ensure they would own the legacy of their powers.

He'd initiated a plan to kill Crane and Armitage and destroy the Vampire Dominion. It would take another twenty years to mature. He closed his eyes thoughtfully; about the same time his new grandson would take to reach adulthood. Anton would have no part to play in the destruction of the Vampire Dominion. No, his role was to remain hidden and carry the Slayne line forward. It would be Anton's children who would emerge back into a world vastly different from the current one.

Arthur turned around, dropping down from the parapet to the concrete roof with a single step. The others stood in a line in front of him, he clapped Gang and Jonathan on the shoulders and grinned as he looked around at his friends. "Let's find a bar and celebrate."

The birth of his grandson was the only bright light in an otherwise dismal year. A drink with the finest the Order had to offer would round out one of the proudest days of his life.

Chapter One

"Lions adapt their hunting strategy to the specific vulnerabilities of their prey – and so do I." – Chloe Armitage

* * *

New York City, South of Brooklyn, September 10th, 23:45

James Haley checked the homeless man he'd abducted forty-five minutes earlier.

He'd used the Panopticon to find someone no one would miss; issuing a simple search targeting the least number of social connections. The man was a habitual loner who made a perfect solution for James' current mission. He'd propped the vagrant up against the left-side rear wheel of his black SUV. The vehicle gleamed beneath the powerful lamps running in two strips down the length of a small warehouse. Shadowstone owned the building through a string of near-untraceable holding companies. Sub-contractors had kept the warehouse spotlessly clean and well maintained for years, and no one had used it – until now.

James pressed his fingers against the man's throat. His pulse was steady, if a little weak. He was not the healthiest subject to shoot with a sleeper dart, but it was more important that no one would come searching for him.

He'd operated with minimal forewarning of the new mission. His last meeting with Chloe in his office had ended less than two hours earlier. He'd spent ten minutes setting a number of tasks and searches running in the Panopticon, and then driven his car to the warehouse south of Brooklyn. She'd wanted a means of fast transport for the chameleons. A drone, newly delivered to Shadowstone was on its way, and would arrive in another five minutes. He'd retracted the warehouse's roof-hangar doors, revealing a rectangular gap twenty yards across and twice that long onto the city-lit night sky.

"Beggars can't be choosers," James whispered in a matter-of-fact tone as he wiped his fingers clean on a handkerchief. He followed up by wiping his prints off the man's neck with the same cloth, before putting his leather gloves back on. There was every chance there would be nothing left of the man by tomorrow, but James was nothing if not thorough in covering his tracks.

He briefly pressed his lips into a thin line. It was a small mercy the man would never wake from the sleeper dart. He was a reward, of a sort, for the chameleons. Small mercies were best, no man wanted to be torn apart by a predator. It was better the nameless vagrant never woke up to the horror of his fate.

James acknowledged he was undoubtedly a killer, perhaps even a murderer, but he wasn't cruel – no, never cruel.

He walked around to the back of the SUV, and lifted the tailgate. He reached inside and flicked a switch on an electronic control. A thin, choking cry emanated in perfectly rendered sound from the car's audiovisual system. Thirty seconds later, it played again. He'd downloaded the sound file from Chloe's TAC helmet after her first encounter with the chameleons. He'd no idea what the sound meant but it sent a shiver crawling up his spine whenever he heard it. At the very least, it should attract the attention of the lizards.

James stepped away from the SUV, brushing imaginary dirt from his gloves. The cry was alien, and yet seemed to carry a plaintive sense of loss, overlaid with an implacable need for vengeance. The implicit threat was palpable. The cry continued to play twice a minute on a continuous loop, raising the short hairs on the back of his thick neck with each rendition. He took a deep breath and let it out slowly. He was carrying an uprated .45 caliber Glock within a shoulder holster beneath his suit jacket. The ammunition was a Shadowstone special load designed for maximum damage to unarmored flesh but he figured if he needed to use it, he wouldn't survive the night.

He snorted in a moment of self-derision. His choices had rendered his survival into a day-by-day proposition. He'd thrown his lot in with Chloe and he'd see it through to whatever end. It was too late to waste time second guessing past decisions. He scanned the entrances. They were all locked, except a large garage roller door that opened onto an alleyway behind the warehouse. The bright illumination within the warehouse spilled through the broad doorway into the gloom. He was at an obvious disadvantage standing in the middle of a large, well-lit space while anyone could be watching unseen within the thick shadows shrouding the far side of the alleyway.

The alien cry sounded again.

A bead of sweat appeared on James' brow and he reflexively wiped it away. The waiting was the hard part. He checked his watch, only three minutes had passed since he'd started playing the recorded sound. He glanced back at the alleyway behind the warehouse, where the hell were they?

The darkness beyond the roller door thickened into terrifying solidity. The first chameleon emerged from the shadows like gray smoke congealing into a living nightmare. James' jaw dropped, then he clamped it shut. It was all he could do to avoid reaching for his gun. Chloe had expressly warned him to avoid drawing a weapon. Any overt show of aggression would invite deadly attack. He took an involuntary step backward, then held his ground, his pulse thumping in his ears. The memory of what the chameleons had done to nearly twenty armed gangsters uppermost in his mind.

The creature advanced a dozen feet. It stood close to eight feet tall, heavy through chest, shoulder and thigh. It's skin, a mottled blend of grays and bone-whites rolled over thick muscles bunching and releasing with coiled power. Its coal-black eyes, filled with a shallow wariness resting over unfathomable depths, flicked with cold deliberation about the nearly empty warehouse.

A second monster stepped from the shadows. A half-foot shorter than the first, it moved to the right, sniffing the air briefly before locking its spine-chilling gaze on James. Its shadow-filled eyes drifted lower by a fraction of an inch – staring hard at his throat. A thin line of clear drool escaped past rows of bared teeth, dropping in wet splats on the pale concrete of the warehouse floor.

For a second, James' mind froze, then kicked frenziedly into gear. Where was the third? There were supposed to be three. He dragged his gaze off the two chameleons he could see, his instincts screaming at him to run. He took a deep breath, let it out slowly, and scanned the warehouse – there was nothing to see.

The choking cry sounded again.

The two chameleons snarled, hissing their obvious displeasure.

James' hand flew into the rear of the SUV and switched the recording off.

The creatures fell into silence, watching him balefully, their muscular tails lashing slowly behind them.

A thin ripping screech erupted from the right-side front corner of the SUV. James jerked away to his left. His right hand reflexively reaching into his jacket for his gun. He stopped himself from drawing it just in time, the two chameleons had ducked their heads and appeared to be on the verge of charging forward.

A third chameleon ghosted into view to the right of the SUV, dragging a single talon along the side of the car. The SUV's inbuilt Shadowstone ceramic armor flaked and shattered, giving way before the creature's black talon like it was tinfoil. The chameleon's gaze locked on his own. Its jaw gaped open, revealing rows of serrated teeth. A thin line of clear drool leaked past the creature's gleaming teeth, splashing in fat drops on the concrete floor.

James guts curdled and clenched. He'd never experienced anything quite like this before. The towering creature looked upon him as prey and clearly lusted to hunt, kill and eat him. His vaunted combat skills meant nothing against such a foe.

The third chameleon took a step forward, and said with a voice that was surprisingly human, "Offer insult? Why play this death call?" It cocked its head nearly one-hundred and eighty degrees to the left. "Foolish man."

"I'm … I'm sorry," James stammered. "It's what Chloe provided me to call you with."

The creature stood up to its full height, easily eight feet tall and pinned James with a glare. "Your master … night stalker, blood thief … chose poorly."

The silence stretched, broken only by James' pulse drumming in his ears.

The creatures raised their heads as one, apparently noticing something beyond what James could sense. The chameleons blurred and then vanished.

"What the hell!" James swore. Although half-relieved by their sudden absence, what if Chloe showed up now? The chameleons had disappeared like ghosts, and he was standing around like an idiot with his thumb up his ass. "What a clusterfuck."

James shook his head, the prospect of using the chameleons as some sort of ally filled him with dread. He frowned and shook his head; this was the first decision Chloe had made that he didn't understand. The creatures were too powerful to control, how could she ever hope to bend them to her will?

A distant thrum came out of the sky. The sound grew louder, a pair of turbines ripping apart the night air over the warehouse. The drone appeared, descending straight down through the open roof into the warehouse. It sported a turbine on the end of each wing. The roaring engines were facing straight up, allowing the machine to land vertically like a helicopter. Once in the air, the turbines could turn ninety degrees to face forward allowing jet airliner performance. The tail of the drone rode high, a wide ramp opening beneath it allowing access to a cargo bay that could carry twenty troopers and all their gear, or easily hide three camouflaged chameleons.

Movement caught the edge of James' eye. Chloe appeared at the entrance to the alleyway carrying a black duffel bag. She'd changed out of her corporate suit into combat fatigues, with her sword strapped to her hip. She shouted over the descending whine of the turbines, "James, are they here? Did they come?"

James nodded. "Yes, but they vanished once the drone showed up."

She pursed her lips. "Stay here, I'll find them."

"They—" James shouted.

Chloe dropped her bag and vanished, her extraordinary speed eclipsing his ability to track her movement.

"—didn't like the recording," he finished quietly. James sighed. Everyone around him completely outclassed him. He glowered at the cooling drone and fingered the two-yard rip in the armored side panels of his SUV – something would have to change.

He would have to change.

* * *

Chloe ascended to the roof of the warehouse and opened her senses up to their vampiric maximums.

The early-autumn night filled her awareness. Five miles to the east, a commercial jet rumbled to its landing at JFK airport. Above her the clouds were a rumpled blanket of silvery grays, and satin blacks lit from beneath by the glowing effulgence of the surrounding metropolis. A gentle breeze ruffled her hair with the faint tang of approaching rain. Her nostrils flared, there was nothing of interest upwind of her position. She whirled to her left, staring down the length of the warehouse. Forty yards away, the three chameleons stood with casual insolence beyond the open roof-hangar doors.

The female Shemina, glared avidly down at James and croaked once, a sound filled with ravenous inquiry. To her right, the leader Gullette, tilted his head and stared at Chloe, a slow grin arching across his reptilian face.

The dark orbs of his eyes reflected the city behind Chloe. A pair of arteries ran in warm rippling trails along the underside of his pale throat. His heart rate was slow and steady, a single beat every three seconds. All visible details that would disappear from view the moment he activated the chameleon power of his skin.

Chloe suspected they were watching her as carefully as she was watching them. Deception would be difficult to hide from a predator with senses at least as good as her own. But deceive them she must. She would never honor her promise to share power. She expected they knew she would betray them in the end and they would plan to betray her first.

If a lion and a crocodile were stuck in a lifeboat, they could agree to row to shore for mutual benefit, but all bets were off once they crossed the shoreline. The chameleons would be useful before she accessed the Metaframe with the Key of Ahknaton safely in hand, but afterwards there would be no place for their species in her world.

An apex predator is by definition singular – it was the last truth they would ever know.

Chloe's eyes tightened and she snapped, "He is protected!"

Gullette urged, "Replace him. He is rich in flesh; strong, wet bones!"

The other large male Kavanne, barked once, his head bobbing forward and back in agreement. Shemina edged toward the entrance into the warehouse her tail lashing, her mouth gaping open to drool.

The Red Dragon appeared within Chloe's grip, the tip of the blade pointing like Death's own finger at a spot in the middle of Gullette's forehead.

The chameleon merely lowered his head slightly. His grin deepened; his eyes gleaming with reflected city light. "No armor?" he asked quizzically, his gaze locked on Chloe's eyes. He waved his hand at the interior of the warehouse beneath them. "Yet you take such risk … he your mate?"

Chloe smiled without mirth and stated with glacial hardness, "He is not for eating. Do not test me on this or at least one of you will die tonight."

The other chameleons stared at their leader, their bodies still as statues but poised for action. Gullette's eyes narrowed momentarily, and he said, "The thin one. He stinks of poison. We not like."

"I'll source a replacement."

Gullette spread his hands wide, talons uncurling in the gloom. His dark mirror eyes flicked over Kavanne and Shemina.

"One each?"

Gullette nodded once.

Chloe sheathed her sword and suggested, "Then let's descend and begin practicing for the first mission."

Gullette stared at Chloe, his eyes flat and hard. He barked once; a low sound filled with menace. "Kavanne's call, it speaks of the dead, use it not."

Chloe blinked, then nodded once. From this moment on, James would manage the chameleons' needs and transport them in the drone. She shouldn't need to call them again. She indicated the warehouse floor below with a flick of her head, and then leaped the sixty feet down to the polished concrete.

The chameleons followed.

Chloe landed in a crouch, stood up, and strode over to where James waited next to the SUV. She indicated the homeless man with a hand gesture, and ordered, "Get rid of this one, we need three more, and no sleeper darts. Be back here in an hour."

"Yes, Ma'am," James replied. He turned away, hoisting the homeless man like a sack of potatoes over his shoulder and throwing him into the back of the SUV. A dozen seconds later, the SUV's tires screeched over the concrete as he drove the vehicle into the rear alleyway.

Chloe turned back to the chameleons and directed, "I need you to catch me without harming me."

Gullette snorted, the others barked and coughed, then Gullette nodded once.

Chloe fell into silence, stopped short of initiating a supreme Ramp, and blurred away.

The chameleons vanished.

Without her supreme Ramp, she couldn't detect them, but then neither would her target. She had to ensure the chameleon's capability to capture someone as fast as her maximum vampiric ability, absent the supreme ramp, without harming them. After all, it was imperative she kept her target alive and unharmed at all costs.

No plan survives contact with the enemy, and victory goes to those who can adapt to advantage when circumstances change. Chloe was willing to bet her life on being the most adaptable player in the game against Crane.

A game for the future of reality.

* * *

Chloe watched the New York City streets rolling past the car's window, her mind a million miles away.

The chameleons had performed well. There had been moments during the training that'd made her gasp. They had not taken advantage of her vulnerability and killed her while they had the chance. They still believed in the lure of power she'd dangled in front of them, at least enough to forestall casual violence.

She closed her eyes, replaying the captures within her perfect memory. Had she been lucky to kill the first chameleon nine nights ago? The question was an uneasy one but necessary to ask. No, her supreme ramp was still a key advantage, but even with her extraordinary speed she hadn't been able to both kill one chameleon and defend against Kavanne's attack. The big chameleon's strike had penetrated her defenses and kicked her across a street.

The chameleons were diabolically fast and dangerous. Her normal vampiric speed, at the top of the upper range for vampires had enabled escape times that ranged from twenty-three seconds at best to twelve seconds at worst. Every vampire in the world was vulnerable to these near invisible creatures, and even a Ramp master with a speed talent would only last a handful of seconds longer.

As dangerous as they were to handle, they were perfect for the mission she had in mind for them.

The black SUV started to slow, Crane's citadel looming over the street in front of them. Chloe glanced across at James. He'd been quiet since the training finished. Withdrawn, wary, he'd need a few words of encouragement. She tilted her head slightly and opened her mouth to speak to him.

A ping resounded though the car, a Panopticon message appearing in a heads-up display on the interior of the SUV's windscreen. It read, 'Timestamp: 02:57:14. Target Hana Tanaka observation warning. Search duration post initiation 4:45:32. 15:00 minutes elapsed since last contact. Recapture protocol initiated.'

"Damn!" James swore.

Chloe watched him closely. Hana Tanaka was the technical specialist who was her best hope of getting rid of the killer implant next to her brain stem linked to Crane's heartbeat.

"I set the surveillance systems running on Tanaka nearly five hours ago. She's bolted."

Chloe frowned. "Did your search tip her off?"

James shook his head. "Not a chance. But she's gone to ground. We need resources in Japan as soon as possible to find her."

Chloe hissed, a terrible frustration rising within her. Her fangs descended into attack position. James blanched, recoiling against the door. She blinked, sighing. Her fangs retracted, and she put her hand gently on his shoulder. "Don't worry … setbacks happen. We can't use Shadowstone in Japan without tipping off Crane. What other resources can we use?"

"I'll have to go myself."

Chloe shook her head. "No, you're needed here with the chameleons. Keep the Panopticon searching for her. She'll have to leave a trace sooner or later. We're talking Japan, there are more cameras in Japan than people. Monitor the situation, she'll turn up."

James assented, pulling the SUV to a halt in front of the towering skyscraper Crane used as the seat of his dominion.

"Try to get some sleep," Chloe advised. "But, assume you're on a war footing at a battle front. Things are coming to a head, be ready to move at a moment's notice."

James nodded. "Yes, Chloe."

Chloe exited the car and walked through the main entrance into Crane's citadel. After all the recent events, Crane would call a meeting before dawn. It was easier to be on site when the inevitable order came, and she could avail herself of a warm meal in the feeding halls while she waited. After all, she mused with a hard glint in her eyes, live food was always preferable to the plastic bags of re-heated blood in her penthouse.

The solution to Crane's implant would have to wait while events rushed forward to their conclusions. Events she planned on being able to shape. Crane had attempted to trap her with his implant technology, but there was always more than one way to deal with a problem.

Chloe expected to exploit something Crane had missed. As clever as he was, it was impossible to anticipate everything.

* * *

Late afternoon sunlight slashed through high set windows and skylights into a deserted Tokyo warehouse.

Winches and industrial-sized gray-steel hooks hung by dark chains from overhead gantries. Ancient shipping containers marked with faded kanji characters stood in orderly rows. Lines of obsolete five-and-nine-ton trucks, many draped with military style camouflage tarpaulins, flanked the ancient post-war containers.

Hana Tanaka moved down an open aisle between a row of steel containers and dusty vehicles. Her movements were barely audible beyond the soft tap of her sneakers, but stood out amongst the stillness of the warehouse. She strode confidently but her mind squirmed with doubt. She was relying on a brother and a sister she hadn't seen or spoken to for more than five years. Fumio and Sakura were three years her senior and had been with the Yakuza for at least five years, and now she was seeking their protection.

They'd not joined an ordinary Yakuza clan. The Akai Kage no Ichizoku, or Clan of Red Shadows, was secretive beyond anything she'd ever encountered. The last time she'd spoken to Fumio he'd warned her to stay away. That his world was not her world. That vampires were real and ruled in secret, and that only the Clan of Red Shadows could protect anyone from them, but she wouldn't need protection if she kept a low profile. He had however, given her the address of this warehouse, and impressed upon her to only come if vampires threatened her life. Sakura had simply warned her emphatically that she never wanted to see her younger sister again.

She'd almost obeyed her older sister, but she had no one else to turn to, and nowhere else to go.

The head of research of the Medical Control Systems unit had initiated the development of implants with a powdered silver payload and exotic sheaths. Sheaths made of exotic materials human flesh rejected. With her specialist knowledge, and her family's awareness of the existence of vampires, it hadn't been hard to join the dots. The implants were for use on vampires, and only their ruler would commission such a technology. There was an obvious conclusion: The king of the vampires owned Control Systems Incorporated.

Then someone murdered her manager two and a half weeks ago, and senior management promoted her as his replacement. She'd been horrified by what had happened, not so much by the deaths of the previous head of research and the CEO, but by the fact a similar fate waited for her.

A pair of government operatives from the Tokyo branch of the Bureau of State Security had interviewed her at length. They'd been polished performers, but they seemed more interested in understanding how much she knew rather than in solving the murders. She'd played her part with a straight face, revealing nothing of her suspicions. When the operatives departed the building and closed the investigation with a verdict of murder/suicide, she'd made her decision.

Hana had spent the next two weeks planning her escape. Her final act at Control Systems Inc was to wipe all the technical data for the 'vampire,' implants from the company's networks, as well as destroying the off-site data backups. She'd downloaded a copy of the relevant engineering files to a portable data stick now resting in the front pocket of her tight-fitting blue jeans. It was best to have an insurance policy if she ever needed to bargain for her life.

Hana reached the end of the line of containers and trucks. A steel trapdoor stood open in the corner farthest from the entrance. There was no sign of her brother or anyone else. She paused for a long moment, then advanced to the edge of the opening in the floor.

The trapdoor opened up onto a flight of concrete stairs. A single ancient fluorescent light lit the bottom of the stairwell.

Hana descended; it was the only place she had left to go.

Chapter Two

"That the vast majority of humanity prefers a comforting illusion to a harsh reality has long aided my cause." – Cornelius Crane

* * *

New York City, Cornelius Crane's Citadel, September 11th, 03:01

Cornelius Crane plumbed the depths of his precognitive powers.

As the risk of death increased and the moment of final confrontation approached, Cornelius' vision of the future solidified into ever greater detail. The normal array of options lit with varying amounts of probability had coalesced into a single bright line of near-term events that approached certainty.

Three threats had matured with terrifying swiftness. The most distant was the Red Empire fist team approaching from the east. Their slow speed indicated they were traveling by ship, most likely hidden within a cargo carrier. He would allow them to advance to landfall in early October; their fates would be determined by a trap he would lay within the island of Manhattan.

Next was the looming confrontation with Mekra. Potentially, the most dangerous opponent he faced amongst the three. The Obsidian Claw ninja vampire sired from her tainted blood continued to elude his forces in China and make its way toward her donjon in the Carpathian Mountains. He dared not make a preemptive move against Mekra, as she appeared to be drawing her offspring toward her. It was imperative he extinguished the new vampire strain before it spread and overtook the world. Waiting for his forces to either catch the ninja vampire as it travelled west, or trap it at Mekra's donjon, was the best strategy. Three of his generals, Franz, Zhen and Mosule and their personal praetorians were scouring the Eurasian continent with the aid of the Panopticon. It would have to be enough; he had no further resources to commit to the search for the Mekrarian vampire.

Then there was Anton Slayne, now shadowed by a second figure. Someone else with a tantalizing familiarity was moving into the frame and a final confrontation was imminent. The events of the last twenty-four hours had accelerated the timeline immensely. Somehow, Anton Slayne had become the most immediate threat to his life and without careful intervention that peril would result in his own death.

Whatever hostility Anton Slayne represented; it would manifest within the next twelve to twenty-four hours. Due to the closeness of the death cusp event, the young Slayne appeared with mystic clarity in his vision, revealing to some extent his location and intent. He was moving west from Minneapolis on an almost straight line toward the Panopticon.

A fact that could not be an accident.

As for the second shadow behind Anton Slayne, he'd never witnessed its like before. It stalked just beyond the boundaries of his supernatural perception. He pressed at it. Attempting to drag the identity of the shadow figure into the light through sheer force of will, a bead of perspiration erupting on his smooth forehead. The shadow slipped away, elusive, his efforts to capture it like clutching at fog.

He pressed again and again, but for no result.

Cornelius dropped out of his visionary state and drew a hand across his damp brow. He sat alone on an elegant seventeenth-century French divan in his library, as still as one of the statues in his personal quarters. Was the Panopticon the younger Slayne's next target? If he succeeded in destroying it, what then? Until Shadowstone commissioned the new Panopticon at the East Coast Hub, the Vampire Dominion would remain blind, deeply compromising his efforts to capture the Mekrarian vampire in the East. In addition, what knowledge would Slayne and his companions glean from the Panopticon before they destroyed it? He must reinforce the defenses of the Panopticon with what remained of his best troops. He would strip the citadel in Manhattan down to a skeleton staff to support the defense of the Panopticon. The remaining staff would continue the citadel's basic function as a command center and draw the approaching Red Empire fist team into a trap with the illusion of a fully functional citadel.

As for the elusive shadow, Anton Slayne was not operating alone. Whether the younger Slayne understood the presence of another or not was a moot point. By the time the death cusp arrived, someone capable of being a threat to Cornelius' life would reinforce Anton Slayne.

However, he would not enter the cusp alone, he would ensure his best weapon was at his side for the inevitable confrontation.

In the meantime, he'd evacuate his library, artworks, and Metaframe lore to a new safe location. Of the Metaframe artifacts, he now carried the Papyrus of Hakron the Scribe in a golden scroll tube sheathed in Kevlar at his waist, and the Key of Ahknaton rested above his heart, dangling from a polished titanium chain around his neck.

He rose from the divan, strode to his desk and punched a button on the console. "Ursula, find generals Maze and Armitage. I want them in the war room in thirty minutes."

There was the briefest of pauses. "Yes, Sir."

Cornelius placed his right hand over the Key of Ahknaton, its cold hardness pressing into his sternum beneath his shirt. The only way someone was going to acquire the Key was over his cold, still corpse. He smiled – with his now appropriately motivated enforcer at his side, that would be all but impossible to achieve.

* * *

"The Panopticon must be protected at all costs," Crane ordered, stabbing a long finger at general Clayton Maze. "Spare nothing in its defense. That system is critical to our world-wide operations and we cannot allow an Order of Thoth force team to destroy it."

Chloe looked on as Crane stared hard at Maze, the latter rubbing his chin slowly, his large dark eyes narrowing slightly. Crane didn't need to mention that the Panopticon was an essential part of the force attempting to apprehend the rogue vampire of a 'new type,' forging his way across China to an unknown goal. The new vampire was a mystery she would love to penetrate, but events were not offering opportunities to do so, and she had little spare time to forge them. She broke the silence hanging in the air between Crane and Maze. "If the location of the Panopticon has been revealed to the remnants of the Order of Thoth it's only a matter of time before they attempt to assault it."

Crane's head whipped around to face her. "And what do you know about that?"

"Nothing more than anyone else here," Chloe said. She arched an eyebrow. "You're the one implying the Order stand poised to strike it. Given there are only two force teams left, it would be either Mirovar or Blake."

Crane studied her briefly, and then turned back to Maze. "In any event, I expect an attack on the Panopticon. I want you to take full onsite tactical command of the defense of the fortress. I will second the remaining praetorians from my citadel force to your command. In addition, I will assign most of the Day Guard currently stationed at the citadel to you, as well as the next tranche completing their training at Fort Dix. That will give you sixteen praetorians and forty-eight Day Guard troopers to bolster the forces stationed at the Panopticon site.

Maze said in measured tones, "Have the praetorians fed?"

"Within the last hour. Our local stock of humans in our feeding halls are almost depleted. They won't need to feed for another two days, which will be more than enough time. The need to protect the Panopticon is urgent, an attack is imminent."

Maze leaned forward slightly and inquired, "Are there any other instructions?"

Crane lips pressed into a thin determined line. He took a step back from the war room table, rising to his full height and stated forcefully, "I have given you the resources you need, and nearly two centuries of life after plucking you from that hell-hole in New Orleans. It's time for you to repay your debts and do your duty. Protect the Panopticon or don't bother to come back."

The threat lay heavy in the air. No one took a breath until Maze replied quietly, "I'm ever your loyal servant. I have never forgotten past debts. I will do my duty. Have no fear my liege, the Panopticon will outlast any Order of Thoth scum that attempt to destroy it."

Crane nodded once; his eyes fierce with passion. "You have your orders."

"Yes, Sir," Maze replied with calm confidence, pushing himself away from the table and standing up. He pulled the sleeves of his dark suit over his wrists, a grim smile caressing his full lips.

As he turned to leave, Crane called him back, "One last thing Clayton. I'm promoting Louise Wesson to head of the worldwide Shadowstone organization. She'll report directly to me from now on. I don't want your attention distracted by other responsibilities."

Maze nodded impassively, and said firmly, "Yes, Sir." Then turned on his heel and left the war room.

There was a long moment of silence as Crane watched Maze leave the room, the door closing behind him. Crane would scramble his remaining forces in the north of the United States to defend the Panopticon. Chloe was fully aware of the site, its inherent defenses and the forces already in place. The addition of seventeen combat trained and war experienced vampires and nearly fifty day guards would make the site all but impregnable.

If the Mirovar force team tried to assault the Panopticon fortress, they would die in the attempt. The Panopticon was the most heavily defended site in the Vampire Dominion. However, the Mirovar force team was fresh off surviving the disastrous defeat of the Order at the conclave in Minneapolis. They, along with the Blake force team operating out of California, were the most dangerous surviving elements of the Order, and only a fool would underestimate their capabilities. Recent operations had culled the weakest members of the Order and only the strongest remained in the fight.

Still, assaulting the Panopticon fortress remained a suicide mission.

The more important and less obvious issue was that Crane was running out of praetorians. His strategy of ruthlessly limiting vampire numbers to less than one thousand had been a highly successful component of keeping his rule of the world secret, but it also exposed him to risk if his opponents put his forces under sustained pressure and they began to take serious losses. Total praetorian numbers were never more than a quarter of the vampire population and now they were dropping like flies, recent efforts to recruit special forces on operations in the Middle East notwithstanding.

His best praetorians, vampires of long and loyal service were dead – some of them at her own hand. There were another sixty seconded with generals Franz, Zhen, and Mosule hunting the elusive rogue vampire in the East. There were another forty in standing contingents throughout the world, but his numbers in the United States were wearing thin.

All this added pressure upon his regime. Soon, the stress would reach a peak that Chloe could co-opt to crash his rule. She blinked slowly, but first she'd have to rid herself of the damnable implant buried next to her brain stem.

She would lose everything if she could not afford to see Cornelius Crane, king of the Vampire Dominion, her lord and master – dead – and dead forever. He must die if she were ever to be free of Allemande's curse and at liberty to wield the Key of Ahknaton to bring her vision for a new world order into reality.

Would Crane respond to his losses by creating more vampires? It was a good question. He had an aversion to creating vampires he could not control, but what actions would desperation lead him to?

Her mind whirled with the possibilities but one truth remained above all others – Crane would be at his most dangerous at the end of the game.

Chloe's eyes tightened, her mind racing. The news Hana Tanaka had gone missing, lost to the Panopticon was terrifying. Tanaka was her best and only hope of defeating Crane's implant. Surely there was a back door, a secondary protocol built into the implant that could disarm it. It was her one hope in her secret war with Crane. She had to have an answer for the implant or else he'd already won. She would devote the rest of her life to defending his life and rule, or die at his side with a dose of silver shot into her brain. The purpose of her life would evaporate like a mirage before she could manifest it with a reality of her choosing.

Rediscovering Hana Tanaka was a priority, but with the sudden focus on the Panopticon, it was a task that would have to wait for a more opportune moment. Chloe would have to return to Japan in the near future, perhaps with James and the chameleons in tow, and confront whoever was protecting Tanaka. No one as intelligent as the young scientist would run unless they had someone they trusted they could run to.

It would be wise to make no assumptions about who might be protecting Tanaka. They could range from simple humans – little more than organized criminals or mercenaries, to rogue vampires, or Ramp masters. The Vampire Dominion had reach but Crane spread the praetorians too thinly to shine light into every dark nook and cranny of the world. Anything could be hiding in the darkest shadows. Things that could inspire madness and strike terror in the bravest souls could escape the most thorough searches.

An unbidden memory arrived with a cold shiver up her spine, transporting her back to the dying days of the second world war. To a dank dungeon beneath a dark fortress hidden within the grim forests of Southern Germany. Russian forces were approaching from the east and Allied forces from the west. They were inconsequential to the powers questing for dominance that night. A cabal of Metaframe sorcerers had captured a young girl with a savant ability to access the Metaframe equal to the Key of Ahknaton. They'd used the Nazi movement as a cover to advance their own infernal plans to inflict unspeakable horror upon the world.

Oh, how the future of the world had teetered in the balance. She didn't need a perfect memory to remember what she'd witnessed that night – the scars were still on her soul.

Crane's voice impinged upon her reverie. "—of course, it is essential that we secure—" Crane's palm slammed into the table in front of Chloe. "Pay attention!" His long pale forefinger cut through the air in front of her nose. He snapped, "Get your head into the game, Armitage, or don't you think this is worthy of your notice?"

Chloe blinked. "My apologies, you were saying?"

Crane sighed. "Never mind. Just be prepared to fight, for today we go to war with the remnants of the Order of Thoth. By dawn tomorrow they will have ceased to exist."

Chloe nodded and said dryly, "An excellent plan."

"Don't mock me," Crane snarled through gritted teeth. "Now get out of here before I decide you're more trouble than you're worth."

Chloe's eyes dropped to half-lidded, and she stood up in a single lithe movement. "Of course, Sir. I'll be ready."

Crane grunted.

Chloe turned and left, foregoing any sign of deference. Crane had inserted a deadly implant beneath her skull. Unless he was about to die, she owed him nothing more than indifference.

The door closed behind her, the world was seething with possibilities, wondrous, terrifying, and horrific. As always, she'd chart her own course and navigate in accordance with her own personal star.

She would see her vision realized or die trying.

There were no other options worthy of her interest.

* * *

Armitage left the war room.

Cornelius slumped back into his chair, his hand brushing over his forehead and through his long dark hair. With a death cusp imminent, he'd keep her close at hand. As much to keep an eye on her, as use her supreme skill set to protect his own life. He shook his head. He hadn't seen a convergence of threats to his life this bad since he'd sourced his previsionary power from the voodoo sorcerer and Metaframe adept, Jean Philippe Allemande back in the 1850s. His plans had been progressing perfectly as recently as six months ago, and now, everything had gone to hell. Well, he wouldn't stand for it. He tapped the intercom and buzzed his executive secretary, Ursula Zielinkski. A brief moment later, the war room door opened and Ursula walked into the room.

"Yes, Sir?" she asked in perfectly modulated tones.

"Ursula, please initiate the evacuation protocol for the Citadel, with the following variations. Secure my collections upon my private yacht, the *Odysseus*. I've ordered it docked in New York harbor. Please ensure you include my personal lockbox in my library along with my books and artworks. It contains private materials you must keep separate from the rest. Materials that are more precious to me than the rest of my collection combined.

Ursula nodded. "Yes, Sir. I'll take special care of the lockbox … what is the timeframe?"

"The task must be complete by the end of September. The command center will shift to a skeleton staff immediately. I have seconded all North American praetorian forces and most of the Day Guard to a mission under the command of general Maze. I want the best of the CC operators to transfer to the new facility in the East Coast Hub. The rest can stay here to man operations until the evacuation is complete.

"Shall I decommission the citadel floors and wipe all evidence of our existence?"

Cornelius smiled grimly. "That may not be necessary, but be prepared to do so during October or November. The citadel must move, it's only a matter of time before our enemies destroy this place."

Ursula's light-blue eyes widened. "We've been compromised?"

Cornelius nodded. "Move all your personal effects out of Manhattan … on second thought, out of New England."

"It's that bad?"

Cornelius nodded again and frowned slightly. "We have time, but it is running out."

"Anything else, Sir?"

"No. That is all."

Ursula nodded and left the war room.

Cornelius hadn't shared with her the notion that he could be dead within the next twenty-four hours. She didn't need to know that, and anyway, he planned on surviving the cusp event and ensuring that Anton Slayne died instead. He smiled, that was a far better outcome. Cornelius glanced at a row of clocks on the wall, it was still at least four hours before sunset in Beijing. He'd have to wait until after sunrise in New York City for a progress report from general Haras Mosule on efforts to capture the Mekrarian ninja vampire.

There was no time to waste, he opened up the main screens to view the Panopticon feeds. It was time to review and organize the disposition of his forces, optimize strategies and update tactics. Mastering the available information was his strength and he would use it to defeat his opponents as he had done for more than nine centuries.

If his enemies underestimated him, they did so at their mortal peril.

* * *

Louise Wesson's smartphone rang, a loud and insistent alarm waking her from deep sleep.

Louise snapped to full awareness. It was four in the morning. She'd been sleeping on a low camp bed in her office at Shadowstone research facility number nineteen. Fort Dix sprawled three levels above her office. She'd been at the fort for the last three weeks, making use of the local gymnasium for bathing facilities, and eating at the officer's mess.

She picked up her phone, the calling number displayed as a line of asterisk symbols – that shouldn't be possible. There was only one person who could have such a number. She asked in a clear voice, "Sir, what can I do for you?"

There was the briefest of pauses, then a strong baritone voice spoke with a slight hint of a French accent, "Your anticipation confirms my judgment Ms. Wesson. I'm ringing you at this ungodly hour as events are approaching a critical convergence. I'm promoting you to the head of the worldwide Shadowstone organization. I'm placing the heads of the United Kingdom, Europe, the Far East, Africa, and South America under your immediate command. Of course, you'll continue to personally direct North American operations. This role consolidates the purpose of Shadowstone to provide stability in a dangerous world. Do you accept this responsibility?"

Louise said what she must, "Yes, Sir. I accept."

"You will have full discretionary authority, reporting to and answerable only to me. Is that clear?"

"Yes, Sir. Have you notified the other heads?"

"They will be within the hour, expect them to report back to you within the next two hours. If they don't report in, contact me on my direct line. I will provide my phone address shortly."

"Thank you, Sir."

The unidentified voice clearly belonged to Cornelius Crane, the mysterious head of Shadowstone and as Louise strongly suspected, the head of the vampires. He continued speaking, "Your recent efforts against the Order of Thoth have not gone unnoticed. Achieving a better than one for one kill ratio in a battle is unprecedented for Shadowstone. While some of the enemy escaped, powers that were beyond any possibility to anticipate or interdict helped them. In summary, your conduct of the operation was exemplary and that is why I have rewarded you with this new position."

"Thank you, Sir. I'm honored."

"Indeed, you are … please continue with this level of performance Ms. Wesson and your future career will be unlimited. Do you have any questions?"

"No, Sir."

"Then get to work young lady – there's a war to win."

The call disconnected.

Louise threw off her blankets and got up. There'd be no more sleep for her this night. The three and a half hours she'd just snatched would have to be enough.

Her strategy was working, she was reaching a position where she could influence the worldwide operations of Shadowstone, the Day Guard and the nascent Panopticon in the East Coast Hub. Before long, she'd be able to turn the weapons of the vampires against them, and bring her enemy to their utter destruction. In time, she'd restore the Republic of the United States, and from that singular beacon, a new human civilization would arise without the blight of rule by a class of parasitic predators.

Her smartphone pinged. She glanced at the screen, her contacts list displayed a new address named, 'Cornelius Crane.' The phone pinged a second time, there was a short-encrypted text from the new contact that read, 'PRIORITIES: [1] Accelerate the rebuilding of facility #34 in Brazil and commence harvesting the fungus for the Day Guard serum. Establish five thousand doses within six months. [2] Accelerate the commissioning of the new East Coast Hub it must be ready to begin operations within three weeks' time. (October the 2nd deadline). [3] Rebuild Shadowstone US and UK as a single organization under your command integrated with the Day Guard.'

She thought to herself, *Yes, Sir! I'll build you an army. One capable of defeating a vampire king.*

Louise dressed herself quickly. She thrived on being at the heart of a revolution against a tyrant, a revolution that was long overdue. She glanced at the clock; it was too early to call the architect. He was notoriously touchy about interruptions before seven in the morning. She accommodated his idiosyncrasies; he was essential to the deployment of the new Panopticon at the East Coast Hub. She made a mental note to call him directly after seven am. She must accelerate the deployment of the new Panopticon.

Crane had ordered her to create weapons, and weapons she'd create.

But with any weapon, the critical question was who had control of it? That was a question she planned to answer decisively in her favor.

* * *

The rain was little more than a light mist beneath an ocean of gray clouds.

The architect ignored the damp beading in drops on his dark trench coat. Today was just like yesterday, and tomorrow would be the same. His beloved daughter was still dead, taken a day before her sixth birthday by cancer. He squatted next to her grave and placed an arrangement of flowers before the white marble of her gravestone. He paused for a moment, regarding the bouquet with empty eyes. He arranged the flowers on his daughter's grave. Then pursed his lips, and rearranged them a second, third, fourth and fifth time. Finally satisfied with their perfection, he stood up.

His daughter's mother had left him before she'd died, leaving in a rush of suitcases and a yellow cab to live with her parents. He'd remained, witnessing the final months of his daughter's fight for her life, and finally losing her to the cellular demon that consumed her from within.

He'd buried her, and tended her grave every morning at sunrise without fail for the last six months.

Her name was Rose.

He'd always called her Rosie.

He fully expected she'd live again.

He knew a way to make it happen. Bringing her back was all he had left to live for and he'd received a chance to do exactly that. An organization was funding his research, building the quantum processors, establishing a hyper-secure data center within his home city, providing him with the resources to create a genuine self-aware artificial intelligence. The first of its kind, an evolutionary leap from the AI emulations that were currently operating in the world.

Little did they know that he was templating the new AI's personality off his deceased daughter.

Rosie would come back to him.

Rosie would live again.

Rosie would be a god.

* * *

The destruction of the Panopticon in Utah was central to Louise Wesson's plan. She didn't need a second system looking over her shoulder as she co-opted the new Panopticon and used it to guide an expanded Day Guard in the destruction of the vampires.

Crane had kept his word. All her designated subordinates had reported in, the last was Gordon Heathmont from the UK division. He'd declared his willingness to serve in her organization with a candid humility that differed from the polished professionalism of the rest of the Shadowstone regional heads. She glanced at the wall clock; it was almost seven in the morning. She paused at her desk and practiced breathing exercises while she reviewed the Architect's profile from memory.

The man was a genius, a high-functioning mathematical savant and freakishly obsessed with the most minute details of his work. Her management technique was simple; keep him facing in the direction she needed him to go and unleash him with every aid that she could supply. It was an approach that had sent the Panopticon replacement project moving forward in leaps and bounds.

The clock ticked over to 07:00 and she dialed the Architect's smartphone address. As always, the phone rang once. He wore a communications rig with ear pieces and a microphone when he was available for communication.

He answered sharply, "I was expecting you."

Louise stated calmly, "We have a new deadline. The Panopticon replacement must be operational by the second of October."

"Morning, afternoon, or night? How am I supposed to work with such ambiguity?"

"Midnight on the second will be sufficient – can it be done?"

"Of course not. The new entity will not even be awake on the second."

"How much time can you shave off the original deadline? Cost is no object."

"The birth of the new entity cannot be rushed," the Architect paused for a moment, "and nor should it be."

Louise frowned. "I'm sure my superior will not see it that way."

"The task will take more than three weeks. I have been monitoring progress closely. We should be ready to begin training the new entity against a number of adversarial emulations by the fourth of October, and she'll be ready to begin operations three days later."

"She'll begin training ... it sounds like a child."

"What makes you think she isn't?"

Louise paused for a moment, just what was the Architect building at the East Coast Hub? The original Panopticon had a lot of AI capabilities, but it obeyed the instructions given to it. There was no hint it was able to think for itself, or that it was – alive. "Will the new Panopticon be able to think for itself?"

"Don't call her that name. It's like comparing a bright child with a congenital idiot. The original Panopticon will always be the throwback

Australopithecine, unable to compete with a generation of technology that surpasses it on all parameters."

"Your design exceeds our requirements?"

The architect snapped, "Exceeds? Surpasses? … the two systems are no longer comparable, in fact the name 'Panopticon,' is an insult. The new system has a new name."

There was a long moment of silence.

"… Yes?" Louise inquired carefully.

"It's the Rational Objective Sentience Interpolation Engine."

Louise spelled out the letters, "R … O … S … I … E."

"Yes."

"Just how sentient is this system?"

"More than you can imagine."

"I can imagine quite a bit," Louise said quietly. This was better than she'd hoped for. It was imperative that Crane and the rest of the vampires never found out how capable R.O.S.I.E would be – until it was too late.

Louise thanked the Architect for his update and hung up the call. She leaned back in her chair. Her gaze drifting up to the white ceiling. Her mind spinning away into a field of tactical concerns impacting her strategy.

One remaining question dominated her mind. How could she help the Mirovar force team successfully assault the Panopticon site in Utah? The site was a supreme vampire fortress and as close to a suicide mission as she could imagine. She rubbed her temples, perplexed beyond measure. The Mirovar force team would have to succeed without any aid from her. There was literally nothing she could do without giving her own position away.

No, the Mirovar force team would have to defeat the strongest vampire fortress in existence and destroy the Panopticon on their own.

There was no other way she could achieve her goals.

Chapter Three

"The scourge of the Mekra worshiping blood cultists has all but been wiped out, only a ragged few remain." – Cornelius Crane

* * *

Northern China, September 11th, 19:59

Mekra floated free of her Carpathian donjon.

Her body lay senseless in its silver prison while her mind ranged over northern China. She'd acquired the ability to astral travel a mere six months ago. Her second transformation into vampiric perfection had been as sudden as her original transformation from human to vampire. Imprisonment in silver was an endless succession of sleeping and waking into darkness, broken only with brief interludes of lantern light and Crane's blood slaking her thirst. Crane's imposition of a dietary regime of vampire blood, constant contact with silver, and vast solitude, had taken her beyond a metabolic threshold and into a new realm of power.

The sun descended below the western horizon; its rays powerless to harm her astral form. She welcomed the night like an urgent lover. She'd given away all attachment to sunlight millennia in the past, now she craved only the freedom and power of endless night.

Her servant lay in a dark, cold place, well hidden from sunlight. The red beacon of his sleeping mind marked his lair. A mind she could easily find, penetrate, control, or destroy. Her mental powers of mastery could only reach those sired from her new blood, but she could lightly touch his mind to impart motivation, or dive deep within, taking control of his body as if it was little more than a puppet dancing to her will.

While Mekra had refrained from taking control of Akimitsu, she knew the extent of her new psychic powers as she knew how to breathe. When the time came, she would use them in full to assert her will upon the world. When there were thousands of her children and she was their undisputed goddess.

She glided lower toward the bright lights of China's leading city. How the world had changed during the centuries of her imprisonment. The Earth teemed with people – enough to run the rivers red with their blood. She'd spent the last six months watching, listening, learning, and planning for the moment of her release. Now the opportunity had presented itself, delivered by the hand of her warden. Crane had made a rare error of judgment, creating a son of her blood. One equipped with the power to evade Crane's forces and free her from her donjon.

Her vision tightened upon the railway yards and serpentine tracks near her offspring's resting place. He was sleeping overlong, the place where he rested was too cold, subduing his normal alertness. Dark figures armed for war, were closing in on his position.

Mekra swooped down to hover above his prone form, her eyes widened with alarm, she shouted into his dreaming mind, "Awake Akimitsu! AWAKE!"

* * *

Mekra's voice resounded like thunder breaking against mountains.

Akimitsu's eyes flicked open to darkness and ice. He lay face down on the floor of a refrigerated shipping container. Above him, dozens of pig carcasses hung from hooks in frozen stillness. The steel floor was greasy with icy puddles of fat and pig's blood beneath his face and hands. Mekra was gone. She'd only appeared in his dreams but now enemies were near – it was time to move. The sun had fallen and he could only hope that his relentless pursuers were far enough away that he could still evade them.

He leaped to his feet, padding silently to the front of the container. He'd purposefully left the door shut but unlocked so that he could readily escape. He nudged it open an inch, his pointed ears twitching, his nostrils flaring, his eyes – great dark orbs – peering into a night lit bright by electric overhead lights. Ahead of him a horn sounded a single long blast. The train shook, metal grinding against metal as wheels began to roll. The shipping container vibrated momentarily, then settled as the high-speed freight train began to gather speed.

Two pairs of boots landed on the roof above him. There were two of the older vampires stalking his carriage. Had they detected him? Had they communicated with their fellows? How many were lurking nearby? He couldn't afford their discovery of him. The train was already picking up speed, the wheels beginning to thrum beneath him. Soon it would be traveling to the west at one hundred and sixty miles per hour. His refrigerated hideaway just one container amongst hundreds destined for other parts of China and the world. The train offered the opportunity to break contact with his pursuers and cut days off his schedule to reach the Carpathian Mountains.

Akimitsu kept perfectly still, his hands resting on the handles of the two straight-bladed ninjato swords crisscrossed over his back. The first of the pursuers leaped to the next container, the second pausing directly over his head. The moment stretched, the forward vampire's footsteps came to a halt, followed by the unmistakable sound of a pivot. Akimitsu stilled his heart, becoming a silent void in the night. Above him, the nearest vampire's heart continued to beat steadily and there was the soft susurration of a slow exhale.

A slight variation in the track jolted through the wheels and the container's unlocked door pushed another half-inch ajar. The polished black toes of a pair of armored boots appeared on the trailing roof-edge of the next container. The two older vampires stood opposite each other directly above the steel platform between the containers.

The train gathered speed. The wind howled past, pressing the container door shut. They must suspect he was there. In a moment they would drop down and slam the locking mechanism shut – trapping him inside the steel container. At best, he could cut and tear his way free – at risk of breaking his weapons against the steel walls of the container, but they'd be waiting for him, perhaps with reinforcements already in place.

Akimitsu blurred forward. The container door smashed open, slamming into one of the praetorians who'd chosen the same moment to drop to the platform between the containers. He flew backward, bouncing off the other container and flying into the night.

The train accelerated, the wind blowing with hurricane force past the containers. The remaining praetorian leaped into the space between the containers. He leveled a minigun at the ninja vampire's chest and pulled the trigger. Bright fire lit up the space between them, hard shadows cutting along the edges of the two containers, 7.62mm rounds lancing toward him with a promise of sudden death.

Akimitsu blurred right, his left ninjato spearing between the minigun's spinning barrels. The weapon jammed. The minigun's electric motor whined. Gears stripped themselves, blue smoke blooming around the base of the weapon. His right hand lashed forward, his second ninjato penetrating through the praetorian's heart, sending a ribbon of blood splashing into the night. He pushed forward to the edge of the platform, his opponent falling free of his blades before whipping away as the train left him behind.

He flourished his swords, ridding them of any trace of his foe. He may have won this battle but he'd revealed his position to his enemies. The full might of his pursuers would fall like a thunderbolt against this location. He had to leave immediately.

Akimitsu turned and leaped from the speeding train, blurring southward into the darkness.

* * *

"How did you lose him?" Cornelius snapped, shaking his fist at the main screen in the war room.

Haras Mosule flinched as if slapped. He rallied immediately, his eyes tightened and he stated, "He had warning."

"From who?" Cornelius snarled.

"Unknown, but he was able to ambush the two praetorians who discovered him."

"Are they still alive?"

"Yes. One nearly died from a sword thrust through his heart. I don't think this vampire knows how to kill other vampires."

"Yet." Cornelius affirmed. "He doesn't know yet. Still, he took out two of our men, and if he knew more, he would've killed them. Form your men into four-man squads. No pairs, no singletons. I want four of us in the fight when we next find him."

Haras nodded. "Understood."

Cornelius waved his right hand dismissively. "Or use a weapon with a broad area of effect. You're authorized for surgical strikes from the shadowstar drones. Drop a pattern of five-hundred-pound warheads on him next time and make sure he's gone."

Haras nodded again.

"I'm sending upgraded weapons. Miniguns with flamers and thermobaric rockets. We can't take chances that he might start siring offspring. It's a miracle it hasn't already happened." Cornelius paused for a long moment, then commanded, "You have your mission, now get to work."

Haras slapped the left-side of his chest. "Yes, Sir."

Cornelius disconnected the call and the screen shifted back to a set of Panopticon feeds. He sighed, his hands dropping to the six-thousand-year-old Huon pine imported from Tasmania for the new war room table. He leaned forward, staring at the smooth butter-pale wood, his mind pursuing internal demons. He rose up, studying the feeds on the main screen and a dozen secondary panels. He assessed the disposition of his forces and began sending out orders. He moved all his remaining praetorians from standing roles around the world to Eastern Europe, seconding them to the command of General Dieter Franz. He added general-eyes-only commands to Franz to ready hypersonic land attack cruise missiles armed with nuclear warheads and to move all his forces into the Carpathian Mountains.

General Franz and the forces he'd assigned to him would be the final defense of Mekra's donjon. If need be, he'd attend in person. There could be no mistakes. He must wipe out the new strain of vampire, even if he had to sacrifice Mekra herself to do it. His eyes darkened with ferocious certainty. He'd sacrifice half a continent if it was necessary, but why do that when a neat surgical strike could achieve the desired effect without revealing his hand to the world.

His long right finger tapped the pale wood. It was essential to operate in secret. Untold damage had occurred in the last few months. Surely much of Shadowstone would begin to work out what was going on. They weren't stupid, and nothing focused the mind on questioning the 'official,' truth like defeat and the death of comrades.

Cornelius' rubbed his chin. The existence of vampires must remain secret. He couldn't allow humans to discover they were little more than cattle. They were far from being the rulers of this world. Awareness of their true status would puncture the thin veneer of rationality masking the depths of insanity lurking beneath. He'd watched Western Europe dethrone the concept of God with science, and the march of progress had radically decentered humanity's position in an ancient and expanding universe. Against the vast sweep of infinite time, the life of any individual human being was little more than a brief spark illuminating an endless darkness, destined only to be forgotten by an utterly indifferent universe.

Most people ignored the cold truths of science, and he must exploit humanity's willful ignorance. If true knowledge of vampires arose, it would fan the world into flames against him as humanity united against a common oppressor. Cornelius sighed again. Yes, an oppressor, it was a title he'd be a fool to disown but he wore it from necessity, not from a lust to rule others. In many ways, he'd organized the world to allow him to operate at a distance, to delegate, to allow him a measure of – peace.

But to no avail; he stared at the high-def images of the Panopticon feeds. He was at war; he was always at war. He'd fooled himself with the temporary peace of the last twenty years. His lip curled derisively. His enemies stood arrayed against him but he'd fought their like before, and he'd always survived. He had more than nine centuries of experience with winning the contest for survival. He'd proven his abilities time and again, and this time would not be different.

He would defeat his opponents through mastery of information, through stealth and secrecy, and with the bloody edge of his blade.

His eyes tightened and his lips thinned. It was time to go to war.

* * *

The yellow and black bio-hazard symbol marked the heavy security door like an evil eye.

Gareth Nightingale, the sole surviving Shadowstone agent in Jerusalem took a deep breath and pushed against it. It gave way, opening up into an extensive bio-medical laboratory. He lifted and panned his heavy-caliber H&K 417 assault rifle, the LED flashlight strapped beneath the barrel illuminating the lab. The air was cool, bordering on cold. The deserted Red Empire facility was deep enough to escape the early afternoon sun pounding the museum above. He'd received orders from General Armitage to check the remains of the facility. She'd provided instructions on how to access the lab from the city's sewer system. He'd equipped himself with urban-camouflage combat fatigues and a high-impact weapons fit out. He'd begun the mission just after breakfast and progressed each step carefully. He was all on his own and the nearest backup was hundreds of miles away.

Gareth stepped over the threshold, his combat boots barely making a sound on the tiled floor. Two long workbenches covered with technical apparatus stretched into the chamber. Beyond them lay an operating table equipped with thick metal restraints. Computers and gray-metal cabinets lined the walls, and a floor-to-ceiling cage stood silently at the far end of the room. He paused, waiting for any sign of movement.

He'd cleared the outer rooms up to a guardhouse leading into a long corridor. Bloated human corpses in various states of dismemberment littered the near-end of the corridor. Smoke had recently filled the facility. The unmistakable reek of burned 'long pig,' overlayed the cloying stench of decaying flesh. He'd quickly established there was no one still living within the vicinity of the guardhouse, and retreated back into the prison section. He'd pointed his gun barrel down several of the cylindrical cells in the floor of the prison. They'd all contained the half-melted remains of things that appeared vaguely human.

Someone used white phosphorous grenades or something like them, he surmised grimly. Whatever had happened here, it had gotten ugly in a hurry.

Gareth proceeded down one side of the long laboratory. The facility was without power, the only lights he possessed he'd brought with him. With no one around, he tapped the edge of his light tactical headset wrapped around his close-cropped blond hair. A powerful LED lit up, providing a wide cone of light in whichever direction he faced.

There was a rustle from the cage at the back of the room.

Gareth snapped the rifle up to his shoulder, a tight cone of illumination spearing into the center of the cage.

A young woman rose up behind the bars, dressed in a grimy hospital gown and little else. Long dark hair hung in lank locks over her thin shoulders. She held her emaciated arms over her chest. Her mouth opened, she swallowed, paused, then pleaded hoarsely, "Help me. Please help me."

Gareth frowned. He flipped the gun over, facing back to the entrance, there was no one there. He twisted back again to face the cell. The woman pressed up against the bars. Her chalk-pale hands gripped the dark-steel bars as if she were about to rip them apart. He stared at her, she stared back, her eyes half-lidded against the glare of his LED flashlight. He closed the distance between them until the tip of his gun barrel lay just out of reach of her grasp, and aimed directly at her heart.

Over the last few months, a question had wormed its way into his mind. At first a whisper on the edge of awareness, it had become a roar dominating his waking moments. He decided to test her reactions and snapped a question at her, "Are you a vampire?"

She giggled momentarily, her right hand flying to her mouth. "I was."

She wasn't shocked by the question and he asked, "What do you mean was? It's a one-way trip, isn't it?"

"Not anymore," she replied with a knowing smile.

"What? How?"

She pushed herself up against the bars and whispered, "There's a cure."

Gareth shook his head. "Come again?"

She leaned away from the bars, peering up at his face. "Cute, but not too bright. They have a serum; it reverts vampires back to human."

Gareth frowned. "Prove you're not a vampire."

"Got a knife?"

Gareth nodded, holding his rifle with his left hand, he pulled a combat knife from a sheath at his waist.

She held her left hand out in front of the bars. "Cut me, not too deep, but enough to draw blood."

Gareth flicked the knife expertly and thrust the tip into the middle of her palm. The blade flashed back, its edge bright red.

She blinked and held her hand up. The blood ran freely down her palm, a red thread against the pale ivory of her thin wrist. "Wait for it," the moment stretched, "I'm not healing from the cut; a vampire would close such a trivial wound in seconds."

Gareth waited another half a minute, wiping his blade clean and returning it to its sheath. The blood flow slowed to a stop but the wound didn't close.

"Look," she said, stepping away from the bars and retrieving a gleaming metal net from the corner of the cell. She passed it through the bars to Gareth, letting it fall into his outstretched hand. "It's silver. They used it to restrain me when I was a vampire. Once the serum reached full effect, the silver ceased to work, and I was able to escape the net. If I were a vampire, there is no way I'd willingly touch it."

The two points of evidence were convincing. Everything he'd deduced about vampires in the last few months indicated they had super healing powers and a powerful aversion to silver. He let the net fall to the floor and gripped his assault rifle with both hands.

The woman studied him. "You're Shadowstone aren't you?"

Gareth grinned lopsidedly and took a step back. "Now what makes you think that?"

"You're not Red Empire or Order of Thoth. If you were, you'd have been a lot surer of yourself, and your main weapon wouldn't be an assault rifle. You don't really know what's going on, do you?"

Gareth's grin vanished and he looked around the lab – anywhere but at her. He finally turned and stared hard at her. "Tell me about the serum. Are there samples? Data packs? What do you know?"

She stepped back from the bars, spreading her hands wide. "Have you got anything to eat? Look at me, I'm starving. Give me something to eat and I'll talk."

Gareth hesitated for the briefest of moments, shrugged, and pulled a protein bar from a pouch on his combat webbing. He tossed it through the bars with a flick of his wrist. The woman caught it easily, stripped off the wrapper and began eating it hungrily. As she ate, he patrolled around the lab. There was an open briefcase sitting on the operating table with eleven vials in it, and space for a twelfth. He tapped it with a finger and remarked, "Is this it?"

The woman smirked. "People tried to leave in a hurry and didn't take it. I think they would have been more careful if they'd more time."

Gareth considered her words carefully. He could easily leave her here to whatever fate awaited her. She would be desperate to prove her worth and more likely to tell the truth.

"Data?" he asked.

"Wiped. It's gone completely, at least from here. They smoked the hard drives."

"These samples are all we've got?"

She nodded.

Gareth put his rifle down on the operating table, flipped the lid closed on the briefcase, and locked it by swiping his thumbs over a pair of sensors on the sides of the case. He picked the briefcase up, retrieved his rifle, and turned to the open door.

"Wait!" she yelled. "You can't leave me here."

"You're not the mission," Gareth said, striding between the lab benches. "Taking you with me is more of a risk than I care to take."

"Leaving me behind is the bigger risk," she shouted behind him. "You're losing everything I know about the serum. Take me with you, I'll tell you everything there is to know about what's really happening in the world. I'll tell your bosses exactly how the serum works. I'm a goldmine of information. You can't leave me behind."

Gareth's eyes tightened with suspicion but he hesitated at the door into the prison section, his back still turned to her.

"Shadowstone serves the vampires," she called out from the cage. "Their king is Cornelius Crane. He set up Shadowstone late in the nineteenth century to help with keeping the existence of vampires secret. He's been alive for nearly a thousand years."

A shiver crawled up Gareth's back. Her words rang true, they were like a series of locks snapping open within his mind, one click after another. He whirled around and strode back to the cage.

"Any keys?" He asked quietly.

She shrugged. "All electric, they default to locked when the power goes off."

Gareth paused for a moment. "How have you survived? It must be more than two weeks since this facility was destroyed."

She pointed at the silver net on the floor. "The silver suppressed my metabolism, and the progress of the serum. The effect of the silver wore off in the last day or so, and yes, I'm thirsty too. I could use a drink of water."

Gareth pointed to the near left corner of the cage, away from the electric door lock. She moved quickly into the corner, making herself small, her thin arms covering her face. He lifted his rifle and aimed at the center of the lock. He fired once. The crack of the round reverberating through the lab, the bullet sparking off the lock, before ricocheting into a cabinet. He frowned, took a step forward and fired another four rounds. The lock broke apart on the last bullet, the cage door swinging an inch ajar.

The woman was on her feet an instant later. "Thanks, there was no way I could break free of the cage by myself." She pushed the door aside, grinning broadly as she stepped into the lab.

Gareth would need both hands free to carry a weapon and the briefcase with the serum samples. He slung his rifle over his back, and pulled a 9mm Glock from a holster on his webbing. There was no point trusting this woman. He'd keep her just where he could see her. He flicked the barrel of the pistol at her and nodded at the open doorway. "You go first. I'll give you directions as to where we need to go."

She smiled sweetly at him. Her eyes flicked down to the briefcase filled with serum vials lying on the tiled floor next to his left boot.

Gareth frowned. She was a fraction too confident. A fraction too interested in the serum vials. His survival instincts flared, his finger pulling tighter on his 9mm Glock's trigger.

She blurred forward faster than his eyes could follow. Her right hand flashed upward, striking his throat like an iron bar. His larynx collapsed and his spine snapped like a twig, his body vanishing beneath him. The room spun as he fell, his head hitting the floor with a crack. He couldn't draw breath, a moment later darkness swept in like a funeral shroud and took away all the light.

***

Chloe knocked on James' front door.

There was a rustle of cloth on the far side of the apartment. *That'd be the curtains.* James' footsteps followed as he walked up the corridor. His steps muffled against the floorboards; *he's wearing socks.* She'd sent him a text fifteen minutes earlier warning him of her imminent arrival. The door handle turned and the door swung open.

James stood in front of her, dressed in combat fatigues, his brown eyes filled with tightly held excitement. "Gareth Nightingale is dead. He died in Jerusalem at 13:39 local time. However, all is not lost; we have footage from his tactical headset. The last ten minutes before he died contain something I'm sure you'll want to see."

"Nightingale?" Chloe mused briefly. "Yes. I sent him to investigate the remains of the Red Empire citadel."

James led her into his lounge room and said, "Watch this."

The main panel on his wall lit up with the feed from a single tactical head cam. The footage bobbed about as Nightingale moved through the ruins of the Red Empire prison and the medical research laboratory. The microphone picked up all the sound, rendering the dialogue between the Shadowstone operator and the prisoner in the cage with perfect clarity. Chloe watched with avid interest. Nightingale was doomed the moment he started talking with the woman. The fatal knife-hand strike was merely the expected denouement. A moment after his skull cracked on the tiles of the laboratory floor, there was a snapping of bone and a ragged tearing sound of ruptured flesh. The same sound repeated a couple of seconds later.

"It's out of shot," James remarked, "but I think she just tore his thumbs off to unlock the briefcase."

"It follows," Chloe agreed, a slight smile curling the edges of her red lips. "She's clearly a Ramp master, who'd become a vampire. Who is she?"

"What we know for sure," James explained, "is she speaks English with a faint Japanese accent. The Panopticon picked it up. We also did a match with Hana Tanaka for face and voice prints. They are sufficiently similar to indicate a genetic relationship; they are most likely sisters. Officially, Hana Tanaka only has one sister, Sakura Tanaka. Sakura is three years older, and has been missing, presumed dead for the last five years. The footage of the tactical cam allowed us to check for facial recognition. There was a ninety-six percent match with file photos of Sakura. The four percent gap was attributable to partial starvation, but she hasn't aged at all since she disappeared."

"So, Hana Tanaka's sister masters the Ramp, becomes a vampire, and shows up in a Red Empire medical lab at the center of research for a way to reverse vampirism. … So, what does she do now? Where does she flee to with her prize?"

"The same place Hana is hiding?" James suggested.

Chloe smiled quietly. There were too many coincidences for this to be random. More than blood linked Hana and her sister's fates. The secrets to disarming the implant next to her brain stem and 'curing,' vampirism rested with the Tanaka sisters. She glanced into James' eyes. "Ready the Spike 512 for a flight to Tokyo. Be ready to move at a moment's notice. We'll need to accommodate the chameleons on the flight and have appropriate transport for them when we arrive in Japan. This needs to be off the books – Crane cannot discover we have gone to Japan."

James nodded. "I'll make it so."

Chloe said, "Include my full combat fit out. I'll need my auto-pistols, we can't be sure what we'll find in Tokyo, but I have a bad feeling about it."

James' face paled with an unspoken question.

"Yes. This is serious. Sakura Tanaka was an unregistered vampire. She was off the books for five years. No one knew of her, no one was cleaning up after her. Either she was a captive of the Red Empire for five years, or there is a cell of rogue vampires in Tokyo that have escaped the notice of the Vampire Dominion for decades, perhaps centuries. There are no novice vampires who could hide themselves from us. There is a secret vampire master in Japan, someone who is old, experienced, knowledgeable, and powerful." Chloe blinked, Crane's words from a briefing early in her life as a vampire coming back to her. *'The Red Empire and the Order of Thoth are not the sum total of the threat of the Ramp masters. There are rogues from both factions operating singularly or in groups, and then there are wild talents on whom the powers of the Ramp come unbidden.'* Her opponents in Japan could be anyone or anything. "They could be someone firstborn of Mekra, stronger and faster than a regular vampire, like Crane. They could be a blood-cultist, or even a Metaframe sorcerer with unknown powers. When your opponent is this well-hidden ... the risks are highest." She tapped her lips with her forefinger, then smiled quietly. "But so is the prize."

She left unspoken the deeper question of why the Red Ghost would commission a difficult and expensive research effort to find a cure for vampirism. Understanding the core of Dalien Morte's motivation would be the key to his future co-option within her end game. His quest to find a cure was a major clue. He cared about someone. Someone very important to him was a vampire and he wanted them back. There were no vampires on record who could be important to Morte, therefore there must be a hidden vampire. The only questions that remained were who was the vampire? Where were they? And who had hidden them?

James looked askance and asked, "Hang on a second. Why on Earth would the Red Empire want a cure for vampirism? Don't they have a religious belief in killing vampires?"

Chloe arched an eyebrow. "Why, indeed?" She sniffed, momentarily bemused. "I'm sure we'll find out in due course." She turned away from

James, her gaze drifting away from the world as her mind speared into plans and counter-plans. A climax was coming, powers were converging, events were accelerating. The near future would test her capacity to ride the rising tide of chaos.

Of that, she was sure.

Chapter Four

"The first question I had to answer was how do you defeat an opponent who can see the future?" – Arthur Slayne

* * *

Utah, The Panopticon Fortress, September 11th, 05:00

The distant Vampire Dominion facility rose in stark contrast to the deserted floor of the valley.

Anton Slayne lay facing east. His body pressed flat against hard rocks, staring with his good right eye through a pair of electronic binoculars at the Panopticon fortress. The equipment enhanced his field of view for night vision, range, and available metadata. Peter lay to his right and Francis a yard beyond him, both holding identical binoculars up to their eyes. Jay and Chiara kept watch on the approaches to their position while Li conducted a netmaster hazing operation from one of the two SUVs parked beneath a stand of trees.

The access road into the low mountains overlooking the western side of the fortress was little more than a dirt track for the last half dozen miles. The road had veered off just before the abandoned ghost town of Cedar Fort, and then headed up into the hills in the general direction of Flat Top Mountain. The Mirovar force team had completed the nearly twelve hundred miles from Minneapolis with hard driving and sleeping in shifts in the cars. Even with a day of driving and broken sleep sitting in the back seat, hot blood thrummed through his veins – here was a target worth taking down.

Anton burned with a deep need to destroy the Dominion facility squatting like a malign and alien horror in the valley below. For the first time, they had useful intelligence about the enemy. They could seize the initiative and strike hard, disrupting the Vampire Dominion's ability to track them. With the Panopticon gone, the Vampire Dominion would be blind and Li could dominate the networks, find out where the enemy were hiding and the war would turn in their favor. Winning the next battle was critical to winning the war against the vampires.

Failure was not an option.

Anton scanned the fortress with his electronic binoculars. It was six miles distant from where he lay. A rectangular thirty-foot-high wall enclosed the main facility. The digital range finder scoped the space enclosed by the wall as a mile long by a twelve hundred yards wide, the data appearing as tiny red digits over lines framing what he was looking at. Tall guard towers surmounted with domes and ringed with weapons rose two hundred feet above the wall on each corner of the rectangle, creating overlapping fields of fire covering every open spot in the valley.

To Anton's right, a landing field centered between two hangars filled the available space on the south side of the facility. A pair of black nightfalcon helicopters gleamed under bright lights on the western side of the dark tarmac.

To his left, on the north side of the facility squatted a multi-story administration building. A massive tower rising at least three hundred feet above the ground dominated the nearside left corner of the admin building. A shiny black hemisphere, eighty feet in diameter and half that high crowned the huge tower. The tower's main weapon, a tri-barreled gun projected forty feet past the black surface of the sphere. Sleek silvery fins ran the length of each barrel, forming a 'Y' for anyone with the misfortune to be facing the weapon.

Half a mile outside the north and south walls sat a pair of large rectangular buildings surrounded by a ring of lesser structures. The billowing plumes of steam rising from three large funnels running along the spine of each building marked them as power stations.

Surrounding the whole complex was an outer perimeter fence six miles on each side. A road ran between the landing pad and the main admin building, exiting the main base through a guardhouse on the nearside western wall. The single access road strode across a vast open plain to a second guardhouse on the outer perimeter fence. The whole extended site glowed with rows of lights running in spoke lines from the main facility to the outer fence, which itself, supported powerful lights eliminating any shadows within a hundred yards of the facility's outer perimeter.

Anton asserted grimly, "A mouse couldn't get across that open area without being seen."

"Peter, what are we looking at here?" Francis asked softly.

"Well, working from the outside in. If you focus on our lower right at the outer perimeter guardhouse, you'll see a couple of things. The outer fence is twenty feet high, electrified and topped with razor wire, but that's just for keeping out the riff-raff."

Peter paused for a moment. "The serious stuff is all at the main facility and we'll get to that. However, the outer guardhouse is just a small, low-key affair, sized to hold about a dozen troops, but see those long buildings behind it – they're drone hangars. I've counted five tracked ground drones so far patrolling the open space and the outer fence line. They're about four feet high, eight feet long and carry a .50 cal machine gun. Bad puppies and no doubt slaved off the Panopticon."

"Slaved?" Francis asked. "Are you suggesting the Panopticon would have direct control of the weapon systems?"

"Yes, for anything that's automated. Once engaged, the drones will respond with lightning-fast decisions and ruthless efficiency."

"What about fliers?" Anton asked.

"Ahh… Okay. Got one. About three hundred yards in, hovering above the road to the facility. Can you see it?"

"Got it," Anton said, focusing on a five-foot wide saucer shaped object hovering above the sole road inside the outer fence. Francis followed a moment later with a low whisper of assent. Anton asked, "Any ideas on what the flying saucer does – apart from watching?"

"Weapons are not obvious, but I'd assume any fliers were armed until proven otherwise."

Francis tilted his head and asked, "No armored personal carriers or other heavy equipment?"

"Nope!" Peter said quickly.

"What, no commander tank?" Anton said, with a straight face. "How are we supposed to break in?"

"No," Peter answered in a low voice. "They don't need a tank, everything in this valley is within range of the specter defense towers on the corners of the inner perimeter wall. If they had a commander tank, and we captured it, they'd kill it and us within the first ten seconds of combat."

"Specter defense towers?" Francis asked. "I've never heard of them."

"Yeah. Total state of the art and this is probably one of the few sites in the world they've been deployed. There are sixty vertical launch cells built into the walls of each tower. They'll contain hypersonic land attack cruise missiles armed with anything up to and including nuclear warheads. Note how each tower looks like a long column with strands of barbed wire wrapped around the neck. There's a command center in the dome at the top of each tower. There are four rails ringing the neck of each tower beneath their command center. Each rail carries a pair of mobile weapon systems. The rails allow the weapons to move and cover a full three-hundred-and-sixty-degree circuit around each tower. The rails are all maglevs, they roll fast, completing a round trip in under two seconds."

Peter paused for a moment. The team waited in silence. The difficulty of what they faced revealed in fascinating and horrific detail. "From the bottom up, I count two 20mm rotary cannons, they'll be anti-personnel weapons good out to two miles. Two 30mm auto cannons to deal with light vehicles out to about four miles. Two lasers for drone swarms and incoming weapons, they're good out to the horizon and will keep firing as long as they have power. Finally, there are two rail guns, same spec as a Commander tank for anti-cruise missile defense and general bad-assery."

It was almost too dreadful to ask, but Anton had to know. "What's the big tower in the middle?"

"I was getting to that." Peter tilted his head left and right, as if weighing up the options of how best to break the bad news. "It's a nemesis defense tower. I've only seen it on the web as speculation. It has everything a specter tower has, but bigger and better. See that huge mother of a gun hanging out of the black hemisphere on top. It's a rail gun phalanx. Each second, it can shoot three forty-five-pound kinetic spikes at eleven times the speed of sound. With satellite targeting networked with the nemesis and specter tower's advanced quantum field sensor arrays, it can hit anything a yard wide within a thousand-mile radius."

"Like the rail gun on a commander tank?"

"On mega-steroids. What the commander tank has is like a Glock 9mm compared to a 30mm auto-cannon."

"How do we take them down? Could we take out those power stations outside the main facility, would that make a difference?"

"Internal fuel-cells in the towers will keep them running for a day or so. Plenty of time for the vampire cavalry to arrive and kill us. In any event, we can't reach the power stations."

"At least not across the surface," Francis said. "That's a lot of steam coming out of those cooling towers. Where's the water coming from? There's no river."

Anton said softly, "No river we can see. It must be underground … could we swim in with air tanks, and gain access via the power plants' water supply?"

"I hate to rain on your parade," Peter remarked quietly, "but we don't know where the underground river is or how to access it. We'd need to map it to find out where the inlets are. Plus, drones linked straight back to the Panopticon will monitor and guard all the access paths."

Anton sighed, then declared, "Okay, we can't approach from above or below, that only leaves a deception. We have to convince them to let us in. Could we steal a nightfalcon from somewhere else and fly it in and provide them with," he put down his binoculars, rested on his elbows and air quoted with his fingers, "'the access code,' to let us land? Could we hack their networks to find out what those codes would be? Li's a marvel at that."

Li piped up over the tactical network running through their earbuds, "You've seen too many Hollywood movies. This is real life, I'm not that much of a marvel." She fell silent again, presumably absorbed with the task of hiding their presence from the Panopticon.

"Perhaps we need more insight into what is possible," Francis said firmly. "Li, are you up for attempting a loremaster vision?"

The silence stretched, then Li replied, "Yes, just need to make an adjustment to give me a window for action. Wait ... okay, now we do it."

Nothing happened for a dozen seconds. Anton found himself holding his breath, then let it out slowly.

Li uttered a low moan of grief.

"Something is wrong," Anton muttered, rising in a flash and blurring back to the SUVs.

* * *

Unbidden, a dark wave of loss swept through her.

Li clenched her eyes tightly shut, but it didn't stop the loremaster vision overtaking her mind. Bright fire burned in her right forearm. The world shuddered, splitting in two. A vivid reality flooded her senses, trapping her soul within a nightmare.

She walked on polished floors between racks of server computers, the subsidiary elements of the Panopticon, the mighty quantum processors remained hidden. Her breath plumed in grey mists in front of her. The air chilled to near-freezing temperatures to support the icy logic of artificially intelligent systems.

Behind her whispers murmured, one was Anton, but there was another voice she didn't recognize. She whirled, but Anton stood alone, he frowned momentarily, running a hand back over his tightly cropped dark hair, then frowned incredulously at his scarlet palm dripping blood onto the immaculate floor.

He started to fall.

The rows of computer racks writhed like giant serpents, transforming into massive industrial pipes. Perspiration slicked her brow from the oppressive stifling heat. Francis and Jay stood before her, their faces set with grim determination, assault rifles blazing, rounds whipping past her. Return fire slashed through the room, deafening, thunderous, overwhelming. Great pipes burst asunder. Ravenous steam billowed in clouds cutting through the space where Francis and Jay stood, turning bright pink with their blood.

The blood-drenched mists evaporated to reveal the fortress beneath her feet. Peter loomed over a console. The air was alive with the tang of electric current. Streams of fire lanced across a bright sky. Behind her steel struck on steel, Chiara cried out in sudden agony. Peter turned to look through her, a fatalistic grin seizing his features, his red hair flying free, his hands blurring to his axes. The floor lurched as inbound cruise missiles detonated against the sides of the tower.

She was falling, falling through concrete and metal debris, she searched frantically for a hand hold, something stable to hold onto. Sharp dark steel impaled her outreaching hand, splashing a warm ribbon of blood across her face.

The world shuddered again.

Tears streaming down her face, she said through sobs. "We'll … die in there. No one … escapes. It's a … death trap!"

Anton cradled her in his arms on the dirt next to one of the SUVs, his eyes flashing with anger. "We need to get out of here."

"The roadhouse back toward Salt Lake City," Francis ordered. "We're too exposed this close to the Panopticon without loremaster overwatch. Peter, Jay, get the SUVs on the move. Team, we're out of here."

She gasped. "There's someone else here."

"Who?" Anton said, lifting her like a child into the back seat of the nearest SUV.

Li looked at him, her dark eyes wide. "I don't know … I don't know."

She lay back in the seat, bringing her knees up to her chest, hugging them tight. A moment later, Anton was next to her, his powerful arms holding her close. Peter was in front of them in the driver's seat. The big car's engine thrummed and it swung forward, driving back down the lonely track and away from the fortress.

She couldn't get away from the place quickly enough. She cursed the information she'd got from the tactical helmet in the stormwater drains beneath the conclave hall. It was a false lead; the fortress would kill them all.

No one could destroy the Panopticon.

* * *

Anton rubbed an itch over his left eye patch and stared at his second mug of black coffee.

The team had polished off a small mountain of eggs, steaks, pasta, and salad greens; refueling after the rigors of battle in Minneapolis and a long, fast road trip.

They sat at the back of the roadhouse away from the entrance. Li had remarked about the lack of cameras or other surveillance devices installed in the building – a small silver lining after the shock of her vision. The building was a dead zone for the Panopticon and practically deserted. A grizzled old man ran the place, thin as a rake with a long wispy beard, he looked like a wizard from a Hollywood movie transported into the twenty-first century. There was a fry cook who knew his stuff working in the kitchen as the food had been excellent and freshly prepared. The roadhouse sat on the 'fortress,' branch of an intersection with the main road heading back toward Lehi. The fortress branch led to the deserted town of Cedar Fort, and then past the Panopticon facility toward the southwest.

With no one around to overhear, the team had freely discussed the options. Li's devastating vision of impending doom had not gone down well, the team splitting into two factions. The Li and Jay faction that advocated avoiding the fortress, and the Anton, Peter, and Chiara faction that were set on proceeding despite Li's dark vision of doom.

Reassured that Li's vision had not harmed her, Anton was willing to discount it. As bright as she was, she was a loremaster novice. How much could they trust her vision, and should they weigh her risks against the opportunity to destroy the Panopticon? Anton was willing to bet she was wrong this time, that the vision had erupted more from unacknowledged concern and love for her team mates, than a genuine grounding in a forthcoming future.

Francis had stayed out of the debate, letting each group explore the options, willing to allow a consensus to emerge before he made a decision. Occasionally, he'd ask a question, or probe a suggested pathway, looking for undue risk or poorly grounded assumptions. With the skills and abilities in the team, Francis would be mad not to let them explore the possibilities and thrash out a solution, then step in and back a direction that everyone had already bought into.

However, a shared solution for attacking the Panopticon fortress was nowhere in sight.

"I can't explain it." Li asserted, spreading her hands apart. "It's just … an overwhelming sense of doom. That place is a death trap. It's built to kill anyone who attempts to get in there without authorization. The vampires designed that facility and protect it with utter ruthlessness. Minds without mercy established it, and it will kill us all if we attempt to infiltrate it."

Anton looked across the wooden table at Li. "We can't just rely on you to guard us. You have to sleep, there's a window every day for the Panopticon to discover us. We have nowhere to go that the Panopticon can't find us. We only need someone to walk past us, talking on their cell phone with the phone's camera pointing at us, for the machine to find us. We have to take it out. It's pivotal. A must do. We have this one God-given opportunity to do it, and we'd be crazy to step away from it now."

"Haven't you been listening?" Jay asked, leaning forward to peer past Francis. "We don't actually have a way in. The place is impregnable." He pointed across the table at Peter. "Peter said as much."

Peter shrugged his massive shoulders in silent acknowledgment of Jay's words and then said, "Sure, there is no way to do a frontal assault."

"Precisely," Jay said. "We need to withdraw and find another strategy."

Anton slammed his right hand into his left palm. "In case you haven't noticed, we've been getting our butts kicked. The Order is all but destroyed. We don't need to find another strategy. We need to destroy the Panopticon. We'll never get another chance to seize the initiative away from the vampires. How many people had to die for us to get this opportunity? We know where it is now. How long before Crane understands we know about it and moves it?"

Chiara asked, "Could the Panopticon be moved?"

"I can't rule it out," Li said with a shrug, "but it doesn't matter if they move it. Attacking the Panopticon fortress is suicidal."

Anton couldn't help but think of Samuel Luther decrying the reliability of loremasters and mind palaces back during the ill-fated mission to rescue Ramin Kain from Armitage's manor house. As much as he hated to admit it, he had to agree with Luther, loremasters could make mistakes, especially someone like Li who was new to the discipline. He faced Peter, lifted his hands and implored, "Come on. How can we turn this down? We'll never get another chance like this!"

Peter frowned, wavering.

Li grabbed Peter's right forearm; her eyes wide. "Peter," she glanced over her shoulder at Chiara sitting on the corner of the table. "Chiara," Li shook her head. Her long dark hair hanging in a loose curtain over her shoulders. "You'll both die in the nemesis tower. You're in it when it goes down."

Chiara pressed her lips together, stared at Li, and said pensively, "Cassandra wasn't believed either."

Anton snapped incredulously, "Greek myth? We're relying on Greek myth now?" He shook his head, his eyes wide. "I'm on my own here." He turned to his force leader and pleaded, "Francis?"

Francis drew his left hand down across the day's stubble on his chin and stated, "I'm not sending anyone into a vampire fortress unless we have a clear plan of how it can be done."

Anton sighed heavily, putting his hands flat on the table. "Yeah, sure. Have a plan. We need a plan. Yeah, agreed, but we need to get one quick before we're discovered skulking around this site." His lips curled into a derisive grin. "We're playing for more than our lives here." He looked around the table. "Can you honestly say we're doing the best we can right now? That we're seizing the opportunity? That we're worthy of the abilities we have? For fuck's sake – what the hell are we standing for if we can't focus a hundred and ten percent," his left hand flashed out, pointing in the direction of the fortress, "on destroying that fucking vampire fortress while we still have a chance to do it!"

Francis glanced back over his left shoulder into the body of the building. The roadhouse's proprietor seemed to be ignoring them, and the fry cook was off in the kitchen and out of earshot. "Anton," he admonished. "Maintain cover at all times. Keep your discipline."

Anton stared at Francis, while his breath hitched in his chest. Suddenly he was desperately alone. Did none of them understand what they had to do? They had to find a way to take down this fortress and destroy the Panopticon. Without their mass surveillance system to warn them, Crane and Armitage would be vulnerable. He could find them without them realizing it. He could confront them, and he could kill them. It was what they deserved.

Justice demanded nothing less than their deaths. Could his friends not see what they must do? Was he the only one who wanted to act?

Anton shook his head, utterly perplexed by everyone's defeatist attitude.

* * *

The roadhouse stood alone; a silent sentinel lit by the bright light of dawn.

Arthur Slayne pulled his one-ton pickup truck into a parking bay in front of the roadhouse. The proprietor had sent him a text that the 'team,' had arrived an hour earlier. He'd told the fellow who to look for yesterday and he'd obliged Arthur's request with a message.

He leaped from the truck, his scuffed and faded work boots raising a puff of dust as he landed on the graveled parking lot outside the roadhouse entrance. He'd spent the early morning sending the last of his tracked ground drones into the cave complex on the eastern side of the valley. After Jon Thunder-Axe informed him of recent events, he'd been expecting the Mirovar force team to arrive to destroy the Panopticon, but now they hesitated after discovering how formidable its defenses were.

A hesitation that was all too predictable.

They had no idea of how to get into the fortress, let alone what to do once they were in there. Exfiltration was another obstacle for the team. How on earth would they escape the fortress and break contact with any pursuit? It was certain they still didn't know that Crane had a precognitive power. They were operating blind, and without his help they would all be dead before the day was out.

His smartphone pinged. He read the message, 'Responding to your information, re vampire coven in Las Vegas. Will stage there late afternoon with full team and investigate reports. J.'

Justin Blake and his full force team would be in Las Vegas later today. He'd assisted Justin with a weapons cache in Las Vegas in the previous year. It was all part of a greater plan.

He picked up a roll of paper from the passenger seat and walked to the roadhouse entrance, pushed the doors open and strode into the main dining room.

Confidence bathed his soul in a warm balm. The whispering voices had been particularly quiet this morning. The voices knew far too much. He would stop his ears with his fingers to shut them out but that never worked because the voices were inside his head. They murmured away in a darkness of his own making and it was essential that he never heard what they had to say.

At least not until the right moment.

* * *

The roadhouse entrance doors creaked open.

Anton's head flicked left to see who was coming in. His one good eye widened and he did a double take.

Li gasped.

Chiara blurted, "Gee Anton, it's your—"

"Fuck it," Jay muttered, his face flushing red.

"Cat meet pigeons," Peter remarked dryly, staring past Jay's shoulder from the opposite side of the table.

Francis sighed, closed his eyes for a moment, palmed his forehead, then looked up and said, "Hello, Arthur."

Anton's grandfather, his dark, gray-shot hair compressed beneath a worn 'Caterpillar,' brand cap, dressed in faded jeans permeated with gray rock dust, scuffed work boots, a checkered flannel shirt with the sleeves rolled up over tanned, muscular forearms, and carrying a long spool of paper wrapped with a black ribbon approached the table with a broad grin on his face.

His dark blue eyes fixed on Jay, his face falling. "Two of the best people I ever met died the night Kain murdered your mother. Don't believe his lies."

Jay drew breath to retort, then sighed. He fell into silence, a deep and troubled frown creasing his brow.

Anton's chair scraped across the floor as he pushed back from the table.

Arthur turned to Francis, clapping him on a shoulder like an old comrade. "Let bygones be bygones old friend. The moment for victory is upon us!"

Francis looked up at him and inquired, "How did you know we were here?"

Arthur shrugged. "Jon Thunder-Axe told me about what happened at the conclave. I was expecting you, and I asked the proprietor to keep an eye out for you. All very simple stuff, Francis." He swept past Francis who was momentarily perplexed, grinned wildly at Anton, and said, "Anton, my boy—"

Anton leaped to his feet, his face pale, his right fist lashing out, catching Arthur hard on the jaw. Arthur flew backward past Francis and Jay, crashing into the nearest tables and chairs, sending them sliding across the polished floor.

Anton stepped forward, his forefinger pointed hard at his grandfather, and shouted, "Where the fucking hell were you when Armitage murdered Mom?!" He paused, his chest heaving, then he snapped bitterly, "and they dragged Dad away. Now he's a vampire!"

Arthur picked himself up, rubbing his jaw, his eyes hard. "They did that did they? Imprisoned Billy in silver? I never knew for sure."

Anton's head reared back like an unruly stallion. He took another step toward his grandfather, his voice shaking with barely contained fury "Where were you? We fucking needed you!"

Arthur rubbed his face, his eyes filled with something beyond definition. "Anton. If I'd known, I would've—"

"Done what?"

"—been there."

"Anton," Li said, "Your grandfather couldn't have predicted that Armitage and Drake would come to your home."

Anton flicked his gaze like a whip over his right shoulder. "Stay out of this Li. This is between me," he tapped his chest with his thumb, and then pointed at Arthur, "and him!"

Arthur scooped up his roll of paper from the floor and stepped up close to Anton, his voice level with ironclad discipline. "You forget, I lost a son that night, and Anna was the daughter I never had."

"All the more reason why you should've—"

"Been there!" An incredulous look swept across Arthur's face. "Don't think for a second that I wouldn't've been there in a heartbeat if I'd known."

Anton stared into Arthur's eyes. There was a tightly held fury hidden behind them. It was like looking into a mirror that provided a glimpse of his own future. Beneath the rage, a jarring agonized regret welled forth, reaching icy fingers through the space between them. Arthur's deeply-held pain hit Anton like a cold, hard slap. He took a step backward, the anger at his grandfather ebbing from his heart like an outgoing tide.

Arthur sighed, his eyes hardened over his pain and looked past Anton. "Every day, I wish I'd been there," his gaze flicked back like a knife into Anton's heart and he snapped, "but I'm not a miracle worker."

Something hollow and tight seized Anton's chest. His lips thinned and he blanched. If Arthur wasn't to blame then who was? He stepped back, pushing the question away. The anger for his grandfather replaced with a flood of dark guilt.

Anton looked down at his boots, anywhere but at Arthur.

His grandfather's left hand appeared on his shoulder and gave him a shake. He leaned in and whispered, "We need to talk."

Anton nodded. Arthur's simple words struck like an electric shock. His grandfather grinned with a smile that never reached his eyes, indicated the table with the roll of paper and stated, "I have something here you're going to want to see."

Anton frowned, a residual spark of suspicion flaring within him, but he took another step backward to give Arthur space as curiosity sallied forth.

Jay and Francis pushed their chairs back, stood up, and cleared the nearside of the table.

Arthur stepped forward, untied the black ribbon and spread the paper out on the table. He picked up a pair of coffee mugs and used them to pin the nearside corners down to the wooden surface.

Peter, his eyes alight with avid interest, helped pin down the far side of the paper with a pair of salt and pepper shakers. "Schematics? How did you get them? I presume they're real."

Anton moved up, standing to Arthur's left, staring at the detailed drawings of the vampire fortress. His heart leaped, his mouth fell open, his gaze consuming the densely packed images like a starving man offered a feast. Here was the game changer that would allow a successful attack on the Panopticon. He glanced back at Arthur who winked at him.

He was no longer alone in his quest to destroy the vampire fortress.

Arthur declared, "The initial contracts for the construction of the fortress came out nearly twenty years ago. I have a number of companies I own through a network of proxies. They successfully bid for the work. In total, my companies built well over half the fortress, including most of the IT and security systems."

Peter gave a low whistle.

Li's eyes flattened. "So, you think you can get into the fortress? What about getting us out again?"

Anton explained. "Li had a vision, it wasn't good. We've been arguing about what to do."

"Leaving was our first option!" Jay declared emphatically.

"Oh," Arthur said incredulously. "You don't want to leave."

Francis frowned, and said with quiet finality, "This is not your team."

"Of course, of course," Arthur added, resting his right hand on Francis' shoulder. "You're in charge Francis. No argument." Arthur grinned, glancing around the team. "I'm just a consultant."

Francis' eyes narrowed, then flicked back down to the schematics on the table top. "So, what do you really have?"

"I can get us in and … out."

"You've had these plans for what? Ten years? Twenty years?" Francis inquired. "Why wait until now to do something? You could've sabotaged this site years ago."

"Who says that hasn't already happened? How do you think the loremaster tech can work against the Panopticon? I had people build a backdoor into the Panopticon's network routines to allow us to haze it.

However, we had to limit the feature so that Crane wouldn't get more suspicious than he normally is."

Francis' jaw dropped. He gathered himself, his face flushing. "And now you tell us?"

"Operational security. The Order is corrupt. If Kain had found out, the information would've leaked back to Crane."

"You couldn't trust me after Juliette did the work to hide your family?"

"It's not about trust," Arthur asserted.

Francis' eyes flashed. "It's always about trust. You didn't trust me enough to bring me into your plans. You withhold information, you use people – and they never know what your real goals are. I'll never forget how you put Juliette at risk."

"She volunteered."

"You used her as bait!" Francis snapped.

"She survived."

"Not good enough," Francis stated. He thrust a finger at Arthur. "We have to know what this is really about!"

"Well, I'll tell you what the real goal is here," Arthur stated in a ringing voice, his gaze roving around the team. "We go in. We kill the power, and force the Panopticon to go into 'evacuation,' mode – and then – we steal it!"

"Steal it?" Anton asked.

"Sure. There's no reason why the vampires should be the only group with this technology. If we also have it, their advantage is gone. We'll be able to track them too."

Anton grinned; he liked the sound of this plan.

"Wait a second," Jay said, scowling. "You said your companies built the IT, why didn't you just build a second Panopticon?"

Arthur frowned for a moment. "I said, most of the IT. The quantum processors and AI core came from elsewhere."

"Elsewhere?" Francis asked skeptically. "There's something you don't know?"

Arthur's eyes tightened and he shrugged his shoulders. "Of course, I don't know everything, but I know enough to get us in and get us out again."

Francis breathed out through clenched teeth, then asked, "How do you get us in?"

"There is a complex of caves to the east of the base, they provide a way in via the same underground river that supplies the pumping and power stations."

Jay studied Arthur. "How do you know all this?"

"One of my companies completed the geophysical surveys for the site," Arthur said with a shrug, a slight smile curling his lips. "Of course, we didn't tell them everything we found out."

Peter and Chiara glanced at Anton, quiet hope on their faces.

Li cautioned into the tense silence. "Let's assume we do get in and get out with the Panopticon. Where would you keep it? You'd need an array of quantum processors to run it and truly massive storage. I'm sure the vampires are tracking the manufacture of quantum tech. They'll know. You'll never be able to start it up without them finding out where it is."

Jay said, "Not to mention that you haven't outlined how we get out of the fortress. I'm sure Crane and the rest are not going to let us just waltz out of there with the Panopticon tucked under our arm."

"And just how is that done anyway?" Li asked, in incredulous tones. "We're talking about a major AI system and all its data. How do you keep it from degrading during transport?"

Arthur smiled confidently, like he'd expected these questions. "There is a suitcase sized evacuation system filled with ultra-dense storage and quantum memory chips. It's designed to hold and transport the Panopticon if the fortress and the power plants fail. We'll use it – we just have to trigger the Panopticon to download into it." He glanced across at Jay. "I have the exfil path planned. We'll be able to escape. With the Panopticon out of business – the vampires will not be able to track us."

"And how do you take out the power plants?" Francis asked.

Peter glanced hard at Anton, and shook his head once.

Not with a commander tank, Anton thought.

Arthur stated confidently, "I have a way to take out the power plants."

"A way? … So, definitive," Francis said, his eyes narrowing with suspicion.

Arthur's lips curled into a knowing grin. He reached past Francis and stabbed the blueprints with a finger. "We start at the pumping station, we use the maintenance tunnels on the level below to send two teams to the power stations," he tapped two structures to the north and south of the base with his finger, "here and here." He stepped back, his eyes flashing. He swept his hand through a flat arc over the schematics. "We shut them down and disable the diesel backups. That'll cause a base wide power outage and initiate the Panopticon's evacuation mode."

"That's all very well," Jay said, looking hard at Arthur. "But you still haven't said how we get out."

"We fly out."

Jay laughed harshly. "And, how the hell do we do that?"

Arthur nodded. "A third team destroys the specter and nemesis towers so they can't shoot us down. We capture a nightfalcon from the hangars, and fly the hell out of there."

Anton, his eyes alight, enthused, "We can do this; Peter and I both know how to fly nightfalcons." All feelings of resentment and suspicion had retreated. Arthur was a legend. He must have planned for decades to create this opportunity. Stealing the Panopticon was more exciting than destroying it. It was a way to not only harm the cause of the Vampire Dominion, but strengthen the resistance against them. Arthur's plan ticked all the boxes.

"And what of the fortress' guards?" Francis asked. "I presume they will not be standing around with their thumbs up their butts watching us steal their prized AI."

Li lifted a hand and inquired, "And cameras? There must be hundreds, if not thousands in a site this large."

Arthur's mouth gaped open as if he was about to say something, then he closed it again. His eyes narrowed slightly and he said quietly, "The risks are managed." He started ticking off his fingers. "Yes, there will be guards, vampires, drones, laser grids, and everything will be designed to find you and kill you, but I tell you this – you'll never get another opportunity like this one to harm the Vampire Dominion and bring them to their knees."

Silence fell over the table. Peter looked up from the schematics and said with a measure of hope in his voice, "All this inside knowledge changes everything. We have a real chance of pulling this off."

"A real chance was all I needed," Chiara stated in heart-felt tones.

"I was sold at 'I can get us in,'" Anton said. "We've gotta do this."

Li shook her head. "It's still a death trap." She stared hard at Arthur. "All you've offered is a way to make my vision come true."

Jay declared, "I'm with Li on this one."

Arthur glanced at Francis. "It's your call. I'm just tagging along for the ride."

Francis stared at the schematics for a long moment, and then said quietly, "We keep our eyes open—"

Li's face fell, her gaze dropping into her lap where her hands twisted around each other.

Francis studied each member of his team. "—and we watch each other's backs. We leave our doubts here at this table and commit to the plan." He turned and stared hard at Arthur. "You'd better be right."

Arthur smiled quietly at Francis and then glanced knowingly at Anton.

Anton grinned back, his heart beating hard in his ears. They were going to strike back and rip the Vampire Dominion a new one. There was one remaining question he had to ask. A principle was involved, something learned from hard experience. "One escape pathway out via the helicopters, what's our second exfil path if that's blocked?"

Arthur smiled quietly. "Back through the caves, Anton. Back through the caves."

"We're on!" Anton said, slapping his fist into his palm. In that moment, he couldn't imagine being anywhere else. He was exactly where he wanted to be, allied with his grandfather and fighting against the vampires.

"Okay," Francis said, glancing back down at the map. "Let's thrash out the details."

Arthur nodded. "Sure, but we need to make it quick. The window of opportunity is closing."

Francis looked at Arthur, his eyes steely. "Even so, we're not simply walking in."

"Of course, it's noted," Arthur nodded. "You're the boss."

Arthur flicked a knowing glance at Anton as Francis turned back to the fortress schematics.

Anton hid his response, his face impassive, revealing nothing.

A slow grin spread across Arthur's face, then vanished as he turned to answer a question from Jay.

I have no understanding of my grandfather's plan. Is it as simple as it appears on the surface, or is there a deeper agenda in play? He's just given us the keys to the kingdom of the Panopticon fortress, but why did he wait for us? He could have used another team, or built his own team. What does he really want?

Anton had no answers, and he turned to the diagrams spread across the table top. He needed to pay attention and absorb everything he could. The next twenty-four hours promised to be the most important of his young life.

There would be only one opportunity to strike the Panopticon and this was it.

* * *

His grandfather's one-ton pickup truck raced along the road into the mountain range. The road snaked back and forth through a seemingly endless sequence of curves and turns. The foothills rose up to become mountains overlooking the eastern side of the Panopticon Fortress valley.

Anton sat next to him in the cabin. The rest of the Mirovar force team following closely behind in their SUVs. Li, once again, hazing their presence from any nearby cameras. They'd sat in silence for the last fifteen minutes after leaving the roadhouse. The raw anger in the roadhouse had ebbed but questions remained. He pressed his lips together, frowned and looked at Arthur. He started to speak, then paused for a second.

Arthur glanced over at him. "Spit it out, boy!"

Taking a deep breath, Anton asked, "Where were you on April the twenty eighth?"

Arthur looked at him for a long moment, casually steering the truck around a curve at speed. "I was deep in the Amazonas region of Brazil. I was working solo on disrupting one of Crane's weapons programs."

"Armitage showed me photos of you at a carnival in Rio."

"They made me that night. That was in February, a couple of months before … well, you know."

Anton nodded; his lips pressed together in a thin line.

"There was a praetorian and a pair of Shadowstone agents. I accounted for all of them. Obviously, they uploaded the photos immediately. Afterwards, I left the remains of the praetorian in a dumpster and pushed the agents into a sewer."

"When did you leave?" Anton asked.

"I left the States in December last year. The last person I spoke too was Gang. At that time, the protection around my family was working perfectly." He paused for a long moment and his face hardened. "It all fell apart while I was in Brazil."

"Why weren't you there? Armitage respects you. She said you're in the top two or three swordsmen in the world. You could have made all the difference. Mom and Dad would still be with us."

Arthur shook his head slowly from side to side. "Nineteen plus years of effective protection. We used the Panopticon itself to hide you. The only thing I can think of is that someone recognized William or Anna for who they really were and word got through to Crane. He would've sent Armitage and Drake looking for the Papyrus of Hakron the Scribe, and you know the rest."

"But what were you doing in Brazil? What was so important?"

Arthur sniffed, a sardonic grin curling the edges of his mouth. "Crane's Day Guard program relies on a serum derived from the Ophiocordyceps Diabolicus fungus. The fungus infects ants, sends them completely insane. They attack each other and quickly destroy the whole nest. The fungus then grows a giant spore stalk in the nest fertilized by the remains of the ants. Crane's pet scientists harvest spores from the tip of the stalk. The spores are rich in an active ingredient that switches on some of the epigenetic factors associated with the Ramp."

"Charming," Anton remarked quietly.

"You've seen day guards in action at the conclave?"

Anton murmured, "Yes."

"Now imagine if Crane had thousands of them."

Anton rubbed the short growth of beard on his chin. "Shit."

"You see the problem."

Anton nodded once. "So, what did you do?"

"I took out his research center in the Amazon. It took me half a year to find and infiltrate it. I was out of all contact from February through to July.

Finally took it down on July the fourth. Had our own little fireworks show." He shook his head ruefully. "They had prototypes of everything they were working on, day guards, smart rifles, the whole kit and caboodle. Near the end, one of the guards got lucky. I barely made it out of there alive. I spent the next month recovering with a local tribe of Indians."

Arthur lifted his checkered flannel shirt revealing a pair of fading bullet scars beneath his ribcage.

"I arrived back in the States in early August. I stayed with Jon Thunder-Axe and began making final preparations for this mission. He told me about Kain dying on the twenty-third of August. He'd heard about it from Justin Blake. That was a pivotal shift for the Order, with the Kain cabal suddenly leaderless and scrambling to consolidate their power. Little did they know they were fighting to be captain of the Titanic. Then Crane smashed the Order yesterday morning and now we're here." Arthur sniffed. "So, how did Kain die?"

"He'd been made into a vampire by Armitage and Jay took his head off."

"Hmmm. Poetic justice. Kain killed Jay's mother. Did you know?"

"There's been speculation. Jay spent his life believing you'd done it."

"No wonder he's pissed at me. Old grudges are the hardest to break."

Anton looked at Arthur. He'd been holding a grudge against him since his mother's death. Was it warranted? Did it even make sense? He was no longer sure Arthur had any responsibility for what had happened to his parents. Anton had lost his mother and father, and his grandfather had lost his son and daughter-in-law. The greatest tragedy for anyone was to lose a child.

Anton sighed. He'd been selfish and stupid to blame Arthur for the loss of his family. Now he regretted blaming him. His previous actions were foolish and juvenile, and he was ashamed of them. He vowed silently to not make the same mistake again. His grandfather was blameless, Armitage, Crane, Drake, and Kain were the true culprits for what had happened to his parents. He grinned mercilessly, Kain and Drake had already paid the ultimate price. Only Armitage and Crane remained with open accounts needing closure.

A contemplative look passed over Arthur's face. He glanced across at Anton and asked, "I wonder why Armitage left you alive? It would have been so much neater for her to kill you."

Anton looked down at his boots. "I don't know."

"Well, I think we can rule out mercy," Arthur's eyes gleamed and he inquired, "What did Armitage say at the end?"

Anton blushed and looked out the side window. He muttered, "Something about how it was my fault."

"You're joking?"

Anton jerked around and stared at his grandfather, his heart twisting in his chest. "No, I'm not."

Arthur's eyes flashed and he ordered, "I want you to try and remember exactly what she said. I want you to repeat it word for word."

Anton's heart sunk. Armitage's words and the events of that night lay etched in blood on his soul. He spoke in quiet tones, as if confessing a long-held secret, "She said, 'You are the one that invited us in. You, in your ignorance and helplessness, became the bait that made your parents vulnerable. It is entirely your fault that they are dead or imprisoned forever.'" He swallowed once, his throat threatening to seize up. "Then she said, 'On the bright side – you get to live.' Then she leaned in close and looked into my eyes and said, 'Your parents have told you that they loved you and wanted to keep you safe, but I ask you this – who spent years lying to you and who told you the truth?' Then she cut me free and vanished."

Arthur stared at Anton for a long moment. His hands directing the truck around a hairpin bend from muscle memory alone. "That old myth about vampires having a mesmerizing power is not entirely bullshit. She was laying one on you. She was fucking with your mind." He stared through the windscreen for a brief moment. "Fuck me dead. You were the target!"

Anton shivered.

"That was why she left you alive at the end. That's why she did what she did, and said what she said. It was all a fucking show to get inside your head." Arthur stared at Anton, lifting his hands briefly off the steering wheel to gesture helplessly. "But, what the hell for?"

Anton shrugged his shoulders. How could he know what Armitage was really planning?

"No. Don't try and answer that. You'll tie yourself in knots," he reached across the cabin and tapped Anton's chest. "She wants you for something special. Don't worry, we can work it out. But you can be sure, she has an agenda where you'll play some pivotal role." Arthur stroked his chin, his eyes flashing. "How dare that bitch use my grandson."

He slammed on the brakes, the pickup truck sliding over gravel to a sudden halt. He stared hard at Anton; his eyes lit from within. "We'll get her. We'll get her together. Mark my words, her days are numbered." He paused for a moment, then smiled. "You can get out now, we've arrived."

Anton looked around. They were in a small clearing next to a cliff face, he reached for the door.

Arthur's hand appeared on his left arm, pulling him back. "Oh, by the way, don't call me Pappy, or Granddad, or some shit like that. Just call me Arthur."

Anton opened the cabin door, and said over his shoulder, "No problem, Arthur." He stepped from the cabin to the ground, and surveyed the mountain side. A single cave mouth, a dozen feet across, stood opposite the small clearing. The interior of the cave dove into the rock, disappearing into a well of darkness.

The two following SUVs pulled to a stop and the team disembarked with their weapons and equipment. Arthur called to Anton from the other side of the pickup truck. "I hope you're not claustrophobic."

Anton shook his head and said under his breath, "Not that I know of."

He turned and stared into the cave mouth. He took a deep breath and let it out. He felt lighter. He wasn't to blame for what had happened to his parents. Armitage was trying to manipulate him and he'd been carrying her poison for the last four months. Well, enough was enough. The true culprit was Armitage; the will to revenge surged through his soul. He vowed her manipulation of him would end immediately.

Hatred for Armitage and Crane swelled in his heart. With Arthur's help, he'd take them both down. Killing them would deliver a measure of justice for their many crimes. With an ounce of luck, he'd kill Crane before her eyes. Let her see what was about to happen to her. Let terror and helplessness fill her for a change.

Anton retrieved the Blue Dragon from the rear shelf of the cabin, grinning mercilessly, his mind filled with visions of bloody slaughter.

* * *

Bright sunlight filled the clearing.

Arthur surveyed the assembled team. They faced him in a semi-circle; he could draw a mental line straight down the middle of the group. To his left there was Anton flanked by Chiara and Peter, and to his right there was Francis flanked by Li and Jay. Three who were fully committed to the mission and three who ranged from hostile to doubtful.

It was time to set all fears and doubts aside. He spread his hands wide and stated, "Firstly, I want to acknowledge you all for accepting this mission. This is unlike anything you've done before. This is entering the very heart of Dominion territory and taking their most strategically useful asset. The courage and determination in your choice to be here is without peer."

His gaze flicked over the team like a whip. "I won't sugar coat it," he lifted his left hand up high. "This is the level of danger we will face." He lifted his right hand up to match his left. "And this is the value of what we can achieve." He paused for a moment, dropping his hands. "This is a high risk, high value mission and once it is done, we will have crippled the operational capability of the Vampire Dominion and gained a resource that can be used to bring the Order back to its full strength."

Francis gave a short nod at the mention of restoring the Order.

"I've been preparing this mission for longer than some of you have been alive. The infiltration will be straightforward. I have prepared way stations along the path to supply us with everything we will need to execute the mission. My inside knowledge of the fortress will give us the edge we need to secure victory against an otherwise invincible foe. I won't lie to you. Once we start the process of stealing the Panopticon, they will hit us with everything they've got. Then it will be down to our skills, courage, and teamwork as to whether we succeed or fail, and live or die."

His gaze flicked over Li, Francis, and Jay. "Now, I know we're not all on the same page here, and I'm not going to insult you with some, 'Once more into the breach,' crap. The honest truth is that we are on our asses with our backs against the wall. Despite Li and Wichowski, the Order loremaster capability is almost gone. Without their strategic cover, the vampires will hunt us down and kill us within weeks. If we don't succeed today, we'll all be dead soon, the Order will cease to exist, and every sacrifice we've made," he looked hard at Francis and Jay, "will have been for nothing."

He swept his gaze back and forth over the group. "I can't promise you survival, but I can promise you an honest chance to survive off your own merits. This mission is the best chance you have to make a difference against Crane's Dominion, and your best chance to seize the initiative against the vampires."

He slammed his fist into his palm, and swept the group with his forefinger. "Your efforts in the next twelve hours will make more of a difference in this world than anyone's efforts in the last twenty years … or the next twenty. The Vampire Dominion has held sway for nearly two centuries. Today is the first day where we'll begin to take back our future from them. Today we'll break the back of their systems of control. Today, we stand together against the vampires, and together we'll break their rule."

Arthur swept the group with his gaze and asked, "Are you in or out?"

"I'm in," Peter and Anton said together, followed a moment later by Chiara.

Francis nodded.

Jay snorted, then said, "Sure."

Li stared back at Arthur, and declared, "Of course, I'm in."

Arthur glanced at her; a sardonic smile graced his lips for a moment. He turned away toward the cave and said, "Follow me."

Moments later, the team swapped the bright sunlight for the darkness of the cave.

Arthur led the team into the deepening gloom. He flicked on the LED on his Order nightglasses and a cone of light illuminated the path before him. The nightglasses always operated better when there was some ambient light. He'd already cleared the cave. There was no risk of discovery at this point in the mission. The LEDs would reduce the risk of accidents. The rest of the team followed suit.

As he delved deeper into the bowels of the Earth, there was a conundrum that bothered him. Anton Slayne was not meant to be part of this mission, and yet he'd recently placed a fresh kit bag with Anton's name on it at the first way station. How did he know to do that? It was a right bother not to know all the details of his own plan.

Or even most of the details. Despite his ignorance, he forged forward into the cave.

He would do what he must, and nothing less.

Chapter Five

"The small mountain range due east of the proposed site of the Panopticon fortress has been deemed a Class B safety environment due to the assessed risk of rockfalls and cave collapses. The area has been re-classified as a natural reserve to provide a barrier to any approach. Access will be restricted to fire roads and [REDACTED].

Assessment conducted by subcontractor 'Geophysical Safety Pty Ltd,' registered at [REDACTED]."

– Shadowstone Site Geophysical Assessment Report H-14301 – Rev B.

[DEFECT ID]: K-000129456
[PROJECT]: Panopticon Security System – External Barriers
[STATE]: Open
[PRIORITY]: Low
[SEVERITY]: Low
[SYSTEM]: Mark 15, Block I, 'Dragon's Teeth,' 8MW Stationary Laser Grid
[LOCATION]: [REDACTED]
[ISSUE SUMMARY]: Grid randomly fluctuates generating outages lasting from 1 to 2 seconds.
[DATE LAST CHANGED]: [REDACTED]
[CHANGE NOTES]: Priority and Severity fields reduced from high to low as the issue is cosmetic only. Deprioritize all maintenance tasks on this grid to lowest available level.

– Extract from a Shadowstone Technical Directorate defect report

* * *

Utah, The Caves, September 11th, 08:05

A distant rumble grew then crashed like heavy thunder back at the cave entrance.

Francis turned back toward the echoes, his headlight slashing across the rock wall as he pivoted to the right "What the hell was that?"

"A rockfall," Arthur remarked in matter-of-fact tones from deeper within the cave. "These hills are notorious for them."

"Wait," Francis said. "Jay, run back and check the entrance."

Jay, who was playing the role of rear-guard turned in an instant, blurring back through the darkness. The light from his headlamp disappearing a moment later.

Everyone stood waiting for Jay to return, taking sips of water from bottles and talking in low tones. Arthur called out from the front of the line, "Is this really necessary?"

"I believe so," Francis answered.

"It'll just be some rocks rolling down the outside of the mountain, it happens all the time."

"Do we still have a way out?" Francis asked.

"Well, it'd be extraordinary bad luck if we don't," Arthur declared. "I've mapped these caves exhaustively over the last two decades. There is only one entrance in and we used it."

Francis said flatly, "I don't believe luck is a factor—"

"And nor should you."

"—around you," Francis finished.

"Do you think I planned this," Arthur asked incredulously.

"I wouldn't put it past you," Francis asserted.

"Do you really think I had an avalanche waiting for the day the Mirovar force team would be in this cave? Really Francis, you might be developing a touch of paranoia."

"In the games you play, the paranoid are the ones who survive."

Dancing cones of light painted the walls with pale shadows as the others tracked the discussion occurring in the darkness between Arthur and Francis.

"Survival, that's a bonus," Arthur declared.

"With your plans – always," Francis agreed with a derisive note.

"Hey, I get people through."

"You almost got Juliette killed."

"Oh, Francis. C'mon, that's ancient history."

"Not to me it's not."

Arthur paused for a moment. "Look, I'm fully aware of your loss. We all feel it, but can we agree to put it aside for now."

"This is not about Juliette; this is about how you operate."

"It's a little late to be having second thoughts, Francis. We're committed now."

"Yes, we are. How convenient is that?"

The silence stretched between the two men, and the lights around them grew still. A light emerged from the gloom and Jay slid to a halt at the back of the line. He swept his right hand through a flat arc. "It's blocked. There's no way out."

Francis and the rest of the team pivoted to the front, their lights illuminating the sole figure of Arthur standing a dozen feet in front of the team.

Arthur squinted into the glare, shrugged his shoulders and spread his hands wide. "Well, like I said. Damnably bad luck." There was a long moment of silence, then he added. "Of course, everything has a silver lining. I know the way out."

"Yes, you do." Francis conceded. He pulled his right hand down his face and came to a painful decision. "So be it. I relinquish this team to your care."

Arthur stared at him for a long moment, and then said, "I accept."

"Don't make me regret it."

"I won't," Arthur replied, turning deeper into the cave. He signaled the team forward with a flick of his raised hand.

Francis turned away, pushing past Anton to the back of the line. "Jay," he called out, "I'm joining you to watch our back."

There was no escape except through the Panopticon fortress. They couldn't back out now or abort the mission. It was do or die. Arthur must have engineered the rockfall. He'd ensured they had to go into a battle that only he had the tactical and situational knowledge to get them through.

Relinquishing command was the only way that Francis could give the team the best chance of survival.

It wasn't a choice, the team had to come first.

* * *

Peter slowed his pace, crowding Li as she advanced behind him.

He murmured in a low voice, just loud enough for her to hear and no one else, "You've got excellent hearing. Did you hear a double-tap just before the rockfall?"

Li thought back to what had happened. Yes, there was a pair of reports immediately before the rockfall that blocked their escape path. She nodded reflexively, even though Peter was facing forward and couldn't see her. She replied quietly, "Yes. For sure."

He whispered back over his broad right shoulder, "Shaped charges. No accident."

Peter picked up his pace again. Li falling in behind him. The avalanche that had blocked the entrance into the cave system was deliberate. Arthur Slayne was lying to them. She tensed. What was his true goal? It couldn't be good if he couldn't tell them about it.

A sudden intuition made her stumble. She caught herself before she fell, her left hand pushing against the gray rock of the cave wall, propping herself back upright. The other voice in her vision. The one who'd been talking with Anton before he fell. The one in the main server room of the Panopticon. It was Slayne, and now he was leading them into the very place where her vision could come true.

An ice-cold river ran through her veins. It was all she could do to stop herself screaming out in desperate warning.

Chiara appeared at her shoulder, her gentle hand catching her beneath her right elbow. "Are you okay?" she asked.

"Sure … sure, sure," Li whispered hoarsely. Her left hand flew to her mouth, sliding down and pulling on her bottom lip.

Chiara asked, "Are you really, okay? You don't look it."

Li nodded, no longer trusting herself to speak. She stepped forward, breaking away from Chiara, whose hand fell away.

Whatever was happening – none of it was good.

She looked forward into the gloom beyond the reach of their headlamps. A faint sound of rushing water impinged on her hearing. There must be an underground river ahead, but a river to where? The power stations? A way into the Panopticon fortress? No doubt – it was where Slayne was leading them, but was he leading them to victory or death?

A cold fear gripped her.

Peter was silent in his knowledge that the avalanche was a deliberate act by Slayne. The old man had cut off their sole path of escape to ensure they would follow him into the fortress. Should she scream out the truth? What difference would it make? Slayne knew more about these caves than anyone else.

Li kept her mouth shut in bitter silence. If the one person who knew the way out of hell was the devil – then best follow the devil.

She took a deep breath and let it out slowly. She steadied her stride, watching her foot placement amongst the rough stones of the cave floor. She glanced forward and back. The team surrounded her; Slayne leading, followed by Anton and then Peter. She followed after Peter, Chiara, Francis and Jay trailing behind her. It was not lost on her, the team had self-organized around placing their sole surviving loremaster at the center of their defenses.

What was she now, warrior or loremaster?

Was it possible to be both or would she have to choose?

She followed in Peter's wake, the shadows dancing like fell wraiths on the cold stone of the cave walls. Li had no answers but she resolved to find out. Her faith in Juliette and her father's legacies carried her forward with a lighter step and the shadows on the walls retreated before her advancing cone of light.

The sound of rushing water continued to grow in front of her, just how big was this underground river? Slayne slowed his long strides, and the rest of the team fanned out behind him. He stepped to the wall and pulled back a long, camouflage-colored tarpaulin, revealing a row of military boxes stacked against the cave wall.

"What's this?" Francis asked.

Slayne replied, "What we'll need to traverse the river and fight on the other side."

"Excellent," Peter said. He opened one of the boxes and pulled out a kit bag. "Look Li, this one has your name on it."

Li caught the bag, and unzipped it. She pulled out a camouflage jacket and checked the size. "It's a perfect fit for me." She looked across at Slayne and inquired, "How did you know?"

Slayne shrugged. "It's all part of the plan."

Li stuffed the jacket back into the waterproof pack and zipped it close.

Anton pointed at the rushing waters of the subterranean river. "We're swimming in there?"

Peter turned and arched an eyebrow. "'Fraid of a little water, are we?"

Anton frowned, and shook his head slightly. "I've …"

"Enough, boy," Slayne said brusquely. "You'll be too busy running along the bottom and dodging rocks to worry about drowning. Now strip down for the swim."

Anton opened his mouth to say something, then shut it again, and started dragging off his gear and clothes.

Li glanced from Anton to his grandfather and back again. They'd only just met and Anton was following him around like a lost puppy. What the hell was going on between them? Whatever it was, Li was sure the risk of drowning would be the least of Anton's problems by the end of the day.

Peter, Jay and Francis had opened the boxes, passing out soft waterproofed bags, and modified Order nightglasses designed to work underwater.

Five minutes later, stripped down to her underwear, the Green Dragon strapped across her back, her nightglass goggles and re-breather unit in place, and carrying a pre-packed bundle of equipment for the other end of the river, Li slipped into the water.

The river was surprisingly warm. There must be a strong geothermal source nearby if the water was this warm this far from the power stations.

The Ramp epigenetic density packing of muscle and bone made her substantially heavier than water. Li sank a handful of yards to the bottom of the river without effort. Peter was striding away a dozen feet in front of her, and Chiara was sinking to the bottom a short distance behind her. A tiny LED light on the goggles cut through the darkness with a cone of illumination. The night vision capabilities of the goggles did the rest of the work. She could see perfectly; the water was almost crystal clear.

Li set out after Peter. She'd be damned if she let her friends walk into a trap. She'd keep her eyes open and watch the elder Slayne like a hawk.

Deception stalked his every step. There was no obvious way to unravel his plans. The Green Dragon rested against the smooth skin of her back. If need be, the Green and Black Dragons would fight. If it had been her decision, the whole team would be long gone from here. But it wasn't her decision, and there was no way she would allow those she loved to enter danger without her at their side to share it.

They would live or die together – there was no other way.

She jogged forward in Peter's wake; her heart filled with staunch conviction.

***

The nightfalcon's twin turbines roared, the helicopter descending smoothly into the Panopticon fortress' underground hangar.

A pair of troop-carrying nightfalcons followed it down into the subterranean chamber, landing as a pair behind the lead helicopter.

A klaxon sounded a sharp ululation. The hangar doors rolled back into place with a barely detectable whirr, obscuring the sunlight and leaving the hangar safely lit with electric lights. The klaxon silenced. A praetorian pulled the helicopter's waist door open and leaped down onto the concrete floor of the huge underground chamber.

General Clayton Maze glanced at the gold watch on his left wrist. It was just before ten in the morning. They had arrived in good time. He waited for the rest of his troop to exit the craft. It was his privilege to be last to leave and last to enter a potential war zone. He adjusted his dark-blue suit and his personal katana strapped at his waist before stepping from the craft to the hangar floor. He strode to a position in front of his troops. The praetorians had already organized themselves into four squads of four beside the lead nightfalcon, their M249 light machine guns held at parade rest.

Shouted commands rang out over the declining whine of slowing turbines. The other two helicopters disgorged their loads; forty-eight fully equipped day guards forming into two lines behind the sixteen praetorians.

A welcoming committee advanced from his right, led by the facility commander, a senior member of Shadowstone named Regina Cormack. She was a stout woman, flanked by a quartet of functionaries and assistants, and trailed by two squads of praetorians permanently assigned to the fortress. She wore a dark-gray business suit with her security badge displayed prominently from a black lanyard around her neck. With pale-blue eyes beneath a head of iron-gray hair maintained in a tight bun, she regarded Clayton with a firm gaze, and said in crisp tones, "Welcome to the facility, Sir. What are your orders?"

Clayton stared at the woman, and ordered in clipped tones, "Commander Cormack, set the base to Orange alert, an attack is imminent."

"Sir?" she queried, a frown creasing her forehead. "Our threat analysis is clear."

Clayton smiled coldly. "Be that as it may, our enemies marshal against us. Unlock your weapons, set all alerts, and steel your men for the defense of this facility."

"Yes, Sir," she replied. "Sir, if an attack is imminent, may I suggest a red alert."

Maze stared at her coldly. "No, you may not. I will not signal our enemies that we are waiting for them by putting the base into visible lockdown. Now take me to the command-and-control center. I will need to refactor the disposition of your forces to take into account the presence of my troops."

The commander stiffened, her pulse pounding in her temples. She stated with cool formality, "Yes, Sir. This way, Sir." She turned around, guiding him to a large subterranean corridor heading north into the depths of the facility.

Clayton smiled grimly. Humans, they were so transparent. He glanced around the hangar before following the disgruntled commander to the command-and-control center, his gaze passing over a lone figure dressed in gray coveralls pushing a cleaner's maintenance cart along the far wall.

He took no notice of the maintenance man – he was nothing more than a sack of blood employed in a drudge's job by Shadowstone. Clayton had the safety of the Panopticon in his hands, and his quest for primacy amongst the generals demanded he protect the Panopticon at all costs.

It was a duty he would discharge in full.

He owed his liege lord, Cornelius Crane, nothing less.

* * *

At the age of fifteen, a stranger rescued Dwayne Washington from vampires. He'd spent the rest of his life in the service of the Order of Thoth.

Dwayne had never forgotten the night a hooded protector had saved his life. He and his best friends had been playing basketball in the grounds of their high school. His closest friend Benny's uncle was the school's caretaker, and he always left the lights on over the outdoor basketball court to allow Dwayne and his friends to play in the evenings after school.

The sun had set at least an hour before, and Dwayne was lining up a shot from the free throw line. They were running a competition to see who could get the most goals in a row. Benny was in the lead with six, and Dwayne was preparing to throw an equalizer.

He bounced the ball three times and picked it up ready to throw. Something moved on the edge of his vision as he looped the ball forward to the goal ring. The ball landed on the ring, rolled around the rim, and teetered on the edge. He leaned to the right, willing the ball to fall in.

The ball started to tip in. A figure blurred from the shadows surrounding the court, leaped inhumanly high, grasped the ball from above and carried it away from the goal.

She landed and whirled, her pale skin shining under the fluorescent lights, her red hair a long tangle over bare shoulders and faded denim. She laughed, a high cold sound that sent an icy shiver running up Dwayne's back.

Benny shouted angrily from across the half-court, "Hey! That's our ball. Give it back."

Her eyes flashed with blue fire. She drew her right arm back, grinned mirthlessly, and said nonchalantly, "Have it then." Her hand blurred. The ball vanished, re-appearing as it ricocheted off Benny's face with a loud crack like snapping wood.

Benny dropped like a stringless puppet, his head canted backward at a crazy angle, blood gushing onto the asphalt in freshets from his mouth and nose.

Hollow shock froze Dwayne's sneakers to the court. His jaw dropped open and he stared at Benny lying crumpled on the ground. Harry moaned from behind him, and Jasper stuttered, "Nnn … Nnn … No!"

"Oh, my gawd what a waste," stated a casual voice from the shadows to Dwayne's right.

He jerked around, Harry and Jasper snapping around to see who was approaching them.

A slim man wrapped in a gray business suit, with narrow features, lank raven-dark hair and a broad mouth, sauntered out of the gloom and onto the court. He glanced once at Benny, lying broken on the ground, and sniffed disdainfully. "Now Carla, you know we shouldn't be careless with our food."

The narrow man kept walking toward them, the heels of his boots clicking over the asphalt, a slow grin curling his full lips.

They started backing away. Dwayne's head swiveled left and right but there seemed to be nowhere to run to. Wherever he looked, one of the strangers blurred into view with inhuman speed.

The red-head circled behind them, a high giggle erupting from her throat.

The narrow man stood stock still, sucking air through his teeth while leering avidly at the boys.

Jasper and Harry both ran in opposite directions at the same time. They didn't get far, the monsters pounced like jungle cats. They seized their throats with gaping jaws, sinking gleaming fangs into their flesh, and dragging them down to the asphalt.

Dwayne backed up a step, hesitating to run. He couldn't leave his friends without fighting back. There was a loud crunch as the red-head tore off Jasper's left arm and threw it casually aside.

The narrow man sucked greedily at Harry's throat, bending his friend's torso back over his knee. Harry's spine let go with a sharp crack, his long legs jerking once before hanging like loose noodles.

Dwayne had seen the movies – he knew what they were – they were vampires. His teenage mind immediately accepting what an adult would have struggled to believe – vampires were real. There was nothing he could do to help any of his friends. He turned and fled for his life.

He made it to the court's edge before a force picked him up from behind and threw him against a shelter shed. His right arm snapped against the wall, agony shooting through his shoulder. Half dazed, he turned, backing up against the cold bricks and staring into the face of the narrow man. Dark eyes as black as coal stared back with frigid and callous enmity.

The creature's hands appeared around his throat. The vampire's grip was steely, lifting him effortlessly up by his neck, his legs swinging, his feet dangling off the ground, a low moan of terror escaping past his lips.

The red-headed girl's voice giggled again for a moment, then cut off into sudden silence broken only by a flopping sound of something crumpling onto the asphalt.

The narrow man's eyes widened; his head flicked right.

Bright metal gleamed for an instant under the fluorescent lights over the court. The lights flickered for an instant as something passed beneath them. A thin ribbon of blood splashed from left to right in a line across Dwayne's cheeks and nose.

A look of shock overtook the narrow man's face. His grip loosened, his hands dropping away. His head fell backwards, blood jetting up in twin fountains from his throat.

Dwayne dropped to the ground, staggering away, reflexively cradling his broken right arm. He groaned with abject horror as the narrow man's headless body jerked upright, and lurched with unnatural vitality for a moment before crumpling to the ground, finally coming to rest in a spreading pool of blood on the asphalt.

In the center of the basketball court, the red-head laid in two parts in a blot of dark blood and spilled entrails – evenly split down the middle of her body.

A tall man with a long blood-dripping sword held in his right hand, his face shadowed by a dark-gray hood, stepped casually over the decapitated body of the narrow man. He put his free hand out and stated gruffly, "You need to come with me."

Dwayne hesitated for a brief moment.

The tall man flicked the sword in a blur of movement, the blood fleeing the blade in a thin spray. The magnificent sword flashed in the over-head lights like something magical or holy – a weapon destined to kill monsters. Something black and shiny gleamed in the hilt. A surreal detail capturing his attention amongst the grief and carnage. It was a pearl, a black pearl resting like a mark of God in the handle of the sword.

Dwayne took a short step forward and grasped the stranger's hand. The man's grip was firm and strong around Dwayne's hand, and he promised, "I'll keep you safe."

In his heart, Dwayne knew he would.

His memories were thirty years in the past. Dwayne pushed his cleaner's cart into the nearest toilet block off the hangar floor. Now he served as a willing agent deep within enemy territory. A man on the inside awaiting the moment he could assist the man who'd irrevocably changed the course of his life so many years ago. A man whose life purpose – the destruction of vampires – he'd embraced with all his heart.

He'd overheard the conversation between the vampire general in a suit and the base commander. His trained mind had missed nothing. An attack was imminent. The base was on high alert. The vampires had arrived in force to protect the Panopticon. He checked the individual toilet cubicles, determining that he was alone. Turning his head away from a nearby camera he tapped the right corner of his jaw three times, just below his right ear, activating a hidden implant.

He took a brush and began scrubbing a perfectly clean toilet bowl, then flushed it – holding the button down to take advantage of all the water in the cistern.

He whispered sotto voce, his voice trembling with emotion, "Arthur. General Maze has arrived with sixteen praetorians and forty-eight day guards. They know you're coming. You're walking into a trap. Abort the mission. Abort!"

The communicator thrummed helplessly beneath his ear. Arthur Slayne was out of range. Dwayne couldn't tell him about the flood of reinforcements that had just arrived at the fortress.

His old friend was walking into a death trap and there was nothing Dwayne could do to warn him.

* * *

"We're half-way there. Everyone take a fifteen-minute break. Drink, eat, rest, and refuel," Arthur Slayne stated with brisk enthusiasm.

The Mirovar force team had emerged from the river onto a sandy bank that ran back another twenty yards to a rock wall dotted with more caves. There were three tracked drones sitting in the middle of the underground beach loaded with locked boxes. A powerful lamp facing up to the ceiling of the cave surmounted each drone. The cave ceiling showered the beach with reflected light. Everyone killed their LEDs and removed their Order nightglass goggles. Arthur opened the first locked box, handing out bottles of water and self-heating ration packs to the team members. He then moved to a second box filled with fresh rebreather units and began unpacking them for the team.

Chiara set a fifteen-minute timer on her Order nightglasses. She wanted forewarning for when Arthur expected her to be ready to leave. She had a mission in mind: Anton Slayne.

Anton, Peter and Li had broken away from the rest and sat on the beach next to the river. She joined them, everyone ate and drank with little conversation for about five minutes. The only remarks directed at the stunning vision of stalactites descending from the ceiling above the inky depths of the subterranean river.

Her friends finished their meals. Peter offering to take the empty packs back to the drones. Li went with him, opening a discussion on potential weapons the fortress defenders could use against the team.

Anton looked across at her. His lone eye lingering on her bare skin. They'd stripped down to their underwear for the expected four-hour swim through the river. She was wearing a black bra and panties, and Anton had a short pair of tight-fitting dark-blue trunks that left little to the imagination. The river water had mostly dried on his skin, a few drops here and there. His dark hair sat damply on his scalp. His piercingly blue eye locked on hers. She glanced back at the caves disappearing into the cave wall, and tilted her head quizzically.

Anton took her hand, and she went with him. Disappearing into the shadows of the nearest cave facing onto the beach. He whirled her around, lifting her off the ground with ease. His lips hot against hers. Her heart thudded, she wanted him, she needed him. She would have him.

Strong, urgent hands moved clothing aside. He backed up against the cave wall. She splayed her knees wide while he held her against his hard-muscled body and entered her. He held her close and tight, his hands dropping to support her hips.

She wrapped her arms around his neck and kissed him hard. Her hands rose to the sides of his head. It was impossible to get too much of him. She'd get all she could, while she could. They could both be dead before the day was out.

She held him as tight as possible and rode him to mutual climax.

She held him afterwards, panting over his shoulder as aftershocks throbbed through her body.

Her skin tingling, she arched back and faced him. "Anton," she admitted. "I love you."

He stared at her in the shadows, his hands gently tracing the lines of her face, but the words she wanted to hear didn't come.

"Chiara," Anton said, "I feel you…"

"But?"

"I'd die for you, but what you just offered I can't match."

She whispered, "What does that mean? Can't you love me?"

Anton pulled her in tight and whispered urgently, "You're beautiful … beautiful … stunning. I'm in awe of who you are. The world needs to know who you really are, but … I'm not in a good place."

"Anton?" she whispered.

"I'm driven by vengeance, hate and death. I know that now. You offer me love, and I fear to accept it."

"Be brave Anton, be brave," she urged. His heart thudded opposite hers. She reached up to his face and discovered his right cheek was wet with tears. She held him tight, a pair of tears tracing thin tracks down her face. Turmoil filled their souls to the brim and flowed like a river between them. No one understood how much he'd gone through in the last few months. He'd been certain he'd understood his life, and then the vampires had arrived in his world and torn it apart. A destruction that mirrored her own recent experiences. Only a few short months ago, she'd been certain of her mission and her faith in her father's purpose. Certainty and faith that had been torn to shreds during the debacle at the Maine safe house, and then annihilated on top of the cliffs above the town of Whitby.

Anton felt unworthy of love because vengeance, hate and death filled his life. She had her own knowledge of such things, and he didn't need to be concerned. She was the one person in his life who could truly understand him. He wasn't ready to commit in the same way that she was. He was willing to die for her. She didn't doubt that. It went with the territory of being a vampire hunter, and she would do the same for him.

For now, Anton only had room for one obsession in his life, and that was vengeance against Armitage and Crane.

Chiara released him and stepped back. She'd give him time. The fact he wasn't in the same place she was, didn't change that she'd fallen for him. She was in love. She was madly in love.

Anton Slayne was the breath of her life, and nothing was going to change that.

Nothing at all.

***

Anton emerged from the underground river.

Water sluiced from the barrel of his H&K 416 short-barreled special-forces assault rifle as he sighted along it with his good eye into the darkness of the cave. He cleared the river, mounting the gray stone of the bank. He dragged off the nearly exhausted re-breather unit and tossed it aside. The only way out was forward, and he wouldn't be coming back this way. The rock fall had cut them off from their only escape route, and the only way out was through the fortress. They had one option left: fight for their lives, and take the fortress away from the vampires.

He was okay with that. He'd been fighting for his life since the fateful night two days after his eighteenth birthday. He waited a moment, and Peter's red hair emerged from the swirling waters, quickly followed by the rest of him as he rose in near nakedness from the underground river.

Peter hefted a pair of oversized waterproof backpacks filled with gear onto the bank and stepped past them with a quiet oath, "How the hell did I end up with two?"

"Because you're twice the size of everyone else," Li suggested with a smirk, stepping from the water behind him.

Peter raised an eyebrow, glancing over his shoulder at her and said, "Only where it counts."

"Ha, I'll believe it when I see it."

"Well, whenever you're ready."

Li just grinned at him, arching her chest and sweeping her wet hair back over her scalp. She'd stripped down to her underwear; everyone had left most of their clothes at the subterranean entrance to the river to ease the long underwater journey to this part of the cave.

The journey had consumed the morning, taking more than four hours to navigate the river with their packs of equipment. There had been times when they could emerge onto lonely stone shelves, the light from their nightglass goggles reflecting off majestic limestone galleries unknown to the world. They'd take a short break to rest, eat, and drink from supplies pre-stocked by his grandfather, before reentering the tepid ink-like water of the river.

One of those breaks had been especially memorable. Chiara continued to surprise him with the depth of her passion. She was an alloy of brutal ruthlessness allied with gentle beauty and heartbreaking vulnerability. It tore at him that he was the only person in the world who really knew her. She was too good to remain invisible, but could Francis and Jay deal with the truth, or would they simply try and kill her. Anton knew he'd never be able to allow that to happen. Yes, Chiara had made mistakes, but none worse than anyone else. The true agent of Juliette and Yvette's deaths was

Armitage, not the young woman who was drawing ever closer to Anton's heart.

Chiara's future was an enigmatic puzzle waiting for resolution. One thing he was sure of, he didn't want to drag her into his quest for vengeance against Armitage and Crane. The world had whipped a hundred and eighty degrees since the arrival of his grandfather. He'd never been seeking justice. That was just a story he'd told himself to avoid admitting ownership of the cold vengeance living in his heart. That pretense was gone. He knew full well what he wanted and who he was, and it wasn't fair or right to drag anyone else into his own personal vendetta.

Anton sighed, and set his rifle down on the cave floor, before wiping his hands down his face. It was good to be finally out of the river, it'd spooked him. One moonless night, he'd almost drowned in a river as a five-year-old before his mother saved him. He'd breathed water and lost consciousness, he'd almost died. Water was not his element – especially dark water. He didn't do water if he didn't have to. He'd spent much of the time within the river with that old memory digging its cold claws into his soul.

He turned away from Peter and Li, arched his broad shoulders and dropped off the waterproof backpack that his grandfather had provided to him at the entrance to the river. He swung the sack to the stone floor of the cave and unzipped it. He pulled out a towel and a dry set of clothes. The rest of the Mirovar team emerged from the swirling waters at the edge of the river. In moments they were all removing fresh sets of towels, clothes, combat boots, webbing, tactical gear, weapons and ammunition from the personalized waterproof backpacks Arthur had provisioned at the entrance of the underground river.

Anton was quietly impressed. His grandfather had completed a mountain of work for this mission. He must be a demon for planning and preparation, more so than anyone he'd ever met. He strapped combat webbing over his perfectly fitted urban-camouflage fatigues, and slotted a half dozen fragmentation grenades and fifty round clips of caseless ammunition for his rifle into position across his chest. He reached up and removed the nightglass goggles, and fitted his eye patch and a standard pair of Order nightglasses. He flicked the nightglasses' tiny but powerful LED lamp on, a broad cone of light opening up in front of him. He fitted earbuds into his ears. They wirelessly linked to the tactical network embedded in the nightglasses.

Li's voice whispered in high-definition clarity in his ears, "How's the tactical link?"

"Super," Anton said, quickly followed by everyone else's answers.

"Everyone ready?" Francis asked, walking around the team, checking equipment and offering encouragement.

Peter closed the final ties on his battle vest. His twin bladed battle-axes strapped to his broad back balanced four tri-bladed throwing axes laced with silver on the front of his deep chest. A multiple grenade launcher loaded with half a dozen 40mm fragmentation grenades, dangled just above his left hip from a strap over his shoulder. He wore a belt with a pair of MP7 sub-machine guns and sets of spare magazines riding around his hips, and a bandolier with another six 40mm grenades for the MGL ran from his left shoulder to right hip.

Jay had his katana at his left hip, and a H&K 416 assault rifle with an under-barrel 40mm grenade launcher loaded with a 40mm HEAP grenade. Spare magazines and fragmentation grenades filled his combat webbing. He drew a darkly gloved hand down his face, and then flicked the safety off his weapon.

Li adjusted the fit of the Green Dragon at her waist. She carried a FN P90 sub-machine gun slung with a strap over her shoulders. Spare magazines lined up in a diagonal row across her chest.

Chiara carried a second FN P90, her katana strapped across her back, the handle jutting up over her right shoulder. She stooped for a moment to check a pair of silver-laced throwing daggers attached to the outside of her calves.

Anton dangled his assault rifle from his left hand and checked the Blue Dragon resting across his shoulders. It remained securely positioned and ready to use at a moment's notice. He ran his right hand over the fragmentation and 40mm grenades, and spare fifty round magazines of caseless ammunition strapped to his chest, familiarizing himself with their exact positions. The caseless ammo for the rifle was mostly high-performance armor piercing explosive tipped rounds with every fifth bullet made of solid silver.

Arthur had prepared a classic mix of ammunition for human and vampire opponents wearing body armor. Precisely the sort of forces likely to be defending the Panopticon. Anton wondered just how his grandfather knew so much about the fortress they were about to attack. Arthur's involvement with the facility's construction could only explain so much. What were the other sources of his information for the many years of operation of the Panopticon? There would have been upgrades, technology renewals, changes of policy and process. How did he keep up to date?

Anton glanced across at Arthur. He stood aside from the group; the Black Dragon strapped to the left-side of his waist. His only other weapon was a custom built, .50 caliber auto-pistol holstered down his right thigh with half a dozen spare magazines on a bandolier strapped diagonally across his chest. He watched the team with quiet eyes, his face an impassive mask. The loss of the escape route back through the caves wasn't an accident. Sun Tzu had written about placing his troops into a killing field so they had no choice but to fight their way out. His grandfather had done the same thing. For whatever purpose he harbored within the secrets of his mind, he needed the Mirovar force team to help him steal the Panopticon. From the plan outlined by Arthur in the roadhouse diner, he needed multiple small teams. Two to kill the power stations, another to capture the nemesis tower and use it to destroy the fortress' defenses, and a fourth to steal the Panopticon. With the Mirovar team at his disposal he finally had enough people to pull this mission off. But it wasn't just people, he'd been specifically waiting for the Mirovar force team, and what did that mean? Anton didn't know.

Anton didn't care that his grandfather was keeping secrets. He must have his reasons and only someone completely ruthless could survive against the vampires for as long as he had. The goal was real enough and more than a hundred percent aligned with what Anton wanted to do. He would keep his eyes open, and his friends safe, but there could be no backing out now. They were committed, there were no alternatives left. His grandfather was their best bet for raiding the Panopticon fortress and surviving to tell the tale.

Francis lifted his H&K 416 assault rifle, checked his grenade launcher, then addressed them all, "Okay, team, we're ready to proceed." He glanced at Arthur, and then down toward a faint crimson light in the distance. "You, know what's next?"

Arthur nodded, and commanded, "Follow me." He strode off, the team falling in behind him.

Anton took a position immediately behind his grandfather. In the distance, the red light flickered for a second and then settled into a faint crimson glow. The team moved quickly forward toward the distant illumination, the smooth and level cave floor enabling easy passage.

Peter appeared beside him, nudged him in the ribs and whispered, "What the hell is that diabolical red glow?"

Anton grinned. "That'd be the gates of hell."

"Then Cerberus should be nearby?"

"Boundaries are always guarded, aren't they?"

Peter nodded solemnly. "Always."

"Yeah, whatever it is, I guess it'd be unfriendly."

"It's a mark fifteen, block one, eight-megawatt, stationary laser grid." Arthur remarked dryly a yard in front of them. "Very unfriendly."

The detail of the grid resolved into view. With the benefit of the Order nightglasses, the lasers were completely visible, creating a lattice of thin red lines crossing each other in foot wide squares. The red grid covered the full extent of the cave from floor to ceiling and wall to wall.

There was no way to pass through the grid.

Anton frowned. "A laser grid?"

Peter glanced to the side at Anton and advised in deadpan tones, "Don't accidentally fall into it." He twirled his fingers around each other, and remarked, "Instant julienne. You'd be two hundred and forty pounds of steak tartare."

Li stepped up next to Arthur and asked him, "How do you know about them?"

"One of my companies installed them. There's a feature whereby they shut off intermittently on a random basis."

"Sounds like a bug," Li suggested.

"No, it's a feature," Arthur insisted.

"It's a bug, isn't it?" Li asserted firmly.

Arthur put his hands on his hips and stated, "Look, there's lots of things that mostly work."

"Mostly work?" Li asked with a derisive snort.

"My company was the installer," Arthur explained. "We didn't build the things. But it turns out, they have this useful feature."

"Bug," Li insisted quietly.

The team stood in a line across the cave, looking at the grid. It flickered for a moment a yard in front of them, and went out. A second later the grid switched back on again.

Arthur remarked casually, "It's simple really, we just wait for it to switch off then step through."

Jay asked, "It looked like it was out for a second or so, is it always like that?"

"Mostly," Arthur answered.

Francis inquired, "Why has this never been fixed?"

"Deprioritization, bureaucracy and budgets," Arthur remarked, a knowing smile curling his lips.

"I knew it," Li said. "It's a defect and you've managed to get the vampires to ignore it for years."

"Okay, if you insist."

The crimson light flickered.

"Now," Arthur commanded decisively.

Anton blurred forward, the team moving with him. He turned, backing away from the rest so that he could see everyone. They had all made it through safely.

If that was the first test, it was simple to pass. Surely the rest of the way into the fortress would be harder. This was too easy to believe. He glanced at his grandfather, he seemed to know everything about how this fortress worked.

Was there anything he didn't know?

* * *

"If this was a typical mission," Peter whispered, "we'd be up to our knees in Shadowstone troopers or vampire scum by now."

Anton replied quietly, "This isn't a typical mission. This is what happens when we have enough information to have an advantage over the vampires. That's why we have to push through to the end. We'll never get another chance like this."

"Amen to that," Peter whispered back, wiping perspiration from his brow with the palm of his hand. "How long before we get out of this sauna?"

Anton shrugged his shoulders. The cave had run for another mile from the laser grid, and then opened up into an enormous cavern snaking for miles beneath the valley. In the middle of the cavern, a river of magma wended its way from one end of the gigantic chamber to the other. If the mission hadn't been as serious as it was, Anton would've taken more time to stare in wonder at the sight of the molten rock slowly moving through the middle of the massive underground cavern.

The team walked single file along the chamber wall, as distant from the glowing subterranean river as they could get. Giant circular fans whirled and throbbed in two rows along the cavern roof. They disappeared into the gloom at either end of the massive chamber. Anton surmised their spinning blades kept the air breathable despite the magma, allowing maintenance crews to descend to this level of the fortress.

At both ends of the enormous cavern, at least two miles apart, colossal metallic structures emerged from the ceiling, reaching pale-gray-dusted walls of steel down to almost kiss the molten rock. At the bottom of each structure, pipes whipped back and forth like wild tentacles inches above the glowing magma.

Arthur pointed toward the nearest complex arrangement of pipes slithering back and forth above the molten stone. "Heat reapers. They capture the heat, transfer it up to create steam to drive turbines that power the base. This one is the southern complex, the one in the distance is the northern complex. We named them 'Kraken dash one,' and 'Kraken dash two,' respectively."

Jay snarked, "So, you devoted your life to building shit for the vampires, huh?"

Arthur put his left fist up in the time-honored signal to halt, turned and stared back along the line at Jay. "The vampires would have built it with or without my help. By being involved, I've ensured we have a way in and a way to destroy this facility. Would you prefer not to have that option? Would you prefer this fortress was impregnable? Might I suggest that you focus on the mission in front of us instead of sniping at me. I'm sure the vampires will demand your full attention before we're finished. Is that clear? Are we done?"

Jay's lip curled derisively, then he glanced at Francis. Francis frowned briefly and shook his head once. Jay glared at Arthur for a moment, then shrugged his shoulders, and said casually, "Of course. Have it your way."

Arthur nodded once, and turned back to the center of the massive chamber. Facing away from the team, he pointed at a steel walkway that threaded a thin line hugging the ceiling between the two power stations. It branched off in the middle of the cavern, and reached across to the top of the near side wall before zig zagging down the rock face to the cavern floor. "That's our path in. There's a maintenance shaft reaching up to a water pumping station on the surface. It serves the power stations and the rest of the facility with fresh water from the underground river. It's also directly attached to the main administration building."

"Come on!" Li said, "Where are the cameras?"

Arthur turned again and looked back at her. "They're up on the structures and the maintenance walkway and linked back to the Panopticon. The Panopticon is surveilling this whole area looking for intruders."

"What?" Francis demanded.

"It's not a problem – they can't see us. I had a team program the system to make the members of this team invisible to the Panopticon within the perimeter of the Panopticon fortress."

"Just us, specifically?" Francis asked.

"Yes."

"There were the personalized backpacks as well. How did you know it would be us?"

"I had faith in you Francis to survive the corruption within the Order. I knew that sooner or later you would come here with your team."

Francis lifted his left hand and stroked his chin, then asked skeptically, "Faith, really?"

"The Mirovar force team has always been destined to destroy this facility and steal the Panopticon. I am simply here to facilitate that outcome."

"Wait a second," Li said, stepping forward. "Why didn't you extend the invisibility coverage to the rest of the world."

Arthur frowned seriously. "Too much risk of discovery. As a matter of course, the vampires would make contact with you. They'd note that you didn't show up on the Panopticon feeds, then they would've come looking to find out why. Sooner or later, they would have discovered this hole in their defenses. Today is the first time we could exploit this gap for effect. I had to protect that vulnerability." Arthur smiled. "I've been preparing for this moment longer than you've been alive."

Li looked at him, her eyes filled with suspicion, and inquired, "So, you left us hanging out in the wind so you could protect this pathway in?"

"That's okay Li," Arthur stated with a sardonic nod before turning away from her. "Your lack of approval is noted. However, I don't need your approval … just your participation." He glanced back, his dark-blue eyes flashing. "Now, follow me. This won't take long." He approached the steel stairs of the maintenance walkway reaching up the wall to the ceiling of the cavern. A moment later he was mounting them. "Quickly now, we don't want to leave an opportunity for the vampires to reinforce the fortress after the battle at the conclave hall. We have a small window of opportunity and we must seize it before it closes."

"And what if they have already reinforced the fortress?" Li asked.

Arthur glanced back at her, his face an inscrutable mask. "Then our mission becomes much more difficult, but not impossible for those with the will to seize victory from the jaws of defeat."

He turned back and mounted the first stairs up the cavern wall.

Anton glanced at Peter, and whispered, "What do you think? Have they reinforced the fortress?"

Peter pursed his lips. "Given our luck lately, this place will be crawling with filth."

"Vampires, day guards, drones and assorted flunkies."

Peter nodded. "A target rich environment."

"Well, we won't be bored."

"More the other way I think. I was disappointed not to find an extra pair of underwear in our personalized packs. I mean, what was your grandfather thinking?"

Anton glanced at Peter. "Do you think it could be overconfidence?"

"More like underestimating the pucker factor."

"Geez, that'd be serious … um, how much of a pucker factor are we talking about here?"

"On a scale of one to ten, I figure a nine with a strong tendency to go to eleven."

Anton said earnestly, "Now, I don't feel properly equipped."

Peter arched an eyebrow and wagged a finger at Anton. "You know what we could do?"

"What?"

"Steal them from the enemy."

Anton shrugged his shoulders and lifted his free hand. "They must have a laundry somewhere."

Peter stated deadpan. "Objective number one. Take over the laundry and secure an extra pair of underwear."

"Well, I'm glad we got that sorted."

"It's good to have clear objectives."

"How else would we know if we succeeded or failed?"

"Exactly."

Anton paused, craning his head back. "How many stairs do you think?"

"A few thousand."

"That many, huh?"

"That's just in the cavern. The shaft up to the pumping station would double that."

"Well, that sucks."

Peter grinned. "Suck it up princess. You're a light weight. I'm carting two-hundred and ninety pounds plus my equipment up there."

"Just goes to show, we should have looked at my idea to steal a nightfalcon and get in with a 'security pass code.' Arthur probably has a pass code we could have used. It'd be easier than all these stairs."

"You're just work shy."

Anton snorted. "We'll see about that."

Anton and Peter continued to banter quietly as the Mirovar force team scaled the maintenance walkway up the cavern wall. Anton estimated that in another ten minutes they'd be at the top of the cavern and ascending the shaft up to the pumping station.

As to what would happen after they reached the base, it was anyone's guess.

* * *

Anton followed his grandfather up the final flight of stairs into the pumping station.

They halted in the stairwell at eye level with the floor. The station's pale, polished concrete floor gleamed softly beneath industrial lights set in the high roof. The chamber was a hundred yards long and half that wide. Four massive pumps thrummed with a low roar, dominating the center of the station. Huge pipes ran from the pumps, turning at right angles into the floor, or punching out through the north and south walls toward the thirsty power stations.

Li rose up from behind them and faced Anton. She pointed at her ear and shouted over the deafening noise of the pumps, "Shift to channel number four."

Anton tapped his earbud four times with his index finger and the industrial thunder of the pumps diminished to a background hum.

"Okay," Li asked quietly, her words picked up and broadcast over the tactical network. "Is everyone on channel four?"

The rest of the team waited deeper in the stairwell. They nodded, assented, or gave a thumbs up sign.

Arthur looked back down at Francis and stated, "The pumping station is automated and should be clear of people but we'll need to check."

Francis nodded. He signaled with his hand and ordered, "In pairs. Peter and Li, Anton and Chiara, Jay and myself. Arthur, watch the approaches." He gestured to the other pairs and directed them off into the station, then tapped Jay and rushed off in the opposite direction.

Anton led Chiara out of the stairwell and across the polished concrete floor, his assault rifle ready to fire, his senses alive and ready to ramp at a moment's notice. They passed enormous thrumming pumps ten yards across, massive pipes threading their way to and from the pumps. The pumping station was drawing water from deep underground and sending it to the power stations north and south of the base.

He brushed his left hand against one of the pipes. The metal was neither hot nor cold, and vibrated faintly as great masses of water flowed within it. There was an enormous amount of water rushing through the pipes. He couldn't help but ask what would happen to the power stations if they cut off the water supply? *Nothing good for the vampires,* he imagined.

Anton stepped past the pump, sighting down his rifle into the far corner of the massive chamber. There was no movement, the station was empty. He turned and glanced back toward the stairwell. It was out of sight. The rest of the team had vanished.

Chiara was in front of him. She moved in close, her large brown eyes staring into his. She reached up around the back of his neck with her left hand.

He leaned into her. His free hand snaking around her back, pulling her close, and lifting her off the floor. Their lips met in a long kiss. He held her tight, every inch of contact becoming a heady thrill racing through his veins.

She leaned back, and he let her drop down to the concrete floor. Her brown eyes looked deep into his own and she whispered, "For luck." She put her finger up and pressed it against his lips. She turned, breaking from his grip and jogged past the nearest pump and back to the stairwell. Anton followed closely behind her, the scent of her hair lingering like a warm summer evening.

A brief moment later the team reconvened at the top of the stairs amongst a chorus of 'all clears.'

"Right," Arthur said. "Time to get this party started." He strode over to a nearby valve wheel, gripped it, and turned it firmly anti-clockwise until it locked.

"What does that do?" Francis asked.

"Shuts off an overflow valve. It'll cause the base to send a maintenance crew."

"But they'll discover us," Jay said, nonplussed.

"Precisely."

Anton grinned. "You want them to come?"

"Yes."

“Why?” Francis asked.

“Because I have a man on the inside.”

The rest of the team stared at Arthur. Francis rubbed his eyes as if he was waking up from a nap. Jay picked at some imaginary fluff on his combat webbing. Chiara rubbed the side of her nose, Li smiled derisively, and Peter snorted with rueful admiration.

“Awesome,” Anton enthused.

Arthur consulted his wrist watch. “He should be here in three minutes.”

“Who?” Francis asked.

“An Order helper.”

“Someone who can’t ramp? In this place?” Jay asked incredulously. “They’ll be a liability.”

Arthur shook his head. “Not at all, he couldn’t be someone who has undergone the transition. Ramp masters run a little hot, have very low heart rates, and high body density. The vampires are looking for those markers. My friend is a perfect match to the role he’s playing.”

Jay remarked acidly, “You have friends?”

Francis looked hard at Jay, and chastised him, “It doesn’t matter who he is. We have a mission to execute.” He looked pointedly back at Arthur. “There is only one way out now. We’ll have to give everything we’ve got to reach that goal.”

“Speaking of which,” Li asked, “are we ready to execute your plan?”

Arthur smiled. “A timely question, Li.” His eyes flicking around the team. “We’ll need to split up. Anton and Li, you’ll destroy the southern power station and the diesel backup arrays. Francis and Jay, you’ll do the same for the northern power station and the diesel backups there. That will cause a base wide power fail-over to emergency fuel-cell backup systems and activate the Panopticon evacuation mode. Peter and Chiara, you’ll take over the nemesis tower and destroy the four specter towers before disabling the nemesis tower. This will enable us to commandeer a nightfalcon and fly out of here without Shadowstone or the fortress shooting us down.”

“And what will you be doing?” Li asked.

“I’ll be down in the main server room stealing the Panopticon. I’ll meet you in the hangars and we’ll escape together.”

Li’s dark eyes widened and she shivered. “You won’t make the hangars. None of us will. You just described at least half of my vision.”

Arthur stared at her for a moment, the team standing like statues around him. “Even so, I invite you to challenge the future you have seen, are you willing to try?”

Li fell silent, a troubled frown creasing her forehead.

Arthur said, “Silence implies consent. So, I’ll take that as a yes.” He lifted his wrist, consulting his watch again. “Our friend should be—”

A door in the nearest wall slid open. A tall, slim, almost gangly man, wearing gray coveralls and carrying a battered toolbox stood in the doorway. His gaze locked on Arthur and he strode across the floor with long strides. Weaving through the team, he dropped his toolbox on the floor, grabbing Arthur on both shoulders and exclaimed, "You shouldn't have come!"

"Why, Dwayne?" Arthur asked quietly.

"General Maze is here with sixteen praetorians and forty-eight day guards. They know you're coming; they're expecting you. The base is crawling with vampires. You have to leave."

"Unfortunately, there is no way back," Jay stated harshly. "Our escape route has been blocked."

"What?" Dwayne asked incredulously. "You're trapped?"

"Not so," Arthur answered. "We still have a clear path forward. Are you ready to guide us?"

Dwayne nodded. "Yes, of course."

"Guide us?" Anton asked.

"The maintenance team have to be able to access all areas," Arthur stated. "They clean and maintain all parts of the base on a regular basis. More specifically, we need Dwayne's pass to access the maintenance tunnels."

Dwayne frowned for a moment, then jogged over to the overflow valve and spun it clockwise until it locked. He turned and glanced around at the team. "Quickly now, the faster this is done, the better your chance of survival."

Arthur glanced around the team and declared, "Dwayne will lead us to the next level down, which is a general maintenance access level below the main base. It will give us access to the relevant mission objectives. Once there, we'll split up." He waved his right hand in a flat arc toward the one doorway leading out of the pumping station. "It's time to move."

Arthur and Dwayne strode for the doorway, Anton falling in behind them followed by the rest of the team.

A man on the inside! Brilliant, Anton thought. *This just gets better and better. We should have joined up with my grandfather sooner. We could have been here months ago. Geez, Juliette and Yvette would still be alive.*

Anton heaved a sigh of regret. What had they been doing all this time? Ramin Kain's lies about his grandfather had blocked Arthur from helping the Mirovar force team. Was that Kain's greatest crime? Dividing the Order and ensuring that an uncountable number of people died at the hands of vampires; lives the Order could otherwise have saved?

He shook his head. The Order had gone mad decades ago. The Order was beyond all redemption. The war against the vampires required a new approach. Now it was time to bring the war to them. Anton blurred to the front next to Dwayne. He wanted to be on point for whatever was coming. It was the best place to be to ensure he could protect his friends and the mission had the best chance of success.

He was sure of it.

* * *

General Maze had sent squads to check every nook and cranny of the fortress.

The maintenance alarm in the pumping station had caught the general's attention and he'd sent a squad of praetorians and two squads of day guards to check it out.

Corporal Max Hendrickson had participated in the take down of the Order conclave the day before. Leading Alpha squad, he'd taken out the two Order guards at the front of the converted chapel and then dealt in blood and death within the hall. If it hadn't been for the 'magic,' mist the day guards would've killed all the hostiles in the old chapel.

An ex-JSOC 'ghost recon,' soldier, the higher-ups had tapped him on the shoulder for an ultra-secret program. It'd seemed like the obvious next step for a man of his specialized skills, but nothing had prepared him for 'the serum,' as they called it. Half the new recruits had washed out and left for home. The rest had gone into extensive training against the praetorians. Who the hell they were was a mystery? As enhanced as he'd become, the praetorians were twice as fast and three times as strong.

Max figured the answers were above his pay grade.

He led his squad behind four praetorians. Oddly, they reminded him of ancient knights in their smooth matte-black body armor and edged weapons. The only concessions to the modern world were their light machine guns, armor made of nanoceramic composite instead of metal, and advanced tactical helmets.

Max hoped the alarm turned out to be an incursion by the Order and not a false alarm. He'd lost good men in the chapel and wanted some revenge. He lifted his auto-aiming smart rifle and flicked the safety off.

The praetorians halted, looked at each other for a moment, then loosened their weapons. The lead praetorian turned back to the two squads of day guards following and said quietly, "We sent one maintenance man to the pumping station, now there are eight people in there. Prepare for contact with the enemy."

Yeah, Max nodded silently, *time for some payback!*

* * *

Anton glanced around the edge of the doorway from the pumping station.

A long corridor, twenty feet wide, and the same high, stretched for fifty yards away to his left before branching into a 'T' intersection. To his right, the corridor terminated another fifty yards away with a sensor locked cage door and a stairwell down.

"To our right," Dwayne said, stepping past Anton and guiding the team toward the cage door. "We have to go downstairs to maintenance sub-level zero dash one. The maintenance levels provide access to all the targets."

Anton broke to the left, instinctively guarding the approach from the main body of the facility. He held his assault rifle up, sighting down the barrel toward the 'T' intersection. He had a 'bad feeling,' in his guts that shit was about to hit the fan.

Arthur hesitated at the doorway for a moment. He drew his auto-pistol from its holster, sidled up next to Anton, and whispered, "What's up?"

Anton shook his head, and lifted a finger to his lips.

Arthur raised his fist to halt the team, then turned and flicked his fingers in front of his throat.

Peter was next in line through the doorway, Li followed behind him. Peter unlimbered his multiple-grenade launcher and stepped to the left behind Arthur. Li took a position a couple of feet behind Anton's left shoulder, lifting her P90 submachine gun and sighting along it.

Anton stared down the corridor. He risked a glance back. Francis, Jay and Chiara had taken up positions down the corridor toward the stairwells. Dwayne was further back, crouched down next to the pumping station wall, waiting, a perplexed look stealing over his face.

Li stilled next to Anton, dropping into a Ramp.

Something scuffed against the wall or floor beyond the 'T' intersection. Was it a footfall? Did he just hear a click? Anton plunged into silence, diving deep into the depths of the Ramp. The corridor snapped into razor-sharp clarity, previously invisible dust motes floating serenely beneath bright overhead lights. He breathed in—

Four armored vampires ran into the 'T' intersection. If he hadn't ramped, they would have simply appeared in the corridor. They were moving hard and fast, light-machine guns blazing, rounds whipping toward the team in bright streams of fire.

Bright blue light flickered on Anton's left. Arthur had his auto-pistol straight-armed and pointing at the lead vampire, brilliant rounds surrounded by blue fire lancing down the corridor toward the oncoming praetorians. He rushed toward them, leaning forward deeply to avoid the lines of bright fire reaching deadly fingers to grasp the team.

Anton slammed his finger against the trigger of his assault rifle. It barked into life, sending a stream of bullets toward the vampires. Their rounds were almost upon him. Li jagged violently left, her P90 submachine gun adding to the hellish environment in the middle of the corridor.

Streams of fire whipped past him as Francis, Jay, and Chiara opened up with their weapons, and Peter's MGL chuffed a fragmentation grenade high along the corridor toward the 'T' intersection.

Power roared through him. Leaping to his right, Anton surged up the wall. The vampire's machine gun fire stitching a line of holes beneath him. He ran along the wall toward the praetorians, the nearest vampire shifting his stance to bring his weapon to bear on Anton.

Arthur was already half way toward the vampires, the Black Dragon flying free of its scabbard, glimmering beneath the bright lights. His auto-pistol stammering a deadly stream of bullets at a stunned praetorian, puffs of ceramic powder ablating from his helmet as he staggered backward.

Swapping his assault rifle to his left hand, Anton descended the wall. The Blue Dragon gripped in his strong right hand rising like a silvery spirit above his head.

The other three vampires were evading the fire from the rest of the team, drawing swords and battle axes, and firing back when they could.

Arthur hit their front rank.

Anton landed beside him an instant later.

* * *

A wall of fire erupted from the corridor ripping white plaster board and brick into plumes of gray and ocher dust.

The praetorians had leveled weapons and blurred around the corner. A moment later, all hell broke loose. The serum had changed Max, now all he had to do was act, and the strength and speed would be there. A seemingly endless well of power flowed through his body. He rushed to the edge of the corridor; his team would be the second wave to confront the still unseen Order operatives.

He'd seen how fast the Order operatives could move in the battle at the chapel. It was best not to get too close, better to keep them at a distance, and use the Panopticon and the smart rifles to hit them with five round bursts. That'd worked in the chapel. In the chapel the enemy had been mostly unarmed. The ones with weapons had done most of the damage to his fellow guards and had escaped.

Would the praetorians survive? If they didn't, the protocol was clear – use area of effect weapons to contain the enemy.

A black armored form staggered back into the intersection, his machine gun dropping to the floor with a clatter. His left hand reached for his face. Bullet holes littered his helmet.

How was he still standing?

The stricken praetorian toppled over, blood gushing from beneath his helmet. A 40mm fragmentation grenade flew above him, bouncing against the wall and falling into the middle of the intersection.

Max twisted around, throwing himself flat while shouting, "Incoming!"

His team blurred behind him.

* * *

Peter's fragmentation grenade bounced off the rear wall of the 'T' intersection, rolling across the floor into the middle of the praetorians.

The Blue Dragon ground along the nearest praetorian's bastard sword in a shower of sparks. Anton pushed and whirled, leaping twenty feet diagonally backward down the corridor, a stream of machine-gun fire chasing him through the air.

Bright streams of fire speared down the corridor from the rest of the team to the right and left of the vampires. The praetorians dodged toward the middle of the corridor.

A strong hand pushed against Anton's left shoulder and he slid into the edge of the wall and floor.

A moment later, Arthur landed beside him.

Peter's grenade exploded. The blast wave caught the praetorians, sending them flying through the net of fire erupting from Peter, Li, Jay, Francis and Chiara. Their rounds ripped through armor and flesh, painting the corridor walls red with vampire blood.

The praetorians crashed to the floor, lying in still, black heaps, surmounted by a spreading plume of pink-tinged gray smoke.

The guns fell silent, spent magazines dropping to the floor in a sharp clatter.

Arthur moved, leaping to his feet and dashing away. He took a position hard up against the opposite corridor wall, staring down at the 'T' intersection. He straight-armed the auto-pistol in front of him, the Black Dragon resting in his right hand.

Anton got to his feet swinging his assault rifle around, shedding the spent magazine and loading another in a fraction of a second.

A two-inch wide chrome tube snaked around the left corner of the 'T' intersection. A dozen slim black canisters shot out of it with a staccato chuff of compressed air. The canisters spun hard and fast, hissing as they shot across the tiles. One exploded, taken out by a round from Arthur's auto-pistol. Anton sighted on the nearest and squeezed the trigger. His rifle stuttered, bright rounds lancing toward the nearest canister. It ricocheted aside with sparks flying, sliding between Arthur and himself.

There was a faint whiff of something sweet.

Arthur staggered.

Sharp reports echoed throughout the corridor; bright sparks leaped from the tiles as the rest of the team fired at the sliding black fizzing canisters.

Someone shouted, "Gas!"

Before Anton could work out who'd spoken the world whirled, the solid tiles of the floor rising to meet him.

A darkness as black as any cave swept Anton away.

* * *

Anton's eyelid flickered open.

Sensation and memory returned with a rush. He raised his hands to shield his eye from the glare of the overhead lights. His eye patch was missing, his fingers coming away from his slowly healing left eye socket greasy with herbal balm. He lifted himself upon his elbows, a queasy nausea roiling in his guts. The room was a study in clinical whiteness, the color dominating every surface. Jay and Francis sat propped up against the opposite wall. Peter slouched against the right-side wall studying the single door opposite him with an appraising look. Chiara squatted next to Arthur, her fingers on his wrist, her eyes staring into the distance. Li paced in the middle of the room; her brow knitted with a troubled frown.

Anton swallowed weakly, his mouth dry as dust and tasting just as foul. He croaked, "What the hell happened?"

Li's silhouette loomed above him. "We got captured."

"What about Arthur?"

Li looked across at Arthur, lying in the recovery position on the floor's white tiles. "He's still unconscious, looks like he got the biggest dose."

"How long was I out?"

"Fifteen minutes, maybe?"

"We're fucked." Jay declared vehemently, rising from the floor. He moved closer to Arthur, his eyes flashing with anger. "We should have stayed away, like Li and I said."

Anton reached for the Blue Dragon. His hand faltered, the familiar weight was missing from his shoulders. All their equipment was gone, their swords, guns, ammo, nightglasses, watches, belts, combat webbing, they'd even taken their boots and his eye patch. Everyone was wearing loose combat fatigues and nothing else. His jaw dropped, Jay was right, they were in deep shit.

Jay took another step closer to Arthur. Chiara glanced up, a sudden frown creasing her forehead. Peter pushed himself off the wall and took a step forward, his eyes wary. Francis rose to his feet and commanded, "Jay, no!"

Jay whirled on Francis, and snapped, "What! You think I'd kick him while he's down." He took a deep breath and let it out. A wild light gleamed within his eyes and he promised harshly, "No. I'll wait for him to wake up."

Li stepped forward to face Jay. "Rein it in, Jay." She swung her left-hand wide back toward the door. "I'm sure they'd love to watch us fight amongst ourselves."

Anton leaped to his feet to back her up, but kept back a yard, he didn't want to inflame the situation further. Li was right, they had to stay united in the face of whatever was happening. If the team fell to division, they'd lose the battle – if they hadn't already lost it. Anton glanced down at his grandfather, perhaps the old guy still had a few tricks up his sleeve. He glanced around the room; someone was missing. He asked, "Where's the Order helper? Dwayne?"

Everyone shook their heads, no one knew what had happened to Arthur's man on the inside. Had the team been betrayed again?

Arthur groaned, rolled over, sat up and pulled a hand down his face. "What the hell happened?" He shook his head once, and answered his own question. "Knock out gas." He rubbed his face again, glanced around the team and stated matter-of-factly, "So, they put us in the brig."

Jay's eyes flashed. "You fatalistic prick." He paused for a moment, breathing hard. "Well, I suppose we can chalk this up to 'no plan survives contact with the enemy.'"

"Well," Arthur said, lifting a finger as if to make a point to a recalcitrant student. "You are no longer at the mercy of the dictum that, 'No plan survives contact with the enemy,' if you truly have no plan – only a process."

A look of perplexity stole over Jay's face and he snapped, "And what the hell does that mean?"

Arthur shrugged. "You'll work it out soon enough."

Jay's face darkened and his eyes tightened into glacial hardness. Francis clasped Jay's shoulder. He whirled away from Francis' grip and strode back to the wall. He turned; his face glacial as he watched Arthur get to his feet.

Anton's heart sank. Whatever plan his grandfather had lay in tatters. They were stuck in a prison cell with no way out. All their equipment was gone and they were at the mercy of an enemy who would show them none.

They were well and truly fucked.

Chapter Six

"If everyone understood the actual rules of the game of dominion, and let's be clear about what that is, 'dominion is the ability to order someone to act against their own best interest and have them obey,' – the world would be transformed beyond recognition. Not because everyone would be scrambling for dominance over each other, that would continue to happen as it does now, but because all the standard strategies and tactics of dominion rely on the ignorance of the common man for their effectiveness." – Cornelius Crane

* * *

New York City, Cornelius Crane's Citadel, September 11th, 16:35

The feed from the Panopticon fortress strung eight six-foot-tall photos across the citadel's main display screens.

The system followed with strips of flashing metadata, DNA analysis, and current locations running beneath the photos. The six Ramp masters of the Mirovar force team and Arthur Slayne were in cell block A of the Panopticon fortress. A spy caught with them sat disconsolately in an adjoining cell. To the right of the main screen, a second panel displayed a live feed from the cell holding the captured ramp masters.

Cornelius' gaze flicked from Arthur Slayne's photograph to the live feed from the cell, his eyes drinking in every detail. He'd just lost another four praetorians, but given the result, the sacrifice was worth it. Triumph surged through his soul like a wild horse. He reined his surging emotion in with a tight grip. The Slayne family ancestral line had been a thorn in his side for nearly a thousand years. He'd wait to enjoy his victory for when the surviving Slaynes were dead and buried.

He tapped a switch on the console in front of him, a video conference opened up between the Panopticon fortress and his citadel. General Clayton Maze's face swung into view. A rare smile gracing his full lips. He asked confidently, "Sir?"

"I want a full brief on the details of how they infiltrated the fortress."

"A team is already working on it, Sir. The Panopticon was deceived somehow. But now we have fully identified them, we're tracking their path through recorded video. It looks like they came up from the magma cavern and into the pumping station. We caught them in the corridor just outside the pumping station with knock out gas."

Maze's confidence left Cornelius with an uncomfortable itch at the back of his mind. The Slaynes and the members of the Mirovar force team were still alive, and while they still lived the threat remained unresolved.

Cornelius stared hard at Maze. "You should have separated the prisoners into different cells."

Maze frowned slightly, his smile disappearing. "Sir, we only have four cells on site."

"What about their equipment?"

"It's been stripped from them."

"Where is it now?"

"In the guardhouse."

Cornelius shook his head. "Get it moved immediately off the base. Send it by nightfalcon to my citadel."

"Yes, Sir."

"I don't trust Arthur Slayne at all. Separate him from the rest. Wait," he turned to the staff manning the citadel's command-and-control center and commanded, "Mobilize all available forces. Yes, I know it's daylight. Ready my command nightfalcon for immediate lift off. Send all our reserve praetorians to Fort Dix. We'll man our shadowstars and leave immediately for the Panopticon fortress."

"Sir, I don't understand. We have the Mirovar force team captured. The elder Slayne is in a cell cut off from all aid."

"And yet, we still don't know how he infiltrated the fortress and made his team of saboteurs invisible to the Panopticon. I wouldn't trust the threat Arthur Slayne represents was over even if I was standing on his cold grave. Move to red alert immediately, lock the base down. Be prepared for anything, I will be there by sixteen ten local time."

Maze's eyes flicked away to a read out. "Yes, Sir. I'll be ready for you to arrive in ninety minutes. Is there anything else?"

Cornelius glanced along the main screen. There was Francis Mirovar, Jay Creeley, Peter Lamb, Li Wu, Chiara Romano – no, not Romano. The DNA analysis included her mother's name. He whispered, "Morte."

The young Ramp master with a Red Empire heritage was a mystery he'd unravel, but she would have to wait, there was a more urgent threat to extinguish. His eyes rested on Anton Slayne, the familiar face haunting his recent visions. Cornelius stared hard into Maze's eyes and snapped, "Execute Anton Slayne. Immediately!"

"Yes, Sir," Maze replied. He turned to his subordinates and ordered, "Separate Anton Slayne from the rest of the prisoners. Take him outside the main complex and shoot him. Make sure he's dead and leave his body for the vultures."

A day guard squad leader assented, turned on his heels with the rest of his team and strode off to the guardhouse and the cell blocks.

Maze glanced to his side at Commander Cormack and ordered, "Send a crew to pick up the gear at the guardhouse, send it to the hangars for transport, and initiate red alert."

Cornelius ended the call before the commander could give her assent. Within minutes the youngest of the Slaynes would be dead, leaving Arthur Slayne as the sole member of that line. With Cornelius' arrival at the fortress in less than two hours, the senior Slayne would soon join his grandson in death, but not before he'd personally squeezed every piece of useful information from the elder Slayne's mind. The Slaynes were on the verge of utter ruin.

He savored the moment for a handful of heartbeats.

He grinned tightly, stepping away from the command console. There was one last thing to do before he left for the shadowstar hangar at Fort Dix. He called Chloe Armitage's smartphone; it was time to bring every weapon at his disposal to bear upon his enemies.

And Armitage was his mightiest weapon.

* * *

The call closed and Chloe flipped her smartphone shut.

She rolled off her bed and began putting on her dark-gray combat fatigues. Two minutes later she emerged into James Haley's living room and said, "We have new orders."

"Yes, Chloe?"

"We need to pick up the chameleons at the warehouse, and use the new osprey II drone to get to Fort Dix immediately. Crane has scrambled his forces. He's stripped the citadel of praetorians, there is only a skeleton staff left there for command-and-control functions. He's converging on the Panopticon fortress with every force remaining in North America and we're going with him."

James looked up at her from his desk. "It's daylight, the only option you have to get from here to the warehouse is my car. Are you okay with that?"

"I'll have to be," Chloe grinned dryly. "It's not the first time I've had to travel in the trunk of a car."

James tilted his head quizzically, then shrugged his broad shoulders. "I have some thick blankets; we can make sure you're covered. Once we are in the warehouse, there's no direct sunlight and the drone has transparent armor for windows, so you'll be safe to travel within it. We can make it to the hangars at Fort Dix where you can transfer to Crane's command shadowstar drone."

Chloe nodded. "Excellent, it's time to move."

James rose from his seat and briefly patted down his dark, urban-camouflage Shadowstone combat fatigues in a final check. His combat bag lay on the floor, tightly packed, in accordance with her earlier instructions to be ready for battle. He lifted it off the floor with one hand and looked at her with steady eyes.

Chloe rested her left hand on the handle of the Red Dragon at her waist, turned and strode down the corridor to the front door. James followed a yard behind her. Less than a minute later, they were descending together within the building's elevator toward the basement parking garage.

The elevator pulled to a stop on the third floor. The doors swished open and a well-dressed elderly woman smelling faintly of lavender entered the elevator. She pressed the ground floor button. She studied James and Chloe for a long moment, her eyes lingering on the Red Dragon, and then nodded and declared warmly, "I just wanted to acknowledge you for your service."

James nodded once, his brown eyes narrowing slightly.

Chloe tilted her head, then remarked kindly, "Thank you. We're both proud to serve."

The old woman looked into her eyes and said, "My husband Ben served in the Air Force, God rest his soul. Which branch do you belong with, I don't recognize the uniforms?"

Chloe took a step forward and nodded. "Special forces, Ma'am. We're shipping out immediately."

The old woman reached out to take Chloe's hands. "You be safe then. I know you're the best of us."

Chloe received her hands and squeezed gently. "And, you too."

The lift door pinged. The doors swished open. The old woman glanced at them both, and said, "Good luck."

Chloe caught her gaze. "Luck won't be a factor but we appreciate the thought."

The old woman nodded, smiled, and left the elevator. The doors closed smoothly behind her.

The elevator began descending and James inquired, "Do we need to do anything about her?"

Chloe arched an eyebrow. "Perhaps a little over-zealous James, she's clearly mis-interpreting what's going on."

James shrugged his shoulders. "Yes, of course."

Chloe sighed. The day was approaching when deception would no longer be necessary but only if she won. There were so many obstacles in her way. She would rely on persistence, adaptability, mental agility and the sharp edge of her blade to win through to victory, but in this game nothing was certain. She frowned slightly as the elevator pulled to a stop at the parking garage. If she could manage to keep the chameleons in line, they would make a difference in the coming battle.

But would it be enough?

She didn't honestly know.

* * *

Arthur Slayne shook his head, throwing off the last traces of the knockout gas. It'd taken about six minutes since he'd woken up in the cell block. He mused, that was longer than expected, perhaps he was beginning to feel his age. He said dryly, "Well at least they haven't killed us yet."

Francis stated, "A small mercy."

"That won't last," Jay snapped. "They're probably coming to kill us now."

"There's no risk of that," Arthur declared with a sardonic smile. "They'll want to torture us first."

"Oh, joy," Jay remarked derisively.

Arthur arched his back, and rubbed his neck. "I think I got a cricked neck from the floor."

Jay swore profusely, uttering a long list of profanities.

Arthur raised his eyebrows and declared deadpan, "Well, that's just anatomically impossible. Clearly, you're upset."

"Ya, think?!"

Arthur pursed his lips for a moment, stroking his chin, his thumb an inch away from an implant beneath the base of his jaw. He stated, "One thing this place isn't."

Jay stared at him.

Li ended the silence. "And what's that?"

"A Faraday cage," Arthur answered, tapping the base of his jaw beneath his right ear three times. "Now get ready, in another minute life is going to get very interesting."

Peter looked up from where he sat propped up against a wall. "Define interesting."

Arthur gave a faint nod toward the camera ball in the ceiling, unfurled all his fingers in front of his chest, and puffed lightly through his pursed lips.

Peter grinned.

Arthur's eyelids drooped slightly. The forces unleashed were unpredictable and there were scenarios where all hell would break loose. But he'd run out of choices. The team was committed, the only pathway forward was to victory or death. If what he'd set in motion got completely out of control they would have to move quickly to survive. There were no more tricks up his sleeve.

This was the last big rabbit he could pull out of his hat. At best, he only had a couple of small ones left hopping around in there.

* * *

Ground drone #500 flicked from standby to active.

An internal clock registered that the drone had arrived in place with its payload of two-hundred pounds of shaped mining charges nearly five hours earlier. There were another four hundred and ninety-nine drones. Together they carried one hundred thousand pounds of advanced shaped rock-cutting explosives. They all rested nose to tail, like a train along a jagged line against the western wall of the underground river.

The drone networked to all the other drones. A pair of cameras opened up on the drone, rising three inches above the main body. A secondary system that managed the shaped demolition charges booted into life. It ran through a series of diagnostics and halted at ninety-seven percent complete. All of the other drones were in the green, only #500 sported an orange flashing light on its back. A failsafe abort timer began ticking seconds down from five to four to three …

#500 was not ready. The other drones would discharge their explosives in three second's time. Fulfilling their essential function would obliterate them while #500 would remain behind.

The seconds stretched out.

#500 pulled its cameras back beneath the shielding on its exoskeleton.

The shaped rock-cutting charges of the other drones fired as one.

The rock beneath #500 reared up, throwing the drone through the shuddering water and against the ceiling of the river's channel. #500 fell back through the surging water. It raised its cameras again, but the right one failed, it's casing too damaged to move. The left camera rose. The water was gray with rock, metal, and debris, rushing in a solid torrent to the left.

#500 activated its locomotors, wheels spun freely on the left, the tracks shattered and swept away by the roiling currents. On the right, something ground and jammed, and the drone shutdown the engine to avoid burning it out.

The water carried #500 along, the drone helpless to maneuver, it's one remaining camera recording whatever passed before it. Gray rock scraped along its left-side, then it was flying through the air into an enormous cavern. Its camera swiveled, mapping the space. The enormous chamber was over three miles long. Two giant metallic structures hung down from the ceiling like gravity defying metal monoliths. Metadata reported that the nearest structure was a hundred-megawatt geothermal power station named Kraken-1.

A river of slowly moving magma snaked its way across the cavern floor beneath Kraken-1 to a second power station two miles away.

#500 fell, striking the rocky floor, sliding and spinning across it. Its tough exoskeleton standing up to the harsh treatment. The drone came to a halt next to the river of glowing liquid rock, facing back toward the underground river. The stone wall of the cavern had come apart. The river was violently changing course, a wall of water smashing through a gaping slash in the rock wall over a hundred yards across and thirty feet high.

Water sluiced and foamed around #500's jammed tracks and spinning wheel cogs, exploding into steam as it touched the magma a couple of yards behind the machine. A dozen systems were already offline, #500 was failing, the raised camera quivering on over-stretched hydraulics. The wall of water reached the drone, lifting it off the stone floor of the chamber and carrying it over the magma river.

The last thing #500 registered through its surviving camera before system failure swept everything away, was white super-heated steam fountaining upward around the base of the nearest power station.

* * *

Li cocked her head and lifted her right hand.

A frown creased her forehead. "Did you feel that?"

"Feel what," Peter asked. He glanced across at Arthur, who returned his glance with a brief knowing smile, before relaxing his expression into impassivity.

"I felt something too," Chiara remarked. "A tremor."

Francis stepped in front of Arthur. "What's happening?"

Arthur flicked his head at the cameras in the ceiling, widened his eyes, and remained silent. He gestured for everyone to form a line near the door. He beckoned Peter with curled fingers. Peter arched an eyebrow and strode to the front of the line. Arthur positioned Anton directly behind Peter, and then himself, followed by Chiara, Li, Jay and finally Francis.

Without turning away from the door, he whispered behind Anton's shoulder, "Get ready."

Anton waited, his hands opening and closing beside his hips. Arthur must expect the door to open. The long seconds stretched by, his heartbeat thudding within his ears.

Jay whispered harshly, "What? The door's gonna open by magic."

Arthur replied quietly, "Its protocol."

"Protocol?" Francis asked.

"Health and Safety." Arthur stated decisively.

Jay snorted derisively. "You're kidding?"

"Actually, no," Arthur said with a shrug. "Please note, it's a brig, not a prison." He glanced at the pale shadow circling his left wrist. "It's been … thirty seconds, get ready to ramp."

The lights flickered. A klaxon began to wail in the distance. Arthur snapped, "Now!"

The door automatically recessed into the left wall. Peter blurred forward. Anton rushed after him. The prison cell opened into a short hall. There was another cell opposite, a surprised Dwayne Washington standing in the middle of it. The remaining two cells were to the left, their doors also open.

Peter surged hard right, heading for the guardhouse. Anton pushed to Peter's left-hand side, coming abreast with his friend. The hall opened up into a brightly lit rectangular chamber, a red light glowered over a second doorway opposite the corridor to the cells. A pair of long desks stood left and right facing the entrance, and a pair of closed doors completed the wings of the room.

There were four dark-suited Shadowstone personnel manning the desks and four day guards in battle armor clustered at the guardhouse entrance. The Shadowstone operatives carried sidearms holstered at their waists. The squad of day guards carried their smart assault rifles. Their leader pointed at Anton and shouted, "He's the one, kill him!"

Anton bent low, blurring behind the left-side counter. The nearest operative was reaching for his 9mm automatic. Anton barreled into him with his right shoulder. The man's ribs shattered in a series of snaps as Anton lifted him off his feet.

The day guards fired as one, four five-round bursts slashing across the room. The operative jerked mid-air as fistfuls of bullets ripped great chunks of flesh and bone from his torso, splattering the wall behind the desk with blood. He was dead before he hit the tiled floor.

The second operative on the left was already spinning away to the floor, barely avoiding his comrade's fate.

Anton's hands flashed forward, seeking the 9mm automatic holstered at the dead man's waist. A moment later, his right hand wrapped around the Glock's handle.

* * *

Bright fire speared through the room toward Anton.

Peter grabbed the first operative on the right at shoulder and hip. His fists clenching with bone snapping force. He whirled, the man shrieked, flying through the room toward the cluster of day guards.

The second operative twisted and began to rise from his chair. Peter stepped into him with the full force of his body, his left hand cocked, fingers up, his open palm striking the man's upper right chest. Peter's right hand mirrored his left, striking low on the operative's left hip.

The simultaneous blows lifted the man and his chair – Peter's right hand blurred upwards – sending the operative rocketing into the right wall with a bone shaking crash.

Peter lifted the second operative's purloined Glock 9mm, and twisted toward the entrance.

The day guard's first volley of fire ripped apart the left-side of the room over Anton's head. They had split into two pairs to avoid the man thrown at them. The two closest snapped their smart rifles toward Peter, the red beams of their laser sights seeking him with deadly intent.

Peter blurred further right past the edge of the desk, relying on speed over cover. He fired across his broad chest, pumping the trigger as fast as he could while he raced across the room. The Glock stuttered, brass cases whirling to the side like confetti, 9mm rounds lancing through the air in a widening fan with the two day guards at the apex.

At the conclave, the 9mm rounds had mostly bounced off the day guard's armor. Peter couldn't rely on them. He sank deeper into his ramp, drawing upon the utmost of speed and strength, pursuing the last of the bullets to their targets.

The day guards fired as he reached them. The tips of their barrels pointing at empty space a foot to his left. Peter still held the empty Glock; he drove it point first under the chin of the nearest day guard. The barrel penetrated its full length, hot blood jetting past Peter's right fist. His unstoppable momentum carried the first day guard into the second, Peter's open hand, shaped like a knife spearing into the throat of the second day guard. Both men, lifted from the floor as Peter carried them through the guardhouse entrance and into the hall outside. He smashed them into the polished rock wall opposite the entrance, gore splashing in wide swathes across the cream-colored stone.

Peter stepped back; the two day guards slumped to the floor in growing pools of their own blood.

The operative he'd thrown at the day guards, had ended up in the corridor. He was scuttling backward on the floor, shouting into his headset's microphone, "Backup! We need—"

Peter threw the empty blood-soaked Glock with all his might. It embedded itself in the middle of the man's forehead. The operative fell backward, sliding half a dozen feet across the floor.

Automatic gunfire erupted from within the guardhouse.

Peter whirled around.

The corridor was empty of other threats. He scooped up a fallen smart rifle and dashed back into the guardhouse.

* * *

Anton grabbed the second operative's ankle and jerked.

The man slid across the tiles. He twisted and flipped, frantically attempting to pull his weapon from the holster at his waist.

Anton lunged forward, slapping the operative unconscious. Twisting aside, he gripped the blood-soaked corpse of the first operative with his free hand and lobbed him blindly over the desk in the general direction of the day guards. The guards fired a second fusillade.

"Trigger happy," Anton muttered. The shots had told him where they were. He ramped hard, blurring back to the right, the 9mm automatic pumping rounds at the two remaining day guards. They'd already moved deeper into the room, the 9mm rounds sparking off their armor.

Arthur rushed into the guardhouse from the corridor and broke left behind the desk.

The guards snapped their rifles around at Anton, red laser sights lining up on his chest.

Anton dived behind the right-side desk. The guard's rifles thundered, rounds stitching holes in the wall above his head.

Arthur lifted a desk chair and threw it with bone-breaking force at the nearest day guard.

Automatic gunfire erupted from the guardhouse entrance, followed by a pair of thuds as bodies hit the floor, and a chair clattering harmlessly into the far corner. Peter shouted, "Clear."

Anton rose to his feet.

Holding a smart rifle in the middle of the entrance, his arms drenched in gore, Peter regarded Anton with a raised eyebrow. "Oh, so that's where you were hiding."

"Did you keep anyone alive to question?" Anton asked.

"Alas, no."

"Well, I did," Anton declared, turning back to the last surviving operative.

Arthur pulled the slapped operative to his feet. The man swayed woozily, then jackknifed forward, vomiting his lunch onto the blood-smeared floor. Arthur danced to the side. Once the man recovered his breath, he lifted him upright again and asked, "Where's our gear?"

The man's eyes barely focused on Arthur's face and he slurred, "Store room." He lifted his hand, pointing weakly at the door past Anton's right shoulder.

"Locked?" Arthur asked.

"Not locked."

"Good." Arthur said. His hands flashed, snapping the operative's neck. The man slumped to the floor and lay still.

Francis, Jay, Chiara, Li, and Dwayne emerged from the corridor. Arthur regarded them with steely eyes and stated, "No prisoners."

Francis' eyes tightened and he remarked, "Clearly." He then glanced to the door on the right. "Our gear should be in there."

Dwayne scooped a plastic card off the surface of the right-side counter and exclaimed, "Hey, there's my access pass!"

"Perhaps they haven't deactivated it yet," Arthur suggested hopefully.

Anton tried the store room door. It opened easily, sliding into a recess on the left. The room was lit. All their equipment lay in neat rows on a pair of long tables. He reached for the Blue Dragon, and called out over his shoulder, "It's all here."

"Two minutes, everyone," Francis called out. "We have to move quickly."

Peter appeared beside Anton. "We're back in business." He grabbed his MGL and reloaded it with a fresh 40mm grenade to replace the spent one.

Anton strapped the Blue Dragon back into place across his shoulders.

Peter was absolutely right.

* * *

Alarms blared, a red light strobing slowly across the command-and-control center's ceiling.

General Clayton Maze shouted, "Kill that damned noise."

One of the staff flicked a switch and the alarm died, a moment later the red light ceased strobing. A diffuse illumination filled the room, eliminating shadows and putting the displays and monitors into sharp contrast.

A ten feet high and twenty feet wide main screen dominated the wall opposite the primary entrance of the command-and-control center. A three-dimensional graphic of the complete fortress filled the display. The primary power station, Kraken-1 had shut itself down. A sharp red line drew a square around the deepest underground structure of the station. Clearly visible text beneath the red square declared that the heat reapers were offline. The base's power supply had shifted to the secondary power station, Kraken-2.

Clayton had felt the vibration through his shoes half a minute earlier. Now he had an answer for the implications of that tremor. He turned to the stout woman standing on his left and snapped, "Commander Cormack, what the hell is going on?"

The woman's heart rate had risen above a hundred beats a minute, and her face had blanched into a damp pasty gray shade. Clayton stared at her. The last thing he needed was someone who would freeze in a crisis.

Cormack reached out and grabbed the chair in front of her, her knuckles pale against the dark leather. Her gaze broke away from the main screen, her head flicking right to stare at Clayton. "Sir, we've just had a fail-over." She took a deep breath, steadied and stood upright, her hands falling to her sides. "The base can run perfectly well on Kraken dash two."

Clayton watched her, his vampire senses penetrating her responses. She'd never studied deception; she was an open book. She seemed to be quickly calming down, but still, he asked in quiet tones, "This has never happened before?"

"No, Sir."

"What happens if the second power station fails?"

"Both stations have auxiliary diesel backups, either of which are capable of keeping the Panopticon and our defensive systems operational."

"And if they fail?"

"Sir? Two power stations, two ranks of distributed diesel backups, that's quadruple redundancy. The probability of all four systems failing at the same time is astronomical."

Clayton smiled grimly. "Assume this base is now under attack."

"Sir, Ma'am," one of the technicians shouted, standing up from his console, one hand outstretched toward the main display. "We have casualties in the guardhouse outside cell block A."

Clayton stared at the huge screen, eight white-cross markers where clustered together in the guardhouse and the corridor outside it. The squad of day guards he'd sent down to execute Anton Slayne were all dead. He snarled and commanded, "Open cameras on cell block A."

The schematic of the fortress vanished, replaced with a series of picture-in-picture views. The cells were empty. The guardhouse was an abattoir of human flesh. The prisoners had escaped. He shouted, "Open views on the nearest twenty camera locations."

Twenty picture-in-picture views lined up in four rows of five on the main screen. The Mirovar force team were still at the guardhouse, clustered in a store room off the guardhouse reception area. They still had them caught in one location. The spoofing of the Panopticon cameras they'd used to infiltrate the base was over. While it was regrettable the Mirovar force team had rearmed, a result of lack of time to remove their gear to a safe location and assuming the cells would be failsafe, it would not save them from destruction.

Clayton glanced at a secondary screen displaying the locations of all friendly forces within the perimeter of the outer fence. He still had twenty-four praetorians and forty-four day guards available. He'd deployed four of the praetorians at the main server room guardhouse – the final vampire defense of the Panopticon core. That left him with twenty that were immediately available. He whirled around and commanded, "Carney, Holdsworthy, Sutter, and Tench, take your squads down to the guardhouse and kill the Mirovar force team."

The praetorian squad leaders assented enthusiastically and strode from the room with their men.

Clayton had to protect multiple assets to keep the Panopticon operational. While splitting his forces might appear inadvisable, in the absence of knowing Arthur Slayne's strategy he had to cover all elements. He turned back to Commander Cormack and ordered, "I'm delegating command of the day guards to you. Secure the power stations, pumping station, hangars, and access to the main server room."

"Yes, Sir," Cormack replied, turning and striding away to a secondary set of consoles manned by half a dozen of her own staff.

His sixteen fully armed praetorians would confront seven Order operatives. Standard Vampire Dominion operating procedure called for better than two to one odds when confronting Ramp masters.

His praetorians should be enough to stop anyone.

* * *

Geophysics had fascinated Wesley Jackson for most of his adult life.

As much as he loved the field, the data he was receiving from the magma chamber beneath the Panopticon base sent a cold chill crawling up his spine. He'd have to alert the general. He glanced up at General Clayton Maze. He was possibly the most intimidating man he'd ever encountered. While the praetorians left him with a cold fear, the dark-blue suited general made him want to crawl into a hole, and pull the earth in on top of himself.

However, the only thing worse than confronting the general was staying silent about what he was witnessing on his data feeds. Wesley rose from his chair, raised his hand and said tremulously, "Sir, … there might be a problem."

Maze glared at Wesley and snapped, "What now?"

"Sir, it's … it's the magma river, Sir."

"What about it?"

"It's getting bigger, Sir."

"And?"

Wesley's words came out in a rush. "The underground river is diverting onto the magma. The water explodes into steam on contact with the molten rock. The stone shelf at the edge of the magma is cracking and exposing more magma. More water is flowing from the river resulting in more cracking and more magma – it's a runaway process. The pressure within the cavern is growing exponentially."

The General's face froze, he snarled then declared, "Well, we'd better lock this situation down before anything," and he air-quoted, "'BAD!' happens." He glared at Wesley and snapped, "Keep the status monitored and keep me up to date if anything changes."

The scientist looked back at his screens. A deep and growing need to flee possessed him. A need he barely managed to hold in check.

Was anything going to change? For sure, but by then it would be too late to do anything about it. No, scratch that. It was already too late.

Wesley had an urgent need to go to the bathroom, and from there, to his car in the parking lot. Perhaps today was a good day to leave work early, but it was too late, the base was in a red-alert lockdown. No one was coming in and no one was going to leave.

He stared at his main console screen. A readout displayed the increasing pressure within the magma chamber in sharp red numerals. The whole base was sitting directly above the middle of the cavern and the pressure cooker within it.

What crazy son of a bitch signed off on this design, he thought bitterly.

Wesley's guts turned to water, cramping hard. Now, he really had to go to the bathroom. His head flicked left and right. All he needed was an opportunity and he'd take it.

It was time to run.

* * *

A new feed overrode the main display.

Clayton Maze whipped around, what new irritant was about to bedevil his world?

Cornelius Crane's face appeared on screen, a few wisps of dark hair escaping from beneath his tactical helmet. Behind him, praetorians arrayed for war filled the main cabin of his command nightfalcon. He'd stripped the remaining forces of the citadel. He stared hard at Clayton and snapped, "Kraken dash one is offline. What the hell is happening down there?"

Maze frowned for a split second, then stood tall and said, "The fortress is under attack, Sir. It appears the Mirovar force team have detonated munitions against the wall of the magma cavern diverting the main underground supply river onto the lava flow."

Crane's eyes hardened. "No. Not Mirovar, it would be Arthur Slayne. The operation against the Panopticon fortress is beyond the likes of Mirovar. Only the elder Slayne could accomplish such a thing."

Clayton nodded. "Of course, Sir. I see that now."

Crane, his eyes dark and flinty, lifted a long finger and pointed it at Clayton. "Have you executed Anton Slayne?"

Clayton's arm pits grew clammy and he swallowed against his suddenly dry mouth. "No, Sir—"

Crane leaned into the camera, his face swelling on the display. "What?" He paused for a moment, his lip curling derisively. "Pray tell, why not?"

Clayton's mind screamed behind his eyes. Did he dare lie to Crane? His king would arrive in less than eighty minutes. Crane would soon discover any lie, and the consequences would be beyond his worst nightmare. He whispered hoarsely, "The Mirovar force team killed a squad of day guards. They have escaped their cell." His voice picked up urgency, returning to normal volume. "Sir, Carney, Holdsworthy, Sutter, Tench and their squads are en route to kill them. The rest of our forces are reinforcing the defenses of the Panopticon and the primary systems of the fortress. We'll recapture them or kill them soon."

Crane fell silent for a long moment, his face paling with thinly controlled fury. His fangs descended into attack position.

Several command-and-control center operators gasped, a technician leaped from his chair and ran screaming for the exit, others swore loudly. One of the praetorians blurred, seizing the fleeing man and silencing him with a gauntleted hand over his mouth. The helpless fellow's feet dangling and kicking six inches off the floor. Commander Cormack rose up from her console, her face blanching with abject terror.

Crane spoke slowly through gritted teeth, his tone acquiring a dark sibilance through his long fangs, "Secure the Panopticon and kill the Ramp masters. I want their heads." He ran his finger in a flat arc in front of the camera. "I want their heads in a line when I arrive." He paused for a brief moment. "Bodies still attached is entirely optional."

Clayton's chest tightened, it was difficult to breathe, let alone speak. He finally managed to say, "Yes, Sir."

Crane stared hard at Clayton. "If not, I'll tear your throat out myself – general or no." He paused momentarily. "Now, get it done," and closed the call.

Clayton whirled on the remaining four praetorians and shouted, "Secure this room. No one comes in or out without my command." He turned and glared at Cormack. "Get your staff under control. If they want to live, they'll damn well obey orders."

Cormack stuttered, "B-b-but, but—" then lapsed into silence. She gripped the back of her chair, then lifted her hands and started issuing commands. Her team hesitated for a moment, glancing around at the hard-faced praetorians surrounding them before complying with her orders.

The praetorian holding the squirming man released him. The technician stumbled and fell, then picked himself up gingerly, glanced once at the armored vampire towering above him, and slunk back to his console.

Every human in the room would be dead within hours. He could not allow any to survive with knowledge of the secret existence of vampires, but until then they could serve a useful purpose. Clayton studied the main screen. Picture-in-picture feeds from twenty different locations within the base filled it from edge to edge. The praetorians had blurred down corridors and stairwells to the subterranean level holding the guardhouse and cell blocks. The Mirovar force team, Arthur Slayne and the traitor Washington were completing the retrieval of their gear and equipment. Unless they moved soon, his praetorians would catch them in the guardhouse, and from there – there would be no escape.

He opened a broadcast channel to all the praetorians and day guard troopers within the fortress. "New orders. Kill all non-authorized personnel on sight. Accept no quarter. Take no prisoners. Win back this fortress!"

In a minute or two, the slaughter would begin; and he'd be able to regain control of the base.

Clayton grinned. The Order operatives were doomed.

Chapter Seven

"The gestalt experience of a loremaster vision often invests everything you witness with extreme, hyper-realized emotion. The experience can be so powerful, so vivid, that it overwhelms your capacity to process it. The loremaster technology is not safe, using it can send you insane. This is why we have extensive training protocols to assist the novice loremaster to safely navigate the technology. Even with those protocols in place, one in four loremasters will kill themselves within the first two years." – Juliette Mirovar

* * *

The Panopticon Fortress, Cell Block A, Guardhouse, September 11th, 14:41:20

The team emerged from the store room into the cell block A guardhouse.

Li walked behind Arthur Slayne's left shoulder. It was the best place to keep an eye on him. He glanced up at one of the corner cameras; it was tracking their movement across the room. He shook his head and declared, "That's not a good sign."

Li's eyes widened. "They can see us again." She cast about while pulling her laptop from her backpack. She dashed behind one of the counters and yanked a security pass from the nearest Shadowstone operative's corpse. She waved the pass over a reader on her laptop. The machine pinged, subverting the operative's identity, and connecting to the base's wireless network. Her implant burned, data streaming through her enhanced nervous system. The guardhouse faded, ghosting away, replaced with an immersive experience of the Panopticon fortress.

"I'm in," she whispered.

The base's schematics appeared as an illuminated map over everything around her. She flew like a ghost through the maze of corridors and maintenance tunnels, pipes and power conduits. The disposition of the opposing forces was clear, including the sixteen praetorians rushing toward their position in the guardhouse.

They were five seconds away.

On the edges of her perception a fell shadow stirred and cold tendrils of terror crept into her soul. She ruffled through the base's core systems like fanning a set of cards. Kraken-1 was a mess and getting worse, then her attention arrested on the fire alarm system. Anyone could set it off, and it would take five minutes to reset it.

Three seconds remained until the praetorians arrived.

The shadow rose, rising, and rising, swelling like a malicious tidal wave over her world. Terror clenched in her gut and she gasped for breath. Li activated the fire alarms – all of them on the main levels. Forty massive fire doors erupted from wall recesses and slammed shut throughout the primary underground levels of the fortress. The nearest trapping the praetorians in a corridor fifty yards short of the guardhouse entrance. It would take the base's operators five minutes to reset the system and free the vampires. The team had gained a five-minute window. It would have to be enough.

The shadow deepened into utter darkness, the fortress fading into it. A malevolent intelligence regarded her with a baleful glare.

A desperate desire to flee ripped through her.

The darkness reached for her with a thousand tendrils of shadow.

A single golden flame broke the dreadful gloom before her.

The darkness recoiled, thundering with deafening malice.

Li burst out of her vision; the guardhouse and the rest of the team snapping back into sharp reality around her. A whoop, whoop, whoop klaxon wailed in the distance, counterpointed by deep thuds from the fire door as the praetorians tried to break it down.

"We are opposed," Li whispered, her words barely audible, her face pale with shock. There was something out there. Something that had regarded her with utter enmity in its alien soul. Nothing human could be that hateful, that pervasive, that dedicated to her total obliteration.

"Good work, Li," Slayne enthused, resting a firm hand on her shoulder. "The fire doors will hold for five minutes," he leaned in a fraction, studying her face. "What else did you see?"

Li looked at him with wide eyes for a long moment, then straightened, brushing his hand off her shoulder. She stepped in close, poking him in the chest with two tight fingers. She needed answers and she needed them now. "What got us out of the cells? What was that tremor all about?"

Slayne frowned at her. "The short answer – the underground river is flowing onto the magma beneath the power stations, it has taken Kraken dash one offline."

"Pressure is rising in the magma cavern – it's heading toward a catastrophe."

Slayne tilted his head half-quizzically, as if Li's news wasn't a surprise. "That so? Well, we have no time to waste worrying about what we can't stop."

Slayne tapped his wrist watch. His gaze whipped around the team and he flung his right hand toward the reverberating thuds emanating from the corridor. "We have less than five minutes before those praetorians trying to smash that fire door down get free, and the clock is ticking." Turning to the members of the team in turn, he declared, "Here's the new plan. Francis and Jay, you've got the second power station and the backup generators on the north side of the base. Peter and Chiara, it's still the nemesis tower for you. Take command of it, and use it to kill the specter towers before disabling it. If Kraken dash one comes back online, or they fire up the southern bank of diesel generators – take them out hard." He stared at Anton and Li, a wry grin curling the edges of his mouth. "You two can come with me. After Francis and Jay take out the main power, we'll steal the Panopticon."

Li shook her head, her eyes filled with horror. "You've just described my vision this morning. I never told you all the details. You're leading us straight to our deaths."

Slayne snorted derisively. He stared at her, his gaze filling with a terrible intensity. "That's unfortunate for your vision then, isn't it? We'll just have to outsmart your anticipation of doom."

Li stepped back, her eyes wide, staring at Slayne with dread.

Francis stepped forward and commanded, "Okay team, we have new objectives." He frowned momentarily at Arthur. "We have to execute the plan as is. Stay in touch via the tactical network. Watch out for day guards with smart rifles, and watch each other's backs."

"Thanks, Francis," Slayne said, then tapped his watch again. "You've all memorized the schematics. The fire doors cover the main corridors. The maintenance tunnels are on a different system. Dwayne, take us to the nearest entrance to the maintenance tunnels."

"Sure," Dwayne said, he rushed to the exit into the corridor, lifted a hand and called out, "Quick, this way. We can reach our objectives before the vampires can try to stop us." He turned, dashing off to the right, and away from the reverberating fire door at the opposite end of the corridor.

Slayne declared, "They can see us on cameras, but they can't intercept us. We have four and a half minutes to complete our missions." He looked hard at Li. "Can you haze the cameras? Can you blind the Panopticon?"

A chill seized Li's heart. This close to the heart of the Panopticon, it could be literally watching her attempt to blind it. She'd only have seconds before it would swamp her efforts with a network backlash that would fry her laptop and possibly burn out her implant. Then there was the 'thing,' waiting in the darkness – an infectious madness filled with utter hate for all life. If that pernicious loathing caught her … she dreaded to think what might happen. At best, it would kill her, and at worst, it would send her hopelessly insane. It was clear she didn't have the defenses she needed to ward off the threat to her sanity.

"No," Li stated, "It's not possible this close to the Panopticon." She didn't dare tell him about the 'thing,' haunting her visions.

Slayne frowned, his lips thinning in disappointment. He turned away to follow Dwayne into the hallway.

Li followed the team into the corridor, past the crumpled, bloodied corpses of the Shadowstone operative and the day guards Peter had killed. Dwayne swiped his security pass over a reader on the wall and lifted back a grill from the floor. There was a ladder descending into a dimly lit gloom. The Order helper pointed down and said, "I'll go first, follow me down." He disappeared through the hole. The rest of the team in front of her quickly followed their guide.

Anton fell in beside Li, his face filled with serious intent. He whispered, "C'mon Li, let's see it through."

Li smiled weakly, her guts churning, and leaped through the square hole in the floor into the maintenance tunnel below. She dropped twenty feet, landing in a crouch on a solid steel mesh floor. Thin strip lights ran into the distance in both directions. She moved aside, Anton landing next to her a moment later. The rest of the team had disappeared into the maze of maintenance tunnels. Slayne stood at the first intersection, he looked back, beckoning them forward.

She couldn't see Dwayne Washington; he had vanished. Li figured the Order helper's chances of survival were no different from her own or the rest of the Mirovar force team.

Precisely zero.

* * *

The fortress command-and-control center's main alarm shrieked a new alert, followed by a klaxon whoop, whoop, whoop siren.

The main screen reverted to the full three-dimensional fortress schematic. Fire alarms were going off everywhere. A wave of deja vu swept through Clayton Maze's soul and he shouted, spittle flying from his lips, "Kill that fucking damned noise."

The room fell into silence.

Clayton growled. "The fortress can't suddenly be on fire. What the hell is going on? Cameras on all those locations, put 'em up!" He thrust his hands at the main screen, his voice rising to a shout, "Put them up now!"

The operators rushed to comply. The screen changed again, revealing corridors and intersections across forty locations. There wasn't a wisp of smoke or lick of flame visible anywhere.

Commander Cormack broke the silence, her voice a strangled whisper. "It's a false alarm. They're back in our networks."

Clayton's gaze flashed over the screens. The Order operatives had vanished. His fists clenched into black hammers and he snapped, "Where the hell have they gone?"

"Sir," An operator called out. "The praetorians have been trapped in a corridor on sub-level dash two."

A second operator called out, "Sir, day guard squads numbers one and twelve, en route to the main server guardhouse on sub-level dash four have been trapped behind fire doors."

"Trapped?" Clayton asked incredulously.

The first operator quailed. "Yes, Sir. By the fire door next to the cell block A guardhouse, Sir."

"Then lift it," Clayton ordered. He raised both hands palm up and shouted, "Lift them all!"

"Ahhh, Sir," Cormack said, her voice reeking of trepidation. "It will take five minutes to reset the fire alarm system and open the doors."

Clayton turned and stared at her. He drew a hand slowly down his face, and stated with deadly calm, "Five minutes." He paused for a long moment. The faint susurration of the air conditioning competed with the drum beats of human hearts to fill his ears. He wanted to rend and tear, but no – he needed these animals to save the fortress and protect the Panopticon. His king would punish him if he failed. He swallowed once and declared with quite forcefulness, "Then we must find them, and position what forces we may to slow them down until our vamp— … praetorians are free and we can hit them hard."

His lip curled. His momentary lapse meant nothing anymore. These blood bags would soon be dead. He could never allow a human to live with the knowledge of vampire existence. That was a given of the world Clayton lived in.

The operators worked their consoles. Three new screens opened up on the main display. They flickered as they swapped from camera to camera. Whatever they were recording was moving fast. Clayton accelerated his senses to match the video feeds. There were three groups of Order operatives ramping to whatever objectives they were seeking. They were using the maintenance tunnels. Why the maintenance paths didn't have fire doors was a question that would have to wait. He'd already memorized their names. Francis Mirovar and Jay Creeley were passing underneath the main northern wall. He slowed down and snapped, "Commander, what forces do we have at the northern power station?"

"I've already sent three squads of day guards to Kraken dash two, they arrived moments ago."

Clayton nodded; his forces were already waiting for the two Order operatives to arrive. A direct assault by Creeley and Mirovar would be suicidal. They'd be sitting ducks in the tunnels approaching the power station, mere targets for the merciless accuracy of the Panopticon guided smart rifles of a dozen day guards.

His eyes narrowed with calculation and he accelerated again. Peter Lamb and Chiara Romano were rising through the maintenance levels, they were on a direct course to the base of the nemesis tower. A chill crawled up his spine. If they dared suicide, they could destroy the whole base with a single hypersonic nuclear-tipped cruise missile. They could kill him. He dropped back to normal speed. "Commander, what of the nemesis tower?"

Cormack blinked. "The towers are fully operational – the weapons are hot in accordance with red alert protocols. They're unmanned, slaved to this command-and-control center, or the Panopticon if the command-and-control center fails."

"Are there manual overrides?" Clayton asked.

Cormack's mouth opened and closed without a sound.

Clayton snarled, blurring across the room. His hands appearing on the woman's shoulders, shaking her back and forth like a rag doll. "ARE THERE MANUAL OVERRIDES?" he thundered, spit flying from his mouth across the commander's face.

Her neck snapped, her head lolling backward, sightless eyes staring upward.

Useless! Useless! Woman! Clayton seethed, throwing her across the room like a broken toy. She crashed into the wall with a coldly satisfying crack of snapping bones, slumping into a heap on the floor, blood dripping from her nose and mouth onto the pale tiles.

The four praetorians standing guard at the corners of the room bared their fangs, hissing loudly at the remaining humans.

Hard and inevitable experience would soon school the surviving operators about their true status as food, but first they had to do something about Lamb and Romano.

Clayton glanced at the secondary screen displaying the disposition of friendly forces. His prized praetorians stood in a cluster on sub-level-2, but there was no indication of the fire doors on the 'friendly forces,' display. He had no way of readily determining which forces could now reach which locations. "You there," Clayton said, pointing at the oldest male operator. "What forces have we got that can reach the nemesis tower?"

The operator paled; his skin chalky beneath his short gray hair. A bead of perspiration appeared on his temple and began sliding down in front of his ear. He lifted a trembling finger and pointed at a slim, young, dark-skinned woman and murmured, "She's next in line."

Clayton's gaze focused on the young woman. Her name tag read, 'Siobhan Ulysses.' For a brief moment, she stared back at him with a steely gaze, then stated, "Sir, we have two squads of day guards guarding the pumping station. They could be at the nemesis tower in less than a minute. There's another squad heading to Kraken dash one, I'd advise bringing them back to secure the saboteurs. We have three squads guarding the hangars, we could send them onto Kraken dash two."

Clayton's lip curled. Here was someone who knew what they were doing. "Do it, Commander."

She turned back to her console, and spoke quiet calm orders into a microphone.

Clayton accelerated again. The last feed showed Arthur Slayne, Li Wu, and Anton Slayne approaching the ladder to maintenance sub-level-3-1. They must be heading for the Panopticon. He blinked. He had to get this situation locked down immediately. He would spare no one in his efforts to protect the Panopticon from Arthur Slayne and the Mirovar force team. He asked the new commander, "What of the Panopticon?"

"Two squads are already en route to reinforce," she glanced briefly at the nearest praetorian, who stared back at her with indifferent eyes, "… the praetorians there, but fire doors have trapped them as well."

"Then send others. Send the squads from the hangars."

Ulysses shook her head once. "Sir, if Kraken dash two goes offline, the Panopticon will go offline. If that happens, the day guard's smart rifles will go offline diminishing a key advantage for us. In addition, the selected targets are significant. Kraken dash one is offline. Shutting down Kraken dash two will initiate the Panopticon evacuation protocol. Given the disposition of enemy forces I think they're attempting to steal the Panopticon, but to do that they have to breach the main server room guardhouse. That guardhouse is in lock down and has four of your praetorians as a final line of defense. The final door is like a bank vault, no one can get through to the Panopticon until the red alert ends."

Clayton snorted, his lip curled and he said, "Pray that you are correct." He stabbed a dark finger at her and demanded, "How long before the fire alarm resets?"

Ulysses pointed at a red counter on a side screen. It ticked over from 02:40 to 02:39. "Once that counter hits zero. The fire doors will retract."

"Send your troops, commander," he ordered, staring at the screens.

For the moment, circumstance had tied his hands, but not for long.

No, not for long at all.

* * *

"Why are there no fire doors in these tunnels." Li asked.

Slayne glanced to his left and stated, "You're a curious young lady aren't you."

"Well, to be honest Arthur," Anton said, "I'd like to know too."

"In another four minutes we'll be knee deep in vampires, and you both want to talk about technicalities?"

Anton nodded, and Li answered, "Yes."

Slayne's eyes tightened as he pulled to a stop next to a ladder positioned against the back of a narrow square alcove in the wall. "Okay, the bottom line is that two companies built the levels of the fortress under different sub-contracts. They each had a requirement for fire control systems, one picked fire doors, the other picked CO2 fire suppression systems. Don't start a fire down here, the CO2 will suffocate you before the smoke does." He stepped into the alcove and onto the metal rungs of the ladder, and glanced back at Li. "Are we good?"

Li nodded.

Slayne let go of the ladder free falling to the bottom of the shaft. He landed lightly on his feet, whirled and swore, "Shi—"

A heavy machine gun thundered into life on the lower level, drowning out Slayne's words. Bright flashes strobing up the ladder shaft. Anton's eyes widened, he lifted his assault rifle, and dived head first into the shaft.

Li blinked. What the hell did Anton just do? He'd kill himself when he hit the bottom of the shaft. She rushed forward twisting to the left, her right hand caressed the right-side of the ladder, her right boot brushing against the same. She dropped down the shaft in free fall.

Anton's assault rifle roared on full auto beneath her.

Individual rounds from Slayne's auto-pistol cracked through the air like an iron whip, blue flashes counterpointing the stuttering roar and fiery flashes of the .50 caliber machine gun.

Li gripped the ladder hard, pulling herself to a halt. She waved her P90 sub-machine gun aside to get a better look down the shaft. Anton was upside down, anchored by jamming his boots against the narrowly spaced walls of the shaft, his legs spread in a 'V.' He held his rifle beneath his head, its barrel reaching just below the bottom rim of the shaft. The weapon ran dry, and Anton dropped it to the steel mesh floor a dozen feet below. He crunched forward, snatching a pair of grenades from his webbing. He pulled the pins with his clenched teeth, and spat the rings away. He shouted, "Fire in the hold!" and launched the grenades deep into the maintenance tunnel.

Time seemed to stretch for a moment, then the grenades exploded with a thunderous roar and a flash of white light.

The .50 cal stopped firing.

Anton released his foothold on the walls of the shaft, dropping and twisting cat-like to land in a crouch next to his empty assault rifle.

Slayne blurred past him on the right, firing a single shot from his auto-pistol. He called out, "Clear."

Li dropped to the floor. Anton and his grandfather stood thirty-feet away next to a tracked ground drone. The machine was a sleek eight-foot dark-gray tube, with four sets of triangular tracks standing four feet high. It carried a .50 caliber heavy machine gun on its back. The gun's trigger mechanism clicked continuously on an empty firing chamber; the ammunition belt feed smashed to oblivion by Anton's grenades. Blue smoke rose from a neat hole near the rear of the drone. The clicking slowed, then stopped. The drone settled to the floor, surrounded by a thin blue haze of acrid smoke.

Slayne and Anton glanced at each other, and the older man instructed him. "Ahh … it's 'Fire in the hole,' Anton."

Anton shook his head. "Huh? What?"

"It's 'Fire in the hole.' You said, 'Fire in the hold.'"

"No, I didn't."

Li came up beside him and declared, "Yes, you did. I heard it."

Anton glanced back and forth between his grandfather and Li. His lips curled into a half-grin and he shrugged sheepishly. "Well, I must've got a little over-excited back there." He smiled broadly, ramming a fresh magazine of caseless ammunition into his assault rifle with a sharp click.

Slayne lifted an eyebrow, turned away and led them past the smoking ruins of the drone. "We have to drop down to maintenance sub-level four dash one, from there we can come back up onto sub-level dash four. The only way into the main server room and the Panopticon core is via the guardhouse on that level."

Li frowned. "Surely, they'd have it locked down by now."

"Yes, they have done exactly that," Slayne said, knowingly. "However, there is another protocol built into the door. One of my companies built the final guardhouse, and they inserted a little extra functionality just for me."

"A back door?" Anton asked.

Slayne smiled in the strip-lit gloom of the tunnel. "More like a front door keyhole," he tilted his head slightly and raised his forefinger, "and I have the key."

Li frowned. "Your biometrics are in the system."

"In the hardware. It's a lot harder to find when it's hardwired into the electronics of the door."

Li grinned despite herself. There was no denying that Slayne had performed marvels of preparation for this mission, and just maybe there was a sliver of hope in the Slayne's ability to do the unexpected.

Her brief smile evaporated, by the same token the elder Slayne could just as easily be leading them all to their deaths, and one day, Anton would do something that wasn't crazy-smart but just plain crazy, and get himself, and those around him killed.

It was only a matter of time until disaster struck.

The events in her vision were still in the future.

***

Peter blurred out of the final ladder shaft and into the dimly lit inner core of the nemesis tower.

Chiara followed a moment later, her gaze locking on the only exit from the chamber, an open doorway leading into a twenty-foot-long corridor.

The room was square, a hundred feet on a side, with twenty feet high ceilings. Yard-thick pillars stood in four rows across the room, industrial piping and heavy power cables laced the walls and ceiling.

Peter moved quickly through the available space, checking to see if there was anyone else in the room. He arrived in the middle of the room. They were alone. Above him, a narrow square shaft rose up through the core of the tower. It was barely four feet wide; a single maintenance ladder set close to the shaft's wall rose up to the top of the narrow column.

Peter's nightglasses adjusted to the ambient lighting in the shaft. Metadata scrolling across his field of view stated the shaft was two-hundred and seventy feet high. It didn't reach the control dome on top of the tower. It wasn't another way in.

Apart from the ladder, glistening cold-blue fuel cells and massive power cables covered the walls of the shaft. Additional power cables snaked into conduits that disappeared back into the maintenance level they'd just come from. He shook his head, he'd love to be able to spend a week deconstructing and understanding the technologies involved in the tower, but there was no time for that. He sighed and turned to the sole corridor leading out of the chamber. Chiara glanced back at him from halfway down the hall, a 'hurry-up,' expression flashing across her face.

Peter shrugged his massive shoulders, and whispered, "I know, no time to smell the roses." He strode forward, unlimbering one of his double-bladed battle axes with his left hand. He held an MP7 sub-machine gun loaded with silver-laced high-performance armor-piercing bullets in his other hand. The Milkor MGL swung from a strap at his left hip.

Chiara glided silently forward to a slatted metal door at the end of the short corridor. The halls beyond were well lit, thin strips of bright light casting tiger stripes on her lithe form. She froze, looking back over her shoulder at Peter and slashing her fingers across her throat – the universal sign for silence.

Peter crept forward and peered through the slats in the door.

There were eight fully armed and ready day guards in the hall outside. One commanded, "Sochi, take your squad up the stairs. Don't let anyone get to the top."

"Sir," a voice responded from the base of the stairwell on the edge of what Peter could see. Four sets of boots tramped up the stairs to Peter's left.

Peter looked at Chiara. She lifted four fingers and pointed up the stairs. He nodded; a squad was going up the stairwell that spiraled around the inner wall of the tower to the command center at the top. She flicked her head to the right, lifting four fingers again.

Peter nodded. There was a second squad guarding the base of the tower. Well, eight day guards weren't that bad. Sure, they were fast, strong, tough, skilled and deadly accurate with their smart rifles, but there was only eight of them. Chiara and Peter could hit the bottom four before the ones above could react. He lifted his hand to signal the attack.

"Hendrickson," a new voice called out. "We've been sent to reinforce this position. The hostiles are in the ground-floor chamber now. Our orders are to hold them in place until the praetorians arrive."

Peter crouched and stared. The guards knew exactly where they were and weren't afraid that Peter and Chiara knew that they knew. Another squad had taken a position thirty feet back from the first squad. Now there were twelve day guards, and the back four would get shots in before they'd dealt with the front four. Worse, the squad up the stairs would come down as soon as a fight started. The day guards could easily catch them in a crossfire, and they'd both seen how deadly the smart rifles were at the conclave.

Chiara tapped him on his chest, leaned in close, and whispered, "How are we going to get past these guys?"

Peter frowned and whispered back, "It's a good question."

It was a damn good question.

Peter glanced at the time readout on his Order nightglasses. It read, '14:44:55.' In a little under two minutes the fire doors would lift and the trapped praetorians would be free. Like Peter and Chiara, they'd take about eighty or ninety seconds to get from the guardhouse to the base of the nemesis tower. Probably faster since they had the benefit of using the main corridors.

Peter frowned, they had less than three minutes left to take control of the nemesis tower and execute their mission. However, they had twelve day guards with smart rifles waiting to kill them as they emerged from the maintenance tunnel to enter the stairwell.

If that wasn't the definition of a 'turkey shoot,' Peter didn't know what was.

They needed help but where was help going to come from?

* * *

Jay blurred down the maintenance corridor.

It had been a long ramp. Francis and Jay had covered more than a mile through the maze of maintenance tunnels to the edge of the northern power station in under two minutes. There was a final dog-leg to pass through and they'd emerge into the lower ground floor of Kraken-2, the sole remaining power station for the Panopticon fortress.

Their mission was simple. Shut down the power station, and disable the diesel backups. They'd discussed the technical details back at the roadhouse that morning. They knew what they had to do and now was the time to do it.

Jay hit the left-hand turn at full speed, he went around the corner in two bounds across the walls, descending to the floor to cover the next fifty feet of corridor to the final right hand turn into the power station. Francis was fifty yards behind him, a distance maintained to allow Francis to react if Jay hit something. Jay was on point; Francis was watching his back. Jay had volunteered for the role, he wanted to be first to contact the enemy.

There'd been a lot to deal with in the last few weeks. The loss of Yvette was at the top of the list. The revelation that Arthur Slayne might not be the murderer he'd always believed was in second place, and the near destruction of the Order was third.

Jay wasn't entirely sure he wanted to keep going with the Mirovar force team. Perhaps it was time to break out and create his own team. The Order needed to be rebuilt and shaped to the modern era, but that was a secondary concern. The main issue was that the spy who'd betrayed Yvette and Juliette to Armitage was still in the team. He'd weighed the available evidence and settled on Chiara as the guilty one, but nothing had been done. The rush of events had conspired to delay the application of Truther and the determination of guilt, and without cast-iron evidence he couldn't act.

He'd made a mistake blaming Anton for his grandfather's actions, and now it seemed most likely that Ramin Kain was the true murderer of his mother. Jay didn't want to repeat the same mistake with Chiara.

In an ironic twist of fate, he'd taken Ramin Kain's head in the dungeons beneath Armitage's manor house without realizing he'd been delivering a long-awaited justice for his mother's murder. With Arthur Slayne absolved of guilt for his mother's death and the real killer dealt with, there was no reason to continue to hate the elder Slayne, but habits nurtured from a young age were hard to break.

The unresolved issue of the spy was setting his nerves on edge. He knew it was a problem and he was less than his best for it, but he couldn't just let it go.

It'd become clear that Slayne wasn't a murderer and Ramin Kain had falsely accused him in an act of rank injustice, and Anton was a brother in arms and a proven warrior against the vampires. But he needed justice for Yvette and both the Slayne's rubbed him up the wrong way. They were reckless in their actions and took unnecessary risks. If they were comfortable with harboring a known spy then that would be the last straw.

Jay set his thoughts aside. He launched himself up the wall to take the last corner. He hit the far wall getting his first glimpse into the bowels of the power station. The final leg of the maintenance corridor was more antechamber than corridor. Sixty feet long, thirty feet wide, and twenty feet high.

A pair of closed retractable doors ran the length of the antechamber's ceiling. The antechamber opened up into the main chamber of the power station. The larger chamber was well lit, with walls of pipes, control consoles, and maintenance ramps and walkways surrounding three huge thrumming turbines.

Ten day guards armed with smart rifles stood in a flattened semicircle facing the entrance. Another two manned 7.62mm mini-guns, positioned deeper into the power station on a maintenance walkway in front of the closest turbine and fifteen feet above the floor. Red laser sights hung like straight strings filling the antechamber he was about to land in.

Jay had time to react – just a matter of a tenth of a second faster than the fastest day guards manning the mini-guns and rifles set to fill the corridor with a storm of sudden death.

All his tremendous momentum was pushing him forward, deeper into the antechamber toward the waiting weapons. Barrels snapped into motion as the guards responded to his arrival, ably assisted by the Panopticon tracking his movement. Fingers pulled on rifle triggers. The electric motors on the mini-guns whirred, barrels spinning into deadly motion. Bright golden fire erupted from the throats of a dozen weapons.

Jay kicked hard, his left hand flying up to grab a steel reinforcing rod on the left-side retractable door in the ceiling. He swung hard, his shoulder snapping, agony lancing across his chest. He pivoted in a sharp arc back into the short corridor in the middle of the dog-leg.

A hail of bullets tore the wall apart at the end of the antechamber behind him.

Jay landed in a crouch, and backed up against the opposite wall facing anything that might come from the station. His left arm hung limply; his H&K 416 assault rifle held like a hand gun toward the corridor to the power station.

Francis pulled to a stop next to him, then dragged him another dozen feet deeper into the dog-leg. He said urgently, "Your arm. Give me your arm."

Jay turned, leaning against the corridor wall, his left arm hanging like a loose noodle from his shoulder.

Francis picked up Jay's left arm with both hands.

Jay braced himself against the wall, his face set in anticipation of what was about to happen. Ramp epigenetics enhanced the ability to operate in the face of pain but everything still felt the same.

Francis twisted and pulled.

The arm slipped back into its joint, a wave of agony ripping through him, then ebbing to background thunder. Jay panted. Something caught his eye. Another gun barrel edging past the far corridor – from behind them. His rifle flashed up and he let rip with a three-round burst. The bullets ricocheted off the edge of the wall around the barrel and it vanished back behind the corner of the wall.

Francis blurred, taking up a position forty feet away facing into the corridor back to the fortress. He fired a 40mm grenade down the corridor and followed with a long burst from his assault rifle.

Return fire ripped into the wall a meter to his right. He glanced back at Jay, frowned, his lips pressing together into a grimace. He snapped into the broadcast link, "Mon Dieu, we're surrounded."

Francis looked hard at Jay, and flicked up his right hand once with three fingers, and then again with four. He'd got a glimpse of the forces that had come up behind them. Another three squads of day guards had cut off any escape route. Twenty-four opponents pinned them down at the entrance to the power station.

They were just short of their mission objective, but the power station might as well have been on the moon. Jay stared at Francis; a fatalistic look passed between them – they were going to die on this mission.

We have less to lose, Jay thought bitterly. *We'll take as many of them as we can with us and have an honor guard when we pass through the gates of hell. They can blow trumpets and beat drums, and know they faced the best of the Order of Thoth before they died.*

He blinked; his eyes suddenly moist with tears. He wiped them away with a hard brush of the back of his hand. It was time to open the gates of hell, and come what may, he'd die on his feet with weapons in hand, and rebellion on his lips. "After all," he whispered to himself. "They can only kill me once."

And Yvette is already there…

* * *

The reports came in over the command-and-control center's audio system.

"Hendrickson reporting in. We've locked down the nemesis tower. Three squads on site. Two hostiles trapped in the ground floor chamber."

"Mason reporting in. We've secured Kraken dash two. Six squads on site. Two hostiles trapped in the maintenance tunnel just short of the Kraken dash two lower mezzanine level."

Clayton Maze demanded, "Commander, what is the status at the main server guardhouse?"

"Still secure," Siobhan Ulysses responded. "Cameras have Arthur Slayne, Anton Slayne, and Li Wu on the lowest maintenance level. They will need to rise to sub-level dash four to access the front of the guardhouse."

"Maintain our forces in position. All we have to do now is keep them where they are. Once the praetorians are free, we can mass our main strength against their weakest positions. Mirovar and Creeley are the most exposed but clearly, they can't move with the number of day guards in position around them. Now open a broadcast link with my praetorian squad leaders, I need to give them fresh orders."

Ulysses nodded and flicked a switch. "The link is open, Sir."

Clayton stared at the main screen. One of the picture-in-picture views showed sixteen praetorians standing in a corridor waiting for the fire doors to retract. He declared, "Carney, Holdsworthy, Sutter, Tench, I have fresh orders for you." Four of the vampires in the corridor looked up at the camera. "Sutter and Tench, take your squads to the base of the nemesis tower and engage the hostiles there. Carney and Holdsworthy, take your squads to sub-level dash four, link up with day guard squads one and twelve and crush any hostiles encountered there. Once you've secured the nemesis tower and the approach to the main server guardhouse, then transfer to the Kraken dash two power station and mop up the last of the hostiles. Is that clear?"

There was a chorus of assents.

The link closed. Events were progressing as expected, it was a marked improvement over the recent past. Clayton glanced at the fire alarm reset counter. It read, '01:20,' and ticked over to 01:19 as he watched. In another eighty seconds the praetorians would be free.

He allowed himself a triumphant grin. Arthur Slayne remained outside the main server guardhouse, and the rest of his forces couldn't move, pinned down and unable to reach their objectives. Arthur Slayne's mission had failed, and soon, very soon, his praetorians would crush the Order forces beneath their heels.

Clayton's smile broadened.

Victory was inevitable.

* * *

The lowest maintenance level was as quiet as a tomb.

Li prayed quietly to herself that it wouldn't become one. She drew comfort from the slight sounds of their footfalls, rustling of gear and drawing of breath. Simple things that proved they were in the real world and not lost in a loremaster vision gone awry. Thin strip lights ran in a single line down the center of the ceiling. They cast just enough illumination to render the Order nightglasses superfluous. Li, Slayne and Anton still wore their nightglasses for access to the tactical networks and situational metadata. She ran next to Anton, following his grandfather through the twists and turns of the maintenance tunnel.

Arthur Slayne paused for a moment before a ladder ascending within an alcove to sub-level-4. The level holding the entrance to the main server room and the Panopticon. He looked around at Li and Anton and declared, "The others should be in position by now, but they haven't reported in."

Anton frowned and opened his mouth to speak, but before he could utter a word Francis called out over the tactical link, "Mon Dieu, we're surrounded."

Peter whispered quietly over the same broadcast channel, "Chiara and I are trapped on the ground floor of the nemesis tower. We have too many day guards outside and no way to maneuver around them."

Li looked from Slayne to Anton and back again, and declared, "Everyone is pinned down."

Slayne stepped away from the ladder. "Well that sucks." He put his hands on his hips and stared hard at Li. "It's time for you to do your thing."

"Do what?" she asked perplexed.

"C'mon. You're the only loremaster we have. Hack into their networks, find a weakness and exploit it. We need to get past these day guards and their damn smart rifles before the praetorians get loose." He tilted his head, and his lip curled derisively. "Or, our goose is well and truly cooked."

Li looked to Anton. His lips thinned and he shrugged his shoulders. He was lost for ideas too.

Her chest tightened and she snapped, "Do you realize how close to the Panopticon we are. I'll only have seconds before it mounts a counter attack with all the might of the main server room behind it. It could fry my implant, my laptop, and leave us blind."

Slayne took a step closer and leaned in. "Then I suggest you ramp as hard as you can before you go in," his gaze nailed her to the spot, "and make it as quick as possible." He put a firm hand on her shoulder and whispered, "We'll keep you safe."

Li looked at him with wide eyes. It wasn't her physical safety she was worried about. It was everything else. A memory rushed through her from the roadhouse that morning. Slayne had said, *'How do you think the loremaster tech can work against the Panopticon?'*

Li's mind raced. Slayne knew about the loremaster tech. He knew all about it. He was the one behind it. He'd probably invented it.

Slayne gripped her other shoulder, leaned in further, his face mere inches from her own. "Ramp as hard and fast as you can go. Accelerate yourself, do what you have to do and get the hell out again before," he arched an eyebrow, "anything untoward happens."

He knows. He knows about the thing in the darkness. A cold fear clenched like a frozen fist in her guts. *And he's sending me in.*

The crackle of automatic gunfire came over the tactical link, followed by the crump of exploding grenades. The team was in dire straits. The elder Slayne watched her with flat eyes that hid secrets beyond counting; while Anton kept glancing away down the maintenance tunnel, looking for threats that weren't there.

Li let her eyes droop and wondered for a brief moment how she could push on. Then she reached for her laptop, sat down cross legged on the floor and opened it. Did she have a choice? It seemed that she didn't; there was nowhere to hide from reality and she wasn't one to look for an escape from responsibility. If she was the only one who could, then she was the one who must. After all, she was her father's daughter.

She centered herself in the moment and smashed through the noise within her own mind, drowning herself in silence bordering on the absolute. Slayne and Anton stood watch over her seated form. She glanced at them; they were as still as statues. Her perception of time had accelerated to a new maximum.

The external world vanished with an electric snap.

The darkness was waiting.

The fortress was no longer a shining thing of modern lights and clean surfaces. It had transformed into a gloomy ruin of dust-laden stone. Power cables and data conduits ran like veins over a corpse of basalt and steel. A dark sky, lit with alien constellations hovered overhead. Her breath came in a misty plume in front of her face.

Li shivered and flexed her fingers, a thin layer of ice cracking over her skin, sharp needles penetrating her flesh.

Something howled in the distance, an alien roar of agony or ecstasy – it could have been either or both.

The fortress writhed, stars whirling away to infinity.

She pulled into herself, gathering everything she was to the hidden center of her soul.

Crisp walls, gleaming tiles, straight lines of networked light hung before her for a moment, then twisted away.

Chaos.

A single drumbeat of time thundered throughout the world.

Was it a millisecond? A minute? A day? How much time had passed while she strove to gain control?

Too many questions.

…

Li let go, sinking deeper into the silence.

She forgot her name and then her own existence.

The fortress was the only reality.

She who was no longer Li reached through her implant into the surrounding networks. A pressure was building on the edges of her awareness. The lightning-fast processors of the Panopticon core were already responding to her presence.

Time was running out.

She reached automatically through the network, there were hundreds of smart rifles connected to the Panopticon. There was no off switch, but there was a diagnostics protocol. She reached for the program and ran it. Every rifle went offline, checking its status, running a set of automated instructions to test its readiness for use. The smart rifles would still operate as regular assault rifles but the enhanced aiming was offline.

She had gained twenty seconds for the team. All she had to do now, was emerge from the vision and tell them before the window for action closed. If only she could remember how.

The fortress peeled away, darkness spearing through the tears in reality like negative light – displacing everything before it.

Icy terror lanced through her heart.

Dark malice swirled around her. A golden flame burst into existence before her. The dark recoiled, the flame spread, an expanding sphere of warm light engulfing her.

The golden light brushed past her skin. She remembered, *I am Li.*

The dark tensed, massed and struck. The flame withered but did not go out. A terrible presence appeared behind her, freezing her to the spot. Cold, heavy hands landed on her shoulders. Something leaned in against her back, its breath rotten with death against the side of her face. It declared in deep tones of terrifying longing, "I've been waiting for you."

Li burst out of the vision, screaming at the top of her lungs. She leapt to her feet. Her laptop flying. She pranced on the spot, knees jerking up and down, wildly slapping at her shoulders. Her skin was alive with goosebumps; shivers rippling over her shoulders, crawling up her spine and sliding over her scalp. Just the 'thing's' touch carried a wretched violation of her soul.

She pulled to a halt. Her eyes wide, panting for breath, bent over, her hands on her knees. Li jerked upright. She tapped her nightglasses and broadcast an order over the tactical link, "Attack now, their rifles are offline – you have seconds to act." She stared wordlessly at Slayne and Anton. Both men were wearing looks of utter perplexity, the latter holding her laptop like he'd caught it mid-air. "Later," she whispered hoarsely. "I'll tell you later."

Slayne looked at her quizzically, a half-frown creasing his forehead. "You, okay? Still good for the plan of attack once we get to the main server room guardhouse?"

Li nodded.

"Okay, then," he said, turning away and blurring up the ladder to sub-level-4.

Anton handed back her laptop and gently grasped her shoulder. "Are you really, okay?"

Li nodded once, glanced up the ladder and said, "Let's do it."

Anton blurred up after his grandfather and Li followed after him.

* * *

"—you have seconds to act," Li called out over the tactical link.

Peter didn't hesitate, his big right boot blurring sole first into the middle of the slatted door. The metal door bowed outward, then snapped free as locks and hinges shattered, flying across a ten feet wide landing before ricocheting up the stairwell. He followed the momentum of his kick, stepping through the doorway. He holstered his submachine gun in a flash, his newly free hand snapping to the remaining battle-axe strapped across his massive shoulders. He lifted both blades in front of his broad chest, their bright metal gleaming beneath the overhead lights, and pivoted hard to the right, his boots screeching across the tiles.

Four day guards stood forty feet in front of him down the main corridor, ready to fire. A pair of guards ten feet away on the left and another pair the same distance on the right either stood, or knelt on one knee. Eight gun barrels lined up on his position in the landing before the stairwell.

Peter pushed deeper into his ramp, power coruscating like lightning through his limbs. He leaped, flying six feet above the floor toward the two day guards on the right.

Streams of fire erupted from all the trooper's rifles – passing beneath his leap, ripping into the wall before the stairwell. Chiara erupted from the maintenance corridor like she'd been shot from a cannon, flying over the hail of bullets tearing the stairwell's landing apart. She flashed toward the other pair of guards, her katana gleaming in the overhead lights.

Peter twisted mid-air, landing on his feet a yard in front of the two guards. They twisted left and right, separating, their guns firing, bullets streaming past him aimed at where he'd been. The rifle barrels swung in toward him. Hot throats spewing puffs of gray smoke, individual rounds resolving, muzzle flashes strobing across his deep chest. Each deadly round cracked like a whip, echoing through the corridors.

His axes fell, sweeping through a pair of diagonal slashes. Striking both men at the point where neck met shoulder, tearing through armor, flesh and bone. Peter's blades completed their arcs without slowing down, and he threaded the gap between the butchered guards as they fell away to the left and right, broad swathes of blood painting the cream walls and white-tiled floor in his wake.

Peter jagged hard left. Across the chamber, Chiara had hit the other two guards with equally lethal results. Their dismembered bodies lying in spreading pools of gore. The squad down the main corridor heading into the administration building stopped shooting. Chiara and Peter were now in the wings of a 'T' intersection and out of the immediate line of fire.

One of the guards deep in the corridor swore loudly, "Shit."

That was good enough for Peter. They had to press the issue before the smart rifles started firing with deadly ·Panopticon guided accuracy. Boots stormed down the stairs; the third squad were descending from the top of the tower to join the fight. They remained exposed to a potential crossfire from the day guards, and they had no way of knowing when the smart rifles would come back online. They could only assume the restoration of Panopticon driven accuracy was imminent.

Well, Peter considered, *they might be smart rifles, but they can't shoot around corners.*

Another guard shouted, "Fire in the hole!"

Four fragmentation grenades bounced off the throat of the corridor, angling left and right into the wings of the intersection.

Chiara blurred backward into the corridor leading toward the pumping station.

Peter turned hard left, blurring toward the corner farthest from the bouncing grenades. He leaped, rotating mid-air, flying backward into the upper corner next to the ceiling. His axes plunged into the walls on either side of the corner, becoming anchors beneath his elbows. His knees snapped up, becoming a wall in front of his torso. He ducked his head, making the smallest possible profile for a man his size. The grenades roared, smoke and fire rushing through the chamber. The edge of the blast struck him. A dozen small wounds opening up on his exposed skin. He dropped to the floor, blood running freely along his massive limbs and from a cut over his right eye.

Peter grinned the fighting grimace of a wounded bull. He re-sheathed his axes over his back and lifted his Milkor multiple grenade launcher from the strap at his hip. The weapon was set for automatic fire. He stepped away from the corner of the corridor and fired against the far wall, ricocheting three 40mm grenades into the squad of day guards lurking back toward the main administration building.

They shouted warnings and began running, then explosions tore through the corridor sending a sheet of flame and smoke into the intersection.

Peter strode into the dying flames, his eyebrows shrinking from the heat. He turned his torso to the left, the MGL chuffing three times, shooting more grenades up into the stairwell. The MGL clicked on empty and he dropped it to the floor.

Chiara appeared from the other corridor. He caught her gaze for an instant, flicked his head right to indicate where he was going, and blurred into the corridor to face the remaining day guards there.

Chiara went in the opposite direction, chasing the explosions rising along the stairwell to confront the squad coming down from above.

Peter passed into the remaining haze of the exploded 40mm grenades, his battle-axes reappearing in his bloodied hands. The gray smoke eddied and swirled, shadowy forms moving through it, rising to strike back at him.

It was a target rich environment.

* * *

Peter's grenades filled the stairwell with flame.

Chiara blurred up the stairs, chasing the flames as they vanished into gray smoke. She'd slung her P90 sub-machine gun, favoring her edged weapons against the day guards in the confined and smoky spaces of the stairwell. After dismembering the two day guards outside the stairwell, she'd flicked her katana clear of gore and sheathed it across her shoulders. Her throwing daggers, pulled from the sides of her boots appeared in her hands. The silver-laced blades gleamed despite the haze in the air. They were a comfortable weight in her grip, perfectly balanced for throwing. Their razor-sharp edges equally lethal for human or vampire targets. She didn't always carry them but had selected them for this mission, and had borne them through the underground river along with her favorite sword.

The first guard emerged from the smoke, his assault rifle swinging around to bear upon her. A second guard was a step behind and to the right, his smart rifle rising to bear on her chest, the laser sight cutting a flickering red line through the gray smoke.

Two six-inch blades flashed through the haze, sinking up to their hilts in the throats of the two day guards. Chiara blurred after her knives, passing the falling men before they hit the floor. Her katana swished free of its scabbard in an instant.

She sank deeper into silence. Power surged through her body and she accelerated up the curving stairs.

Flames burst through the haze from above her on the left, lines of fire ripping through the confined space. The final day guards were emptying their clips, bullets spraying everywhere.

Chiara pushed up to the right, wall running along the outside wall.

The guards responded, lifting their weapons, the final rounds in their magazines stuttering along the wall.

A bullet slammed into her left hand, dragging it and her katana back to the right.

A second bullet missed her chest by a hairsbreadth, drilling a hole through her right bicep.

Chiara snarled, flying over the guards' heads to land on the stairs behind them.

They whirled, dragging on their triggers, their rifles clicking on empty.

She stepped into the two men; her long dark plait mirrored in their visors rising like an enraged serpent above her. Her katana swept through a flat arc from left to right, collecting first one head and then the other. Their bodies slumped away, fountaining blood. Their helmeted heads bouncing and rolling down the stairs, disappearing around the corner of the stairwell.

Chiara staggered back to the inner wall, lifting her left hand up. There was a neat hole through the middle of her palm running blood down her forearm. She looked to her right arm. Her bicep had been perforated like a piece of meat with a sharp knife. Blood was streaming from the entry and exit wounds, running in rivulets down to her elbow where it dropped away to splatter on the tiled stairs.

She clenched her right fist around the handle of her katana. Her grip was strong. They'd missed the bone in her arm. Her left hand was another matter. She flexed it and agony ripped up her forearm.

She looked at it dispassionately. She'd dealt with worse before her ninth birthday at the hands of her father and her master instructor – Taipan. She descended several steps and retrieved her throwing daggers. She paused for a moment to clean them on the guards' uniforms before sheathing them back in her boots.

Mounting the stairs, she stooped and picked up a pair of smart rifles and a satchel of fresh magazines. She'd rather use their ammunition first when more day guard reinforcements arrived. That would leave the silver laced ammo in her sub-machine gun for the inevitable vampires. She picked up her pace. It was time to secure the nemesis tower, and once they'd accomplished that, she would bind her wounds.

The sounds of battle faded behind her. She had no doubt Peter would join her shortly after dispatching the last squad of day guards in the corridor. She flexed her injured hand again, pain shooting like barbed lightning along her left arm to her shoulder. Chiara circled the tower another three times. The last thirty feet of stairs, reflected a metallic sheen, and curved heavily to the left, contracting into the midline of the tower.

Chiara emerged from the stairwell onto a twenty-foot-wide metallic landing directly above the tower's midline. Ten feet high circular metallic walls surrounded the landing. A single wide doorway opened onto the command center of the nemesis tower. She stepped off the landing and onto the polished metal floor of the nemesis tower command center.

She circled the dome once. The barely audible scuff of her boots and her breathing the only sounds breaking the chamber's silence. Above the squat column over the stairwell, sat an operator's cockpit. Beside the column was the rail gun phalanx. It sat on a heavy cradle, its barrels punching through the barely visible wall of the dome. Thin strips of metal in the interior of the dome showed where the gun would rise or lower on the vertical axis. She presumed the dome could rotate left or right to point the gun in any direction.

Hence the metal stairs. The top thirty feet must reconfigure as the dome rotates. She whispered quietly to herself, "You don't have to be an engineer to work this stuff out."

Chiara surveyed the valley beyond the fortress, it was quite a view. She glanced at her hands. Blood was dripping from them onto the floor. She mused fatalistically to herself. *We were never going to get out of this unscathed.*

* * *

"—you have seconds to act," Li called out over the tactical link.

Francis was already moving. Jay launched himself forward, coming aside his force leader as they curved into the last corridor leading into the lower mezzanine level of the power station. The enhanced aiming of the smart rifles should be off. They had a slim window of opportunity to break through the screen of day guards and complete their mission.

The final corridor into the power station's main chamber had become sixty feet of waiting death. The only saving grace was its thirty feet of width and twenty feet of height. They would need every inch of maneuvering room to make it into the power station alive.

Jay hit the far-left wall fully ramped, blurring through the corner a yard above floor height. Francis was above him, wall running ten feet off the floor. The important thing was to present the enemy with two targets that were moving too fast to follow, and to never run in each other's wake – that's where the bullets would be – until the Panopticon aiming came back online and the day guards sharpened up their accuracy.

The ten day guards stood in an arc sixty feet back from the corridor exit. Without the benefit of the Panopticon, they'd lost their ability to co-ordinate on a single target per squad. Each man aimed for themselves.

The first two seconds were critical.

Jay leaped, arcing diagonally over the floor to the far-right wall, his finger pressed hard against his H&K 416 assault rifle's trigger. His weapon stuttered, high-performance rounds spearing away toward the guards on the far left of the arc. Francis opened up on the far-right edge of the arc. The day guards were fast, they had demonstrated that at the conclave, but they weren't as fast as a Ramp master – they couldn't dodge bullets.

The day guards fired, ten smart rifles opening up at the same time. Every guard was attempting to hit either Francis or Jay, and their streams of bullets flooded into the corridor. Their laser sights led the bullets. What would have been a tactical advantage to assist aiming against a normal opponent simply provided advance warning to a Ramp master of where the bullets were going.

The first two day guards spun away in plumes of pink mist, struck down by Francis and Jay's armor-piercing rounds. The nearest guards began reflexively sidling toward the middle of the arc in front of the maintenance corridor exit.

Francis and Jay fired continuously. The mini-guns positioned on the maintenance walkway a hundred feet inside the power station opened up. Bright streams of fire spearing down toward them.

Jay cut left, leaning low to avoid a laser sight string. He leaped, rolling over another two red strings and the golden stream lancing down from one of the mini-guns. He fired back, leaping to the left-hand side of the corridor. More guards staggered back, rounds punching through their armor and opening up fist sized holes in their backs.

Francis and Jay burst free of the corridor. Four guards remained standing on the floor of the chamber, desperately dragging on their rifles to bring their weapons to bear on the two blurring Ramp masters.

Jay cut hard left toward a giant pipe rising out of the floor, Francis cut hard right, running away from Jay. The day guards were a tight group in the middle of the open area and then began scattering. Francis and Jay kept firing, pale-gray smoke shrouding their weapons. They caught the remaining guards in a deadly cross-fire and cut them to ribbons before they ran ten feet. Their opponent's smart rifle return fire dwindled to nothing, stray bullets ricocheting off walls and industrial sized pipes behind the two Ramp masters.

The mini-guns on the maintenance walkway tracked them to their cover behind identical rising pipes on opposite sides of the chamber, bullets ricocheting off the polished concrete of the power station floor.

Jay glanced at his rifle; a counter indicated he had two rounds left in his magazine. He looked across at Francis who was ramming a fresh magazine home.

Francis lifted a pair of fingers and pointed in the direction of the walkway. He chopped his hand down and blurred forward. Jay went with him, bringing his gun to bear on the day guard positioned on the far right. He fired twice, and continued blurring forward to escape any return fire. There was none; the mini-guns didn't have time to spin up, their operators taken out by double taps to the head. Jay and Francis met in the middle of the chamber. They looked back, staring hard into the corridor leading back to the fortress.

"The other three squads are coming," Francis warned. "They'll have the Panopticon back online. They'll be a lot more dangerous than these fellows were. I need you to hold them off so I can shut this station down."

Jay nodded. "You got it, Boss."

Francis smiled grimly and blurred away to the power station's control room. A small office built above the level of the turbines on the far-right wall. There was no one inside. The normal operation of the station was fully automated but they could control it manually from the office.

Jay ejected his rifle's spent magazine and rammed a fresh one home. He cocked the under-barrel grenade launcher, loading a 40mm grenade into position. Cover and speed would be his defense. He just had to hold the squads off long enough for Francis to shut off the main power. Arthur Slayne had explained the Panopticon would then go into 'evacuation mode,' eliminating all the primary Panopticon systems including the day guard's smart rifles.

He stepped behind a screen of pipes, taking a position where he could see down to the end of the last corridor. The squads would be on him in moments, their smart rifles would be back online.

He'd have to hold them off for up to a minute.

Jay took a deep breath and let it out. He couldn't lose; if he won, the mission won, but if he lost, he'd be reunited with Yvette.

He grinned and laughed harshly.

He had nothing left to lose.

* * *

Peter stepped off the stairwell landing and entered the nemesis tower command center.

Chiara was there to greet him. He placed a warm hand on her right shoulder and suggested, "You'd better bind those wounds."

Chiara looked up at him, and slung her sub-machine gun at her hip. "I know, I was waiting for you to get up here." She studied his wounds briefly and declared, "You got lucky, all that bleeding you're doing looks superficial."

Peter shrugged and shook his head once. "I'll cut the fragments out once I get a spare minute." He backed toward the nearest wall and surveyed the nemesis tower command center. It was a hemispherical dome eighty feet in diameter. The tower's primary weapon system – the rail gun phalanx – dominated the space. The rail gun's three barrels, two above and one below in a triangular formation, cut through the armor skin of the dome and ran another forty feet past it. Three silvery six-feet-tall heat-dissipation fins describing a 'Y' ran the length of the barrels outside the dome.

The previous evening, the dome had been shiny black when observed from outside. From the inside it was transparent. Peter shook his head in awe, the Vampire Dominion had the best technology. The rail gun rested on a massive cradle that allowed it to rise to nearly vertical or depress well past the horizontal. A strip of transparent armor two yards wide intersected with the barrels. The strip would move with the weapon to allow it to rise or fall. A pair of power cables thicker than Peter's thighs rose out of the floor, snaked over the cradle and connected to the rear of the weapon. The weapon stood off-center to the left. An open cockpit rose directly above the stairwell exit. Within the cockpit, a single chair and control console sat in the exact center of the sphere.

"This I've got to try," Peter enthused, his eyes filled with awe. There was a ladder running ten feet up to the top of the central column. He quickly mounted the ladder, hunched, and squeezed himself into the cockpit, muttering to himself, "Damn equipment, always built for dwarves." He gave up on attempting to strap himself in and studied the command console.

"Right," Peter said, and grinned. "Time to put this gun to good use." He flicked a switch and a three-dimensional holographic battlespace display painted the interior wall of the sphere surrounded the cockpit. There was a single joystick mounted on the right-hand arm of the cockpit chair. He grasped it and leaned it to the left.

The whole dome began rotating to the left. The cockpit followed it, rotating above the central column. The stairwell humming and clanking beneath him as it automatically adjusted to the new position of the dome.

"Nice," Peter whispered, bringing the gun to line up on the southwest specter defense tower.

A set of pale cross-hairs appeared on the wall aligned with the center of the specter defense tower. There was a black button on top of the joystick. Peter depressed it.

Bright red bold-faced letters appeared on the battlespace display. 'NEMESIS SYSTEM COCKPIT LOCKED. SYSTEM CONTROL SLAVED TO C&CC.'

"Well, I should've expected that," Peter observed. He tapped his earbud. "Li, are you online?"

Li's voice came back shrouded by gunfire, "Wait!" The firing ceased. "Another drone. We're on sub-level dash four proceeding to the main server vault. What do you need?"

"The vampires have locked the nemesis tower down. All weapons control is with the c-n-c center."

Li paused for a moment. "I can't unlock those weapons from outside the main server room. I need more access."

Arthur declared, "Li can do it once she logs into the core networks. We have to get into the main server room first. You'll have to hold for another two minutes."

Peter glanced at the time readout on his Order nightglasses. He'd set a countdown timer on the fire doors. In another forty seconds the praetorians would be free, and in two minutes time they could be at the base of the tower. It was going to be a close thing. If they sent two squads, there was no way Chiara could hold off eight vampires by herself while he dealt with the specter defense towers. He'd have to help her, and if he was helping her – he wasn't executing the mission and destroying the vampires' ability to stop them escaping in a captured nightfalcon by shooting it down.

In a worst-case scenario, the vampires would overwhelm them before they could execute the plan, and the rest of the team would lose their opportunity of escape. As the possibility of failure clawed at his guts, Peter grinned ironically and silently vowed that he would not fail the mission – he'd see all his opponents dead before that happened.

There was constant background gunfire over the broadcast channel. Jay and Francis were silent, which meant they were ramping and fighting. The mission to shut down the second power station was undecided.

Peter wiped blood off his forehead with the back of his hand and suggested, "Those fire doors aren't going to hold forever. We'll have vampires on our six in less than two minutes."

"There's only one way out of here," Arthur declared. "We're almost at the main server room vault now. You have to hold for another two minutes – make it happen."

Peter bit his tongue. *Sir! Fucking yes, Sir!* "Don't worry!" he half-shouted, his gaze locked on Chiara's face. She simply took a breath, her eyes closed and her face filled with a deathly calm. Peter blinked, he'd never seen an expression of such conviction on someone's face before and it took his breath away. Chastened, he said quietly, "We'll get it done."

"Noted," Arthur answered.

The line silenced.

Peter glanced down to his right, where Chiara stood facing down into the stairwell. A lot was riding on Chiara's ability to stop anyone coming up the stairs. She'd opened her eyes and he caught her gaze. "You, good?"

She smiled, her eyes glistening. "Of course," she patted the bandage around her right bicep with her patched left hand. "Never better." She turned to look down the stairwell and snapped a fresh magazine into a captured smart rifle. Her FN P90 submachine gun slung at her left hip from a strap over her shoulders and a second freshly loaded rifle rested at her feet.

Oh my God, Peter thought. *We're cutting it fine.*

* * *

Francis dragged on a pair of giant black levers on an enameled cabinet attached to the wall of the power station's control room.

They came down half way, then snapped down and locked in the 'off,' position. Giant valves opened, while others closed in the bowels of the power station, sending fresh steam from the magma cavern through pipes bypassing the first turbine. It began spinning down. He repeated the process for the second and third turbines, and sharp whines filled the power station as the turbines began slowing down. He flipped a series of switches disabling the diesel backups. The power station was going down and going down hard. A cold start would take a week and by then the mission would be long over – one way or another.

Dials lining the wall of the control room began sliding to the left, down, and anticlockwise, every direction indicating shutdown. Kraken-2 was coming to a halt.

"Gas! Gas! Gas!" Jay shouted over the tactical link.

Francis looked through the control room's windows. A dozen or more gas grenades were spinning across the open floor of the power station.

"Get out of there," Francis shouted.

"Moving."

Francis turned back to the controls. The guards would follow the grenades into the power station. Their tactical helmets would protect them from the invisible gas while it would knock Francis and Jay out if they got so much as a whiff of it.

"How long can we hold our breath," he whispered to himself.

Machine gun fire erupted from the throat of the corridor leading back to the fortress. A burst of rounds starred the window on a straight line to his head.

"Contact," Jay shouted, returning fire.

There was a faint vibration in the floor. Francis grabbed the front edge of the console. Nothing else happened and he stood up tall. He wiped his forehead, his hand coming away slick with perspiration. He glanced at a dial recording ambient temperature in the power station. The needle was past ninety degrees Fahrenheit and well into the yellow zone. The red zone began at a hundred degrees. The power station wasn't meant to be this hot and shutting it down should make it cooler – not hotter.

"What the hell is happening?" he whispered to himself, looking at all the available readouts for a clue.

The floor vibrated for a couple more seconds.

The guns in the power station fell silent.

Francis tapped his ear bud. "Jay, did you feel that?"

"I sure did, the guards have disappeared – they're bugging out," Jay shot back. "I think we need to get the hell out of here too."

"I think you're right. Up to the surface, now!"

Francis blurred from the command room, dashing across a maintenance walkway to a set of stairs leading up to ground level.

Jay blurred across a nearby maintenance walkway running above the second turbine. They hit the exit door at the same time, bursting out into the afternoon sunshine. Behind them, the thunder of roaring steam overwhelmed the descending whine of the slowing turbines.

Chapter Eight

"I am an initiate of the third rank of the test of the Olgoi Khorkhoi. I have mastered the disciplines of the Red Empire. I will honor the way of my ancestors. I will honor the faith of my mother and father. I will bring ruin to my enemies and see them choke on their heart's blood before I die. This I vow before God and let my life be forfeit before I break this oath."

– "Oath of the Princes," from The Way of the Faithful, a book of Red Empire lore.

* * *

The Panopticon Fortress, Main Server Room Guardhouse, September 11th, 14:46:20

Arthur, Anton and Li arrived in front of the main server room guardhouse on sub-level-4.

A thin square outline ten feet across and ten feet high marked the location of the vault door. Rows of cameras ran across the top of the entrance. A pair of bio-metric readers rested five feet off the floor to the right of the door.

Anton and Li, took up a position to the left of the door, their weapons slung and their hands free. Arthur approached the readers, looked up into the cameras and grinned insouciantly. "Hi guys, I haven't seen your lot since Brazil."

A gravelly voice came over the intercom and said, "Ahhh, Slayne."

"Still alive, huh! You guys are in 'B,' company. Be here when they leave, and be here when they come back. What are you really doing? Waiting for the pension plan to kick in?"

"What's your strategy Slayne? Bore us to death with your talking?"

Arthur placed his right hand over the first reader. It glowed green around his palm. He stated, "Well, you do have us at a disadvantage. You being behind a vault door and all."

"Do you really think we're so dumb that you can insult us into opening it for you?"

Arthur leaned down and positioned his left eye over the retinal scanner. A light above it flicked from red to green. He stepped away from the door to the right, turning to face Anton and Li. His right hand appeared in the gap between his thigh and the wall. He thrust out four fingers and said, "Of course, not. I know you're smarter than that." He thrust out three fingers.

Anton and Li grabbed pairs of grenades from Anton's webbing, pulling the pins, and releasing the arming catches.

"I know the row of cameras above the door gives you a good view of everything—" Arthur said, snapping two fingers out in a downward 'V,' "—except for the bio-metric readouts."

A seam appeared in the middle of the door. It split into a pair of foot-deep halves, sliding smoothly and silently back into the walls. The gap opened up to a foot wide.

Arthur nodded firmly at Anton and Li. They threw their grenades through the gap and into the guardhouse. He whispered, "A bit of an oversight really."

Four gas grenades shot back through the gap, bouncing against the far wall, landing and fizzing across the corridor floor in front of them

Arthur's eyes widened. He spread his hands through a wide, flat arc, blurring away from the door. Anton and Li vanished in the opposite direction.

Three of the fragmentation grenades returned back through the doorway. They exploded with whip-like cracks, flame and smoke consuming the space in front of the door. The last grenade exploded within the guardhouse, eliciting a howl of pain and furious swearing.

"Flame burns the knockout gas off," Arthur called over the tactical link. "Quickly, attack now."

Anton hit the doorway first, Arthur a yard behind him, and Li a yard behind them both. The Blue, Black and Green Dragon swords gleamed beneath the overhead lights within the guardhouse.

Four praetorians attacked. The one at the rear shouted, "Kill them all! Accept no quarter!"

"Fabulous advice," Arthur declared with a straight face, leaping into the fray.

* * *

For the third time, an alarm blared its warning note through the fortress' command-and-control center.

Clayton dismissed the alarm with a chopping motion of his right hand and shouted, "What the hell is it now?"

"Kraken dash two has shut down," an operator called out.

"The backup diesels have not come online," a second operator declared, panic seeping into her voice. "We're running on emergency fuel cell power."

A third operator shouted, "The Panopticon has initiated its evacuation protocol!"

Clayton opened his mouth to issue a command.

The main screen shifted to a full view of Cornelius Crane's pale face, his fangs in full view jutting past his bottom lip. His brown eyes bored into Clayton's like a pair of pitiless lasers. He hissed past his fangs, then said, "The Panopticon is offline! What the hell is going on? Do you understand the operations you are putting in jeopardy with your incompetence?"

Clayton snapped to attention. A thin sheen of perspiration appearing on his smoothly shaven head.

An operator called out, "The fire doors are open."

Commander Ulysses, her voice an island of calm within the thinly held panic in the command-and-control center, declared, "Carney, Holdsworthy, Sutter, and Tench are all en route to engage the enemy with their squads, Sir."

Crane paused for a moment, his fangs retracting. His long forefinger loomed in the middle of the screen and thrust in the general direction of Ulysses. "Promote that woman, she's keeping her head while those around her are losing theirs."

"Yes, Sir," Clayton replied, a touch too quickly. "I already have."

Crane stared hard at Clayton and rubbed a finger above his left eyebrow, as if he was developing a headache. He glowered. "Both power stations are offline. They have disabled the diesel backups. In less than four minutes the Panopticon will complete the evacuation protocol, downloading itself into the P-Case. They have captured the nemesis—"

Crane broke off speaking, his gaze suddenly distant. Clayton glanced around the command-and-control center. Horror filled the staff's faces, except for Ulysses who maintained a grim impassivity. He followed her gaze to a secondary screen displaying a scene of utter mayhem in the main server room guardhouse. The room was awash with blood, the last of the praetorians falling into five separate pieces beneath the blades of the two Slaynes and the Wu girl.

"Catastrophe," Crane whispered. In harsher tones he commanded, "Secure the P-Case and evacuate it from the fortress. Under no circumstance allow Slayne to depart the fortress with it. Recapture the nemesis tower. He no doubt plans to use it to facilitate his escape. Take back the tower, or if necessary, destroy it to block his escape. Above all else, secure the P-Case, or see it and Slayne destroyed!"

"Yes, Sir!" Clayton shouted.

Crane stared at him for a long second, then vanished as the screen reverted to a fortress schematic littered with red boxes surrounded by flashing warning messages.

Evacuation? Yes, perhaps it is time to secure my own survival. Clayton demanded, "Ulysses! Status report!"

"Sir, Carney and Holdsworthy are en route to the main server room with their squads. Day Guard squads one and twelve are en route as well and will arrive first."

"Set a cordon with the guards."

Ulysses nodded. "Sutter and Tench are en route to the nemesis tower, and another three day guard squads are evacuating Kraken dash two."

"Evacuating?"

"Large amounts of steam are issuing from pipes rendering the station impassable."

One of the technicians, a thin man with a crew cut, and a 'geophysics is cool,' badge on his left chest, lifted a trembling hand. Clayton ignored him and commanded, "Send the guards to secure the underground hangar and prep the nightfalcons for immediate lift off."

"What about us," the geophysics technician asked in a tremulous voice.

Clayton stared at the man, who promptly looked down at the floor, and said with complete surety, "We stay here until the P-Case is secured and the nemesis tower recaptured, then we evacuate." He sneered silently. *Of course, you're not coming with us. There's no room for useless baggage on our nightfalcons.*

He turned back to the screens, watching sixteen praetorians advancing through the corridors and tunnels of the base toward their objectives. There was still time to take back the P-Case, defeat the Ramp masters, and win the battle.

Nothing was beyond saving.

* * *

The timer on the bottom right-hand corner of Li's nightglasses flashed zero.

"The praetorians are free," Li said briskly, striding from the blood splattered guardhouse into a short corridor to the main server room.

"I know," Slayne remarked, flourishing the Black Dragon to clear it of blood. He strode beside her on the right, Anton flanking her on the left. "You need to break into the fortress' core networks."

Li nodded grimly.

"You have to free up the nemesis tower," Slayne stated. "The praetorians will hit it and us in eighty to ninety seconds from now."

Li stopped walking for a moment. "Can you keep them off me?"

Slayne nodded. "Actually, you will. Once you're in, you can disable the bio-readers on the door. No one will get in or out until you open it again. Anton and I will head back there now and guard it until you close it. Then we'll be back for the P-Case. Okay? You good with that?"

Li pursed her lips and nodded. They had no idea what she'd faced in her last loremaster vision. She watched them blur away for a moment, then turned away, opening and passing through a final doorway into the main server room.

She entered a large circular chamber. An outer rank of racks hosted hundreds of servers. She shivered, suddenly enveloped by a strong current of freezing air rising through the steel mesh floor. Li strode forward past three concentric sets of full server racks surrounding the core of the server room.

At the center of the chamber, six quantum processors arranged in a hexagon six feet on a side, maintained an intricate shifting lattice of blue light between them. The Panopticon AI was a thing of light and now it was dying, but its crypt was a resurrection chamber called a P-Case. The P-Case slotted neatly into a large briefcase sized holding bay next to a desk-console with a chair facing the near side of the hexagon.

Li strode to the chair. Time was evaporating away. The praetorians were on the march and she had to act quickly. She placed her laptop down on the console. A cable was available for administrators to plug into the core networks and she attached it to her laptop. A moment later, she connected into the core network and … went nowhere, but—

The chamber vanished for a moment and then reappeared – was it real or a vision?

Cryptographic characters streamed over every surface like a living skin with a mobile technophilic tattoo. The vision washed over her, an intense layer of encryption surrounding her. She'd have to break through it before she could do anything else. Her implant pulsed. Beating like a living thing, faster and faster until it burned like an iron spike driven through her flesh.

The cryptic characters flowed and swirled in patterns beyond prediction. On the axis between the ranks of server racks the shadows thickened and darkened, swelling with a living presence, promising nothing but abject horror.

The temperature dropped, her breath misting before her face. The cryptic characters ran in rivers, fractal patterns teasing her mind with broken slivers of recognition. They swirled and churned, mesmerizing in their movement. The shadows advanced, but with them came a soporific calm: a settling quietude. "What is the urgency?" they whispered. "There is none," they answered with a comforting surety.

The cryptographic characters danced at the edge of her skin, probing against a thin golden glow lying defensively a fraction of an inch outside the boundary of her flesh.

Li looked at the soft, golden luminosity, half-curious, her eyes drooping. It was beautiful, fragile, temporary – like a summer flower destined to last a single fragrant evening before the night extinguished it forever.

Like all living things.

Eternal darkness swelled in the depths of the shadows, beckoning with fluttery fingers.

If only she could remember.

Golden light flashed on the far edges of her vision, like a wedge opening a distant door. Gunfire reverberated from somewhere behind her.

What?

Li blinked. She lurched to her feet, slamming her hands on the console. A hot, indignant rage surged through her – *how dare they trick me!* The light on the edge of her skin flaring into hot golden flames – alive with her will.

Something clicked into place within. She had to establish control over her environment within the loremaster visions. The golden flame was the key, she was sure of it. Somehow, it linked directly back to Juliette. It was her legacy. A protective gift she'd accepted over her former teacher's grave, and it kept appearing whenever she needed it the most.

She looked around, seeing the chamber with new eyes. In this place – the rules were different. Li centered herself, drawing the flame forth from her deepest sense of being. Instinctively, she lifted her hands up, palm outward, describing a pair of circular arcs. The golden flame followed her hands, billowing outward to form a thin luminous sphere a dozen feet across centered on her heart.

Beyond her sphere of flame, the shadows hardened, thickening into a tangible darkness filled with malice.

Li focused and pushed with everything she had, expanding the boundary of light past the hexagon of six quantum processors. The Panopticon was gone, the intricate web of light abandoned. Her sphere of light spread, encompassing the whole of the hexagon lattice. The web of light hosted by the quantum processors shifted in color, matching the flame wreathing the boundary of her sphere.

The cryptographic characters fled with the stalking darkness. The shadows remained, but now they were simply shadows cast by her own light.

Warmth suffused her being, she broke out in a broad spontaneous smile.

Golden light flashed behind her again, shouted warnings ripping through the guardhouse. "Watch out!" automatic fire tearing from the throats of multiple weapons behind her.

Her smile vanished. What was the time? Numbers washed through her: 14:48:05. "What!" she called out, bursting out of her vision. She whirled around. At the end of the corridor, Anton and his grandfather traded shots with opponents down both sides of the corridor.

She remained connected to the core networks via her implant and the laptop. She passed through the encryption like it wasn't there. She reached through the networks, snapping invisible commands. The vault doors began sliding shut.

She tapped her tactical link. "Peter, your weapons are hot."

"Thanks, Li," Peter called back.

Li rubbed her right forearm. Her implant was warm, no longer a fiery spike. She'd become a living conduit for information. She turned back toward the quantum processors. The blue light of the Panopticon had vanished. The web of light glowed with the warm golden color of Juliette's flame. Li rode the quantum processors like a goddess within a limitless chariot. She reached for information, filtering, integrating what she found with the vast power of the quantum machines underpinning every operation of her mind.

"Oh," she whispered. "Oh … OH … OH!" Now she could see, she could really see what to do. She smiled grimly, a frown creasing her forehead. There was very little time left to act.

Almost no time at all.

* * *

He'd get one free shot before the enemy reacted.

Peter selected four of his seventy hammerhead land attack cruise missiles armed with conventional warheads. It would take each missile three seconds to launch, rise, maneuver, and spear into its designated target. Firing a hypersonic cruise missile at a specter tower less than a mile away was an unusual tactic at best and at worst madness. But still, it would give the towers an immediate and inescapable threat to deal with and buy him essential time.

Time was his most precious resource.

Peter flexed his fingers; it was time to kick ass. He set off the hammerheads. Four long panels came out of the sides of the nemesis tower and slid aside. Four bright steel frames pushed out, each loaded with an eighteen feet long silvery dart. The four missiles leaped away on vertical columns of gray smoke, vanishing into the bright afternoon sky.

Four dark blue tracks appeared on the holographic battlespace display, leaping above Peter's head toward the apex of the dome.

* * *

Chiara stared into the entrance of the stairwell.

The muffled roar of the cruise missiles a footnote to her readiness to fight.

Li called out over the broadcast tactical link, "Two praetorian squads are about to hit your position at the tower."

Chiara glanced up at Peter, he glanced back for an instant. His expression said everything, 'how will you survive?' before he turned back to the cockpit controls.

She turned and faced the stairwell. *Don't worry about me.* She lifted a pair of captured assault rifles, and paused at the doorway waiting for the vampires to hit the bottom of the stairs. A heartfelt whisper, like an old and honored friend slipped into her mind, *I am an initiate of the third rank of the test of the Olgoi Khorkhoi. I have mastered the disciplines of the Red Empire. I will honor the way of my ancestors. I will honor the faith of my mother and father. I will bring ruin to my enemies and see them choke on their heart's blood before I die. This I vow before God and let my life be forfeit before I break this oath.*

Heavy footfalls fell on the first of the steps at the base of the stairwell. They became a rush. The praetorians and day guards were coming as fast as they could. There was no stealth and no finesse. Their strategy was as simple as it was obvious, swamp the tower with numbers and kill all within it.

Chiara dived deep into silence. Her hands becoming utterly still, her gaze piercing the air. There was no point in allowing the enemy to advance to the top of the stairs. No, she'd make them fight for every step, bleed for every yard. Let them question their purpose while life fled from their eyes. Let them wonder in their last moments of life at how she'd beaten them. Let them know the true fury of a gifted initiate of the third rank.

It was time to reveal to the world who she really was. To uncover her true self. The Raven was a dim memory. Chiara Romano a discarded mask. Now there was only Chiara Morte, a true princess of the Red Empire.

She blurred to the left and clockwise down the stairs.

* * *

Peter locked the rail gun phalanx on the southwest specter defense tower.

It was time to see what it could really do. He depressed the trigger on the joystick. There was a brief, almost innocuous hum. The rail gun phalanx fired; three forty-five-pound kinetic spikes accelerating to eleven times the speed of sound as they left the barrels. They covered the three quarters of a mile to the southwest specter defense tower in three tenths of a second. The spikes punched through the specter tower's nano-ceramic armor and hardened ferrous shell, shattering the tower's primary support structures a yard below the command center before passing through the other side and vanishing into the distant floor of the valley in plumes of gray dust.

Fuel cells caught in the passing shockwave detonated, sparking a near instantaneous chain reaction down the tower.

The specter defense tower lit up like a two-hundred-feet tall firework, the command center evaporating in a brilliant glare of blue-white light as the fuel cells consumed all their energy in a single moment. The blast wave blew out the southwest corner of the fortress, obliterating anything standing within a hundred yards of the base of the tower.

"Ghosted it."

Peter re-targeted the rail gun to the southeast specter defense tower. The thunderous crack of the evaporated southwest defense tower smashing against the nemesis tower like the whip of a vengeful god.

* * *

Thunder slapped against the side of the nemesis tower.

Chiara almost flew down the stairs. The enemy were rushing the stairwell, rising upward against her. Four grenades appeared, hurled by men who were still out of sight around the curve of the tower. She feathered the triggers on her captured assault rifles. The barrels blurring from side to side as she simultaneously shot the two leading grenades, and then the two trailing grenades an instant later. The grenades ricocheted back down the curved stairwell before exploding amongst a mass of armored figures.

She descended on the chaos, her guns firing on full auto. She blurred from side to side. Survivors in the front ranks returned fire, bullets whipping past her, cracking against the walls in a staccato racket.

The vampires had stacked the front ranks with day guards. Her speed outclassed them. The four grenades and her concentrated assault rifle fire cutting them down where they stood. Behind them, the praetorians maneuvered violently, avoiding the hail of bullets.

Her magazines ran dry and she dropped her empty guns.

In a single motion the vampires reformed, the front rank of praetorians dropped to one knee, the second rank stepped to the left and right, the third rank closed to the midline of the stairs, and the final rank stood tall. Eight squad automatic weapons snapped up and forward, barrels spitting flame, bright lines of fire flashing toward her.

Chiara pulled back behind the curve of the inner wall, fire slashing past her face, bullets smashing against the main column or ricocheting against the wall behind her in a drumming roar. She snapped her P90 submachine gun up from her left hip. The vampires were already on the move, chasing their bullets up the stairwell. She had forty rounds of caseless high-performance armor piercing explosive tipped rounds in her magazine, and ten more made of solid silver. She leaped backward up the stairs, firing into the empty space in front of the onrushing vampires. They couldn't see her, and she couldn't see them – yet.

The leading praetorian ran into her fire. Her rounds punctured his armor, ejecting plumes of bloody spray out the back of his torso. The first silver bullet hit him and he lost control of his body, his forward momentum smashing him against the outer wall.

Chiara cut backward out of the streams of return fire, rushing back up the stairs and firing behind her. She needed to slow them down long enough for Peter to complete the destruction of the fortress' defense systems. She would do it or die trying.

She would keep her oath.

* * *

Peter swung the joystick to the left.

The sphere rotated with his guidance. It only had to travel a short arc to bring the rail gun phalanx to bear on the southeast tower. The rail gun automatically reloaded. Threat markers appeared on the holographic battlespace display painting the interior of the sphere. The other three specter towers were turning weapons to bear upon the nemesis tower. They all had to do a full one-hundred-and-eighty-degree rotation as their default positions were facing outward.

Peter had at least a second to react before the surviving three towers simultaneously attacked him.

He glanced overhead; the four hammerhead hypersonic cruise missiles were maneuvering a mile above the fortress. In less than a second, they'd be spearing down like the fist of God upon the four specter towers. One destined to pound rubble, its target already destroyed. But the other three missiles must be on the threat matrix for the surviving towers.

Peter was betting they would defend against the incoming strikes. It would be the default protocol. The towers would defend themselves first and then the fortress second on the principle that if they fell to an attack, the fortress would be undefended against the next assault.

The two class II rail guns on the southeast specter tower halted halfway around their rails, their long barrels reaching for the sky. The other secondary weapons continued to slide into position against the nemesis tower.

As soon as the opposing towers could bring weapons to bear, they opened fire. The 20mm chain guns ripping into life, streams of fire reaching for the hemisphere atop the nemesis tower. The 30mm auto-cannons opened up, seeming to operate in slow motion firing three rounds per second, each one pinging off the transparent armor of the sphere with dull thuds.

The dark blue threads of the hammerhead tracks streaked down over the battlespace display. The hypersonic cruise missiles shredding the air over the fortress in their race to their targets.

***

Chiara was running out of stairs.

The vampires were pushing her back too quickly. Machine gun fire ripped up the stairs, filling the stairwell with plumes of ceramic dust. It was enough to haze sight and provide a moment's desperate cover. She dove deep into her ramp, reversing her momentum and leaping left and up against the outside wall, running horizontally along it. She pulled the trigger on her submachine gun, riffing through the last of her armor-piercing and silver bullets.

The praetorians rushing up from below twisted away, grimacing as the tang of silver hit their nostrils. One lagged, crowded by the others, and took the brunt of her fire from point-blank range. His torso ripped open as the explosive rounds tore him apart. A pair of silver bullets sent what remained of him spinning away down the stairs.

Chiara drew her katana mid-air, one of her throwing daggers appearing within the grip of her bandaged left hand, the other silver-laced blade now strapped to her right forearm.

The praetorians reformed in pairs, wielding their edged weapons. Guns left holstered for close quarters combat against an opponent who could dodge around a barrel.

It was six against one. Chiara landed three stairs in front of the leading two vampires, her sword slashing down just right of the first praetorian's midline, inviting him to deflect her attack toward the second vampire on her right.

The first vampire took the bait, swatting her katana aside.

Chiara went with the strike, her blade flashing through the second vampire's right arm, taking his limb off just below the elbow.

He howled, spinning back into the internal wall, his sword held tight by his gauntleted fist clattering to the stairs. He clutched his stump, blood sluicing through the fingers of his remaining hand.

Chiara's hands blurred, swapping her katana to the left and her throwing dagger to her right. She ignored the excruciating agony pulsing from her left hand. She'd suffered worse at the hands of her instructors. She blocked the first vampire's counter attack with her sword, using the force of his strike to push her to the right. Her dagger flashed upward, diving to the hilt beneath the second vampire's jaw. She stepped back a pair of stairs. The silver-paralyzed praetorian, eyes glazed with sudden death, falling like stiff timber across the stairs in front of her. His colleagues would have to step over his rigid, partially dismembered corpse to attack her.

Chiara liked that idea – let them witness their impending doom.

The odds had improved to five against one.

* * *

Above the southeast specter tower, the descending hammerhead missile evaporated in a glaring ball of white-gold fire as a pair of defensive kinetic spikes struck home.

The rail gun phalanx locked onto the southeast specter tower. Peter pulled the trigger. The phalanx hummed and fired. The three kinetic spikes decapitated the second specter tower and detonated the fuel cells within it. The southeast specter tower went the same way as the first specter tower, taking out the southeast corner of the fortress a moment later.

The second hammerhead disappeared in a cloud of fire above the northwest specter tower. The third pummeled the remains of the southwest tower. The fourth managed to avoid the less than righteous kinetic spikes of the northeast tower, planting its one thousand pounds of high-explosive warhead on top of its target.

The warhead didn't detonate until the missile had penetrated half a dozen yards into the throat of the specter tower. The combined forces of the cruise missile strike and the stricken tower's fuel cells created a massive blast, ripping a crater more than two hundred yards across, obliterating all evidence of the specter tower's existence.

Only the northwest specter tower remained. It was in the opposite direction to Peter's rail gun phalanx and its rail guns were already halfway to bearing on the nemesis tower.

A fatalistic dread gripped Peter's soul. He was going to be too late. The last specter tower would get in at least two rail gun shots before he even got a lock on them. There was nothing he could do to stop the specter tower's kinetic spikes detonating the nemesis tower's fuel cells. He'd just witnessed three examples of exactly what would happen if the fuel cells exploded.

He dragged the joystick to the left. It was always going to be the last specter tower that would be the most trouble. Peter fought the tower's controls with nothing but hope and a prayer, and he hated it. In seconds, there would only be one tower left standing.

In the moments left, Peter offered the shortest prayer of his life that the gods of fate would spare his tower – and armed his secondary weapons. They'd been turning with the rail gun phalanx, now they whizzed on their magnetically levitated rails to point northwest.

Lining up dutifully on the last specter tower.

* * *

Thunder cracked and roared against the walls of the nemesis tower.

The vampires surged up the stairs. Chiara had to give ground or they'd overwhelm her with weight of numbers. Allowing them to surround her would surrender her defense of the tower and result in certain death.

The two nearest vampires, the original first on her left and a new one on the right, slashed, feinted and ground their blades against her flashing katana.

Chiara double feinted left and right, drawing both vampires' defenses. She flicked her left wrist, sending her silver-laced dagger into the throat of the praetorian on her left. He froze. She smashed hard to the right against the other vampire's blade, then whirled back, her katana flying through a high horizontal arc, beheading the stationary vampire.

Her strike collected the silver-laced dagger embedded through the vampire's Adam's apple, knocking it free. It bounced against the outer wall, ricocheting behind her. She leaped backward, giving ground while catching her flying dagger mid-air.

She landed, her katana whirling, blood flicking off in thin ribbons. She wore a merciless grin, her long plait snaking over her right shoulder, ready to face the remaining four vampires. They growled and snarled like a pack of wild animals, rising up the stairs in a dark-armored wave.

* * *

The northwest specter tower brought all its weapons to bear on the nemesis tower.

The nemesis tower's rail gun phalanx had reloaded, but was still pointing into the valley to the right of the last specter tower. The dome still rotating to bring the massive weapon to bear on the last specter tower but not quickly enough to matter.

The specter tower's class II rail guns fired as one. Kinetic spikes tearing through the barrels and heat fins of the rail gun phalanx. The nemesis tower shivered, steam pouring from shattered heat dissipation fins. Two of the three rail gun barrels shattered, spinning debris falling three hundred feet to the ground below.

Peter focused on his remaining weapons.

The specter tower's chain guns, auto-cannon, and lasers were hammering the armor of the nemesis tower. The nano-ceramic ablative was doing its job, absorbing energy and evaporating away – but under these weapons it would be a short-lived defense. The rail gun phalanx's heavy forty-five-pound spikes had proven to be lethally effective against the specter towers. Peter didn't want to find out the hard way the class II eleven-pound spikes were just as effective at penetrating the nemesis tower's protective skin. What he'd been able to glean about nemesis and specter defense towers over the years suggested that the nemesis tower's armor should be better but he had no specific facts about it.

The specter tower's rail guns shifted aim to the base of the nemesis tower.

Peter aimed his rail guns at the specter tower's rail guns.

It was going to be a slug fest.

All four rail guns fired at the same time. The spikes traveling at two miles per second covered the distance between the towers faster than the eye could follow. The nemesis tower shuddered. The opposing rail guns evaporated in clouds of shredded metal and silvery fire. They'd never fire again.

A roar thundered up from the base of the nemesis tower.

Peter arched an eyebrow. The absence of instant incineration indicated the fuel cells hadn't detonated. He swung his rail guns in. A pair of cross-hairs painting the location just below the command center dome on top of the specter tower.

A double tap to the throat. He pressed the trigger. The rail guns fired, a pair of spikes slamming into the neck of the specter tower. Flames shot from the impact points. The specter tower's lesser weapons continued to fire, raining rounds and searing threads of heat against the nemesis tower's fraying skin.

He fired a second time, sending another pair of spikes onto the same impact points as the first two. These penetrated deep within the tower, sending whips of fire shooting back out of the entry holes. A moment later, the tower evaporated in a massive fuel cell detonation, obliterating the northwest corner of the fortress.

The last of the specter towers had fallen.

Peter dropped the controls, leaping from the cockpit, his hands reaching for two of the tri-bladed silver-laced throwing axes strapped to his chest.

He landed on the floor of the dome, his boots slamming against the polished metal.

Blade against blade combat crackled like a fire storm from the stairwell.

* * *

Chiara traded blows with the advancing praetorians.

The silver-laced dagger grew slick in her grip; blood seeping through the bandages wrapped around the palm of her left hand. The quick stitches she'd applied minutes before were no longer holding under the stress of combat.

The tower shuddered, a roar thundering from deep within the stairwell, blue-flecked shadows dancing fitfully against the walls beyond the vampires.

The praetorians pressed forward. A vampire from the second rank leaping over the front two, diving and twisting overhead.

Chiara reflexively threw her dagger. It slipped in her wet grip, deflecting off the praetorian's armor before spinning away down the stairwell.

The praetorian landed behind her.

She whirled, ducking instinctively, a double-bladed axe whistling over her head. She launched herself past him, other weapons crashing against the stairs behind her. She ran the outer wall, passing behind his left shoulder to land further up on the metal stairs.

A thin wedge of light cut a line on the outer wall of the stairwell. The landing at the top of the stairs was within view. Explosions thundered against the tower. Peter was still fighting the specter towers. She had to keep the vampires at bay.

Her last silver-laced dagger gleamed in her left hand. She blurred in close to the battle-axe wielding vampire, deflecting his attack to the side. Her next move had to succeed, or she'd fall within reach of a much stronger opponent. She thrust up with her blade, driving it beneath his jaw and into his brain.

He froze. The other three vampires rushing past him.

She pushed backward, slashing desperately, leaping back to the forward edge of the landing at the top of the stairs.

The paralyzed vampire's throat opened up, blood gushing over the smooth lip of raw flesh beneath his jaw in red freshets. He remained standing, frozen in spot and bleeding to death.

Chiara retreated to the middle of the landing.

Three vampires followed her, the two nearest blades grinding against her own desperate defense in a shower of sparks.

A pair of gleaming tri-bladed axes spun past her. The first axe slashed past the nose of the nearest vampire as he jerked his head backward. The second axe collected a second praetorian in the chest, lifting him off his feet and throwing him into the third vampire behind him – sending both falling down the stairs.

The nearest vampire recovered from Peter's near miss. He slashed down hard against Chiara's sword, sending it out of her blood-soaked grip to clatter against the stairs.

She fell backwards to the wall, her last silver dagger her only defense.

The praetorian surged forward, his sword rising through a vicious arc.

Peter blurred past her, his battle axes flailing at her assailant. Sparks flew, the vampire's sword shattering under the onslaught of thicker, heavier metal. Disarmed, he lost his head a moment later in a fountain of blood, Peter kicking his headless corpse down the stairs.

The last vampire rushed back up, leaping over his beheaded comrade. He pulled to a halt a dozen steps below the carnage on the landing. He stared at Peter's twin battle-axes dropping great splotches of gore onto the metal floor and Chiara's bloodied silver-laced dagger. His eyes widened and he broke, vanishing back down the stairwell. A moment later he howled in abject misery before falling deathly silent.

"Hell," Peter swore, nonplussed. "What was that?" he advanced warily down the stairs. Chiara picked up her fallen sword and followed at his right elbow. In moments they came upon the vampire who'd cried out. He was face down in a growing pool of his own oozing body fluids five steps below them. Wisps of gray vapors rose from every gap in his armor. The whole of his body lay covered by a blue mist that gently roiled and billowed.

Her lost silver dagger gleamed softly beneath the mists.

Peter put his arm out to stop Chiara advancing, and shook his head. "It's no good. Some of the fuel cells have spilled into the stairwell. We have to go back up."

Chiara stared at the miasmic funk of fumes shrouding the stairwell, they rose over another stair and began lapping at the base of the next one. The deadly mist trapped them in the tower and there was no way out. Her first silver dagger, a family heirloom, rested on one of the submerged steps – lost for all time.

She turned and followed Peter back up to the dome.

Chapter Nine

"The proposed site of the Panopticon fortress is directly above a multi-chamber magma feature. The geology of the proposed site is deemed to be moderately to significantly unstable. While the chance of a geological event is deemed highly unlikely [< 5%] over the expected life of the proposed facility. In the event of the nearby underground river being redirected into the top-level magma chamber, the risk of a geological event increases to highly likely [> 90%]. A geological event is defined as an event that would result in the total destruction of the proposed facility and would render the site to a radius of ten miles unusable for a replacement at any time during the expected life of the proposed facility.

Internal assessment. 'Geophysical Safety Pty Ltd,' registered at [REDACTED]."

– Draft document not sent to the customer.

* * *

The Panopticon Fortress, command-and-control center, September 11th, 14:48:20

'Secure the P-Case and evacuate it from the fortress. Under no circumstance allow Slayne to depart the fortress with it. Recapture the nemesis tower. He no doubt plans to use it to facilitate his escape. Take back the tower, or if necessary, destroy it to block his escape. Above all else, secure the P-Case, or see it and Slayne destroyed!'

Those had been Crane's last words to him. Clayton mopped his brow with his handkerchief. What the hell was wrong with the air conditioning. No doubt that was breaking down too. Everything else was well and truly fucked up beyond all recognition. He cast a quick glance around the command-and-control center. The four praetorians of his personal guard stood grimly around the walls of the chamber. The humans were barely under control, only the newly promoted commander Siobhan Ulysses, showed any real capability to manage her emotions.

The last two minutes of mayhem had been writ large in high definition on the multiple screens lining the walls of the chamber. The fortress was a shambles. The specter towers lay in rubble. Both the main power stations were down. The Panopticon was in 'evacuation mode,' transferring itself into a P-Case for transport offsite, leaving only 'dumb,' secondary systems in operation.

He'd witnessed two praetorians lose their weapons. Their blades disappearing in plumes of super-heated metal as their owners fell apart in the main server room guardhouse. It seemed most of the Mirovar force team carried dragon blades, siblings of the Red Dragon wielded by Chloe Armitage. While one young woman, little more than a girl, had fought eight praetorians to a near standstill in the stairwell of the nemesis tower. He hated to admit it, but he'd horribly underestimated the true threat of the Mirovar force team. It was clearly a collection of the elite of the Order of Thoth, and demonstrably superior to the other Order teams they'd defeated.

"Sir," Ulysses called out. "The Panopticon download will complete in two minutes time."

The nemesis tower was teetering on destruction but still partially operational. The praetorians sent to recapture it were dead to a man. Of the twenty-eight praetorians on site after he'd landed with his four squads of reinforcements, only twelve survived. The day guards had been culled from forty-eight to twelve men. The two squads outside the main server room slaughtered in an extended gun fight with the two Slaynes. The other personnel on the base were standard Shadowstone operatives who were functionally useless against Ramp masters and not worth counting.

Or were they?

The Order of Thoth were famous for avoiding 'innocent deaths.' It was a weakness of their philosophy and eminently exploitable, all he needed was a group of hostages to use as human shields and he could snatch victory from the jaws of defeat.

A tremor vibrated through the floor for a solid three seconds.

Clayton's eyes widened. He still had an ace up his sleeve. He'd shift all his effective personnel to the hangar, and have Slayne bring the P-Case to him. He loosened his katana at his belt. It was time to put every last resource he had into the fight in a final do or die effort.

He cast a steely glance over the humans. "Ulysses, assemble your staff and get them to the underground hangar. Quickly now, we are evacuating the fortress immediately. Recall all praetorians from the cordon on sub-level dash four and send them to the hangar to provide a security force to ensure a safe evacuation of all personnel."

"Yes, Sir," she replied, quickly issuing a series of commands.

Clayton smiled dryly and glanced at the praetorians. They all gave knowing looks back. The humans were utterly expendable but may yet prove useful in securing the return of the P-Case.

He followed his unwitting hostages from the command-and-control center, the four praetorians of his personal guard flanking him.

* * *

Li sent a silent command through the core networks.

The vault doors began opening again.

"What the hell!" Anton swore, whirling to face the expanding gap, his assault rifle snapping up against his shoulder, pointing into the gloomy corridor. He glanced at a counter on the side of his rifle and back at Li. "I'm almost out of ammo."

Slayne peered into the corridor, strip lighting flickering fitfully within it. "There's no one there," he remarked, momentarily perplexed.

"They've already gone," Li declared, emerging from the short corridor leading back into the main server room, her eyes blazing with urgency. "The day guards sent here are dead. All the vampires have left for the hangars. They're evacuating."

Slayne grinned derisively. "They're taking control of the one way out of here. They're hoping we'll bring the P-Case to them and hand it over."

Li frowned and nodded. "That too, but," she grabbed Anton's shoulder, pushing him toward the open vault door, "Anton, you must go. You must help Francis and Jay secure the hangar. It's the only way we can escape. Run, Anton, run as fast as you can. We need you there."

Anton frowned for an instant, then grinned with a promise of dire consequences for any foes in the hangar. "Consider it done." He glanced once at his grandfather, and blurred through the doorway, vanishing down the corridor.

Li turned to face Anton's grandfather. Her head was full of quantum processor fueled insights and it was time for a reckoning. She opened her mouth to ask her first question.

The floor, walls and ceiling vibrated. She crouched reflexively, the flickering lights casting shadows across Slayne's impassive face.

The elder Slayne closed his eyes for a moment, then stared at her, a knowing look in his eyes as stillness stole back into the room. He didn't seem surprised by the tremor, and after integrating her mind with the quantum processors – neither was Li.

"This site's going to blow, and you knew!"

Slayne nodded.

* * *

Peter placed his fifth and last 40mm grenade into his multi-grenade launcher leaving the sixth chamber empty.

He slung the weapon back at his hip, positioning the empty bandolier over his right shoulder. He grimaced, rubbing his big fingers through the short growth of red beard covering his chin. He lifted his hands, pulling the hood of his combat vest over the rough mess of his flaming red hair. The toxic vapors from the leaking fuel cells were steadily rising. They were only a dozen feet from the top of the tower and rising at two feet per minute. In another six minutes they would seep over the landing and begin spreading across the floor. The cockpit was the highest structure above the floor but retreating to it would buy less than an extra five minutes.

Chiara looked at him. "You're the technical genius – how the hell do we get out of this one?"

Peter frowned, wracking his brain. They needed a way to stop the vapors from rising. If they could bleed them off it would buy time. If they could get rid of them entirely, they could escape the tower through the base. Many of the fuel cells were still intact and working, despite the destruction of the rail gun phalanx, the tower was still mostly operational.

"I might just have a way." He leaped to the cockpit and activated the controls. The battlespace display lit up above his head. He set all the hammerhead missiles to pre-launch mode. Over eighty panels pushed back and slid aside. Metallic frames pushed out on all sides of the tower, blue vapors spilling from most of them.

Chiara reported from the stairwell landing, "The vapors are falling. It's working."

"That's great—"

A shudder rolled through the tower. The structure wobbling for what seemed like forever. In a true anal-puckering moment, Peter envisioned the tower falling to the ground, a stray spark igniting the fuel cell vapors. *Well, at least it would all be over in a moment…*

"—what the hell!" he finished.

Peter looked to the north. The Kraken-2 power station was returning back to Earth in fragments of blackened concrete and darkened steel. Its previous foundation of solid rock replaced by fountaining plumes of super-heated steam laced with molten ribbons of fiery rock.

The battlespace display overwrote the falling debris of Kraken-2 with red squares marked with the words, 'SYSTEM FAILURE.'

Chiara whispered in awe, "Look to the south."

Peter twisted around in the cockpit chair. The southern power station was sliding into the Earth, pools of bubbling rock oozing up around it. The process suddenly accelerated as jets of super-heated steam cut through the roof of the power station like it comprised tissue paper rather than yard thick layers of steel-reinforced concrete.

They were out of time. He leaped down to the floor and strode to the stairwell landing, stowing his Order nightglasses in a protected inside pocket of his battle vest. He hefted his MGL with his left hand, and declared with absolute conviction, "If we don't get out of this tower we're going to die.

Chiara nodded in grim agreement. "Do what you have to do."

Peter looked down into the stairwell. They had to get rid of the toxic vapor. The quickest way was to burn it off. However – would enough of the explosive force flow out through the missile launch cells to avoid killing them? Would the eighty plus hypersonic missiles hold together or would they catastrophically cook off, adding rocket fuel and thousands and thousands of pounds of very-high-tech explosives to the mix? Would the W80 nuclear warheads on twenty of the hammerheads survive without detonating?

There were so many ways this could all go wrong – but doing nothing was to accept certain death. Peter was not one to go quietly into the night. The W80s were unarmed and should be safe enough. The hypersonic missiles were tough beasts, built to withstand massive heat and pressure. Perhaps there was a slim margin where they could snatch life from the jaws of death.

Peter's lips pursed together, his will to act locked in a rare moment of hesitation. It was like playing Russian roulette with a revolver with only one empty chamber, but the alternative was a quick and certain death.

He glanced at Chiara. "Best get back to the opposite side of the chamber."

"What about you?"

Peter grinned momentarily, then sucked air through his teeth.

Shit! I'm honestly lost for words. He finally said, "Just get back, this is gonna suck."

He took a step onto the landing above the stairwell.

"Yep," he whispered to himself, a shiver crawling up his spine, "this is gonna suck big time."

* * *

Jay and Francis blurred across the scorched tarmac of the VTOL landing field on the south side of the fortress opposite the administration building.

To their right, the wrecks of two nightfalcons burned amidst bubbling pools of bitumen. Heat shimmered through the air, and thunder cracked and reverberated across a cloudless sky.

Jay and Francis rushed into the canted structure of an above ground hangar on their left. Working together, they heaved aside fallen debris, uncovering a stairwell leading down. The fortress was falling apart. They had witnessed the destruction of the specter towers by Peter and Chiara as they'd run south from Kraken-2. The day guard squads had used MRAPs to drive back from Kraken-2 to the fortress, beating them here by a small margin.

The three squat MRAP vehicles stood abandoned on the other side of the landing field next to another entrance within a second half-destroyed hangar. The southern wall of the building was alight, a growing plume of black smoke gouting from a wide tear in the roof. They'd thought better of simply chasing the guards down through the same entry site. That could be a quick and easy way to get a bullet in the face. It was better to infiltrate the underground hangar from another direction.

To the north and south of the fortress, plumes of steam and thick black smoke billowed from the ruined power stations. Jay felt small and insignificant before the ferocious powers emerging around him. Whatever the mission had started off being, it was now a matter of simple survival. But survival was not so simple – he wasn't going to leave anyone behind – not on his watch. They had to capture a nightfalcon and get everyone out. And if possible, more than one chopper; after all, not everyone was a vampire.

With his head on a swivel, movement behind his left shoulder caught Jay's eye. He glanced around to the nemesis tower. At least forty missiles had emerged from the near side of the tower, blue vapors tinging the air around them. Whatever Peter was up to was beyond Jay's comprehension. He trusted the big guy must have a plan in mind. He glanced at Francis, who nodded, and then dashed down the stairs, weapons drawn. Jay followed on his heels, holding his H&K 416 assault rifle at shoulder level ready to fire. His combat webbing was light on his shoulders. Only two full magazines remained, including the fresh one in his rifle. He had a pair of fragmentation grenades on his webbing and a 40mm HEAP grenade in the launcher beneath his rifle's barrel, but they would be of limited use in the tight and dangerous confines of the underground hangar. The last thing he needed was to set off a chain reaction of exploding fuel bowsers. Francis' ammunition was also running low. They couldn't afford a long fire fight.

Thin strips of flickering light lit the stairwell. Their only hope was that at least one nightfalcon was still operational and they could open the hangar doors and escape. Anything else would leave them at the mercy of the titanic forces erupting from the bowels of the Earth.

They hit the lower level, running out of the stairwell into the massive underground hangar. The chamber was easily six hundred yards long by two hundred yards wide. There were four nightfalcons lined up in a square three hundred yards away in the middle of the underground hangar. A dozen gray-clad technicians were swarming over them. Their turbines were idling in a low rumble. They were ready to fly.

Long rows of crates, spare parts, mobile fuel bowsers and other racks of equipment lay between the helicopters and the two Ramp masters. They ran to the nearest pallet holding a shrink-wrapped turbine and stood up flat against it.

"'Ware the choppers," Francis warned. They'd have to be careful with their shots. The last thing they needed was to destroy the means of their escape.

Jay glanced around the end of the turbine. A dozen day guards were fanning out from the nearest row of nightfalcons. They spread out in pairs; their smart rifles held high. They raced across the pale concrete floor with more than human speed. "We've been made."

"It's a maze fight," Francis advised. "Draw them into these rows of equipment. Don't give them time to take a shot. It's do or die!"

Jay nodded, keeping his assault rifle ready, his katana resting in its scabbard at his left hip.

Francis whispered, "I'll take the south side."

"I'm north."

"Expect no quarter."

"I'll give none."

"We'll meet in the middle at the helicopters."

"Got it," Jay said, blurring away from the turbine. Assault rifle fire cracked through the hangar, rounds sparking off a pallet of locked military boxes behind him. The guards were closing the distance. They were quick to fire, but lacked the deadly Panopticon accuracy they'd demonstrated at the conclave. He had to deal with them. Capturing at least one nightfalcon helicopter was a must do. The Mirovar force team would end without it and there was no way Jay would let that happen.

Jay fired a quick three-round burst at the nearest pair of guards, they dived aside, the rounds cracking away into the depths of the hangar. He crouched, darting forward deeper into the stacks of equipment.

It was game on.

* * *

Li stared at Arthur Slayne, who studied her quietly. She looked hard into his eyes and demanded, "How long have you known?"

"Since the design phase of this fortress."

"You built it didn't you?"

"Pretty much all of it."

"Do you realize what the existence of the Panopticon has cost us?"

Slayne smiled. "Do you realize what it's about to cost Crane and Armitage?"

Li paused for a second, suddenly out of her depth. She changed tack. "Your grandson is becoming a killing machine. Is that by your design too?"

"It's good he's on our side then, isn't it? But no, it wasn't my intent." Slayne looked past her to the main server room and the P-Case unit. "Come, walk with me."

Li fell in beside him, smiling sardonically. "Is this where you impart some time-honored wisdom to allay my concerns and convert me to a devoted follower?"

Slayne sighed as he walked. "What have I done to earn such cynicism from someone so young?"

Li snorted. "For a start, lying about placing shaped charges to fake a rockfall. Blocking off any form of retreat and ensuring that we would go forward with you."

Slayne turned, his eyes sparkling. "Well done, I knew you weren't a fool, but what principle am I following? As a student of your father, you know of what I speak."

Li answered without hesitation, "Sun Tzu. He wrote, 'At the critical moment, the leader of an army acts like one who has climbed up a height and then kicks away the ladder behind him. He carries his men deep into hostile territory before he shows his hand. He burns his boats and breaks his cooking-pots; like a shepherd driving a flock of sheep, he drives his men this way and that, and none knows whither he is going. To muster his host and bring it into danger – this may be termed the business of the general.' You kicked away the ladder, burned the boats and broke the cooking pots forcing us to this course and none other."

"So, you understand why, and yet you harbor resentment."

"We're not sheep to be driven."

"You've been spending too much time around Francis, he's a good man, but—"

"But, what? I happen to think he's right – you don't share enough of what you know. You play your cards too close to your chest and you do it all the time." She wagged her finger at him. "You don't let anyone in. You don't trust anyone."

"Geez, Li – you're so insightful."

Li tilted her head and frowned. "And then you deride us. Do you have any idea why no one trusts you?"

Slayne paused for a moment, a faint smile playing at the corners of his mouth. "What makes you think I need to be trusted?"

Li opened her mouth for a second.

"I don't care if you trust me or not," Slayne continued. "I don't need your trust and I never have. Why on Earth do you value it so much? … Wait, don't try and answer that question." Slayne spread his hands, his lips curling into a derisive grin. "It's because you're completely fucking naive, which is a dangerous combination when allied with a native genius level intelligence."

Li's eyes flattened and she stated, "If you're trying to win friends and influence people you're failing badly."

Slayne looked at her, his eyes wide; his voice heartfelt. "Li, you're the daughter of my best friend and in my honest opinion the brightest hope for the future of the Order, but you have so much to learn about how the world really works."

"Brightest hope, huh? What about Anton?"

"I think we both know that Anton could rise to the job, but he'd have to ditch a lot of baggage first."

"You're not backing him?"

Slayne shrugged his shoulders and spread his hands wide. "I know my own grandson."

Li's eyes flashed. "Then share with me. Tell me what I need to know."

Slayne looked down the short corridor to the main server room and strode forward. "I could tell you. Simple things like the Mirovar and Blake force teams are 'deliberately,' the best the Order of Thoth has to offer. Along with some of the independents you are the foundation of the future of the Order. I'm sure with your newly acquired powers you're already thinking about it, so you tell me – who are the real talents within the Mirovar team."

Newly acquired powers? Just how much does he know? Striding next to Slayne, Li looked up at him. "Peter for strength," she paused momentarily. "Anton for more than speed. He has a whole new way of ramping."

Slayne tilted his head and arched a quizzical eyebrow. "Or a very old way of ramping. One forgotten due to rarity. But there are more talents than Peter and Anton, how many people do you think could insert a loremaster implant in their arm and integrate with a quantum network less than two days later."

She glanced up at him, her eyes widening.

"Yes, Li. It was a theoretical possibility in the implant design but it took you to prove it a reality. You have a talent for what you're doing, but," Slayne's eyes tightened, a coldness creeping into them, "talent alone will not save you."

Li hesitated, then asked, "You know of the Shadow?"

Slayne nodded. "Our final enemy. The one behind the existence of vampires. He can appear in visions and dreams. Loremasters are particularly vulnerable." He hesitated for a moment as if distracted and shook his head once. "That feature wasn't anticipated during development of the implants."

Slayne stepped over the threshold into the main server room. Li followed after him. Once she came abreast of him, she asked, "He's real, isn't he? Who is he?"

Slayne's face froze into a mask of dreadful certainty. "Oh yes, Li. He's very real. The ancient Egyptians worshiped him as the god Set." He strode forward and stood beside the P-Case. It was a burnished silvery box the size of a large solid briefcase, sheathed in dark nano-ceramic armor and resting in a solid metal cradle jutting a yard above the floor. A flashing green light nearly filled an indicator strip on the outer side of the case. The Panopticon would complete evacuation in a matter of seconds.

Li's heart jumped. "A god?"

"Might as well be a god."

Li sighed. She was full of questions. Slayne was telling her the truth. He wasn't holding back or being evasive. She'd so many more questions to ask. Information gleaned from her integration with the quantum processors told her much but hinted at far more. They had barely scratched the surface of what she wanted to ask. He stood next to the P-Case with his hand on the handle. Ready to pick it up as soon as the download process was complete. It was infuriating, why didn't he understand the urgency and just tell her what she needed to know? Weren't they on the same side? Her shoulders slumped and she pleaded, "How do I resist a god?"

Slayne looked at her, his face an inscrutable mask for a moment. Then he reached over with his free hand, grasped her shoulder, and smiled warmly. He said, "There always comes a time in life where you can either give up or step up." He paused for a brief moment. "Your time is coming soon." His gaze dropped back to the green strip. It flashed once more and became a solid glowing line. He glanced back at her, and ordered, "Follow me!" he lifted the P-Case from the cradle and blurred away.

Li looked back at the shining golden light of the hexagon lattice. The approaching cataclysm doomed the quantum processors. The pressure building beneath the floor would soon destroy the entire facility. At best they had fifteen minutes to make good their escape. At worst, they were already beyond saving themselves. She found it hard to tear herself away from the golden glow illuminating the center of the chamber. It felt like she was leaving the best part of herself behind.

She blinked, whirling away from the gleaming web, striding forward to the vault doors. The light behind her casting a long silhouette of her body across the tiles beneath the flickering strip lighting. Where was Slayne leading the team? Where was he leading her? She had no idea. No quantum processor enhancement could shed light on the deepest secrets buried in Slayne's mind. She would have to wait for events to reveal the truth.

It was time to open some doors. She sent silent commands traversing the core networks. Hundreds of yards away, the underground hangar doors responded, massive localized fuel cells and dedicated engines engaging for effect. Two hundred slats moved, dropping and sliding aside. In less than two minutes the hangar doors would be fully open, allowing the helicopters to launch into the safety of the sky.

Regretfully, it was time to leave the quantum processors behind. She whispered to herself, "Too many questions and all unanswered."

Li stepped over the dismembered corpse of an armored praetorian and exited the guardhouse. The corridor was a slaughter house of dead day guards, overwhelmed by Anton and his grandfather while she dreamed her lucid loremaster dreams. Their names came to her unbidden, information sent along the core networks fed by the quantum processors. They were all young men; men who were heroes in other times and places. Betrayed by lies to a battle they couldn't win for a cause that wasn't theirs. Images flooded her of their personal lives. Photos of family members, girlfriends, partners, and soldiers in arms on distant battlefields. One after another, images flashed through her mind and left her soul in tatters. She sank to her knees. A pair of tears spilled from her eyes and rolled down her cheeks. One of the men lying dead in this corridor had been holding his newborn daughter only three months earlier.

I have tarried here too long.

A dreadful urgency lifted her to her feet. She ran, rapidly picking up speed. She needed to leave this doomed place and the scarred ghosts haunting it. She blurred, heading for the underground hangar. The slaughter in the corridor was but a foretaste of what may come. One thought pushed the ghosts away, *Would Arthur Slayne reach the hangar soon enough to stop Anton?*

For Anton must be stopped, and his grandfather was the only one who could do it.

* * *

Peter pointed the MGL down the stairwell and squeezed the trigger.

He'd already ramped hard, dropping deep into silence. The propellant ignited, sending the grenade out of the barrel with a drawn out 'chuff.'

Peter moved hard right, out of the landing and back into the nemesis tower's command center.

The grenade snicked against the outer wall of the stairwell, ricocheting deeper into the tower.

Peter turned one hundred and eighty degrees, leaping upward.

The grenade passed through the surface of a roiling cloud of blue mist, striking a stair and detonating—

The cockpit sitting on top of the central cylinder passed beneath Peter's feet. He sailed above it, pulling himself into a tight defensive ball. In front of him, Chiara crouched down against the far wall of the dome as far from the entrance of the stairwell as she could get.

The fuel cell vapor ignited. A wave front of flaming gas traveling down to the base of the tower in a fraction of a second. Super-heated gas expanded, seeking every possible path of least resistance, shooting out through the open missile launch cells in massive sixty-yard jets of blue tinged flame.

Above the detonation point of the grenade, the ignition wave front traveled upward, seeking any point of egress. The top of the stairwell became a funnel, super-heated gas roaring through the doorway into the tower's command center opposite where Chiara hid.

Peter flew through the air, holding his hands over his eyes, plugging his ears with his thumbs, his little fingers squeezing his nose shut. He held his breath, clenching his jaw as hard as he could, threatening to smash his own teeth with the forces at play.

A giant fist thundered into his back, accelerating him into the curve of the dome. Heavy bones, toughened far beyond any human norm by ramp epigenetics, shivered and flexed to their maximum extent but didn't break. Heat washed over him in a wave, igniting spot fires on his clothes, flames haloing his hood.

Peter slid down the wall in a smoking, smoldering mess, landing next to Chiara. She huddled in a ball, a low moan of pain escaping her lips.

The tower rocked, the remaining intact fuel cells detonating in rapid succession. Secondary explosions reverberating throughout the tower. Flashes of blue light cut through the lower edge of the dome like the knives of an angry god. Metal squealed like a tormented demon. The floor canted, Peter and Chiara sliding and rolling across the polished floor to the other side of the dome. The wrecked rail gun phalanx rising up into the air like a bizarrely indignant metal finger.

The dome was coming apart from the tower supporting it.

Peter scooped Chiara up, and with her tucked under his left arm he bolted across the slanting floor for the stairwell. The phalanx continued to rise, accelerating as the dome separated from the rest of the tower.

He dived, sliding into the stairwell, pushing off the outer wall, rattling and diving down a dozen feet of stairs.

Metal roared and ripped with an unearthly screech. Bright sunlight speared through a giant horizontal tear in the base of the dome. The dome split apart, peeling away from the neck of the tower and spinning away to oblivion.

Peter looked up at bright blue sky, a fresh breeze washing across his face. He batted at a stray tongue of flame licking at the tatters of his clothing.

Chiara muttered dryly beside him, "We should do this again some time."

Thin trails of blood were seeping from her ears and her eyes were horribly bloodshot. He could barely hear her, his tactical earbuds were dead – overwhelmed by the explosions, but they were both still alive. He plucked the ruined earbuds out of his ears and his hearing instantly improved. The low reverberating rumble from the north and south now unremitting in its titanic intensity.

Peter stood up. A mile to the north and a mile to the south of the tower, dark smoke formed two funnels reaching like cyclopean fingers into the vault of the sky. Of the power stations, there was no sign they'd ever existed. In their place fire raged, lightning sheeting through the hellish conditions beneath the gigantic, towering columns of gray-and-black-shot smoke.

He looked down, within the remains of the fortress perimeter. The doors to the underground hangar were sliding back, revealing four nightfalcon helicopters.

Lightning crackled across the blue sky, stretching a bright whip from north to south. Thunder bellowed in its wake, a warning shout to the world.

Peter lifted his gaze, frozen in sudden awe by the raging firestorms hanging like hell drawn stains against the cobalt sky. He looked back down at the underground hangar and the men scurrying like ants around the helicopters. Their efforts rendered puny and futile by the forces arrayed against them.

Chiara fell into position next to him and whispered hoarsely, "Is there enough time?"

Peter glanced down at her and then back at the tortured sky. His eyes widened before the impending doom closing in from the north and south. Everyone had to get out of here before the two fire storms joined in the middle and became one. That could be a handful of minutes away – or less.

Only one thing was certain – time was running out.

* * *

The underground hangar doors hummed, sliding smoothly apart.

A strip of bright sunshine appeared, resting like the finger of God between the two lines of nightfalcons. The six day guards had vectored in on Jay's position, their footfalls echoing off the concrete floor. The hangar hadn't been designed for stealth operations – that was for sure. The east side of the hangar was more warehouse than anything else. Pallets loaded up to seven or eight feet high with anything ranging from computer spares, through long-life rations to spare helicopter engines, stood in a checkerboard of crisscrossing rows.

Jay's last burst of fire had sent two of the guards diving for cover, and he'd dashed forward to the cover of the next stack. The trick would be to get them to fight him on his terms. Up close and personal with an edged weapon where his superior speed, skill and strength would decide the outcome. If they were smart, they'd give ground at every opportunity and try and surround him in a cul-de-sac and bring superior numbers to a gun fight.

He blurred around the next left corner. There were four guards. Everyone fired, his three round burst matched by four equal answers spearing down the aisle between the pallet rows. Jay pushed hard, his left shoulder flaring back, slamming his body into a pallet of shrink-wrapped cartons. Half a dozen rounds zipped past his chest. One of the guards swore profusely for a moment as all four disappeared into the stacks.

Where the hell were the first two guards? Jay blurred back to his original pallet, turning and spraying a burst of automatic fire down the aisle. It was empty, running footfalls sprinted along the concrete in the next aisle in front of him – and behind him.

They were attempting to surround him. In the southern stacks, gunfire flared from multiple locations. Francis was still in action. Someone screamed, accompanied by a low guttural groan, a ribbon of blood splashing above the top of the distant pallets.

Four grenades rose into the air, they were going to bracket Jay's position. He blurred forward, leaping and flipping over the nearest pallet, rising above the next aisle. His rifle flamed left and right, sending bursts of fire at two of the guards who'd just thrown grenades. The one on the left staggered backward in a pink mist, his rifle clattering to the floor before he turned and slumped face downward onto the cold concrete. A silver round sparked off the shoulder armor of the one on the right, spinning him around. The hit spoiled the guard's return fire, bullets spraying up to the hangar roof.

Jay landed in the next aisle over. The grenades exploded in a rapid series of thunderous cracks, shrapnel slashing through the air in the vacated aisle. He reversed immediately, blurring back the way he'd come over the middle aisle and into the smoke-filled aisle. He landed, surrounded by the stench filled aftermath of four grenades, and zagged hard left. The guard who'd got behind him in this direction, would be running forward to trap him again.

Jay emerged from the grenade smoke, catching the guard as he barreled past. Jay picked him up, sweeping him off his feet, whirled and bounced him against the nearest pallet. He stepped back, his right hand drew his katana from his left hip and whipped it around in a single motion, slashing through the guard's neck in an instant. Jay blurred in the direction the guard had come, the hapless fellow falling to the floor behind him, his helmeted head rolling away from his blood gushing body.

Two down, at least one wounded, and three at full strength. Jay needed to bring this to a close. He looked around. The smoke from the grenades was dispersing, he rushed forward a dozen steps. The guards had vanished. He slung his rifle to his left, pulled his last two grenades from his webbing and ripped out the pins with his teeth. He spat the pins away and shouted, "Oh, fuck it!" in desolate tones, giving away his position at an intersection between the aisles.

If they wanted to surround him, then let them, but only on his terms.

Jay slotted the grenades next to the base of the pallets. They were on a four second fuse, he figured that'd be about right. He turned and blurred between two pallets. He turned hard, clambering up onto a set of locked military boxes standing seven feet high and lay prone. He held his rifle in one hand and his katana in the other.

The pallet started shaking, another tremor reverberating through the fortress. Thunder cracking overhead – whomever the gods were – they were shifting from angry to demented.

"Shit!" a guard swore from ten feet away.

"Grenades!" another yelled.

The guards scattered. The grenades exploded, fragments ripping through the nearby pallets, and pinging off the heavy military boxes beneath Jay. He was up and moving in an instant, holding his breath against the clouds of smoke. His eyes slitted, diving into the intersection cleared by the exploding grenades. His assault rifle erupted into life, a long burst of fire claiming two of the guards still attempting to flee the grenades. He whipped about taking the second pair a moment later.

He rushed toward the nightfalcons, clearing the rows of pallets.

Francis blurred into the open a hundred yards to his left, his katana whirling through a deadly arc, slashing a guard across his chest. The man fell away in a spray of blood. Francis whirled toward Jay his eyes hunting for another foe.

Beyond him, a dark armored form emerged from an aisle against the far wall of the hangar.

Francis stood between the guard and Jay, blocking his fire.

Jay dashed right, shouting, "Watch—"

The guard's rifle barked. A trio of bullets slammed into Francis' back, punching out of his chest and pushing him forward into a pink mist of his blood.

"—out! Francis!" Jay screamed in fury and horror, sending a long burst of fire thudding into the last day guard. The lone guard staggered back a step, stumbled, and sat down like a broken toy against the distant hangar wall.

The Mirovar force team's luck had run out.

* * *

A stuttering rip of assault rifle fire came to a halt on the far side of the hangar.

Ignoring the gunfire, General Clayton Maze shouted, "What the hell! Who opened the hangar doors?"

His eyes flashed over the praetorians and the humans huddling in front of them. The intolerable sunlight was spreading in a widening rectangle. In moments it would cover the four nightfalcons in the middle of the hangar. The doors were supposed to remain shut until he was safely onboard a helicopter. Then they would open to allow him to escape. How could he approach them now with bright sunlight cutting an ever-widening toxic perimeter around the blessed helicopters?

Commander Siobhan Ulysses, stared at him nonplussed. "Sir?"

"Get them closed."

Ulysses shook her head. "We can't do that from here, Sir. We'd have to get back to the command-and-control center or," she pointed at the nearest helicopter gleaming in the bright afternoon sunlight, "we operate the hangar doors from the cockpit controls."

Clayton snarled.

"Sir," said Holdsworthy, one of the three surviving praetorian squad leaders. He pointed past the nightfalcons with an armored fist to the eastern side of the hangar. "Order operatives."

Clayton's head flicked left. Slumped armored forms littered the concrete past the helicopters. In their midst, a young man with dirty-blond hair kneeled and rocked back on his heels, cradling an older man who was lung shot and spitting blood.

Francis Mirovar was at death's door and Jay Creeley was alone and distracted. Clayton smiled with avid glee, at least two scalps would be his before he departed the doomed fortress. "Carney, Holdsworthy," he snapped, pointing at the vulnerable Ramp masters across the hangar. "Secure the nightfalcons. Kill Creeley and Mirovar, and bring me their heads." The two squad leaders and their praetorians blurred away, veering left and right around the sunlight encased nightfalcons.

Once they'd eliminated the two Ramp masters, it would be a simple matter to get the nearest helicopter to lift off, slide twenty yards out of the sunlight and into the shadows. He and his remaining praetorians could board the craft, and protected by the armored skin of the nightfalcon, they could escape the coming disaster.

But first they would have to play out the final act, the use of the hostages to secure the Panopticon P-Case when Arthur Slayne inevitably arrived with it in hand. Clayton whirled upon the cowering humans, his fangs bared, he hissed once then commanded, "Strip off your uniforms. You are no longer part of Shadowstone. I free you of your oaths of service. Strip!"

The humans fumbled and stumbled, attempting to obey his orders. Only Ulysses maintained her composure, frowning briefly before unbuttoning her shirt.

Once he'd secured the P-Case, only the vampires would escape. He'd leave the humans behind. Let the raging forces rising from beneath the fortress consume them. Of course, it was only fitting the mortals perished while their betters survived.

It was the natural order of things.

Chapter Ten

"The berserker is the rarest of the Ramp talents. In fact, it is so rare the Ramp masters have forgotten Ramp berserkers exist. But I remember, how could I forget the most dangerous foe I ever faced." – Cornelius Crane

– Cornelius Crane's personal diary.

* * *

The Panopticon Fortress, Underground Hangar, September 11th, 14:50:35

"Vampires," Francis whispered past a hacking blood-drenched cough.

Jay's eyes flicked up. A dozen praetorians had entered the hangar on the far side of the nightfalcons. They hesitated, disconcerted by the growing strip of sunlight spreading across the four helicopters. There was a narrow corridor of shadow north and south of the nightfalcons. The vampires would come as soon as they saw them, but they'd have to veer hard left and right. The sunlight would funnel them into a pair of narrow paths. The opportunity to attack them while the sunlight corralled them would only last a moment.

Jay carefully pulled his hands back, letting Francis drop gently back onto the concrete.

Francis coughed once, his head barely rising and whispered, "Leave me."

Jay ignored him, rising to stand astride his force leader's body. He slapped his last fifty round magazine of high-performance rounds into his rifle. Every fifth bullet was a silver hollow point, designed to fragment upon impact. He pumped the under-barrel grenade launcher priming the 40mm high-explosive armor-piercing grenade within it. He pushed aside the impending loss of his beloved mentor and best friend, and plunged deep into silence.

The hangar resolved into crystal clear view. Every noise resounded with sharp and distinct clarity. One vampire, a tallish black man with a bald head dressed in a fine suit with a katana at his waist, shouted, "Carney, Holdsworthy, secure the nightfalcons." He pointed directly at Jay and shouted again, "Kill Creeley and Mirovar. Bring me their heads."

Jay waited to see which way they would run. If he was really lucky, they would all bunch up and run to one side of the hangar to avoid the sunlight.

They split up. One squad of four running to the right-side and the other squad running to left-side of the helicopters. Their paths describing an oversized baseball diamond as they skirted the growing rectangle of sunlight covering the nightfalcons in the middle of the underground hangar floor.

Jay snapped his rifle around to the right. He triggered his launcher, sending his only 40mm grenade spearing away toward the shadowy strip between the nearest nightfalcon and the right-side hangar wall. The long body of the helicopter obscured the flight of the grenade from the vampires. If Jay had timed it right, they wouldn't see it until it was too late.

The second squad had further to run, they would show up after the first squad came into view.

The first praetorian rounded the nightfalcon on the right, closely followed by the rest of his squad. The 40mm HEAP grenade lanced into the space between the nightfalcon and the hangar wall, striking the lead praetorian in the chest. The grenade flexed for a microsecond, grinding into the nano-ceramic plate of his armor, then it exploded. A molten copper whip shot through the vampire's chest, carving a six-inch-wide hole through his body. The detonation of the grenade opened the rest of his body cavity like a can of tuna hit with a sledge hammer. His helmeted head sailed off his body, rising high on a tide of super-heated air. The rest of his body down to his knees evaporated in a red streaked ball of white fire. His legs below the knees skidded off in opposite directions. The three vampires near him, caught on the edges of the explosion flew aside like leaves on the wind, cartwheeling into the nose of the nearest nightfalcon and the hangar wall.

Jay had to leave Francis; his best option for saving their lives was to get the praetorians into an edged-weapon fight. He scooped up the gore-slicked White Dragon where it lay on the concrete floor with his left hand. With his right hand holding his assault rifle like an oversized pistol he blurred to the left.

The first of the praetorians in the second squad rounded the nightfalcons and opened fire, a stream of bullets spearing toward him.

Jay zagged violently to the right, returning fire with his assault rifle. Bullets whipped past him on the left. He dove deeper into the silence, as deep as he could go. He was Francis' last defense.

It would have to be enough.

***

Carney evaporated in a blinding glare on the left-side of the hangar.

Clayton hissed past his fangs and swore bitterly, "What the fuck?"

The rest of Carney's squad were bouncing off the shadowed wall and the sunlit nightfalcon next to them. One slid screaming off the helicopter's armored nose, bright flames licking around his dark helmet. A moment later, raging fire immolated his head, a great tongue of orange flame rising a couple of feet above it. The vampire howled, staggering for the nearby shadows. He never made it, slumping to a smoking heap a yard short of dark sanctuary.

A brief queasiness assaulted Clayton's stomach. He wrinkled his nose in distaste. The praetorian's fiery death by sunlight was not something he needed to witness with a great block of bright light shearing through the air mere yards away. He steadied his nerves and accelerated his senses to vampire maximums. The world slowed down, snapping into razor sharp clarity. Holdsworthy's squad were disappearing round the far-right-side of the nightfalcons. Gunfire erupted from his vampires, followed by immediate return fire.

Creeley wasn't so vulnerable after all.

They needed to finish the lone Ramp master quickly before Arthur Slayne showed up with the P-Case. He needed all his forces and the human hostages to force the elder Slayne's hand. He opened his mouth to shout a new order.

Something new moved on his far left.

The younger Slayne blurred out of the sub-level-1 corridor from the main administration building.

Crane's orders swept through his mind like a cold wind. *'Execute Anton Slayne. Immediately!'* What a stroke of good luck the Mirovar force team had so thoroughly divided their forces. They were all over the place, just waiting for their dooms to arrive. Anton Slayne paused a dozen feet inside the hangar, his attention arresting on something on the far side of the great chamber.

Clayton jabbed his left forefinger at the young Slayne and shouted to his personal guards, "Kill him!"

His four praetorians blurred toward the hapless, gawping fellow. Clayton followed the young man's line of sight. His gaze fixed upon something lying past the nightfalcons. Something barely visible through the space between them slumped on the cold concrete.

Mirovar.

Clayton's head flicked back to the left.

Anton Slayne's face paled, a thin foam appearing at the corners of his mouth. The rest of his body becoming incredibly still.

Clayton stared.

Slayne's right eye darkened, the pupil expanding to its maximum extent. A red ring of engorged blood materializing around the dark pit at the center of his eye. He threw away his rifle, a magnificent katana twin to the one borne by Chloe Armitage appeared in his hands with astonishing swiftness.

A rare chill crawled up Clayton's back.

His personal guard attacked.

* * *

Francis lay on glacial ice, his heart's blood pooling around his shoulders and chest on the hangar's polished concrete floor.

The world drifted, the agony of battle fading away. Someone was near, an invisible presence hovered over him. Francis tried to lift his right arm, but his flesh was heavy, oh so heavy.

Juliette ghosted out of the air, a gentle smile caressing her face. She whispered, "Francis."

She was here. She'd come back for him. Francis lifted his hand; now it was easy, everything was easy. He rose up from the floor, his fingers tracing the smooth curve of her cheek.

His heart glowed with light.

The world vanished behind him.

* * *

A red mist descended.

Francis was dead. The vampires had killed him. Francis had given him a home. He'd defended Anton when the Order had wanted him dead. He'd given him a new place to belong. He was family.

Something touched upon at the burial test at the Maine safe house snapped. A barrier hidden deep within himself disintegrated in a blue flash. A cobalt fire, as cold and implacable as a glacier, roared through him with terrible urgency. It was beyond containing, shooting out of the top of his head in blue sparks and violent pulsing silvery streams.

There could be but one purpose – to bring utter ruination upon those who opposed him. He might have grinned, a rictus smile promising sudden death – he was lost, floating freely, beyond all self-awareness – possessed by an overwhelming need to kill and kill again. Every fiber of his being devoted to a singular end – the delivery of death to his enemies.

Four praetorians surrounded him, their swords and battle-axes swinging toward him. Anton blurred forward, snapping the Blue Dragon down through a short chopping arc. The vampire in front of him didn't have time to defend himself. The Blue Dragon's gleaming blade shearing through his raised sword in a shower of super-heated metal droplets, slicing through helmet and chest armor, sweeping down and exiting though the creature's groin.

Anton barreled through the vertically bisected vampire – his twin halves flying apart in a Rorschach sheet of gravity resistant gore.

The vampires behind him thrust and slashed through empty space.

Anton pivoted, reversing course.

The three praetorians spread out, flanking him to the left and right. The last vampire held back a yard or two, swinging a pair of battle-axes and looking for an opening to attack.

Anton rushed upon them. His clothing awash with the first praetorian's blood, gore running in rivulets down his face.

The flanking vampires launched overhead strikes with sword and battle-axe from the left and right.

Anton halted on a dime, the weapons shearing through empty space a hairsbreadth in front of him. He slashed the Blue Dragon from behind his right hip through a wide horizontal arc. The gore-soaked blade stuck the right praetorian above the hip and continued through armor, flesh and bone, exiting in a spray of blood. Anton pivoted with the strike, using his momentum to strike at the vampire on the left.

The left praetorian escaped death, rolling over the Blue Dragon as it swept beneath him.

Anton pushed off his left foot, pivoting hard to the right.

The two praetorians shouted and rushed him, attacking him high and low with a long sword on the left and twin battle-axes on the right.

Anton leaped, blurring beneath the sword and above the battle-axes. He angled the Blue Dragon to the right, taking off the battle-axe wielding vampire's arms below the elbows. The stricken praetorian recoiled back, his face lifting to the hangar's roof, unleashing an unearthly howl of anguish.

Anton landed, stamping his right foot, pivoting hard to the left.

The fourth vampire thrust desperately with his long sword; a stabbing blow aimed to gut Anton before he could recover from his leap.

Anton batted the flat of the fourth vampire's sword blade to the side with his left hand. He stepped forward. His right foot lashed out, taking the sword-wielding praetorian in the groin.

The vampire curled forward over Anton's boot, grunting loudly in agony.

Anton veered to the left, slicing down on the back of the leaning praetorian's neck. The Blue Dragon continued on without slowing, the vampire's head leaping forward through the air on twin jets of arterial blood.

Anton turned, leaping on the armless praetorian. He ended the vampire's wailing with a slashing diagonal cut through his chest wall, leaving the praetorian writhing in two halves in a spreading pool of blood and entrails.

He paused, the Blue Dragon hovering at a diagonal an inch in front of his right knee, blood dripping from its tip onto his left boot. His night-shadowed eye flicked toward the nearest opponent. A dark-skinned vampire with a bald head, dressed in a fine dark-blue suit, standing thirty feet away.

The blue fire of cold rage burned hard and true.

The vampire's agonizing death was the only worthy outcome.

* * *

Clayton's personal guard rested in dismembered blood-soaked fragments.

The agent of their doom was staring at him like a death-obsessed fiend.

Something had gone horribly wrong. His 'hostage,' plan was in tatters. He'd not seen the likes of Anton Slayne in the near two-hundred years of his life. He shouted across his tactical network, "To me! To me!" His surviving praetorians would come to defend him. Jay Creeley and Francis Mirovar would have to wait.

The gore-soaked apparition advanced toward him. His sole eye burning with an implacable will to murder.

Clayton drew his katana from the scabbard at his waist with a clean easy sweep.

It was time to prove why he was a general of the Vampire Dominion.

* * *

Dust motes rose in flurries in the afternoon sunlight spearing into the underground hangar.

Anton took a step. A drop of blood fell from the tip of the Blue Dragon, dropping slowly to the cold concrete floor. The vampires were coming. It was good that they came – the sooner the better. He hungered for their deaths. There was no battle plan, they would come into range of his blade, he would strike and they would die.

The dark-skinned vampire general backed away, shouting, "Fire! Kill him!"

Two vampires blurred from the narrow strip of shadow on the left, and another three from the far right of the hangar. They all leveled light-machine guns at Anton, firing as they rushed across the concrete. Streams of bright fire lit the air, reaching greedy fingers toward him.

Anton grinned, a mirthless veneer over darker depths, blurring toward the general.

Bullets slashed through the space behind him, then the guns fell silent. He was too close to the general for the praetorians to risk further machine gun fire.

Maze lifted his katana, angling it for defense.

Anton slammed the Blue Dragon through it – the general's blade shattering in a cloud of blazing sparks. The vampire twisted away; he'd anticipated losing his sword. The blade's sacrifice saving the general's life.

Anton strode forward a step. The five praetorians arrived, machine guns slung, armed with a variety of swords and axes. Three flowed past the general like river water around a rock, two more came from behind Anton.

A moment later they swamped him.

* * *

Clayton had moments left to act.

The five praetorians whirled around the lone figure of Anton Slayne. He should have died in the first second and yet he lived. One of the praetorians slumped to the right, his knee shattered. Another opposite stepped back, blood spraying from the stump of his right arm.

He had to save himself, and to do that he needed a nightfalcon and a pilot. But first, he needed a shield. Someone who'd baulk the demon carving his men into sushi. He'd pick the best-looking girl amongst the hostages, someone Slayne would find it next to impossible to ignore. He blurred over to the cowering Shadowstone staff, grabbing Commander Ulysses in an iron grip. He lifted her bodily, carrying her back to the swirling fight between his surviving praetorians and the younger Slayne. Surely Slayne, being a member of the Order of Thoth would hold scruples about killing the innocent, and Commander Ulysses, with the face of an angel, her athletic curves, and dressed in nothing but her dark-red underwear would create the perfect image of a damsel whose life Slayne would not risk.

Clayton took a position between the fight and the nightfalcons. He pursed his lips. *If only I had a thick blanket, I'd take my chances running across to the nearest helicopter.* The young woman was struggling within his grip. He tightened it and whispered harshly, "Stay still and shut the fuck up, and you just might live."

She stilled, her heart beating just a little bit faster than normal. In quieter times, he would have valued her as a useful member of the Shadowstone organization. Someone with a cool head under pressure who could have risen far, perhaps all the way to the ranks of the vampire elite. But today, she was a blood bag. A meat sack whose only value would be realized through his own survival.

He rested his 9mm Glock just beneath her right ear and called out, "Men, stand down. Slayne – drop your weapon or she dies!"

Two of his praetorians blurred backward a dozen feet each, the third fell backward, a terrible wound opening across his chest. He joined the other two slumped on the concrete floor in spreading pools of blood.

Slayne's head jerked left, his single eye boring into Clayton's.

There was no hint of mercy or respite within that darkened orb. It seemed as devoid of feeling as the black eye patch covering Slayne's left eye socket. Slayne raised his katana, the meteoric-iron blade slanting into perfect stillness over his right shoulder.

Despite the vulnerable curves of the vital young woman held tightly to his chest, the bastard was going to attack. Clayton straight armed the Glock, pumping the trigger. Bullets streaked down range toward Slayne, shockwaves trailing after them. Slayne pulled his right shoulder back, avoiding the first round. Then he moved hard and fast. Clayton's hand tracked him, round after round slamming through the air without striking home.

A sudden pressure arose on Clayton's groin. The Ulysses woman was clutching his testicles. She clenched her fingers with an iron hard grip. He threw her from him, the crotch of his suit coming away in her right fist. Agony roared through him; he didn't have time to assess the damage. The young demon was upon him and his Glock was clicking on empty.

Slayne lunged forward, his gleaming katana describing a wicked horizontal arc.

Clayton veered violently away, but all his vampire speed was for naught – defeated by the vicious razor-sharp blade sweeping across him from left to right. The lower half of his body vanished, a thin ribbon of blood splashing to his right. He started to fall, a hollow agony rising in a wave from his lower abdomen.

Slayne's rear foot flashed forward, the sole of his boot sinking into the lower part of Clayton's sternum like a sledgehammer.

His breath burst from his lungs. He left the lower part of his body behind. His torso rising in a high arc thirty feet above the concrete, flying backward into the scalding sunlight bathing the central interior of the hangar.

The agony began the moment the sunlight struck the dark skin on his face and scalp. Flesh burned, melting and evaporating into bright flame and greasy smoke. His eyes sizzled and popped. Bone disintegrated, turning to dust. Brain tissue boiled and spat. His limbs spasmed in abject horror. The fire spreading in an all-consuming chain reaction throughout his torso and arms.

He was still flying when death swept everything away.

* * *

Arthur blurred into the underground hangar past the bodies of four thoroughly gutted vampires.

Half a vampire dressed in the flaming tatters of a suit was immolating in the sunlight in front of four nightfalcons. There were at least a dozen maintenance staff staring at the vaguely human remains sparking and smoking on the concrete. Another twenty or so people dressed in their underwear were cowering and backing away. Half of them were crying. One whimpered. Another sobbed loudly, wringing his hands in front of his thin chest.

Beyond them, a striking young woman dressed in dark-red briefs and bra was picking herself up off the concrete.

Anton strode away from the lower half of a dark blue suit, spilled entrails, and a pair of dismembered praetorians spurting fresh blood onto the hangar floor. He progressed through a circle of another three broken armored corpses, his boots leaving bloody footprints on the pale concrete. He advanced on the frightened Shadowstone staff; a merciless grin fixed on his face. His dark eye stared through them like they were beneath his notice – their impending deaths nothing but an afterthought of something far greater. The Blue Dragon, barely visible beneath the gore, hung loosely in his right hand. He lifted his left hand, sweeping blood from his forehead revealing unnaturally pale skin.

He's gone, shuddered like a chill wind through Arthur's mind. He summoned the wild Ramp, tapping into a deep well of emotion. An abiding love suffused his being. Silvery blue light coruscated through his limbs. Time slowed precipitously. Anton became the sole focus of his attention. A drop of blood hung from his grandson's right ear; it began to stretch—

Arthur blurred forward.

Anton's sword rose reflexively against him, Anton was fast – as fast as Armitage in Michelangelo's secret vault, and operating with a deadly instinctive style.

In a burst of blinding speed, Arthur slipped past Anton's outstretched blade. The Blue Dragon passing over his right shoulder. He locked Anton's right arm, stepped past him, throwing his grandson to the concrete floor. The Blue Dragon clattering away from Anton's grasp.

Arthur flowed over him, pinning Anton's arms with his knees on Anton's biceps. He ground his left forearm into his grandson's throat. The short-lived burst of his speed talent ebbing away to a regular Ramp.

Anton flexed his chest muscles, pulling against Arthur's knees. Squeezing his arms off the floor through pure power.

It was like wrestling a vampire, Arthur was losing his grip. He reared back, his right hand flashed forward, slapping Anton hard across the face. He leaned back down, shouting into his grandson's face, "Wake up, Anton!"

Anton squeezed harder, his eye still berserker dark, a ring of red around the expanded pupil, blood vessels writhing like worms.

Arthur's knees began to slide inward off Anton's arms. He backhanded his grandson, his knuckles cracking like a pistol shot against Anton's jaw, turning Anton's face hard to Arthur's right, a splat of blood jetting onto the nearby concrete.

"WAKE UP!" Arthur screamed. He let go of Anton's throat and grabbed the sides of his grandson's head, bringing his face down to Anton's and staring hard into his eye.

"SEE ME! FOR GOD'S SAKE SEE ME!"

Anton twitched beneath him. He blinked, his pupil contracted, the red vessels retreating from his eye. Color returned to his forehead and his arms fell back, releasing the terrible pressure against Arthur's thighs.

Arthur rocked back on his heels, squatting next to his grandson. He pulled Anton up into a sitting position and insisted, "You'll be alright. Yes, you'll be alright."

Anton looked past Arthur's shoulder at the half naked Shadowstone staff, as if seeing them for the first time. His jaw dropped, his eyes widened, and he murmured, "I wanted to kill them. I was going to kill them all."

Arthur dropped forward onto his knees. He leaned forward, hugging his grandson and patting his back. "It's okay now. It's alright."

Anton panted against his shoulder, his chest heaving with half-choked sobs.

Arthur's stomach clenched and his chest tightened. He didn't want this for Anton. The wild Ramp was hard enough to master under the best of circumstances but to recover from the intoxication of the 'berserker,' – that was something else.

He held his grandson and vowed to keep him close.

I have to keep him safe.

* * *

A tremor struck the underground hangar.

The hangar roof doors ground to a halt, giant cracks appearing in both directions across the ceiling. People screamed and started running for the nightfalcons.

Anton shook his head, rising to his feet with his grandfather. The last few minutes seemed more like a nightmare than real life. Another shock rocked the floor, and he steadied himself on his grandfather's shoulder. He glanced back at the nearest nightfalcon; a grinning face greeted him from the bay doorway.

Arthur prodded him with a firm hand at his hip and they ran toward the closest helicopter.

Anton veered to scoop up the Blue Dragon where it lay on the concrete. Leaving the famous sword behind was not an option.

Dwayne Washington waved the other maintenance and Shadowstone staff off to the other three nightfalcons. Arthur and Anton reached the open bay door, clambering up into the main cabin. Dwayne doffed his maintenance cap and said dryly, "Welcome aboard the Washington express."

"We ready to fly?" Arthur asked quickly.

"All the birds are ready. These tremors have got everyone motivated to get the hell outta Dodge," Dwayne declared. He flicked his head at the smoldering remains of the vampire general. "And seeing a vampire burn to death in sunlight has made true believers out of everyone here."

"Get the other choppers away," Arthur ordered.

Dwayne ran to the cockpit, and flicked a switch on the main console. A set of sirens started ululating throughout the hangar. The other nightfalcons, packed with every living human left from the fortress, lifted off en masse. He looked back, grinned reflexively and said, "I'm amazed that's still working."

Anton looked around the empty cabin. "Where are the rest? Where's Chiara and Peter? Where's Li? Where's Francis and Jay?" He began to move to the other side of the helicopter to see where Francis had fallen. Perhaps he'd been wrong. Perhaps Francis was still alive and would appear in moments, hobbling, and leaning on Jay's shoulder for support.

Jay appeared on the other side of the helicopter, leaping into the cabin with a single bound. Francis lay in his arms, his face blanched and still, blood coating his chin. The front of his chest swam in more blood. Jay put him gently on the floor of the cabin, his eyes searching the interior of the helicopter. "Have we got a damn medical kit?"

Arthur squatted near Francis' head and felt for a pulse. Jay stared at him for a moment and called out again, "C'mon, have we got a fucking medical kit?"

Arthur's face turned grim, and he looked hard at Francis' chest. Three bullet holes were clearly visible through the blood-soaked tatters of his shirt. They were close to the center of his chest. Anton's heart fell, there was no hope left for Francis' survival – he was dead.

Dwayne emerged from the cockpit with a large first aid kit. Arthur looked over his shoulder at Dwayne and shook his head.

Jay swore, "Oh shit! Oh fuck! Fucking hell."

Dwayne grimaced, and returned back to the cockpit. Arthur put a hand out to grasp Jay's shoulder, and Jay slapped it away. He sat back, leaned up against the hull and raised his hands to his face.

Arthur stood up and shouted over the din, "Peter and Chiara are on the tower. We'll pick 'em up in a minute."

Anton's lips pressed together and he glared at the sub-level-1 corridor. Francis was dead. It was horrible but nothing could be done about it. Peter and Chiara were still on the nemesis tower and could be rescued, but not everyone was accounted for. He shouted, "Where's Li."

Another tremor hit, sending cracks rippling over the concrete floor. Fountains of steam began erupting through the concrete. A gray haze filling the distant corridor.

"Where the hell is she?" Anton muttered. The helicopter lifted, its turbines thundering, hovering a foot off the shaking floor. He yelled, "What the hell, we're not leaving without Li." He moved to the edge of the bay doorway, his eyes narrowing. He'd have to go back into the fortress and get her. Something must have happened to stop her from reaching the hangar. Was she trapped? Why hadn't she called out for help? He shouted, "What's happened to the damn tactical links?"

Dwayne called out from the cockpit, "Offline. The shit erupting outside has fried the uplink towers."

"I'm going back," Anton declared, surging forward.

A pair of strong hands pulled him back. "Wait!" Arthur shouted, pointing toward the entrance into the sub-level-1 corridor.

Li blurred from the haze into the hangar. She dodged past a pair of steam plumes, leaping into the open bay of the last nightfalcon. Anton grabbed her, hugging her tightly. "You're safe."

Arthur called out to Dwayne, "Go! Go! Go!"

The turbines roared. Another tremor hit, the strongest yet. The cracks in the hangar roof ripping apart, great chunks of concrete and metal crashing left and right. The nightfalcon leapt upward like a wild thing. The spinning rotors clawing for purchase. It cleared the hangar roof, soaring into the open air.

Li pushed against his chest, leaning away from him. Her eyes were dark and flat, her lips pressed together. She snapped, "No. Not safe at all."

Anton let her go. They stepped away from each other. The light in the world dimmed, and Anton wondered, *Why?*

Li glanced past Anton's shoulder and spotted Francis lying dead on the cabin floor. Her eyes widened, and her hands flew to her mouth. Anton barely heard her over the thundering engines as she half-shouted, "Oh my God! Francis!"

Arthur called out from the middle of the cabin, "Dwayne, the top of the nemesis tower. We have two more to pick up."

"Roger that, Arthur," Dwayne called back. A sudden gust of hot wind hit the side of the nightfalcon like a fist. The airframe shuddered but held together, Dwayne swore before recovering control, ascending as fast as the nightfalcon could go.

The nemesis tower loomed in front of them. Beyond it, darkness and fire stained the sky. An Earthborn storm of molten rock and sheet lightning claiming the valley for its own.

* * *

The sun warred a losing battle with titanic demons composed of dark-gray smoke, raging tongues of flame, sheets of bright lightning, and vaulting steamers of glowing molten rock.

Chiara and Peter stood tall on the slanting neck of the beheaded nemesis tower as violent shadows overtook the valley. Another tremor struck the fortress, the whole tower wobbling on its base. Four nightfalcons had lifted off from the underground hangar. Three powered away at top speed to the northeast, toward Salt Lake City.

The last nightfalcon rose through the encroaching gloom. It shuddered and bucked, struggling against wild gusts of hot air rising and swirling around it. Chiara reached over and grasped Peter's hand. "We'll only get one chance at this."

Peter nodded. "Don't worry, we'll get there." He grasped a nearby prong of exposed steel – a temporary anchor against the rising winds.

The nightfalcon shuddered again. The screaming turbines cutting through the bass rumble rising from the Earth. The helicopter swept closer, tilting and turning to make a pass. It swept forward. Chiara prepared herself to ramp and leap, Peter stilled next to her, doing the same.

The nightfalcon bucked like a wild thing. It leaped forward, charging toward the top of the tower. Its engines roared like tortured demons. Peter and Chiara twisted and fell flat against the floor of the tower. The helicopter roaring above them, occluding the sun. Then it was gone.

Chiara flipped to her feet. The nightfalcon rose, then dipped, hovering fifty yards away – out of reach.

The tower wobbled again. Chiara looked down over the edge. A forest of hammerhead cruise missiles greeted her with upturned noses, beyond them twin plumes of steam erupted from the base of the tower. The tower shook, tilting a handful of degrees over toward the waiting nightfalcon. Anton and Li were visible within the cabin. They were grim faced, turning and shouting instructions to Dwayne, their voices smothered by the roar around them. The tactical links were offline. The molten demons rising from the Earth had destroyed all the satellite relays operating within or near the fortress.

"Fuck it," Peter swore in frustration.

"What are they waiting for?" Chiara asked, thoroughly perplexed.

Peter grinned lopsidedly. "Our last chance."

The pilot tilted his head, the nightfalcon followed his body language and shuffled across. The distance between the top of the tower and the helicopter dropping to forty yards.

The plumes of steam thickened and darkened. One of the remaining fuel cells cooked off sending a blast of blue flame shooting through the wall of the tower. The tower rocked again. Steam and smoke rose in plumes, obscuring the nightfalcon with a wall of smoke thirty yards from the tower.

"Where are they?" Chiara whispered. Would the nightfalcon survive, or would Anton and the rest of the Mirovar force team plummet to their deaths in a flaming wreck.

The nightfalcon emerged from the smoke, turbines roaring, sweeping toward them.

Another fuel cell cooked off, exploding with a deafening crack beneath them. A flash of blue light reflecting off the bottom of the nightfalcon. The tower shuddered, tipping hard toward the nightfalcon. The nemesis tower began toppling to its doom.

The helicopter swept within ten yards of the tower. Chiara and Peter leaped at the same time. Anton and Li reached out from the open cabin doors, each anchored by an arm reaching back into the cabin. Chiara reached for Li's hand and Anton reached for Peter's. Hands met, gripping tightly. A moment later they landed safely on the cabin floor.

Arthur Slayne shouted, "Punch it, Dwayne!"

The nightfalcon soared away. Beneath them, the nemesis tower toppled. The crash lost in a round of secondary detonations that blew it into a cloud of debris, flashes of azure light reflecting off the clouds of dark smoke above them.

"Francis!" Peter shouted, his face blanching with shock.

Chiara whipped around to face where Peter was pointing with a shaking hand. Francis lay in blood-soaked clothes on the floor toward the front of the helicopter cabin. A trail of blood attested to the fact that someone had moved him forward and away from the open bay doors. Her throat tightened. There was so much she needed to tell him about what had happened the night Juliette and Yvette had died. She had wronged him and now he was dead. There could be no atonement for what she had done. No forgiveness for her betrayal. Something moved and settled deep within her soul. She'd been ill-used as a child, forged in agony into a living weapon to fulfill the will of her father. A man who had betrayed The Way of the Faithful by treating with vampires. Her life had become a lie, a false life that had brought nothing but the deaths of good men and women.

She stared out through the bay doorway at the geological chaos unleashed upon the Panopticon fortress. She rose out of an ocean of dark regret and found sanctuary on a new purpose. Her father stood fixed before her mind's eye.

There would be a reckoning written in blood.

* * *

The nightfalcon cleared the immediate vicinity of the fortress.

The helicopter flew southwest, flying a hundred feet above the valley floor at one hundred and eighty miles per hour.

Anton rubbed the sides of his nose, and then his temples. Francis' death was hard to accept, but it was a miracle they hadn't all died within the fortress. The Mirovars had saved his life, and helped him find a new home. Now that home no longer had a head. He sighed, and perhaps it no longer had a heart too. Perhaps the heart of the Mirovar force team had died on the cliffs above Whitby and they had been proceeding on momentum more than anything else.

Anton glanced across at Li. He set aside his thoughts about Francis and the Mirovar force team and wondered what had kept Li back at the main server room. She whispered, her gaze distant, "Seventy-two percent … ninety-four percent … gone." Her face bore an odd expression, like she'd just lost a dear friend but was also relieved. She looked at Anton and stated enigmatically, "They're gone."

"What's gone?" Anton asked.

"The quantum processors."

"What?" Anton asked. Her response leaving him perplexed.

She said in a tone of quiet intimacy, "I was networked with them." She frowned at him, her dark eyes filled with something that could have been concern for him or fear of him. But she didn't approach him or offer further explanation, and whatever was in her eyes remained absent from her reserved and alert posture.

"Oh," Anton said weakly, nonplussed by Li's comments and sudden standoffish attitude. *What do I say to that?* He shook his head and stared past her at the fortress imploding into a small lake of fiery lava. What had really happened in the last five minutes? He'd seen Francis die and it had triggered something deep within him. He'd fought like a man possessed, but possessed by what? There'd been a wild freedom to it. A loss of all inhibition that'd felt like being some sort of god, answerable to no one and nothing. But who was he? If his grandfather hadn't stopped him, he'd have killed everyone there.

He shook his head. Murdering a bunch of unarmed people wasn't him. A memory exploded into his mind, of driving a commander tank through a military base in England. How many people who'd only turned up to work at a job, that as far as they knew was just another government job, had he shredded with rail gun spikes and cannon shots? He took a deep breath and sighed. He'd felt entirely justified when he'd done it. He was just trying to save Peter, but now it didn't sit well with him anymore.

The world was a helluva lot more complicated than a Boston boy on an ice hockey scholarship could expect to understand. Anton sighed, that boy was dead. As dead as yesterday. He could fill in the gaps of what had happened. He'd gone berserk, and worse – part of him had absolutely loved it. He had no answers, and he looked around the cabin. Peter was sitting in shock opposite where Francis lay, occasionally gesturing in a 'what the fuck?' manner. Chiara sat near him, her face filled with sadness and something deeper that spoke of adamantine purpose. A cold chill ascended Anton's spine. It was not a look that he'd ever want to see on an enemy. He reflected briefly for a moment. Sometimes Chiara could be truly frightening. There was a kind of remorselessness about her that exceeded any he'd ever witnessed before, and he wondered what could have caused that in her.

He turned to his grandfather. He was wrapping the P-Case in what looked like green kitchen cling wrap. Anton asked, "What's that?"

"Faraday tape. It's a smart material for blocking the P-Case's beacon. We can't disable the beacon without disabling the case, but we can shield it."

Anton nodded. With the Panopticon down and the P-Case shrouded in a mobile Faraday cage, they were well on their way to escaping the Vampire Dominion.

Arthur put the finishing touches on the tape and looked up at Anton with a gleam in his eyes, and declared, "Mission accomplished."

Anton flicked his gaze at Francis lying on the cabin floor and asked sadly, "At what price?"

Arthur followed his gaze. "A high price, but one we all volunteer to make once we become a vampire hunter." He stepped to the side of the cabin and strapped the P-Case to webbing on the cabin wall. He turned back to Anton and reached out, placing his right hand on Anton's shoulder. He leaned in close and stated firmly, "What happened to you can be controlled."

"I damn well hope so."

Arthur advised quietly, "Don't fear it." He leaned in and patted Anton's chest with his left hand. "Embrace the power within you." He gazed into Anton's eyes and stated confidently, "You're very fast and strong, between the two of us we could kill Armitage." His mouth opened into a tight, hungry grin. "Perhaps even Crane and her together."

Anton rubbed his jaw and whispered just loud enough for Arthur to hear, "What really happened back there? I lost it completely. I was berserk."

Arthur grabbed both his shoulders with strong hands, and squeezed hard enough to cause pain. "It's called the wild Ramp. No one else knows about it. But, don't worry. I can do it too and I'll show you how to master it."

"But, I … I just … wanted to kill everyone." Anton leaned in; his eyes lit by an intense light. "And I loved it. I really wanted to do it." He stepped back and Arthur released his grip. Anton pulled his left hand down over his jaw. He looked away, the last of the fortress was sinking out of sight in the distance.

Arthur pulled him around and declared authoritatively, "The Order is like a monastery full of monks, all full of clarity of mind, will power, and silence. You and I," he tapped Anton on the chest again, "we don't belong there. We belong on a wet, windswept cliff face. Thunder and lightning sheeting overhead. Our blades drenched in the blood of our enemies and a wild roar on our lips."

Anton looked into Arthur's eyes.

A slight smile curled Arthur's lips. "We're not built for a quiet life." He stepped aside, staring to the south. "Come with me Anton, we'll take Crane and Armitage together."

Anton frowned, then stepped next to Arthur and declared, "Yes, let's do it. Let's do it for Francis, Juliette, Yvette, and everyone who's been lost to the vampires."

Arthur smiled at him and clasped his shoulder. "Good, boy."

The nightfalcon raced through the mid-afternoon sunlight.

Anton mused to himself. They were doing everything they could to maximize their chance of escaping but would it be enough. His gaze drifted with thoughtful speculation. Given his recent experiences, Crane and Armitage were devilishly difficult opponents. Against them, it was always best to assume the worst. For all their efforts to avoid detection, the vampires would find them, and this time Crane and Armitage would come for them.

He glanced across at the P-Case strapped tightly against the webbing on the cabin wall. They had the Panopticon, and there was no way that Crane would allow them to keep such a prize. There was only one question worth asking.

What would they do when Crane and Armitage caught up with them?

* * *

The nightfalcon fled across the valley floor.

Li watched the red and gold glow of exploding lava playing against funereal clouds of smoke hanging like a shroud over the valley. Barely taking in what could've inspired a vision of hell by Hieronymus Bosch, she devoted herself to digesting the insights gained while connected to the raw power of the quantum processors of the Panopticon. As terrible as the loss of Francis was, her sudden grief remained overwhelmed by the experience of merged insight with the Panopticon's quantum processors. The same way a rogue wave could overwhelm a fishing trawler: wiped out, obliterated and lost to all awareness. A sinking hulk of grief remained beneath the surface of her soul. Still there, not forgotten, but ignored for a short time.

Francis' death left her with one core truth – war will cost you the ones you love.

The insights from merging with the quantum processors had come thick and fast. Crane's citadel was a 108-floor skyscraper at number 350 on Fifth Avenue, Manhattan, New York. All the floors above the hundredth remained dedicated to the operations of the Vampire Dominion, and included Crane's personal quarters.

And now, it lay mostly abandoned.

Crane had stripped all the remaining praetorians in North America from their posts and was converging on this valley. They would arrive in a little over an hour's time at approximately ten minutes after four in the afternoon. Armitage was sharing a command shadowstar drone with him.

Crane was building a second Panopticon at the East Coast Hub. A location so secret, even the Panopticon knew nothing of it. The new worldwide head of Shadowstone, Louise Wesson, was overseeing its construction. Shadowstone would complete the new machine in a month's time.

They had a window of a month where the vampires would not have pervasive surveillance technology. The window would then close and the vampires would have a new system of greater power than the one the team had just destroyed. All the danger they had just gone through, all the lives they'd taken, and the death of Francis would buy them at most a month of advantage.

The mission was a strategic disaster.

Li turned away from the smoke and flames, and looked through the cabin to the front of the helicopter. Slayne had joined Dwayne Washington in the cockpit. Where was he leading them too now? What were his plans for the Panopticon locked away in the P-Case? How did he expect to escape the imminent wrath of Crane and the might of the Vampire Dominion?

She glanced around the cabin. The team members were a mess. Chiara was … Chiara Morte, daughter of the Red Ghost. Li blinked. Her heart sank. There really was a spy within the Mirovar force team, and she was staring at Francis' body with her face filled with grim purpose.

Li kept her silence. There was nothing to gain from telling the truth at this time. Peter and Chiara were both wounded, but could still serve. Jay was in good shape, coming through the battle mostly unscathed, as had Anton – a dark future opened up before her – no, not Anton. Anton had awakened something within himself that could threaten the team and everything beyond. What if he failed to master his new berserker powers? What if Armitage captured and turned him? And, Armitage had an unhealthy interest in Anton; that was clear from the evidence in the Panopticon. She could do it. She could turn him into a vampire to further her own ends. Anton Slayne could become an unstoppable force for evil in the world.

As for Slayne? He was hiding something; something beyond imagining.

Li vowed to keep her new knowledge to herself, at least, for the time being. One thing was crystal clear; she couldn't trust Slayne – no one could. She leaned against the rear bulkhead and stared along the midline of the helicopter through the front windscreen. They were tracking southwest at three miles per minute. Where they ended up rested in the hands of someone she didn't trust.

Li stared at the back of Slayne's head. As the man had said himself, he didn't need her trust. Well, she'd watch him like a hawk. She'd work out his plan and if it was going to put the team into danger without gain – she'd put a stop to it.

Li took a deep breath and let it out slowly.

* * *

Arthur leaned back in the co-pilot's chair.

Dwayne nodded in acknowledgment and asked, "All good, Arthur?"

He smiled grimly and answered, "Sure, sure … it's solid."

"We've got forty-five minutes flight to the ditching site. We're in full stealth mode flying nap of the Earth. With the Panopticon down, the vampires would have to have a shadowstar drone within line of sight to find us."

Arthur nodded. "Good, good. I might rest my eyes for a few minutes."

"Sure," Dwayne said. "You do that. I'll wake you if anything happens."

"Thanks," Arthur replied, leaning back in the chair and closing his eyes.

What remained of his mind spun away. Francis was dead. Only Jon Thunder-Axe and himself had survived from his original force team. Francis, Juliette and Gang were all dead. He took a deep breath and sighed. Sometimes he felt really tired and this was one of those times. He sighed a second time and put his feelings aside. There was nothing more he could do for Francis. He'd been a good soldier, one of the best, and his death in battle was always the likely outcome – no Ramp masters died of old age.

Arthur's attention returned to current events. There was no way he could leave Armitage and Crane a single breadcrumb. They knew he was careful; a breadcrumb would standout like a neon sign that he was asking them to enter a trap. No, he had to be immaculate. He had to do everything he could to ensure they could escape without leaving a trail. He had to keep the escape believable.

As to the nature of the trap – he had no idea.

He'd partitioned a sizeable fraction of his mind away. The part that understood the plan in full, that knew what the end game was. That part of his mind he'd cut out and cast away in a process as dreadful as it was agonizing. No one fully understood the process of personal division. It was risky, he may never re-integrate what he'd lost. It was a risk he had to take – there was no one else who could confront Cornelius Crane.

What remained of himself was an instrument of his original whole-self's will. He would do what was right. He would respond to each situation as he must. But he had no idea what end he was leading the Mirovar force team too. He would always do his best with the circumstances as he found them, he was sure of that much, and the plan he'd devised would assume his behavior.

Arthur hoped his hidden plan was a good one. He hoped the Mirovar force team would survive. He hoped that Anton would live long enough to overcome the addictive power of the berserker version of the wild Ramp and find a good future for himself with a family of his own.

He hoped for many things, but he feared that none would come to pass because in his heart of hearts he knew that he was an utterly ruthless bastard with a genius for strategic and tactical planning. What he'd planned could be anything and he'd only discover what it was as it played out.

Arthur summoned silence. The voices were coming back. They always seemed to be worse after a fight. He'd chosen this path. He'd chosen to suffer insanity in his quest to deflect Crane's precognitive power. How else could you defeat someone who could see the future? Deliberate madness was the only answer he'd been able to come up with.

He spent the rest of the flight wrestling with the whispering voices of his other discarded selves.

* * *

The abandoned nightfalcon sank into the sandpit and the body of Francis Mirovar disappeared with it.

Jay snapped at Slayne, "That P-Case had better be worth it."

Slayne stated with deadly certainty, "This is a strategic game changer for us. We've blinded the vampires, and soon we will be able to see everything they've been hiding from us. This changes everything and shifts the strategic balance to our favor."

Jay's gaze slipped back to the sinking helicopter. It held an awful fascination for him. Slayne's 'kinetic' sand slurry crawled pale fingers over the top of the rotor blades, returning the dry lake bed to its natural pristine state. Francis and the nightfalcon vanished from the surface of the Earth. Entombed forever in a secret grave beneath the dusty surface of Lake Sevier.

An unmarked grave – the natural legacy of a vampire hunter. One day, he'd own an unmarked grave too. His tears had dried in the fifty-minute flight to the dusty lake bed. Francis was gone. His mentor was dead. His best friend lay consigned to the Earth with only a handful of survivors as witnesses to his passing. Francis had deserved better.

Slayne spoke quietly behind him, "You were the second in command of the Mirovar force team. You're Francis' designated successor. You have to take command of the team."

Jay whirled to face Slayne, a cold sliver piercing his heart.

"They are your responsibility now." Slayne paused for a moment. "Can we work together to finish this mission?"

Jay's chest heaved, a bolt of nausea shooting through him. He gritted his teeth and answered, "Yes. To the end of this mission. Once we have completed our escape, we go our separate ways."

Slayne nodded. "Fair enough."

Jay pivoted, and glanced back at the dry lake bed hiding the nightfalcon and Francis' body. It had taken fifteen minutes to sink the nightfalcon and remove all evidence of their presence. He looked around at Peter, Li, Anton and Chiara. They were looking at him with studied acceptance, wondering what he would say and do. He would honor Francis' memory and give them the best he had to give. He looked back at Slayne. He had to know more about what was going on. How else could he do his duty to the team?

Jay flicked his head back toward Francis' grave and asked, "So, you must have prepared this site for today?"

Slayne nodded. "Over the last few years, we developed a variation of 'kinetic sand,'" he smiled and shrugged his shoulders. "It's little more than a modification of a child's toy, but in large quantities and colored to match the environment, it's a superb solution to hiding a nightfalcon. We have also laced the sand with additional ingredients to suppress any metal or mass signatures. To all intents and purposes, anyone scanning this site will assume it's all just," he spread his hands wide, "dry lake bed. Someone would have to step on it to realize it's not natural."

"We?" Jay asked.

"One of my corporate fronts."

Jay gestured to Peter and Chiara and asked, "Why didn't we fly to the safe house, drop off our wounded, and then have a minimal team ditch the chopper?"

"Operational security," Slayne replied. "Crane's hunting us. Flying the chopper to the roadhouse and back here only increases the risk of discovery. We have a fully equipped medical team, food, water, clothing, weapons and transport at the safe house."

"This safe house, how long has it been in operation?"

"Years."

Jay's eyes widened and he addressed the team. "Armitage had half a day to question Ramin Kain in Whitby. We have to assume she knows about this safe house."

Li exclaimed, "Jay's right! With everything that's been going on we've forgotten that Armitage had almost a day to question Kain. We have to assume she drained him of all useful information."

Peter lifted an eyebrow. "As well as all of his blood."

"Look," Slayne said. "I'm not up on what exactly happened with Kain, but even if Armitage knows about the safe house. She's not here. She's inbound with Crane and heading for what remains of the fortress and we're ahead of them. We can use the resources at the safe house and then move on. We have a window for action. The Panopticon is down, and it will take time for the Vampire Dominion to adapt to its absence. We can break contact and disappear with the Panopticon. We'll be in and out before Armitage, Crane, or any other vampire can react."

"Clearly," Jay stated. "Okay, let's move." He glanced at Slayne and directed, "You know the way, take us to the safe house."

Slayne called out, "Follow me to Black Rock." Then broke into a run the lean and rangy Dwayne Washington would be hard pressed to keep up with.

Jay glanced up at the sun. It was halfway down from its peak. They had less than four hours of sunlight left. They needed to be far from here by then and back under the vampire's radar. They had to break contact with the inevitable vampire pursuit before daylight failed, or else they would be fighting the vampires on their terms.

And that was something Jay wanted to avoid with all of his heart.

Chapter Eleven

"The immortal ruler must keep their immortality hidden from the great mass of humanity, lest they rise up against him in a fit of envious fury." – From the unpublished chapter, 'On Immortality,' from 'The Prince,' by Niccolo Machiavelli

– An unpublished document from within Cornelius Crane's secret library

* * *

Utah, The Panopticon Fortress (Ruins), September 11th, 16:10

A bubbling lava pit spread for two miles across the floor of the valley.

Chloe sat next to Crane in the cockpit of his command shadowstar drone. They both wore their personal body armor, their weapons and tactical helmets stowed with them in the drone's cabin. Unlike a standard shadowstar drone, the command version could only carry two crew. Additional computing, communications, and weapons arrays filled the spaces that another two praetorians would have taken.

The command drone hovered on pale jets of blue fire two miles above the floor of the valley. Crane had pulled to a halt three miles back from the plume of smoke and flame rising from what had been the Panopticon fortress. Three additional shadowstar drones filled with the remaining twelve praetorians from the citadel flanked the command drone.

Crane stared at the lake of fire and uttered a single word with a strong French accent, "Catastrophe."

Chloe coughed, her right hand flying to her mouth, shielding a sudden smile from view. The loss of the Panopticon would throw Crane's world into disarray and allow her to seek the Tanaka sisters without fear of discovery. She regained her composure a moment later, raised an eyebrow and declared, "Despite his sacrifice, General Maze was unable to thwart Arthur Slayne's plan."

Crane turned to face her. If he felt disturbed by the loss of one of his generals, he hid it well. His eyes narrowed with a calculating look. "And what do you think Slayne's plan is?"

"Let's start with what we know," Chloe said. "Shadowstone are already de-briefing the staff who escaped the inferno and reached Salt Lake City. A single nightfalcon evacuated the site with the Mirovar force team, Slayne, and the Panopticon P-Case. It's feasible, he has an unknown source of quantum processors and an appropriate power supply. Once on a suitable network, he could restore the Panopticon. The first thing it will do is requalify the root user account. That would be Slayne, all else will follow from that. Everything the Panopticon knew – Slayne will have access to, including all our current systems."

"We have to get it back, or destroy it," Crane stated emphatically. "The necessary hardware at the East Coast Hub is already operational. If we re-acquire the Panopticon, we could restore it in less than twelve hours."

Crane left unsaid that he needed the Panopticon to help find the rogue 'vampire of a new type,' heading west across China. Chloe watched him closely. The next few hours offered a once in a century opportunity to deliver Crane into a world of chaos, allowing her to seize the initiative against him. She chose her next words carefully. "The staff from the fortress know about vampires. They saw you bare your fangs on the screens in the command-and-control center, and by all reports they watched Maze burn in sunlight." Her eyes widened and she spread her hands wide. "The secret of our existence is disintegrating before our eyes." She pursed her lips. "Perhaps a new strategy is called for?"

"We'll have to sanitize those who survived," Crane paused for a heartbeat, "and those they have spoken with."

Crane was doubling down on secrecy. Chloe decided to be politically expedient and conceded his point. "Agreed. But, in the next few hours we need to act without constraints to reacquire the Panopticon or see it destroyed. We have a small window for action. If Slayne gets away, he could disappear with the P-Case, and without the Panopticon – finding him will be more than difficult."

"Finding Slayne when we had the Panopticon was next to impossible."

"We found him in Rio."

Crane snorted dismissively. "And lost contact with him almost immediately with all our assets butchered."

Chloe stared at Crane, portraying concern and attentiveness. A believable posture given the loss of the Panopticon struck at the heart of the foundation of the Vampire Dominion and was therefore a strike against Crane, and via Crane's implant, a strike against her own interests. She could back Crane's desire to retrieve the Panopticon in full while covering her own agenda to free herself from his rule.

It took all her will power to avoid screaming in triumph. The Mirovar force team and Arthur Slayne had surprised her. An unusual outcome she was pleased to wear this time. She'd overestimated the defensive systems of the fortress and underestimated the resourcefulness of Slayne allied with the Mirovar force team. She would have to be wary of what Slayne and the Mirovar force team could achieve together. Underestimating them a second time could prove fatal. After all, what had just happened to Clayton Maze. The five generals had been in place for nearly two centuries, and now there were four. How long before more fell? She arched an eyebrow in silence. It was only a matter of time before Crane's rule resembled the remains of the Panopticon fortress.

Crane snapped, "What are you so amused with?"

"I'm considering the effectiveness of Slayne with the Mirovar force team. They are a foe to be reckoned with." Chloe smiled broadly, revealing her fangs. "I'm looking forward to collecting their heads."

"Indeed, it goes without saying," Crane stated. "Now let us focus on the problem at hand. It's been seventy-five minutes since Slayne left the site. He could be anywhere within a two-hundred-and-thirty-mile radius by now. He could be past Idaho Falls to the north, nearing Denver in the east, approaching Las Vegas in the south, or heading toward nowhere important in Nevada to the west. It's a big territory and growing in all directions at three miles per minute."

"Are they still flying, or have they already abandoned the nightfalcon for a different form of transport? A nightfalcon flying nap of the Earth in full stealth mode will defeat our satellites, and without the Panopticon we can't integrate other sources of information. However, they won't be able to evade line-of-sight detection by this drone's sensor array."

Crane shook his head. "Slayne will expect our shadowstar drones. He will abandon the nightfalcon and go to ground. If only we'd been able to fully penetrate their organization and discover the whereabouts of their safe houses. They are most likely going to one now. They will proceed from there on something that will blend in," he shrugged his shoulders, "cars, trucks, motorcycles. They could resupply at a safe house, move quickly to a final exfiltration point and leave the country from there."

"Clearly," Chloe agreed. It would be stupid to underestimate Crane's mind or his ability to work out what was really going on. Chloe had to work with the utmost care to avoid discovery as she maneuvered for advantage. She knew all about the Order of Thoth network of safe houses. She'd known ever since she extracted the information from Ramin Kain in the dungeon beneath her family manor. Crane was right. Slayne and the Mirovar force team would not stay with the helicopter longer than they had too. Even without the Panopticon, a nightfalcon was too obvious, too visible, too easy to find with the sensor arrays on their shadowstar drones.

The nearest safe house was a roadhouse in Black Rock. The location was well within the perimeter of territory a nightfalcon could reach in seventy-five minutes. They could be there now, but could they hide a helicopter near there? It had to be possible, Slayne would have planned for the disappearance of the nightfalcon as a necessary part of the exfiltration of the Mirovar force team.

She looked at Crane and said, "I agree. Slayne will run for a short time to break contact with the fortress site. He will either know or correctly assume our shadowstar drones can detect a nightfalcon if it's within line of sight. To mitigate risk of discovery, he will abandon the nightfalcon at a location where he can make it disappear. He will proceed to another nearby site where the team can resupply and rearm. They will then proceed from there to an exfiltration site with fast international transport," she shrugged, "such as a private jet. Within a matter of hours, he'll be out of the country with the Panopticon."

Crane shook his head ruefully. "A typical private jet could use a straight piece of road; they just have to have one hidden. Not to mention the fact they could ignore filing a flight plan and simply hug the surface of the Earth to a foreign destination. This problem grows apace." Crane paused for a moment. "Can we identify the P-Case beacon?"

Chloe glanced at the displays in the cockpit. "Nothing is showing on our scopes or satellite feeds. The P-Case beacon has been conspicuous in its absence. There are suppression technologies. Faraday tape comes to mind."

"We should assume Slayne has used such a technique to hide the beacon. He's not going to leave us a trail."

Chloe tilted her head slightly. "And if we found a 'bread crumb' or two?"

"It would be a trap."

"No breadcrumbs so far. Can we assume he's not laying a trap?"

"And there's the core issue," Crane stated, his eyes narrowing with suspicion. He tapped the armrest of his seat with a long forefinger and then sighed. "It can't be ruled out. But how can he plan on us finding him if he leaves no clues? Especially, given his ability to evade us over the course of his life." He pressed his lips into a thin line, then declared, "I'm not convinced this is an elaborate trap but I cannot ignore the possibility. However, trap or not, it remains a moot point if we can't find Slayne and the Mirovar force team."

Chloe asked innocently. "Are there any other ways to identify their movements?"

Crane stared at her for a long moment, shadows moving behind his brown eyes. He tilted his head slightly, his dark leonine hair sliding across his shoulders, and said, "It remains to be seen. We need to determine the direction Slayne and the Mirovar force team have escaped in, and their final exfiltration site in country before they go international … our time to act grows short."

Chloe paused for a microsecond, relishing Crane's lack of denial. She must keep him alive for now, but once she'd rendered her implant harmless his time would be short indeed. She stated calmly, "Shadowstone reported they were traveling to the southwest in the opposite direction to everyone else."

"Indeed. Then southwest shall be our first direction of inquiry. Our objectives are simple. Re-establish contact with Slayne and the Mirovar force team. Recover the P-Case intact, and destroy them without mercy. If absolutely necessary, the P-Case and the Panopticon must be destroyed lest they remain in Arthur Slayne's hands. Is that clear?"

"Crystal."

"Then give me a few moments to rest my eyes and consider my strategy in full."

"Of course," Chloe agreed. A slight smile curling her lips as Crane laid back in his seat and closed his eyes. While he no doubt sought to engage whatever sorcerous power Philippe Allemande had gifted him with, Chloe would consider her own options. Arthur Slayne with the Panopticon would become a measurably more difficult opponent. Crane with the Panopticon restored would have a better chance of capturing the elusive rogue vampire in China, but he would also be able to entrench his position and re-establish the status quo. A circumstance leaving Chloe unable to pursue Hana Tanaka and therefore compelled to remain Crane's dedicated protector.

The destruction of the Panopticon was the best option, or at least lost to Crane and Slayne. Slayne would not be able to leverage his position against her, and Crane would have to deal with the crisis in China without the aid of the Panopticon. There was a very real chance he would take personal control of the hunt for the rogue vampire. Chloe could go back to Japan without the Panopticon tracking her. Use the chameleons to find the Tanaka sisters, and extract a solution for the removal of her implant and source the cure for vampirism. The last could be extremely useful when she dealt once more with Dalien Morte and the Red Empire.

Furthermore, with the Panopticon down, Crane's own ability to avoid being tracked was compromised. If she could source a simple but powerful Shadowstone tag, she could track his movements whenever he used the command shadowstar drone. Something he was likely to do, given his single-seater drone was down for a maintenance cycle.

Crane's eyes were vibrating beneath their lids. Was he dreaming or experiencing a vision? Perhaps one day soon she'd have the opportunity to find out. Chloe lifted her smartphone and sent James Haley a quick message. It read, 'I need a micro-tracker immediately. Do you have one?'

James replied back in a handful of seconds. 'Yes.'

Chloe lifted her eyes for a moment, struck by a sudden inspiration. Her interrogation of Ramin Kain would now bear fruit. She sent another message. 'James, go to the intersection of Utah state route 257 and Black Rock road. There is a roadhouse on the southeast side of the cross roads. It is an Order safe house and the likely exfil target for Slayne and the Mirovar force team. Re-establish contact with the Ramp masters but maintain stealth and do not engage.'

Twenty seconds later, James replied, 'Found it. ETA of 17:25 +/- 5 minutes.'

It was time to take a calculated risk. To leverage her knowledge of the Order safe house network acquired from Ramin Kain. It was likely Slayne and the Mirovar force team had used the closest safe house on the exfil path. She could send James and the chameleons to Black Rock to confirm the path of the Ramp masters. She could then maneuver Crane to the Black Rock safe house where one of the camouflaged chameleons could apply the micro-tracker to one of the command drone's landing struts.

Chloe composed another message to James and sent it. All she needed to do, was put Crane and the command drone within the vicinity of James and the chameleons and she could track Crane's movements through the Vampire Dominion's co-opted military networks.

James and the chameleons were flying in the osprey II drone. Its performance was similar to a commercial jet liner. If the Mirovar force team lingered in Black Rock they would be discovered in a little over an hour from now.

Chloe smiled. Slayne and Mirovar were not stupid, they would not stay at Black Rock longer than necessary. With both Crane and Slayne in the field, the situation was very fluid. She'd have to find a way to ensure the P-Case was lost, and remained lost, and that she gained the capacity to track Crane's movements. She was not yet ready to deploy the chameleons against Crane. What if he had a voice activation method for the implant resting beneath her skull? He could kill her in a heartbeat. She'd trained the chameleons to capture a vampire without harming them. A technique designed to be used against Crane without activating Allemande's curse.

It would have been poetic justice to imprison Crane within a silver coffin within his own facility at Rikers island, but paralyzing him with silver would likely activate the curse and kill her. Instead, she could use the safe house in Arizona. She could lock Crane below ground in a prison cell reinforced to defeat vampire strength and guarded by an elite Red Empire fist team answerable only to her.

Then all she need do was induce the Mirovar force team to discover the Arizona safe house and its prisoner and her problem with Crane would be solved forever, but before that glorious event occurred, she'd have to relieve herself of the damnable implant pointing half an ounce of powdered silver at her brain stem.

And for that – she needed Hana Tanaka.

* * *

Shadows fled to the perimeter of Cornelius Crane's precognitive vision.

A cusp event was imminent. The direction and distance to the location revealed via pure intuition. In less than four to five hours he'd face a test to his life his precognitive powers could not see beyond. The near future resolved into sharp clarity. The shadowy second figure behind Anton Slayne revealed as his grandfather. The two Slaynes would fight him together within an aircraft hangar, each armed with one of the dragon swords.

A formidable pair, but Cornelius would have the combat prowess of a king of vampires and his bastard sword forged from meteoric iron by a peerless Damascan genius, and Chloe Armitage would stand at his side armed with the Red Dragon. Together, they should have sufficient power to best the Slaynes, but he must avoid hubris. The Metaframe inspired sorcery would not display a cusp if the risk was negligible. Wisdom called for due caution. He approached the pair across a pale concrete floor. Armitage emerged from the shadows, and took a place at his side. The Red Dragon poised in perfect stillness over her left shoulder. The figure of Arthur Slayne responded to their presence, turning toward him, his eyes flicking back and forth between Armitage and himself. He was holding the Panopticon P-Case in his left hand and the Black Dragon in his right.

Slayne would keep the Panopticon close, not trusting to leave such a prize in the care of another. His inability to trust the protection of the Panopticon to anyone else would give Cornelius the opportunity to end the Slayne line and retrieve the Panopticon at the same time.

However, … he pressed his lips into a thin line. This opportunity was too good to be true. How could he trust this vision? Slayne had proved to be a diabolically clever opponent. There was no way he would offer his grandson, himself and the Panopticon at the same time … not unless he believed this was the true end game that would give him decisive victory over the Vampire Dominion.

Cornelius hadn't survived for nearly a millennium by taking unnecessary risks. The way of power demanded the elimination of risk, the betting on one sure thing after another. A ruthless operator would search for self-deception and eliminate it. Arrogance, hubris, over-confidence, these were the traps of fools.

The recent discussion with Armitage returned with a snap. Arthur Slayne was offering a trap, but its shape was superbly hidden. A trap Cornelius may have to spring to discover its true nature. He needed the Panopticon back to support his efforts on the Eurasian continent. He had to quell the threat posed by the single Mekrarian vampire traveling to the west, before thousands more rushed upon the world in a wave of destruction he could not contain without revealing himself to the world.

The new Panopticon would not be ready for up to another month. Mekra and her spawn could overtake half a continent in that time. Everything was at stake: stakes that called for the utmost in effort and sacrifice.

Cornelius was well aware that many would see him as the villain but few would understand that he also championed a cause. He ensured that most people, day after day, got to wake up in the morning. To live their lives without fearing demons in the night. To live in a shield of ignorance many of them would fight vigorously to maintain. Few people welcomed the illumination that declared their cherished beliefs to be lies.

He kept the world safe from harsher masters who would extract a greater price.

Cornelius opened his eyes and looked across the cockpit at Armitage.

She watched him with her vivid-blue eyes, her left eyebrow arching quizzically. She asked, with a touch of insolence, "Did you have a nice nap?"

He frowned, sat up straight, and stated, "They are fleeing to the southwest. A matter of a few hundred miles to a location northeast of Las Vegas."

"That narrows it down. I won't ask how you know."

"An excellent decision on your part," he said sardonically. She clearly suspected his precognitive power. Well, let her continue to speculate. She'd get no confirmation from him. Cornelius studied her for a long moment, then declared, "The Slaynes and the Mirovar force team are heading for an airport. It will be a location they can reach within the next five hours using common transport."

"We need a new strategy."

"And you have something in mind?" Cornelius asked derisively, "Perhaps a strategy you have already prepared for just this contingency?"

Armitage ignored his sarcasm and leaned toward him. "We have too few praetorians, and the Blake force team operates in the southwest. We could end up facing both force teams at once."

"Do you fear such?"

She grinned. "Yes. Even I would fear to face the two premier and might I say the only surviving force teams of the Order of Thoth. And you should fear them too."

Cornelius grinned wolfishly. "Then what do you propose?"

Armitage tapped her lips with her right forefinger.

* * *

The shifting images on the command drone's displays cast shadows across Crane's face.

He watched her expectantly. Chloe knew this game well. Crane would ask her for advice, and then do whatever he wanted to do anyway. He did it to double check his strategy and test it against another point of view to avoid blind spots. However, he knew full well he couldn't trust her advice, except that she wouldn't send him to his doom – not with the damnable implant beneath the base of her skull ready to send a lethal dose of powdered silver into her brain stem on the event of his death.

This was a game she'd have to play with the greatest subtlety. She suggested, "We need to activate the militia."

Crane paused for a moment. "To what extent?"

He was at least willing to consider the idea. The Vampire Dominion maintained a register of every vampire. They had an allocated territory in which they could hunt. They had to obey the rules for kills, disposals, and maintaining the secrecy of vampires. If they behaved, the Vampire Dominion protected them from the Red Empire and the Order of Thoth. If they broke the rules, the praetorians would come looking for them, and if necessary, Chloe herself would intervene.

Chloe's dire reputation had kept the Vampire Dominion an orderly community for over a century. The average vampire feared her more than they feared the Red Empire and the Order of Thoth, and justifiably so. She could find any of them in minutes and be on their doorstep in less than twenty-four hours. However, now it was time for the vampires to repay the Dominion for their protection. Crane needed them; it was time to raise an army. "Given the short timeframe, I propose we call up every vampire in the west from Tucson in the south, to Portland in the north. Then through an arc from Denver and Dallas in the east and Monterrey in the southeast. If we notify them now, they still have time to converge with private jets on Las Vegas."

"That would raise forty to sixty vampires for immediate action," Crane replied. "If Justin Blake arrives with a second force team, that may not be enough to bring an overwhelming force to the fight."

"They must also bring their familiars and wannabe vampires. They are easy converts and just as easily disposed of afterwards."

"How many?"

"Another two hundred or two hundred and fifty for a total force of more than three hundred vampires, plus we'll control the air with our shadowstars."

"And afterwards?"

"Bunch them up and wipe them out. The wannabes and lesser vampires are disposable. A pair of hypersonic missiles from this drone will be enough to eliminate them. If we really need to sanitize Slayne's exfil site completely, we can use a nuke. We have two on board this craft."

"Indeed, but perhaps a little difficult to explain to the world."

"Not in the least. The United States Air Force could easily be transporting a live warhead from one site to another and have a 'terrible,' accident. There would be an official inquiry, reviews of operations, updates to protocols, and a two-star general would lose his pension. In less than twenty-four hours the attention of the world will move on to the latest scandal involving a Hollywood celebrity and their over-indulged pet llama."

Crane arched his eyebrows. "Everyone believes they know the truth."

Chloe tilted her head. "Human arrogance is so useful. No one bothers to look beyond what they already believe. We can use that to our advantage. We can create an army of vampires, use it to effect, and then destroy it – all within a matter of hours. We can obliterate the evidence of the new vampires before it can get out, and we can use the blunt force of hundreds of vampires to swarm attack Slayne and the Mirovar force team."

"And if the Blake team is coordinating with Slayne and shows up on the field of battle?"

"We'll have over three hundred vampires, and our praetorians in reserve. If needs must, we can enter the battle too."

"Such forces are not without risks of their own. They will be difficult … perhaps even impossible to control."

"Those risks are less than the risks of failure."

Crane frowned briefly, then commanded, "Wake them up, and get them in motion."

Chloe nodded. "We'll coordinate them via your skeleton staff at the citadel."

"Make it so," Crane ordered.

Chloe nodded again and got to work.

***

The remains of the Panopticon fortress were a faint smudge on the northern horizon.

Arthur and Anton led the Mirovar force team past a 'Closed for Renovations,' sign and pushed through the front doors of the Black Rock roadhouse. There were two men and two women in the main dining room dressed for performing surgery.

Arthur addressed a middle-aged woman with iron-shot short hair, "Rebecca," he nodded toward Peter and Chiara, "we have two who have taken hits and need to be assessed."

Rebecca ordered, "Mike, Jess, you look after the big guy." She gestured toward Chiara and the third surgeon. "Ben, you and I will work on the girl."

There was a brief chorus of assent and the four doctors went to work.

Arthur caught Anton's attention and pointed at another table next to the kitchen. It was laden with an abundance of food and drink, and he said, "Better fill up. We won't get another chance to eat for a while."

Peter called out, "Anton, could you get me a tray." He looked down at the dark-haired woman prying a sliver of black metal from his forearm with forceps and winced. "I could've just dug that out myself."

"And make a right mess of it too, no doubt," she said, without taking her attention off what she was doing.

Arthur called out, "Everyone, our helpers have combat surgeon experience from Iran, Venezuela, and South Korea. They might not be Ramp masters, but they know what they're doing. Come over here and refuel."

Jay shrugged and approached the food-laden table.

Arthur continued. "Jay, Anton – eat fast, take a tray if need be and go out and set a perimeter watch."

Anton looked at Arthur, a question poised on his face. "Peter asked—"

"Don't worry, I'll make sure everyone gets fed," Arthur said, and clasped Anton's shoulder. "Go with Jay and set up a perimeter. Our asses are hanging out in the wind here and I want to know if anyone shows up."

Anton nodded and replied, "Sure."

"By the way," Arthur suggested with a slight grin, "don't shoot Dwayne when he catches up with us."

"I'll make sure to keep a special lookout for Dwayne."

"Good boy," Arthur enthused, patting Anton on the back.

Anton loaded a tray with three steak sandwiches and a couple of bottles of water, and strode back out into the sunshine. Jay came up beside him, similarly ladened with a tray and his assault rifle.

Jay said, "I'll go around the back and check the east side."

Anton nodded.

Jay paused and instructed Anton in terse tones, "Watch out for the Order helper. It wouldn't do to shoot him."

"Yeah, I get it," Anton responded, somewhat nettled.

Jay clicked his tongue. "Well, I saw what happened in the hangar. I just hope you're okay. Are you okay?"

"Yeah, sure, … sure, sure. I'm okay."

Jay looked at him strangely, then shrugged and made for the northern corner of the roadhouse.

Anton watched him go and whispered, "Does everyone think I'm a freak?" He shook his head and turned to the west. Dwayne Washington appeared in the distance, running at a good pace for a normal. Five minutes later he passed Anton with a nod of his head and made for the roadhouse entrance.

Anton downed the last of his second bottle of water as Dwayne pushed through the doors.

As strange as his life had gotten since his eighteenth birthday, could it get any stranger than today?

He shook his head and sighed.

What the hell is normal anyway?

***

One of the surgeons clicked away with a micro-suture gun on Chiara's wounded hand. Another dropped a fragment of metal plucked from Peter's chest onto the floor. Arthur leaned back in a wooden chair and took another bite of a turkey on rye sandwich.

Dwayne Washington, his shirt soaked with perspiration, pushed through the roadhouse doors.

"About time," Arthur declared, putting down his sandwich.

"Geez, Arthur. I'm not Superman. How am I supposed to keep up with you guys?"

Arthur smiled. "It's okay. Just playing mother hen here. Grab a quick bite to eat and some water." Arthur glanced at a clock on the wall. It was nearly ten minutes to five. "We need to be out of here as soon as possible." He glanced across at Peter and Chiara and the surgeons attending to their wounds and stated, "We don't have any time to waste." He looked hard at Dwayne and said, "Out the back room, I have something for you." Arthur glanced around the main dining room again. Li had filled a tray of food and was eating from it. Jay and Anton were both outside watching the perimeter.

Arthur had something he must do. A subliminal command given by his previously whole-self overtaking what remained of his mind. An imperative to take Dwayne to a back room and open a cabinet. The command had kicked in as soon as Dwayne arrived at the roadhouse.

Dwayne avoided the food and grabbed a bottle of water, following Arthur into the back room.

Arthur made a beeline for a tall, gray metal cabinet at the back of the long room. He unzipped a pocket on the jacket he'd worn since the underground river, and pulled out a key. The sliver of cut metal filled him with surprise. He hadn't known it was there until he needed it. Arthur put the key into the lock on the cabinet and turned it. The door sprung loose and he pulled it aside.

Resting on the floor of the cabinet was a common black duffel bag. It appeared to be holding something. Arthur lifted it out, placed it on the floor and unzipped it.

Dwayne looked past his shoulder and whispered, "Arthur, what the hell is that?"

Arthur lifted a second P-Case from the duffel bag and replaced it with the original P-Case from the Panopticon fortress. He glanced back over his shoulder, then turned around and thrust the duffel bag into Dwayne's hands. What he said next felt like it'd been inspired by God, "Take this to Jon Thunder-Axe in Arizona. You know where he lives. He'll know what to do with it."

"Yes, Arthur," Dwayne replied, his eyes wide.

"Go now. There's transport for you out the back. Take what you need and go."

Dwayne looked at him, clasping the duffel bag containing the original P-Case with both hands. "I'll guard it with my life."

"I think the plan is that won't be necessary."

"I hope so."

"So, do I. Godspeed my friend."

Dwayne put his hand out and declared quietly, "It's been an honor."

Arthur took his hand firmly. "For me too. Now be off, time is wasting."

Dwayne nodded. Turned on his heel and left without a backward glance. The back door swung shut behind him. A handful of seconds later a motorcycle engine roared into life. Wheels spun on loose gravel for a moment and then the revving engine receded into the distance.

Arthur looked down at the second P-Case. It was wrapped in Faraday tape exactly as he'd wrapped the original P-Case. He couldn't have told the two P-Cases apart even if he wanted to.

He had no idea what was in the second P-Case. That information remained hidden within the community of his other selves and they never spoke of it. There were two new imperatives within his mind: treat the second P-Case as if it was the original P-Case containing the Panopticon and never attempt to open the second P-Case.

Arthur carried the second P-Case from the back room into the main room of the roadhouse. In another fifteen minutes or so, they would all have to leave. The vampires were coming for them and they would never give up.

There was a certain satisfaction that the vampires would persist in their hunt. Arthur didn't know why he felt that way, not for sure, but he needed them to persist in seeking him.

It was all part of a greater plan.

* * *

The afternoon sunlight cut across the ocher gravel behind the roadhouse.

Anton joined the rest of the team and the Order helpers in the shadows beneath a broad porch. Before them, lay a line of black Kawasaki KLR 650 motorcycles. Each bike had a yellow post-it note sticker on it with a name. Anton spotted his name on a nearby motorcycle. More preparation by his grandfather. The man was a demon for planning.

Arthur gestured to the team of surgeons. "Rebecca, Ben, Mike, and Jess, your work has made a world of difference. Now it's time to get out of Dodge. You know the exfil paths. I'll be in touch, and if not me, then Jon will be. Now make yourselves scarce."

The medical team turned and mounted their motorcycles. A minute later, the four doctors disappeared at speed toward the east on Black Rock road.

"Where's Dwayne?" Li asked.

"He's already left," Arthur answered. "There was no point in him sticking around. The sooner he left the safer it was for him. The same holds true for us. We should assume Armitage and Crane have breached the safe house network via Ramin Kain. They will send resources to this site or come here themselves. Our advantage is speed and stealth. We're in front of them and we need to stay ahead of them. They will be on the back foot after the loss of the Panopticon," he raised the P-Case for everyone to see, "and we need to exploit that to make our way southwest to my airport."

"You own an airport?" Jay asked.

"Yes. Well, it's the done thing if you need to ensure an exfil path. Now, the bikes are full of fuel and all good to go. They all have a GPS unit and it will guide you. If for some reason the GPS fails, or we get widely separated, the airport is just before the intersection of US route 93 and Interstate 15 in Nevada. If we get that far, you can't miss it on the left as you head toward Las Vegas. Now about fuel, you should be able to get to my airport on a single tank of fuel from here but you won't have much juice left at the end. If you need to re-fuel, do so at Enoch or Panaca. We can afford a couple of minutes to refuel more than we can afford someone running out of fuel. Okay, it's more than two-hundred and seventy miles by road. It will take us a few hours and we're running out of sunlight. Make the best time you can but don't take too many risks with speeding. The last thing we need, is to be picked up by a local cop and given a ticket. The vampires will shift to military and civilian systems of surveillance. We must assume they retain effective co-ordination of those resources. We must blend in with the local population as much as possible. From here to Milford, hammer the bikes. There are no cops out here but whenever you get within ten miles of each town, pull back to the speed limit. As a last resort, each bike has a pair of H&K MP7 submachine guns with spare magazines in their pannier bags. That is for emergency use only. I hope I don't have to remind anyone that stealth is now king."

Arthur touched his Order nightglasses. "Our tactical network is operational again." He glanced across at Li. "Li's loremaster laptop has been fully recharged. However, with the Panopticon down, we're not hazing it. What we have to watch out for is standard military and civilian systems. Li, I don't expect you to haze those while you ride a motorcycle. That's asking too much, even of you." He looked around the team. "Stay in touch via the network and be prepared for anything. We are on the run and we will be hunted."

Arthur paused to let the last point sink in then continued. "We'll split up into small teams so there isn't a," Arthur air-quoted, "'group of six,' to draw the vampire's attention. The teams are Jay riding solo. Peter, Chiara and Li as a group, and Anton and myself. I'll leave first, followed by Li's team, followed by Jay. Maintain a thirty second separation between the teams." He looked around the group. "Last but not least, I have supplied everyone here with a complete fake identity. You have a valid driver's license and debit card, and your bikes are registered in your fake names. Check the lanyard wrapped around the handlebars for the details. Okay, are we all good to go?"

Everyone nodded or murmured assent.

"Then let's saddle up and get going."

The team moved quickly. Anton approached his bike and pocketed the lanyard with his new driver's license and debit card. He mounted the motorcycle, tilted it to the right, lifting the kick stand with his heel. He hit the starter button and the engine fired into life. He glanced at the metadata streaming down the sides of his Order nightglasses. The bike had a top-speed of a hundred and thirty miles per hour, and a maximum range of three hundred miles. It was already quarter past five in the afternoon. The stop had been necessary to patch up the team, but it'd taken a lot of time.

He looked across at Arthur. His grandfather nodded. It was time to go. He engaged first gear and revved the engine, pulling away from the roadhouse. The pair cut right around the southern end of the roadhouse before turning left onto Utah state route 257, the main road heading south. They quickly accelerated to a hundred and ten miles per hour. They would make the best time they could while they were outside the towns. They would have to stay within the rules. They needed to blend in. A speeding ticket would alert the vampires to their location, and that would be a disaster.

Li's voice came over the tactical link, "Leaving now."

The team were exfiltrating from the roadhouse. What sort of lead they had on the vampires; Anton didn't know.

All he could do was hope they had enough.

* * *

Twin turbines thrummed through the hull with a muted roar.

The osprey II drone descended behind the Black Rock roadhouse, landing halfway between the main building and a pair of railway tracks running north to south. A trio of wheeled legs descended from the main body and planted firmly on the hard ground. The twin turbines on the wings began spooling down. The rear cargo door opened, folding down to the ground beneath the high tail of the craft.

James Haley descended the ramp, fitting a pair of sunglasses to his face. His heavy weapons remained stowed in the drone, he only carried his uprated .45 Glock in a shoulder holster over his combat fatigues. The scopes on the drone had revealed the site was deserted. He glanced at his wrist watch; it was 17:25. The roadhouse's kitchen still showed warmth on the drone's scopes. The Mirovar force team had evacuated the roadhouse recently. James had missed them by less than fifteen minutes.

He'd activated a blanket sweep of the site from five miles out using the drone's sophisticated sensor and computing suite. There was an older model Order sensor array built into the building. James had disabled it remotely before landing the drone. The cameras installed in the roadhouse would continue recording, but couldn't see his drone, the chameleons or himself.

They were as ghosts pursing the Mirovar force team.

The chameleons followed him out of the drone and into the late afternoon sunlight bathing the roadhouse. They lifted their pale-gray snouts, sniffing the air. Rising to their full height they stared at the horizon. James figured they could see in spectra beyond normal limits, both infra-red and ultraviolet. His orders were clear. Re-establish contact with the Mirovar force team, maintain stealth and determine where they were taking the Panopticon.

That is, find the bastards and avoid discovery and death while doing it. They were simple enough orders to follow while the Mirovar force team were doing their best to get away. James walked through the rear door of the roadhouse, pushing his sunglasses up to rest on his crew-cut scalp. He walked past a long room with an open and empty gray cabinet, a kitchen redolent with old cooking smells, and into the main dining room.

There were a couple of chairs covered with blood-stained sheets. IV poles stood nearby, empty fluid bags and IV lines dangling from them. Bloodied swabs and fragments of gray metal littered the floor. The Mirovar force team had taken some injuries. There was another table with the scattered remnants of a small feast. James sniffed the food. It was still fresh. He lifted a ham, cheese and egg sandwich. The aromas of fresh egg and ham making him salivate. He put the sandwich down. There was no guarantee the Order hadn't poisoned what they'd left behind.

There was a lot of circumstantial evidence to suggest the Mirovar force team had used the site. They'd fed, drunk, got patched up for whatever injuries they'd sustained at the Panopticon fortress, and then bugged the hell out of there. James turned on his heel and strode back out of the roadhouse, dropping his sunglasses back into place as he stepped out into the late afternoon sunlight. It was time to find out what the chameleons had discovered.

The three chameleons stood in a triangle facing each other. The two males focusing with sharp intensity on Shemina.

James froze. Were the two males about to attack the lone female?

Shemina bowed low, like a seven and a half feet tall ballerina pretending to be a swan, and made a soft, low coughing sound for almost a minute.

He didn't move. The males were not about to attack. No, this was something entirely different.

Gullette and Kavanne gave a loud croak in unison. Shemina rose to her full height, gave a long coughing cry and then settled back to her normal resting-alert posture. Her eyelids dropped halfway over her eyes and she studied James with a slight smile lifting the edges of her lipless mouth. The two males flicked their heads around and stared through him. James stood reflected in their black eyes, a military statue staring back at them, his face pale with fear.

He lifted his right foot and backed carefully away. If the male chameleons were about to get feisty with each other over the female, he didn't want to get in their way, or become a snack the victor offered to the lucky girl.

Gullette shifted on his feet, his tail lashing once. He lifted his right hand, his long fingers uncurling like an alien machine. "What you see? Nothing important." The chameleon paused for a long moment and stared silently at James, a thin line of drool dangling from between his shark-like teeth.

James stared up into the big lizard's great yellow eyes. The message was clear. Gullette raised his head an inch and finished with, "Search complete."

"What did you find?" James asked quietly, just managing to keep his composure.

Gullette flung his right hand out, pointing east along Black Rock road. "Four go there." He turned to the south to look down Utah state route 257 and said, "Six, all changed, and one not."

"Six?" James asked, nonplussed.

Gullette nodded. James allowed himself a grim smile. One of the Mirovar force team was missing – did they leave someone behind at the fortress? Did they have a casualty? His smile evaporated. Had they split up?

"What sort of transport?"

Kavanne mimicked perfectly the sound of motorcycles.

"Motorcycles?"

Gullette nodded.

"How long ago?"

Gullette smiled and held up ten fingers.

Excellent, the Mirovar force team had left ten minutes ago, riding motorcycles south on Utah state route 257. They possibly had an Order helper with them. Another four Order helpers had left to the east. And it looked like they had taken a casualty or split up. He'd report back to Chloe and await orders.

As for the chameleons and their strange behavior, he'd wait until he was well and truly alone with Chloe before mentioning it. What was it? His best guess was a mating ritual, and with two males and one female – that could only spell trouble.

"Back to the drone," James declared, moving past the chameleons and up the ramp. He settled into the pilot's chair, opened the drone's communication console, composed a brief report and sent it to Chloe.

"Now," he whispered to himself. "She wanted a micro-tag." He reached for his combat bag, searched briefly inside it and withdrew a small black box marked with Shadowstone technical directorate symbols.

He was ready for the next step in Chloe's plan.

* * *

James Haley's report flashed across the command drone's screens.

The report read, '17:31:24. Six Ramp masters identified fleeing south along Utah state route 257. Estimated to be currently located north of Milford and using motorcycles for transport. Five Order helpers identified. Four heading east on Black Rock road, and one heading south with the Ramp masters. Roadhouse on the intersection of Utah state route 257 and Black Rock road identified as an Order safe house. Order Sensor array identified and disabled. Suggest that the Mirovar force team have taken a casualty or split up. Remaining on site pending further orders.'

Chloe arched her eyebrows and declared, "Haley has done well."

"Outstanding," Crane enthused sardonically, a dry note entering his voice. "However, while I find this sudden advance welcome. It does seem," he spread his hands wide, "overly fortuitous. I'm at a loss to explain how James Haley could find so quickly what we could not."

"For many years, James Haley was our best Shadowstone operative."

Crane frowned. "It seems insufficient."

"Perhaps this is simply a fortunate turn of events?"

Crane stared at Chloe and declared, "I haven't survived nine centuries by being lucky." He steepled his fingers and looked over them at her. "However, we will take this discovery on face value and monitor what happens. It seems the Mirovar force team has taken a casualty. Do you concur?"

Chloe nodded. "Arthur Slayne is the only operative likely to go off on their own. As a strategy, it would lower the risk of us finding him, but increase the risk of us killing him if we do discover him. It is difficult to assess his options in this instance."

Crane looked into the distance for a moment and stated decisively, "He will stay with the team. Proceed on the basis they have taken a casualty."

Chloe wanted to say, 'One for team vampires,' because it would irritate Crane enormously if she did so, but she held her tongue and said instead, "Four helpers have left for the east. Shall we pursue them?"

"No."

"What if they have the P-Case?"

Crane paused for a moment. "Slayne will keep the P-Case with him. He will not trust the care of the Panopticon to another."

"You are certain of this?"

Crane stared at her for a moment, as if considering his answer. "Yes."

I'm not allowed to ask how he knows this, Chloe thought. "Do we take them on the road?"

"We have to preserve the safety of the Panopticon. That rules out aerial bombardment by our shadowstars. We will have to fight hand to hand, and this team has defeated nearly thirty fully armed praetorians today. We have too few praetorians left to ensure an overwhelming force and none to waste. No, your first proposal is a good one. We will raise a militia army and destroy them at their exfil location. They are heading to an airport northeast of Las Vegas; we only need to identify it and marshal our forces there before they arrive."

Crane waved his hand over the display screen and a detailed map appeared. He stabbed a location to the southwest and suggested, "Somewhere here, there is an airport."

Chloe's fingers flashed over a keyboard and the map expanded to much finer detail. She looked at the screen for a second and stated, "There is a privately-owned airport just northeast of the intersection of US route 93 and Interstate 15 in Nevada."

"Yes," Crane nodded decisively, tapping the airport on the display screen with a long pale finger. "That's where we will find Slayne and the Panopticon. We can get our militia to converge in sunlight protected aircraft and land at the airport." He glanced at a clock on the screen. "Sunset is at 19:43, a little over two hours from now. How many covens have we woken up?"

Chloe answered, "Fourteen. We have forty-seven registered vampires ready to go within a thousand miles of Las Vegas."

"We have a target. Get them moving, and make sure they bring every wannabe vampire they can find. I want three hundred plus vampires on the ground by sunset." Crane smiled grimly. "It'll be a meat grinder, but we can use the militia to exhaust their Ramp capabilities, then attack them with our fresh praetorians when they are at their weakest." He nodded quietly. "Yes, first we exhaust them, then we overwhelm them."

Chloe nodded, and hid her concerns. Her proposal for raising a vampire militia might actually work. She silently prayed Arthur Slayne had sent the P-Case away with the Order helpers. If he still had it with him, Crane could retrieve it and re-establish the Panopticon before the next dawn and she'd lose her opportunity to seize back the initiative.

She looked past Crane for a moment. There was another opportunity rising amongst the chaos. In the hurly-burly of a battlefield, her pet chameleons could move like ghosts. Chloe needed to separate the Panopticon from both Slayne and Crane, perhaps the creatures could play a pivotal role in the drama that would soon unfold. It remained to be seen if Slayne still possessed the Panopticon. He was a wily opponent. If she were in his shoes, she would have passed the Panopticon off to another and then led her pursuers away from it. She pursed her lips. Of course, she would then lead her opponents to a suitable field of combat and chop them into small pieces with the Red Dragon. But Arthur Slayne wasn't her, what would he do?

She focused back on Crane and asked, "Are you certain this is a trap?"

"Undoubtedly, it's a trap."

Chloe smiled. "And your plan is?"

"Well, not to spring it." He waved his hand across the desolation of the Panopticon fortress. "Look at this. Slayne has smashed the fortress, he clearly had a way in and an Order helper on the inside." Crane shook his head. "How did that happen? Then he guts half the remaining praetorians in North America, and steals the Panopticon. I'm sure I know where every damn quantum processor on the planet is, and he doesn't have any. So, he can't be intending to set up the Panopticon as his own system. No, it's bait – pure and simple. His targets are you and me. He wants to cut off the head of the snake."

Chloe shrugged. "Well, you could be right."

Crane grinned derisively and steepled his fingers. He stared into her eyes. "I'm going to stake your life on it."

Chloe arched an eyebrow and said in a low mocking tone, "Indeed."

"You really are a piece of work," Crane declared, a dark intensity lighting his eyes.

Chloe looked at him in silence. Crane needed her and he admired her skills. There was nothing else between them.

Crane's face darkened. "No, this mysterious trap of Slayne's will become his grave. We'll play along while we put our temporary army in place, then let him draw us in before we turn the tables against him and destroy him utterly." He collapsed his steepled fingers and tapped his thumbs against his lips. "The next few hours will decide more than all the conflict of the last century. By the dawn, the Panopticon will be restored, the Order all but destroyed, and the Slayne's extinguished from the planet."

Chloe nodded; he could well be right. She suggested, "We could relocate to the Order safe house and land. We could save fuel while the militia mobilize and converge on Slayne's airport."

Crane nodded. "It's as good a place as any, make it so."

"Yes, Sir," Chloe replied, a slight smile gracing her lips.

Now it was time for James and the chameleons to show their worth.

* * *

The hangar doors slammed shut, plunging the interior into dimly lit gloom.

A long heavily-shielded limousine pulled to a halt before a private jet with blackened windows. The doors of the long black car opened and four people emerged from the cabin. They were uniformly pale of skin, youthful, beautiful, richly dressed and adorned with top-end sunglasses.

Tamsah al Ramil, aka 'the Sand Crocodile,' had been tracking this vampire coven since arriving in Portland before dawn. The Red Empire had identified a number of covens in North America over the last five decades. The Portland coven was a listed target awaiting the opportunity to send a fist team. The heavy presence of the Vampire Dominion in the United States had limited the feasibility of inserting a team to destroy the coven. A fact Tamsah welcomed as he'd lost contact with the truth speaker after the daylight battle in Minneapolis the day before.

The previous day, he'd killed four of the strangely enhanced Shadowstone troopers, and a squad of praetorians in the sewers beneath the Order conclave hall to enable the truth speaker to escape. He'd then exploited old contacts to use Red Empire assets active on the West Coast of the United States to locate the Portland coven. He still had status on the Red Empire networks as an undercover operative. His conversion to a vampire remained a well-kept secret from his former comrades. The Red Empire would seek to bring him back into the fold now the secret alliance with Armitage was over. However, if they found out he'd become a vampire they would seek to deceive, trap, and kill him. He wondered what had happened to the other Red Empire operatives assigned to Armitage. If she had forbidden them to contact the Red Empire, they would remain ignorant of the truth and continue to obey her orders.

Tamsah had stayed hidden at Portland International Airport as the day dawned, and the sun crept over the sky. The latest news reports on his smartphone told of the eruption of a new volcano in Utah, south of Salt Lake City. An eruption assumed by serious-faced reporters to be due to natural geological forces. No, the news reports were propaganda promulgated by the Vampire Dominion and their agents in the PSYOPS directorate of Shadowstone. Instead of a natural event, the remnants of the Order had staged an attack on a Vampire Dominion facility.

He'd radically overshot his mark, ending up in Portland, Oregon instead of a valley southwest of the regional city of Lehi in Utah. Still, all was not lost. As a member of the elite leadership cadre of the Red Empire, Tamsah had participated in multiple war games to evaluate conflict scenarios with the Vampire Dominion and the Order of Thoth. Crane had lost praetorians in Minneapolis, and no doubt had lost more in Utah. One question that had stimulated vigorous debate was Crane's willingness or lack thereof to raise a vampire militia to replenish his losses in the event of losing large numbers of praetorians.

Now, it seemed that events were producing that exact scenario. Tamsah had originally considered stealing the Portland coven's private jet, but now it looked a lot more feasible to simply hitch a ride. The Vampire Dominion militia would take him to the Mirovar force team, and back into the presence of the truth speaker.

He reflected upon the truth speaker; a young Order operative named Li Wu. Armitage had established an elaborate gossamer trap for her within the dungeon beneath her manor house in Northern England. Armitage and her henchman Marcus Drake had converted his fist team and himself into abominations. She had ordered them to dress as praetorians and conduct a bizarre theater of murder in front of the rest of the Mirovar force team. At the final moment, Li Wu had looked into his eyes with proud defiance and filled him with the most dreadful shame. Her words seared into his soul, *'Who are you? You're not a praetorian.'* She was right in the deepest way possible. She had spoken the most profound truth while staring with courage into the face of death.

The shame had been overwhelming. He'd used the strike of hidden death to fake her execution and she had survived, borne away from the dungeons by her team mates. From that night on, he'd devoted his life to her protection. His destiny bound to the truth speaker in an unshakable bond of honor. He lived for her honor for he had none himself – for no vampire could have honor.

Tamsah returned his attention to the Portland coven. His strategy for re-establishing contact with the truth speaker was to infiltrate the vampire community and follow trouble to its source.

A dapper young man, dressed in upmarket casual wear and the finest Italian shoes read a message on his smartphone. He turned to the other three and declared, "We have new orders from the Dominion. We have to go to a private airport northeast of Las Vegas."

"And what of our familiars and their poor ignorant friends?" a tall, slim brunette asked with mock concern, shrugging her shoulders and opening her hands wide.

"They'll be arriving shortly," replied the dapper man. "We'll convert them here before we fly."

"Oh, darling," the brunette remarked flamboyantly, "tonight will be such a delightful soiree!"

"Exactly," the dapper vampire agreed with a grin. "There will be hundreds of us versus a handful of them. The lucky few who arrive first will feast on their blood tonight."

The third vampire smirked, his full lips parting around perfect teeth. "There was a great victory yesterday morning. Crane has smashed the Order forever."

"There are only a few stragglers left to mop up," the fourth vampire remarked, casually leaning against the limousine and lighting a cigarette.

The vampires grinned at each other.

Tamsah emerged from the shadows and strode confidently toward them. He was clad in close-fitting dark clothes and a matte-black leather jacket. His pair of blackened twelve-inch tri-bladed knives securely hidden next to his ribs.

The nearest pair whirled around, all their smiles vanishing. The dapper vampire snapped, "Who the hell are you?"

With their supernaturally keen senses the recognition of Tamsah's vampire status was a foregone conclusion. He was betting on it. He needed quick acceptance, and to fit in with the coven. The last thing they would expect would be that he was a former operative of the Red Empire.

"I hear there's a fight coming up," Tamsah stated.

The vampires stared at him for a moment. The dapper vampire inquired, "You've seen the broadcast from Crane's citadel?"

"Yes," Tamsah lied. "But I lack transport."

The brunette sniffed imperiously. "You seem oddly ill-equipped for a vampire."

Tamsah raised a quizzical eyebrow. "I like to travel light."

The fourth vampire pushed himself off the limousine and suggested, "If there wasn't a war on, we'd send you on your way. Oregon is our territory."

Tamsah raised his open hands to shoulder height and said calmly, "Of course, I'm not a poacher."

The dapper vampire stated, "None of that matters now. You can come with us. The more the merrier." The dapper man's smartphone pinged and he glanced at it. "The familiars and wannabes are arriving by minibus now."

"Fabulous," the brunette remarked breathily. "I'm really quite parched."

Tamsah prepared to participate in the feast. He wanted to be at his best in the coming battle. The truth speaker deserved nothing less than everything he had to offer her.

A side door opened, a bright splash of sunlight cutting through the gloom. A line of well-dressed, clean-cut, young men and women walked through the doorway and into the hangar. There were twenty-six of them, they doffed their sunglasses, blinking and murmuring excitedly at the vampires waiting in the shadows.

The Vampire Dominion would harvest thirteen new vampires in the next ten minutes. The rest would be food. The Portland coven would bring seventeen vampire militia to the coming fight, and one former Red Empire operative of the second rank.

Tamsah bared his fangs.

***

The blood thief's aircraft descended on jets of blue flame.

Gullette stood in the shadows next to the osprey II drone. Kavanne and Shemina rested inside the vehicle. Meat-that-talks, the prey animal that worked for the blood thief had given him a task. It was simple enough, deposit a tiny dot of technology smaller than the tip of his smallest finger upon the landing strut at the front of the nearest drone.

Gullette's skin tingled constantly, maintaining the trick of light that rendered him invisible to all but the blood thief. He crossed the forty yards to the drone, reached down and pressed the dot against the metal surface of the front strut supporting the craft. The dot gripped the metal with minuscule clamps, tiny screws automatically penetrating the surface of the strut. A moment later, the surface of the dot changed color to match the surface of the strut and the dot vanished from view.

Gullette stepped away. The blood thief was tracking the movements of the craft. She must expect its pilot would go somewhere interesting, somewhere secret. The vampire general answered to one entity alone – the king of the vampires. Her treacherous nature stood revealed. As expected, the vermin breathed nothing but treachery, but advantage lay in anticipation of deceit. She would lie to them, she would attempt to deceive them, but in the end, he would turn the tables and defeat the blood thief.

He retreated up the ramp and into the cool shadows of the cargo bay of the osprey II drone. His nostrils flared at the faint whiff of Shemina's female glands. She was entering her reproductive cycle. He stared at Kavanne, who stared back, his nostrils flaring with barely restrained threat. The spines on Kavanne's long arms and down his back began to bristle. His long talons emerging from his fingers for the death strike.

Gullette leaned forward, humming low in his throat. A rich, complex melody filled the cabin for ten seconds, and Kavanne quieted, his talons and spines retreating to a relaxed posture.

Gullette blinked in the gloom, his head bobbing forward and back. The song had worked this time, but as the mating instincts waxed over the next few weeks, the song would lose its potency as a greater power overwhelmed it. It had been two thousand years since the last mating cycle of the people.

While he welcomed the opportunity to spawn an egg, the timing was terrible. He needed Kavanne to help defeat the blood thief. It would lower the risk if there were two of the People. She'd already killed one of their number, one whose name they could no longer voice, and he was loathe to risk Shemina in combat with the vampire general.

He needed events to move quickly or he'd lose the opportunity to bring the People back to primacy on this world.

And if Gullette didn't win, what did the future hold?

Nothing but extinction.

Chapter Twelve

"All conception of horror is defeated by the possible realities hidden within reach of the Metaframe. It is imperative that no one ever accesses the Metaframe again. Further change could unleash worlds of darkness, chaos and evil beyond anyone's imagination."

– An entry dated [REDACTED], 1945. Cornelius Crane's personal notebook kept in his secret library

* * *

Utah, Enoch, September 11th, 18:01

The late afternoon sun cut long shadows through the gas station.

Three young men whooped and jeered. The driver floored the big V8 engine of their Ford pickup truck. The light-blue truck spun its wheels across the concrete as it veered onto the main road. Once on the bitumen, the wheels got traction and the truck took off with a roar.

Li arched an eyebrow at the rapidly vanishing vehicle, and wondered briefly at how frivolous people could be. The sound of rushing fuel peaked within the motorcycle's gas tank. She lifted the fuel nozzle and slotted it back into its holder on the gas pump.

She flipped the cap closed and glanced around. Peter, Chiara and herself had decided to refuel at the first opportunity. They now had plenty of juice to reach Slayne's airport with some to spare if trouble showed up. They had covered seventy-two miles from the Black Rock roadhouse in a little over forty-five minutes and were making excellent progress. She swiped Slayne's debit card over a reader and paid for the fuel. The fake identity provided by Slayne stood the test and the transaction went through.

Li pivoted, lifting her left leg to mount the bike. The world tilted, a sudden wave of dizziness washing over her, and she fell back down to the cold concrete between her bike and the gas pump. Somewhere in the distance someone called her name.

She blinked, rising to her elbows. The world flipped to a photographic negative, all the shadows glowing with their own light, and then snapped back into something that resembled the real world. Her breath rasped in her ears. Her heart thudded in her chest. The lights of the Enoch gas station continued to shine but no one was home.

Li leaped to her feet and looked around in growing terror. The dizziness had vanished along with everyone else. Peter and Chiara, other drivers, the gas station staff were all gone. The road past the station was empty of traffic and the town of Enoch lay as silent as a tomb.

A familiar voice not heard for years called out behind her, "Hi, Sis."

Li whirled around. Standing ten feet away was a young man with dark brown eyes, spiky gelled hair, and an insouciant grin. It was her dead brother Qiang, dressed in the street casual clothes he was wearing the last time she'd seen him alive. Love burst through her heart. She took a step forward and whispered past a half-choked sob, "Qi?"

Qi took a step back, maintaining the distance between them.

Li pulled to a stop, her chest heaving. Disappointment flooded her. "This isn't real."

Qi tilted his head and declared, "Everything you perceive is real somewhere."

Li frowned. "You're not my brother."

"I could be. I could be anything you wanted me to be." His features twisted, melting like wax. He shrank, dropping six inches, his clothing transforming into a pleasant dress. Li looked upon her mother with horror.

"This is no good," her mother stated authoritatively. Her features melted. Her clothes transformed. A moment later Qi's smile twisted into a derisive grin. "You carry a blindness within you. Give up the witch's infernal flame and see me truly."

"No!" Li shouted. She reached for the Green Dragon, her hand clutching empty air. She looked down at her waist. The Green Dragon and its scabbard were gone.

"Such distrust," Qi remarked, his voice reflecting her brother's tone of voice perfectly. "Do you really believe your blade would work here?"

Li centered herself, drawing upon Juliette's legacy. She raised her right hand drawing a broad circular arc. Golden light flared around her, expanding outward in a protective sphere.

Qi watched her, raising a quizzical eyebrow, a slight smile curling the edges of his mouth. The edge of the golden sphere stopped about halfway between them. His gaze intensified and he started walking toward her.

Naked panic screamed at the back of Li's mind. The need to flee flooded her soul. She stood fast, barely managing to hold back the waves of terror assaulting her.

Qi's eyes sparkled. His shadow writhed behind him, drawing inhuman shapes upon the pale concrete. He stepped through the boundary of the sphere. Golden fire played in a narrow halo around his body, pale wisps of smoke rising from his form. His face froze for a moment, then the sphere contracted with a snap. He approached calmly and halted just beyond her reach.

Cold terror ran a thousand knives through Li's heart. She gasped out, "You're filth."

"Your perspective is twisted by Thoth's legacy," Qi declared. He reached out his right hand and implored, "Put your cursed burdens down." He brought his hands in, pointing to his heart. "All that you have lost can be restored."

Grief wracked her, as fresh as the day she stood at her mother and Qiang's gravesides, and the night when she held her father's hand on the dock in Boston.

"You don't have to be alone, Li. I can bring them back as if they'd never left."

Li sobbed, tears streaming down her cheeks, she whispered between gasps, "No … No … No."

Qi implored, "Free yourself from false masters and embrace the truth."

She sobbed again, then spat angrily, "There's no truth in you."

"No, truth?" Qi wagged his finger at her, his dark eyes regarding her avidly. "Let me prove my good faith by warning you of your future." Qi's shadow twisted behind him, stretching and darkening with fell power. He waved his hands sharply aside and snapped with quiet intensity, "This, will come to pass."

The gas station and the town whirled and disappeared, and Qiang Wu vanished with them.

Night swept over the world. Li floated like a ghost a foot above a tarmac runway. Thirty feet away, Justin Blake and three others battled a small army of rabid, screaming vampires. The world twisted away … she hovered in mid-air over a pile of smoking rubble. Crane stood glaring at a distant Blake force team, armed with shoulder launched surface to air missiles, he whispered, "Fire." The world twisted away again … she stood beneath the wide-open doors of a hangar. Four hypersonic missiles speared toward her. In the middle of the airport, four more detonated just above the Blake force team in blinding flashes.

The gas station snapped back around her. She lay on her left side in the recovery position and someone's leather jacket served as a rough pillow beneath her left cheek. She blinked and turned onto her back.

Peter was squatting next to her head and asked with a voice filled with concern, "Are you okay? You cried out in pain."

"I think so." Li replied, rising to her feet, wiping stray tears from her cheeks.

Peter picked up his jacket and stood up. Chiara looked across Li's motorcycle and stated, "Nothing on the perimeter."

"How long was I out?"

"About a minute," Peter answered, putting his leather jacket on over his weapons vest. "What happened? Did you have a vision?"

Li nodded.

Peter and Chiara looked at her expectantly.

Li shook her head. "I don't know if what I saw will happen but it looks bad."

"Sounds like business as usual," Peter remarked with a shrug.

Li looked at him and smiled weakly. "My first vision about everyone dying in the Panopticon fortress didn't come true."

Chiara said, "Thankfully."

"So, why should this one?" Li asked.

Peter put his hand on her shoulder and gave her a reassuring squeeze. "Perhaps it's more a case of seeing risk, and we can mitigate risks. Don't underestimate the impact of your own actions in the fortress. You delayed the praetorians and allowed us to get into position. You cracked open their core network and helped everyone escape. Without your actions, the mission would have failed and we'd all be dead."

"Francis still died," she stated sadly.

"Not your fault, Li. You did everything you could do."

Li pursed her lips. "Maybe you're right."

"Are we okay?" Chiara asked. "We need to get going."

Li nodded and mounted her bike. She glanced down; the Green Dragon remained strapped securely to the side of the bike. A handful of seconds later, she was following Chiara out of the gas station. Peter followed, watching her back. Whatever had just happened, she couldn't trust a vision inspired by a fake Qi. Was it really Set who was wearing her brother's form? If it was Set, why was a god paying her so much attention? What could a god possibly want from her?

Li shivered. Nothing good could come from this. Her defensive sphere had barely slowed him down. If he was so strong, why hadn't he been able to attack her in the Panopticon fortress main server room? Her mind clicked like a snapping trap. The quantum processors, she'd been in union with them, but now they were gone and the power they had lent her was gone with them.

She needed to find a new way to defend herself and soon.

* * *

Paragraphs of sharp white letters scrolled down the command drone's screens.

Chloe collated the police reports at a glance and declared, "We have six riders spread across a five-to-ten-minute window. They completed passage through the towns of Enoch at 18:04, Beryl Junction at 18:32, and they should arrive in Panaca at 19:00 give or take five minutes."

Crane raised an eyebrow and asked sardonically, "Why do I need the Panopticon when I have you?"

Chloe looked at him askance and raised her hands with a shrug. "I doubt I can be both a glorified computer and your chief enforcer at the same time."

"Indeed," Crane stated with a half-smile, "and what of the Order helpers?"

"They have all vanished."

Crane pressed his lips together and snapped, "It matters not. We will pursue Slayne into his trap and turn his strategy against him. What is the status of the militia?"

"Your army grows. New reports sent from the citadel indicate a total of nineteen covens for sixty-two registered vampires. They are bringing their familiars and wannabes with them. Total conversions amount to another four hundred and twelve vampires for a total of—"

"Four hundred and seventy-four," Crane said. "Slayne and the Mirovar force team have never seen such a force before."

Chloe arched a questioning eyebrow.

"They will be tactically unprepared," Crane said with a wave of his hand. "The new vampires have all recently fed, but their blood lust is still fresh and easily stimulated. They will be both strong and well-motivated. They will make perfect shock troops," he frowned momentarily. "Ensure the registered vampires are provided with clear descriptions of the P-Case to pass onto their new coven members. Whomever captures the P-Case and returns it intact," he raised an eyebrow and grinned slyly, "will be greatly rewarded."

"A reward?"

"A territory for their coven without restriction on hunting."

"You have somewhere in mind?"

He snorted. "Eastern Europe."

"It'd be a death sentence. Unrestricted hunting would draw the attention of the Red Empire. A new vampire would be lucky to last more than two weeks in Eastern Europe."

"Indeed," Crane remarked with a sardonic grin. He left unsaid that the new vampires would have little real understanding of the ruthless threat the Red Empire posed to their continued existence. Crane's gaze intensified. "Of course, there will be no vampire survivors of the coming battle apart from my praetorians and ourselves." Crane sniffed and shook his head once. "Humans that want to be vampires mystify me. They have no idea of how the world really works. They imagine they will be immortal, powerful, and able to act on their whims. The reality is far from their expectations. These covens we have drawn to this fight, and their familiars and wannabes disgust me." Crane paused for a moment. "Promise them a great reward. In the end it will all be for naught," he shook his head and spread his hands wide, "by the time this battle is done they will all be dead."

Chloe nodded. She had long despised wannabe vampires. The vast majority reeked with selfish, short-sighted needs and vile urges. In her long vampire life, she'd not found a single one with a vision to match the opportunity of immortality. Certainly, none possessed a vision to match her own. She stated, "The militia will be in place before Slayne and the Mirovar team arrive. We'll disperse each coven to a different hidden location at the airport. The citadel staff have assigned them to waves, so we can mass their attacks when needed."

"Monitor progress and ensure there are no unforeseen circumstances."

"Of course," Chloe remarked.

"Our strategy is in motion and now we wait." Crane lifted an eyebrow and inquired, "What is the modern phrase? Ahh, yes, 'The ball is in their court.'"

Chloe responded with a slight smile, giving nothing away. The vampire militia were flying into Slayne's airport northeast of Las Vegas. Slayne and the Mirovar force team were going to arrive after sunset. The militia would park their aircraft out of sight in the hangars and then take position ready to attack. No doubt, Slayne would have prepositioned an Order sensor array at the airport to forewarn him of the arrival of the vampires.

How would he respond? If he proceeded into the airport, he either had a massive ace up his sleeve or he was willing to risk suicide.

Chloe frowned slightly. She couldn't be sure what was going to happen. She took a breath, released it and centered herself. The battle would go to whomever could best adapt to changing circumstances.

Her frown vanished; she was the most adaptable player in the game.

* * *

A message scrolled down Arthur Slayne's Order nightglasses.

The letters and numbers gleamed bright red against the surrounding night. Arthur feathered the throttle of his motorcycle, dropping his speed down to seventy miles per hour. He glanced back at the display. The message read, '20:03:14: Multiple contacts. Multiple incoming tracks. Landing aircraft imminent, list follows.' A list of aircraft model and registration numbers scrolled across his view, thirty-four in total. There was no chance the aircraft were arriving by accident. Vampires were arriving at his airport in overwhelming numbers.

A wave of satisfaction washed through him. This was meant to happen. Despite his best efforts, Crane and Armitage had discovered he was leading his grandson and the Mirovar force team to the airport.

The warmth flowing through him jarred and tore, evaporating away. He feathered the throttle again, downshifting through the gears and sloughing off speed. A cold shiver ripping through his heart.

Anton appeared beside him. His grandson let go of his handlebars and lifted his hands in an obvious, 'what's the matter?' gesture. His dark full-face helmet hiding any expression.

Arthur started to pull his motorcycle to a halt. They needed to rethink the exfiltration. They couldn't simply drive into an airport that could be holding three hundred plus vampires. His decision lasted for less than a second before it vanished into shadow. He twisted the throttle, the motorcycle's engine roared and the bike leaped forward.

A new imperative flooded his mind. He had to take the second P-Case to the airport. Crane and Armitage would come for it and the final end game would begin. The compulsion was familiar, he'd laid it upon himself during the partition of his mind. He must have anticipated he'd have second thoughts about the strategy and put in a number of insurance policies against the possibility of his own rebellion.

How do you ignore a command that comes from the deepest version of yourself?

Anton's voice came through the tactical link on a private bi-directional channel. The rest of the team could not hear them. Anton asked, "Arthur, what's up? Is there a problem?"

He heard himself speak before he thought the words. "There are vampires at the airport. Lots of them."

"Oh my God! How do you know?"

"My sensor array has picked up their arrival."

"We'll be there in half an hour. Should we abort? Is there another way?"

Arthur shook his head. "No, there is no other way." He opened up a broadcast channel. "To all members of the Order of Thoth. I am Arthur Slayne, more than three hundred vampires have converged on my airport at the intersection of US route 93 and Interstate 15 in Nevada. I will be there within thirty minutes. We cannot ignore this vampire threat. We must not turn away from this fight – tonight we go to war. Who is with me?"

The silence stretched.

Justin Blake was the first to respond. "The Blake force team will join you. We will bring extra weapons. We have an ETA of 20:30."

There was a long pause, then Jay responded, "We must win through or die. The Mirovar force team are with you."

Jon Thunder-Axe's voice resounded over the line, "Godspeed to you all."

The line went silent. There were no other Order of Thoth left in North America who were able to answer. Arthur said, "There is a gas station and road house opposite the main entrance to the airport on US route 93. We'll stage there."

"On our way," Justin responded.

Arthur accelerated back up to a hundred miles per hour, his grandson pacing beside him. The time for stealth was over, the time for war had begun. He wished he knew what the end game was. What on Earth had he planned? Why had he laid compulsions upon himself? What fate was he leading his grandson and the remnants of the Order to?

A cold sliver of fear rested in the pit of his stomach and wouldn't go away. Whatever happened, he wouldn't sacrifice Anton.

He'd rather die first.

Chapter Thirteen

"Truth is a locked box filled with everything we dare not question." – Arthur Slayne

"If it is imperative that you forget, then have someone else remember it for you." – Arthur Slayne

* * *

Nevada, Arthur Slayne's Private Airport, September 11th, 20:15

Floodlights gleamed off a sleek dark-gray hull. Vertical turbines howled, and rough grass bowed flat beneath the backwash.

The osprey II drone descended to the ground. James brought the drone down well outside the buildings surrounding the 'X' of the airport's runways. The two runways made a sort of squashed cross. The first running one and a half miles long from northwest to southeast. The second running north northeast and south southwest for a mile. He landed the drone in the middle of what could have passed for a sheep paddock, opposite and almost a mile away from the airport's administration building. He was an easy half mile away from rows of hangars clinging to the eastern side of the runway 'X.'

Three long rectangular warehouses stood to the right of the admin building, all marked by heavy steel doors sized for trucks rather than airplanes.

He'd been scanning the site for the last fifteen minutes as he approached it. There was an Order sensor array buried in the admin building. It had taken most of the last fifteen minutes of his drone's approach to hack into it and disable it. It was an up-to-date version of the older sensor array he'd taken down at the Black Rock roadhouse. The drone's sensor and computing arrays were state of the art, and up to the task of disabling the airport's Order security system. He couldn't spoof the new model with a fake feed, and he'd resorted to a hard shutdown. The system would go dark alerting its owners to the fact that it'd failed, but someone would have to manually reboot it before they could use it.

James figured that anyone on site at the airport would be too busy fending off a mass vampire attack to bother with rebooting a system that would simply tell them what they could see with their own eyes. While landing thirty-four private jets without anyone noticing was the preferable option, it was not feasible given the lack of preparation of the site. The

Order would have some idea of what was coming their way, that was a foregone conclusion. Whether they would walk into a suicide battle versus hundreds of vampires was another matter. James refrained from making a judgment call. It was better to wait and see. He had his orders from Chloe and he intended to carry out those orders in full.

He flicked a switch and let down the rear ramp.

One of the chameleons sniffed loudly behind his right ear.

James whirled half out of his seat. His eyes wide. Gullette looked at him with a baleful glare. "Vermin stench. Too many to destroy." He unrolled a long forefinger at James. "Your problem."

James glanced back through the drone's windscreen at the deceptively quiet and well-lit airport. No, the problem belonged to the Mirovar force team.

He was in position with the chameleons, all he had to do now was wait for the 'go,' command from Chloe.

* * *

Tamsah al Ramil studied the vampires crowding the hangar.

Seven private jets, all but one with blacked out windows filled the building. The last jet was long-bodied and sat by itself at the back of the hangar. Standing singularly, in pairs, in small groups surrounding the aircraft, or sitting on the aircrafts' wings were ninety-seven vampires listening to music, smoking cigarettes and drinking alcohol. Ninety-eight including himself.

Tamsah arched a bemused eyebrow. He'd never imagined himself surrounded by so much vile evil. It was either a nightmare of demonic death come to claim him, or an opportunity to spend the last of his heart's blood dealing death to those who deserved it based on their very existence.

He sighed. The evil within these others, their lust for blood, their need to feed on people – these things he must own as well. Whatever evil he saw around him also resided within his own heart.

There was an obvious solution. Simply walk into the dawn and allow the sun to claim him. He had recoiled from the idea of such feckless suicide. He grimaced, he could not claim that his current path was honorable or his rejection of self-slaughter would expiate his vampire shame – for honor remained forbidden to a vampire.

Yes, he'd lost his honor beyond all hope of recovery, but he might redeem his life through faith, an iron-clad purpose and absolute service to justice. The essence of the Way of the Faithful was fearlessness in the face of truth. He could redeem his new half-life from the vile muck in which it lay by protecting the truth speaker. The one who could see truth in a glance and never feared to speak it. The one who'd sparked a righteous fire in his soul that only death could extinguish.

Tamsah relaxed, his spiral tri-edged blades would drink deep tonight. He glanced around at the nearby vampires. One slapped another on the back and made a crude joke about what they could do to the corpses of the Mirovar team. The other responded with an even more abominable suggestion. Both laughed – a cold grating sound.

Tamsah memorized their faces. They would not survive tonight; he would make certain of that. He could not abide such filth to live. He would acquaint them with the sharp edge of his faith. Sharp edges were best for serving justice to the wicked.

He promised to give them all the justice they needed.

Tamsah looked hard at them with eyes flat like dark river pebbles. Truly, he would be generous when the time came.

After all, justice was not a frugal master.

* * *

Two black Chevrolet Suburban SUVs pulled to a halt at the rear of the gas station.

Justin Blake emerged from a front passenger seat, rising to his full six feet, eight inches of height. The skies were clear, a swollen orb of a moon rested over the eastern horizon. A slight breeze hinted at the coming fall. A coyote howled in the distance; a series of short yaps answering it a second later. He took a deep breath of the fresh night air and exhaled mightily. He ran his big hands though his thick head of dark hair, quickly wrapping it into a tight ponytail with a red tie.

He glanced around at the horizon, his eyes missing nothing. He tapped his Order nightglasses. The tactical network ran through a self-diagnostic and reported its good health with a soft chirp.

It was a good night for hunting vampires.

His team emerged from the two vans and circled around him. His eyes flicked across them. They were all ready and poised for a fight. Their weapons waited in the backs of the SUVs. It wouldn't do to scare the locals by wearing them openly. There would be time to arm themselves once they'd established the plan.

Justin's second in command, Samuel Taylor, six-foot-two-inch tall, built like an Olympic gold medalist track and field athlete, with coal-black skin and short, tight, black hair stood opposite him. Standing next to Sam was his constant companion, Taylor Feury. Taylor was an even six-foot tall, an almost white blond, with an innocent face that led people to underestimate his abilities. A warrior specialist, he was the other half of the pair of blademasters known as the Two Taylors. Along with Justin, they were the sharp end of the spear of the Blake force team. In any conflict, they were the first in and the last out. Next to the Two Taylors, stood Tim Leung and Max Guerra, a pair of Californian netmasters who knew more about cyberwarfare than most people had forgotten and who could handle a katana like the veteran vampire slayers they were. Rounding out the team were Red Cevarre, and Patrick Wichowski, a red-headed combat surgeon, and the team's loremaster respectively.

Sam asked, "What do you make of this call?"

Everyone had heard the broadcast request from Arthur Slayne. The Blake force team had diverted from the investigation of a Las Vegas coven of vampires to support the Mirovar force team in a battle against a massive vampire force at Slayne's airfield. They had answered the call and converged behind the gas station opposite the entrance to the airport. Justin replied, "It'll be a real shit storm, but Arthur is right. We can't leave these vampires alive."

Patrick tapped his nightglasses and suggested, "Slayne and the Mirovar force team must be close to arriving."

Justin nodded. The sharp notes of a group of approaching motorcycles cut through the night air. Less than half a minute later, the first of the riders rolled past the north end of the roadhouse behind the gas station. The other five quickly followed after the first rider. Arthur had sent through a private message alerting Justin to the grim news of the death of Francis Mirovar. The pace of the war had accelerated and death was stalking the Ramp masters, ever ready to snatch their lives away in an instant. He'd passed the grim news onto his team, and they had accepted it well enough.

Arthur Slayne and the Mirovar force team rolled to a halt and parked their bikes in a line next to the Blake team's Chevy Suburbans. Arthur got off his bike and strode over to Justin. He gripped his hand firmly and declared, "Thanks for coming. I knew I could rely on you."

Justin grinned and shrugged it off. "I can't turn down the opportunity to kill more vampires in a night than the Order has claimed in the last decade."

Jay approached and shook Justin's hand. "Well met, it looks like we will finally fight together."

Justin's lip curled sardonically. "Let's hope it's not for the last time."

"Amen to that!" Arthur said in heart-felt tones.

Justin stroked his broad chin and then pointed his index finger at Arthur. "Tactics? We've rushed in here. What is the real situation?"

Arthur lifted the P-Case, and showed it to the combined team. "This is the Panopticon in evacuation mode. You will have seen the news. It wasn't a naturally occurring volcano in Utah. The Panopticon fortress has been destroyed. The Mirovar team, and I infiltrated the fortress, stole the Panopticon, and barely escaped with our lives." He patted the P-Case. "Now Crane and Armitage want the Panopticon back. The vampires are here in great numbers precisely because of this P-Case. I've wrapped it in Faraday tape, so they can't track the beacon, but somehow they worked out we were exfiltrating via my airport."

Sam asked, "Have you got any other exfil paths?"

Arthur pursed his lips. "No. We had an advantage of speed and stealth. Somehow, they penetrated our defenses. They picked up our trail and anticipated our destination here in Nevada. We can't simply divert at this time. For the rest of the night, Crane has at least three hundred plus vampires to throw at us or hunt us down. Plus, he's got shadowstars in the air. We have to pull him into a battle here and take his forces down. Then we can fly out before he can respond with further reinforcements."

"There's another issue here," Sam said, "There weren't three hundred plus vampires within flight range of Las Vegas six hours ago. Crane has ordered the creation of a lot of new vampires."

Justin said, "It begs the question. Is Crane still committed to the secrecy of vampires or are we seeing a massive shift in his strategy?"

"Oh my God," Jay swore. "If we do nothing, what is to stop Crane sending all those vampires into Las Vegas just to draw us out against them? That many could kill a thousand people a minute, and keep doing it hour after hour until dawn."

"It's clear we have to go in," Justin stated, "but what if Crane nukes the airport?"

"Well, all bets would be off," Arthur replied. "But he won't do that while we have the P-Case. He wants the Panopticon back. Growing a new AI from scratch would take longer than he can afford. There's something going down in China. Crane's forces are massed over there and I'm sure he's got a powerful need to get the Panopticon back in one piece – and that means one thing and one thing only – hand to hand combat. He can't afford heavy weapons or some fool vampire trashing the P-Case. He's called up a militia force, a bunch of numpties and wannabe vampires who I doubt he'll trust with weapons. He'll throw them at us as cannon-fodder to wear us out."

"So, what do you intend?" Justin asked with a frown.

"We need to break the vampires here and then exfil the country. I have a secret location in South America where I can stage at. The new Order site of the Panopticon is in Hong Kong, but I have to get there first. We have Huawei quantum processors secretly manufactured in China based on stolen US designs, and the latest Hyundai hydrogen fuel-cells to power the site. Once the Panopticon is operational, we can run its feeds via satellite uplinks to our Order nightglasses."

"That's all well and good, but it's a moot point if we don't survive tonight." Justin stabbed Arthur with his gaze and swept his forefinger through the air between them. "What are your immediate plans to get from behind this gas station to inside an aircraft flying out of here?"

"Hold your horses, big fella, there's a bit more to go," Arthur instructed, placing a hand on Justin's shoulder. "They've already disabled my first sensor array about fifteen minutes ago. There is a second array which is currently on standby and the encryption is my own personal suite which will be impossible for them to break without the benefit of the Panopticon's quantum processors. Right now, they think we are blind. Once I switch the second array on, we'll know the full extent and disposition of their forces. Not only that, I can slave the feeds to our Order nightglasses and everyone will have the same tactical information."

"Okay," Justin said. "That's a plus."

"A big plus." Arthur paused for a moment, pursed his lips and waved his hands in circles as if wafting smoke upward between them. "Look, I know this is going to sound strange." A stillness fell over the team. "My plan was always to make a clean getaway with the Panopticon. However, I always build vampire traps wherever I go." Arthur looked across at Li and Anton. "You saw it in Boston. The warehouse on the docks was a big vampire trap. We didn't get as many as we would have liked and lost a great friend too, but that happens in life. Nothing is certain." Arthur looked around the assembled Ramp masters. "Truly, Crane finding us has a massive silver lining if we seize the moment. This is a once in a lifetime opportunity to seriously hurt the Vampire Dominion."

"Team, heads up." Justin stated firmly. He pointed his finger at Arthur. "I've got the context. Let's get the details sorted, the longer we wait the more likely they'll think of a better way to take us all down."

Arthur nodded. "Agreed. It's quite simple really. I have prepared an aircraft in hangar number one on the southeast corner of the runways. It's fully fueled and prepped to go. However, the hangar is swarming with filth."

Sam inquired, "How are we going to get rid of the vampires and shadowstars?"

"A great question," Arthur turned and clasped Jay on the shoulder. "I need your team to go in with me." He raised the P-Case. "This is both a shield and bait. We go into the airport on our motorcycles. The sensor arrays on the drones will pick up we're all Ramp masters, and Crane will send in his militia. I'm not expecting him to send all of them in at once. He'll want to probe us first and see what we've got. I'm sure he doesn't know that Justin and his team are here, but he has to suspect the Blake team could arrive, given we're in Justin's normal area of operations." Arthur grinned. "So, we'll give him what he expects."

Jay frowned momentarily, then nodded. "We go in first and draw their initial force into battle."

Anton stated, "So, we'll be bait to draw the vampires into a fight." He looked across at Peter and smiled a lopsided grin. "Just like England?"

Peter lifted his hands and remarked back at Anton, "I told you it would happen again."

Jay scowled at Anton and Peter, and then asked, "Then what?"

"We head to warehouse number two – which is anything but – it's actually a fortress. I've reinforced the doors to defeat vampires. There are walkways around the inner walls with shooting slits in the walls. There's heaps of spare ammunition and weapons. I have miniguns built into the corners with two thousand rounds of paired silver and lead 7.62mm hollow-point each. There is a cleared four-hundred-yard kill zone around the building. There are fake doors on the roof, but no external access from above. The walls are smooth hard unscalable synthetic rock. The roof is too high to leap up to for a vampire. It's a vampire trap." He waved his hands expansively. "It's designed to draw vampires toward it and then kill them en masse." He wagged his finger at Justin like a school master instructing a student. "This is where we thin their numbers."

"What if they hold back and establish a cordon around your trap?" Justin asked, seeking to explore all angles and cover contingencies.

"There are multiple levels of tunnels beneath the airport. It's a maze that's easy to lose your way in, but if you have a pair of Order nightglasses hooked up to my sensor array you'll be okay, and as backup I have a map application for the nightglasses. We can use the tunnels to get from warehouse number two to hangar number one."

"What's stopping the vampires from swarming through the tunnels and coming up in the middle of your warehouse?" Sam asked.

"One, the entrances are all hidden. Two, if they manage to work out how to access the tunnels and do that, we'll know as my sensor array monitors the tunnels."

"What about shadowstars? Crane, Armitage and the praetorians?" Justin asked. "This won't be happening without Crane's approval. He's going to be all over this."

"I have surface to air missiles."

"Against shadowstars?" Sam asked non-plussed. "They'd have to be kick-ass."

"Shoulder fired evolutions of the Stinger II," Arthur declared. "They have a hypersonic engine. Next to impossible to defend against, and with a two-stage warhead that operates like a shaped charge followed by a thermobaric explosive. They are advanced working prototypes and we have the only ones available in North America."

"How many do you have?" Justin asked, frowning.

"Eight here. In two caches of four each – it should be enough. Crane only has about twelve shadowstar drones worldwide. And over half his fleet is deployed in China. I don't think we'll see more than four drones here."

Justin and Sam nodded.

Jay stated, "There's a lot of moving parts in your plan. This could get real messy real fast."

Arthur turned to Jay and said emphatically, "The bottom line is that we can't let hundreds of vampires leave this site."

"Crane has shifted strategy and is creating vampires in large numbers," Justin stated. "What does he really expect to happen here?"

Arthur shrugged his shoulders and suggested, "Perhaps he's got a plan to get rid of them at the end of the battle, but we can't assume that's the case. If we let these vampires live, they'll kill five hundred to a thousand people a week until they die."

Everyone fell into silence as Arthur's words soaked in. This many vampires were like an appalling disaster happening every week.

Arthur pressed his lips together and declared, "These vampires are like the road toll. If we don't kill them tonight, we are signing death warrants for close to a thousand people every week forever. No one else is here to stop them. No one else could stop them. It falls to us to stop the spread of this evil. To cut it off at the root before it grows beyond this airport. Whatever else you may have achieved in your lives before this night, it will pale into insignificance when compared with what we must do tonight." He tapped his nightglasses and said, "Now look at this."

Arthur's hidden sensor array activated and a virtual tour of Arthur Slayne's airport opened up before Justin's eyes. The rest of the team murmured in the background as they watched the same feed.

Arthur stated, "I've just activated the primary sensor array at the airport. Crane's forces have already shutdown the secondary array. It was a 'lizard's tail,' designed to distract their attention. They will quickly realize that a new sensor array is in operation, but without the quantum processors of the Panopticon they have no hope of breaching my own encryption tonight. We will have dominant situational awareness on the ground."

Views opened up onto the hangars' interiors and the massed vampires within them. Baring praetorians, no one in the combined team had ever seen more than four or five vampires in one location. The Ramp masters fell silent as the enormity of what they faced struck home.

"No one's going to be short of a dance partner tonight," Peter quipped quietly.

No one laughed.

"We go in two teams, two minutes apart," Arthur instructed. "The first team has to be the Mirovar team, as they are expecting us and we will be on our motorcycles. The second team will be," Arthur swung his finger around the Blake force team, "you guys. We'll draw the first attack, and possibly the second. You'll have situational awareness from your Order nightglasses. Be ready to intervene and meet us in warehouse number two. We'll use that as an anvil they can kill themselves on. Once their numbers are well down, we'll cut through the tunnels, pick up the SAMs, take out the shadowstars in a crossfire and get the hell out of Dodge before they call in reinforcements. Now this primary array is operational, download the maze map to your nightglasses. You'll never lose your way down there."

Justin nodded. He'd heard worse plans in his life. He was going to have to stake the survival of his team on Arthur's ingenuity and do his best to carry out the plan. They had some advantages, the key being the Order nightglasses, and Arthur's sensor network, but having great situational awareness might just be a box seat for watching the vampires wipe out the Mirovar and Blake force teams.

A sliver of dread pushed into his gut. No one had fought so many vampires at once. It was unprecedented in the modern history of the Order or the Red Empire. He struggled to recall what he'd learned of medieval and ancient history, but the only thing that came back to him were lots of images of people getting impaled and he wasn't sure if it was the Order or the vampires doing the impaling or the dying.

His team were already supplementing the weapons of the Mirovar force team from their own spares. In less than a minute, the Mirovar team would be on the move, and less than two minutes later so would his own team.

Sam slapped Justin's shoulder and whispered so only he could hear, "It's like any battle, consign your soul to the care of God, and do what you have to do to win."

Justin grinned wholeheartedly and whispered back, "Amen to that."

They stared into each other's eyes for a moment, and then broke contact and looked away at the same time. Would any of them see the dawn? Justin glanced into the feeds flitting over his Order nightglasses like ghosts. The vampire count was above four hundred.

How the hell were they going to kill so many? He frowned, the only answers he had were hard ones.

Justin's lips pressed together into a thin line as the Mirovar and Blake force teams swirled around him. His gut was telling him a basic truth; this mission was going to be a real shit storm.

He trusted his instincts; they had always served him well.

* * *

The other surviving members of the Mirovar force team bustled around the backs of the SUVs, outfitting themselves with new weapons from the Blake force team's abundant stocks.

Jay approached Patrick Wichowski, pulled him aside and asked in a tight whisper, "You're an Order traveler. Have you got Truther?"

Patrick stared at him for a moment, and then said, "Sure."

Jay tightened his grip on Patrick's arm. "When we exfil, I need you to do a Truther inquisition."

"On who?"

"That doesn't matter for now."

Patrick nodded. "It's your team."

"Thanks," Jay replied, and let Patrick go.

He'd get to the truth about Chiara one way or another. He owed Yvette, Juliette and Francis nothing less.

* * *

Multiple displays of the battle space lining the curved walls and ceiling lit the command drone's cabin.

Chloe would have preferred to come to grips with the Mirovar and Blake force teams face to face and blade to blade. However, such an outcome remained momentarily denied to her by Crane's current tactics. However, tactics invariably changed as circumstances evolved – so, there was always hope.

"Let these worthless vampires spring the trap," Crane declared, staring at a display of cool gray blobs massed throughout the airport hangars. "This is why I favor having a small number of long-lived vampires and slow turnover – stability. Look at these new vampires, imagine the chaos if I released them upon the world. Why would they imagine we would value something we can create in five minutes or replace just as quickly?" he shook his head, "and now they are hot to fight the Order and they have no idea of what they face – unbelievable."

Chloe arched an eyebrow and stated, "I always begin with the premise that humans are irrational, it works for me."

Crane grinned in derisive agreement.

The command shadowstar drone circled the airport at a height of two miles. The other three drones carrying the remaining twelve praetorians of Crane's North American forces flanked it in a wide 'V.' The command drone's sensor arrays blanketed the site. It networked with the other three shadowstar drones to produce a comprehensive view of the airport out to a radius of ten miles around it.

Chloe studied the feeds and the disposition of forces. A red light started flashing in the middle of the admin building. Metadata scrolled through a window next to it. There was a second Order sensor array and it had just become active. She dialed James' number. He picked up the call and she inquired, "Have you seen this new sensor array?"

"Yes. Running penetration algorithms now."

"Have you got an estimate on how long it will take to bring it down?"

"No," James answered. He paused for a second. "It's got a bitch of an encryption layer."

"Keep trying, we need it—"

Crane snapped, "Bring it down Haley. If need be, go in there and rip it apart."

After a brief hesitation, James replied, "Yes, Sir. I'll reposition the osprey to the administration building's parking lot and access the array directly."

"Be quick about it," Crane demanded. "When this battle starts, it will move fast. Now, take out their damn eyes."

"Understood, Sir. Firing up our engines now."

Chloe pursed her lips. James was her asset; it wasn't for Crane to reach past her and order him about. But there was nothing she could do about it. The osprey II drone and the chameleons would be closer to the action then she'd like, but behind the admin building would still keep them out of the direct line of fire.

Crane asked, "Have all the vampires been assigned to waves?"

"Yes," Chloe answered. Unlike James, she could get away with not saying 'Sir.' "First wave is thirty-seven, second wave is sixty-two, third wave is a hundred and sixty, and the fourth wave is two hundred and fifteen."

"Excellent," Crane enthused, "The aim is to exhaust their weapons, get them to expend their silver rounds and deplete their capability to Ramp. Each wave will be bigger, until they fall. Then we swoop in and take back what is ours. Then we stand off and pound this site into rubble with hypersonic cruise missiles."

Chloe didn't bother to answer. The silence stretched. The scopes displayed the osprey II drone taking off and swinging low over the airport toward the parking lot behind the administration building.

A set of six yellow markers appeared on the screens. Motorcycle riders were passing through the main entrance of the airport and riding in two files down the singular road into the airport. They would ride directly past the main parking lot behind the admin building.

Chloe remarked, "James, the Mirovar force team is entering the airport."

"Yes, Ma'am," he replied. "I've got them on my scopes now. Rising out of range of small arms and RPGs." The osprey II rose in the air. The metadata numbers beside the image on the screen rising rapidly as the craft climbed vertically under full power. The Mirovar force team rode past the administration building without slowing down and turned left as a group toward a trio of widely spaced warehouses on the western side of the airport.

Crane declared, "Only the Mirovar force team is visible. Send in the first wave. Let's see who we can draw out of hiding."

Chloe sent the command. The first wave of vampires would originate from a hangar almost eight hundred yards opposite the administration building. They would come upon the Ramp masters from their right rear flank. The hangar doors swung open. The thirty-seven vampires blurred from the building. It would take them a little under thirty seconds to cross the open space to engage the Mirovar force team.

The battle was about to begin.

* * *

The deserted two-story administration building loomed on the right. Beyond it were a pair of runways and a number of hangars. On the left, three large, rectangular warehouses stood in a row to the north.

The Mirovar force team followed Arthur past the administration building and into a left-hand turn toward the warehouses. Anton had joined the rest of them in stowing his motorcycle helmet on the back of his motorcycle. Having full visibility of his surroundings was more important than retaining the limited protection of a helmet. Flood lights lit the whole airport. The nearly full moon added to the illumination. Anton's Order nightglasses rendered the available light into a crisply delineated and fully visible world.

Anton had joined Jay on rearguard duty at the back of the team. Jay rode to his left. On Anton's right, a nearly north-south runway ran for a mile in parallel with the access road. A second, longer runway ran northwest to southeast. Seven large hangars on the opposite side of the airport flanked the northern and eastern runways.

Hangars that Arthur's sensor array revealed were swarming with vampires.

The team had rearmed themselves from the stores in Justin's SUVs. Anton had picked up a now familiar H&K 416 assault rifle with a strap around his neck and shoulders. He wore a bandolier with six spare magazines of fifty-round caseless ammo, every second round was silver, the others were all lead hollow points designed to maximize damage against unarmored targets. He wore the Blue Dragon strapped over his back, the handle jutting up over his right shoulder.

Even though Anton had his head on a swivel, Arthur saw them first. "Heads up, hostiles at five o'clock."

Anton looked over his right shoulder, there were thirty plus vampires blurring across the tarmac and grass between the hangars and the warehouses. Their origin hangar was at least eight-hundred yards away. They were covering a hundred yards every three seconds. Watching them run toward the team was strangely disconcerting. The vampires seemed to be taking too long to close with the Mirovar force team. If they were praetorians; they would already be shooting at him by now.

He grinned; they were too far away to stop the team reaching the fortress-warehouse that Arthur had prepared. All they needed to do was accelerate to escape them.

Arthur started slowing down. The riders in front of Anton began slowing as well and spreading out. Anton feathered his throttle to avoid running into the back of Li's motorcycle.

Anton's head snapped to the left. There was a second posse of vampires twice as large as the first rushing across the airport toward the middle warehouse. They were going to cut them off.

Arthur shouted, "Make for the warehouse. We have to cut through them. Follow me." His bike leaped forward, racing away toward the second warehouse. The second group of vampires advanced, blurring to cut the Mirovar force team off.

Anton twisted his throttle, his motorcycle's engine roaring in response. The bike's tires bit into the tarmac and he rushed forward after the others. Jay was in front of him and pushing further to the left. Anton was on the back-right corner of the team. He glanced behind him. Damn, the vampires were fast across open ground – any hint of slowness had vanished. They had already halved the distance between them to four hundred yards. One of the leading vampires pointed at Arthur and shouted something lost amongst the sharp thunder of the motorcycle engines.

Anton's heart sank. They must have seen the P-Case strapped to Arthur's bike. He leaned forward, shifting gears, the bike accelerating to catch up to the team. But the rest of the team were already moving faster. They had drawn an easy twenty yards ahead of him.

"What the hell?" Anton muttered. He was getting left behind.

Arthur called out over the tactical link, "Justin, go now. We need you. Everyone else, keep them off me at the entrance to the warehouse so that I can get us in."

"We're already on our way," Justin replied.

The two groups of vampires and the Mirovar force team were converging on a wide swathe of pale tarmac in front of the middle warehouse.

Anton unslung his assault rifle and held it in his left hand, gunning his bike with his right hand. His grandfather's voice came over the tactical link, "Save your ammunition, wait for them to get close."

The vampires were swarming in from two directions.

"How close is close?" Peter quipped.

"Last hundred yards."

Anton pursed his lips. A vampire could cross a hundred yards in less than three seconds. He scanned his Order nightglasses, tiny red dots were converging across his lenses. Vampires moving like high-speed ghosts within his heads-up display. They would be within range in seconds.

This shit was about to get real.

* * *

Chloe had already committed the second wave of sixty-two vampires to cut off the Mirovar force team before they reached whichever warehouse was their objective. It had to be one of the three western buildings. There was nothing else beyond the third warehouse except unkempt packed dirt and tough Nevadan weeds.

The second wave of vampires were on course to intercept them before they reached the middle warehouse. However, the Mirovar team were accelerating – it would be a close thing as to who would arrive at the warehouse first.

"There's a second team on the move," Crane snapped. "Two vehicles coming fast down the main entrance from the west."

Chloe glanced at the screens surrounding the cockpit. Multiple text messages from the coven leaders were running across the screen. "They've spotted the Panopticon P-Case. Arthur Slayne is with Mirovar."

"Kill the second team," Crane ordered. "It's Blake."

"Dropping Hoffman's drone into range. We'll use the 30mm cannon. The targets are too close to the osprey," Chloe said, sending a command to the nearest flanking drone. The craft immediately peeled away, diving down toward the airport.

She glanced back at Crane. He looked hard at her and asserted, "Surely, the Blake force team is a bigger prize than Haley's life."

Chloe couldn't risk either James or the chameleons. She'd invested too much time and effort in both assets. Together they were an edge she'd not willingly surrender. The osprey II drone parked in the administration building parking lot was too close to the main entrance roadway and the approaching Blake force team to risk a cruise missile attack. However, she'd be damned if she was going to apologize for her tactical choices in the middle of a battle. She asked archly, "Do you want me to skin this cat or not?"

Crane frowned, his gaze flicking back and forth between the displays and her face. "Do what you must before we run out of time."

She contacted the praetorian commanding the deployed shadowstar drone. "Hoffman, your targets are clear. Fire at will."

"Yes, Ma'am," he replied.

Chloe glanced at the screen displaying the two SUVs racing along the main road into the airport, and whispered, "Mr. Blake. Welcome to hell."

* * *

Arthur screamed over the broadcast link, "Get out, Justin! Get out now!"

Justin's Order nightglasses had picked up the descending shadowstar drone. Now it hovered a mile above the airport in the sweet spot to use its 30mm cannon against a ground vehicle. He shouted to his team, "Blur."

He ramped hard, pushing explosively against the front passenger side door. It spun away in a squeal of tearing metal, flying into the night. He followed it as fast as he could.

Light flashed a yard in front of the Chevy Suburban. The tarmac vaporizing under the hellish blows of 30mm cannon fire. The storm of metal reached the front of the car, evaporating it with a thunderous roar.

Justin's boots hit the ground and he accelerated away. To his right, Patrick and Max were at most a yard behind him. He glanced back. The storm of fire ripped through the SUV's cabin. The Chevy fell apart, two smoking halves falling left and right. The fuel tank exploded with a whip crack, a plume of flame and smoke rising into the night sky.

The attack continued, running into the slowing second Chevy Suburban. The rest of the team had already evacuated the second vehicle. The 30mm rounds lingered for another half second and the SUV evaporated in a bright glare as the remaining stores of weapons and ammo ignited, vaporizing the vehicle into fragments of burning metal.

The edge of the blast wave from the detonating ammunition flattened his team and blew him twenty feet into a hedge lining the parking lot. He rolled away from the thick branches and rose to his feet. He scanned his team; they were all rising to their feet. They had salvaged whatever arms they were carrying with them in the cars, a mix of assault rifles, MP5 sub-machine guns and a lone multiple-grenade launcher. "Damn!" Justin swore. His team had just lost most of their firepower.

The drone continued to patrol overhead. Another attack was imminent, the team needed to find cover as quickly as possible. Justin thrust his right hand out toward the closest warehouse and commanded, "Follow me."

He blurred across the road. They would follow the lines of the buildings to minimize the opportunity for the shadowstar to have another shot at killing them. Ironically, they would be safer in the vicinity of Arthur Slayne and the P-Case than out in the open and in the cross-hairs of a shadowstar drone.

His team blurred behind him. Moments later they were following the wall of the nearest warehouse, looking for the entrance.

The snap and crack of gunfire erupted over the tactical link.

The vampires had caught up with the Mirovar force team.

* * *

No one can become a trick motorcyclist on a first ride.

Anton couldn't aim and fire effectively, and ride and steer his motorcycle at the same time. He spun the bike to a stop, snapped his assault rifle up to his shoulder and ramped hard. The airport resolved into razor-sharp clarity. Time slowed, the blurring vampires resolving into men and women sprinting across the grass and tarmac toward him. It struck him how ordinary they looked, dressed in casual street wear, or occasionally a business suit. It was as if someone had trawled a shopping mall and collected these people at random. None carried weapons, their hands clenching spasmodically. Their eyes reflected the flood lights, dark mirrors filled with blood lust, staring at him with avid hunger. Their excited shrieks cut through the night air like knives. They didn't need weapons, they had numbers. As strong and tough as a Ramp master was, just a single vampire with a good grip on an arm or a leg could tear him apart.

Despite his Ramp, an unsettling disquiet crawled into Anton's gut. These were not disciplined praetorians expected to make rational decisions. A palpable aura of madness infested the air. A dire infection that echoed the berserker within him. He dared not go there again. What use was a deadly power that could kill everyone he loved. He couldn't risk becoming a danger to the rest of the team.

He constrained his ramp, holding it steady at just below his maximum capability.

Tiny numerals ripped down toward zero on his nightglasses' heads-up display. The leading vampires closed past a hundred yards. Anton pulled his weapon's trigger. The assault rifle's configuration was set for three round bursts. The weapon spat flame, three bullets lancing toward the closest vampire.

The vampire moved aside, two of the bullets whipping past him. The third, a silver round passed through his left arm in a splash of blood. His face froze with shock, and he stumbled, falling to the tarmac in a cartwheeling jumble of arms and legs. A hollow-point round struck a second vampire half a dozen yards behind the first in the lower chest. She jerked backward in a pink mist, then recovered, running hard toward Anton.

Gunfire speared from behind Anton's right shoulder. One of his team mates had swapped to full-auto. A withering burst of mixed silver and hollow-point rounds cut through the vampires, dropping another three, with a fourth limping forward on a shot out knee.

The vampires dodged, leaped and twisted, fanning out into a broader front as they sought to avoid the rounds streaming toward them from Anton's right.

Behind Anton's left, light flared, reflecting off the pale faces of the swarming vampires. The crack of an exploding 40mm grenade arrived a moment later. Peter had opened up on the second swarm of vampires with his multiple grenade launcher. A handful of assault rifles barked and stuttered as the rest of the Mirovar force team engaged the larger force.

The range to the nearest vampires dropped to fifty yards. Anton slid his leg over the bike seat and took a step away from the motorcycle. Gray smoke puffed from the barrel of his gun with each round. He snapped the weapon from vampire to vampire. Some were fast enough to twist aside; but combinations of silver and hollow-point rounds shredded two more. The hollow points exiting in plumes of pink mist. Silver stricken vampires fell to the ground, sliding for yards across the tarmac or grass.

Continuous rifle fire lanced past him on the right, ripping ragged holes in the vampire line.

The range dropped to less than twenty yards. There were at least two dozen vampires sprinting toward him, some were branching off toward Anton's right to attack whoever stood behind him. The gunfire from that direction fell silent as his team mate ran their first magazine dry.

Anton held the trigger down, his assault rifle riffing through its magazine on full-auto. The vampires screamed with hate and fury. They converged on his location, bunching up into a nearly solid wall of howling terror. His bullets couldn't come fast enough to slow their advance. For every vampire taken down, another took their place.

Light flashed from behind him, casting shadows across the advancing vampire's faces. Automatic gunfire cracked and echoed across the airport, counterpointed with the sharp crump of exploding grenades. His rifle clicked on empty, gray smoke issuing from the barrel in a rising wisp. A vampire appeared on the far side of the motorcycle. She leered at him, her long dark tresses a ragged curtain around her pale face and gleaming fangs. She snapped, "Your empty."

Anton stabbed her through the left eye with the barrel of his rifle. She recoiled back like a cut snake, her hands flying to her face. The five nearest vampires leaped at him, eyes wild, fangs bared, pale hands outstretched to grip, rend and tear. Their screams rising in excited expectation of triumph.

Anton launched himself up and back, flipping midair. He released the rifle, letting it swing from its straps. His right hand snapped up, grasping the handle of the Blue Dragon. It swished free from its scabbard, its magnificent blade gleaming in the airport's floodlights. He landed on the tarmac, the Blue Dragon arcing down upon the closest vampire. The blade sliced into the creature at the point where the neck met its left shoulder and exited just above the opposite hip.

Anton spun away, his katana trailing a line of blood. The stricken vampire fell in opposite directions, his comrades rushing past him. Their faces twisted with a ferocious madness bordering on frenzy.

Jay stood ten feet away. He rammed a fresh magazine home and opened up at point blank range on the rest of the vampires rushing them. He backed away from the advancing creatures, tongues of fire licking from the barrel of his gun with each round. The vampires were less than ten feet away from him, so close the flames from the barrel were reflecting off their dark eyes and multiple rounds were tearing chunks of flesh from their bodies.

A counter on Anton's nightglasses displayed nineteen hostiles within twenty feet. The vampires were overrunning them. He called out, "They're surrounding us." A sliver of fear pierced Anton's heart. He'd never faced anything like this before.

Jay leaped backward in the direction of the rest of the Mirovar force team, firing his rifle with one hand to provide what cover he could. His other reached for his katana. He raked the tarmac beneath him with rifle fire before he landed. The nearby vampires spinning away. Landing in a crouch, he rose in a classic fighting stance, his rifle slung at his side, his katana held with both hands pointing nearly vertical above his head.

The vampires surged forward again. Anton twisted and turned, rushing to get closer to Jay. Together they could cover each other's back. A vampire grabbed Anton's left ankle. It was like his foot hit an iron bar. He fell down flat on his face upon the tarmac, the Blue Dragon skidding clear of his right hand.

Strong hands flipped him over onto his back. Bodies crowded around him. The vampire he'd stabbed in the eye appeared over his face. Her left eye was a ragged mess of raw flesh dripping blood onto his face. Her head flicked right, lining up across his neck. Her fangs gleamed in the floodlights as she cocked her head back for the downward plunge into his throat.

Something snapped deep within Anton's soul. A cobalt fire ripping through him like an Arctic gale.

The vampire hesitated above him.

Anton convulsed, wrenching his right hand free. His stiff fingers speared upward into the vampire's throat. He clenched his fist, tearing down in a flash, ripping her jaw free from her face in a shower of blood.

He crunched forward, leaping to his feet, another four vampires hanging off him like rats harrying a wild dog. He whirled and spun away, breaking their grip on him, vampire bones snapping like a volley of drums. The creatures howled, then launched themselves forward in a mad frenzy of blood lust.

A voice resounded in his ears. A distant part of his mind recognized it as his grandfather. The voice called out, "Cut through to the warehouse." The meaning of the words lost in a howling gale of noise. Someone was roaring. A deep throated counterpoint to the shrill shrieks of the vampires.

Anton gave way to the berserker Ramp, retreating into a world of instinct where the only rule was kill or be killed.

A red mist descended and cast all restraint away.

* * *

The command shadowstar drone hovered two miles above the airport.

"What the hell is that?" Crane snapped.

Chloe followed the line of Crane's finger to the lower-right-hand corner of the battlespace display. One of the Ramp masters was fighting the vampire militia with his bare hands.

Crane manipulated the feed, and the vision expanded until a ten-yard square around the fight filled half the available display. Anton Slayne blurred through the remnants of the first wave. A counter at the bottom of the screen indicated living militia vampires within the field of view. It was down to twelve, and dropped to eleven as Anton tore the head off the nearest vampire.

The vampires struck back. Pummeling and tearing at Anton. He rocked beneath their blows, but what should have taken off an arm or a leg, or caved in his chest wall, left him standing.

A memory of summoning the hardness of the supreme ramp flooded through Chloe's mind. The night she lay trapped in the foul mud on the bottom of the Mystic River opposite the Boston docks. She'd made her bones harder than the skin of a nightfalcon helicopter. She'd punched through its armored nose with her bare hands and torn it apart. Anton must be doing something similar to avoid the militia vampires tearing him to pieces.

She glanced back at Crane. He did something she'd never seen him do before. He shuddered. He stared at Anton for a long moment. The counter at the bottom of the screen making steady progress toward zero. He then uttered in a voice of quiet amazement, "A berserker." His gaze flicked to Chloe's face. He pointed a long finger at Anton Slayne, a finger betraying a barely perceptible tremble, and commanded, "Kill him. Kill him quickly."

Chloe pressed her lips together and nodded. Her hands flashed over the display. A red cross-hairs appeared over the image of Anton as he smashed the last of the first wave vampires head first into the tarmac, splashing the militiaman's brains over the ground. He rose up from the kill, and looked around, apparently perplexed by the lack of immediate opponents. He spotted the Blue Dragon lying a dozen yards beyond the circle of partially dismembered corpses surrounding him. He blurred to it, scooping it up in a single movement and rushed off toward the second wave vampires assaulting Arthur Slayne and the Mirovar force team.

That fight was at least three hundred yards away from Anton but getting closer with every second as he blurred across the airport. The shift in targets to Anton would give relief to the Blake force team who'd disappeared into the first warehouse. Another Ramp Master two hundred yards in front of Anton opened fire on the rear of the second wave vampires. It was Jay Creeley, he'd obviously thought better of hanging around a berserk Anton Slayne.

Chloe opened a communications channel to the deployed shadowstar drone a mile beneath their position. "Hoffman, a new target has been designated," she said with a level voice. "Avoid collateral damage, no cruise missiles."

"Copy that, Ma'am. Weapons are hot," Hoffman responded.

The time of Anton Slayne being her asset had come to an end. Chloe issued her next command without hesitation, "Fire at will."

She drew in a breath and sighed quietly. Anton exceeded her expectations for him. It was a shame to lose him now before he could fulfill his purpose.

She studied the screens. There was nothing else she could do.

* * *

He barely remembered his name. The enemy massed in front of him. He surged toward them, a bright blade in hand. He would kill them all and rejoice in their spilled blood and dismembered flesh.

Li's voice called from deep within his mind.

Anton staggered. His left hand slapping the left-side of his face. A jagged spear of agony lanced behind his eye patch, driving through his skull like a pile-driver.

The agony lifted, the red mist clouding his mind dissipating like a half-remembered dream. Her voice called out again like a clarion trumpet, "Above you!"

He glanced upward. A shadowstar drone loomed above him. His nightglasses zoomed in. The weapons bay was open, a multi-barreled cannon pointing directly at him with deadly intent.

Anton panic ramped, jagging hard right.

Light flashed behind him. Hot air bathed the back of his neck as the night thundered around him.

Anton kept moving – it was the only thing keeping him alive.

He twisted, turning hard left, bursting forward like a demon escaping hell.

The sharp light and ripping thunder of excoriated tarmac and earth followed him. The firestorm followed his steps, a burnt metal stench flooding his nostrils, promising nothing but sudden death.

Anton dug deep into the silence and blurred to the right.

* * *

Anton avoided the third attempt to kill him.

"Damn it," Crane snapped. "He's too fast."

Chloe asserted, "It's the wrong weapon. It's designed to defeat vehicles. A single Ramp Master can avoid it through continuous random direction changes." She tightened her lips momentarily, suppressing a smile. "We'd have to get lucky to kill him this way."

"Indeed," Crane growled. "Maintain the attack. We'll see if his luck holds out."

Chloe nodded, there was nothing to say to Hoffman, he had his orders and would continue to attempt to kill Anton with his 30mm cannon until he was successful or ran out of ammunition.

She scanned the screens. Arthur Slayne and the Mirovar force team had made it to the front of the second warehouse. The second wave vampires had taken more than fifty percent casualties. Not surprisingly, the use of thermobaric grenades by the Mirovar force team had been devastating against unarmored vampires. The Ramp masters stood in a close group in front of the warehouse, firing automatic weapons on full auto at the advancing second wave vampires. The use of 40mm grenades had ceased. They must have exhausted their stocks. The second wave vampires continued to blur toward the Mirovar force team. They would swamp the Ramp masters in moments.

Chloe doubted that would actually happen. Surely Slayne would have a way into his own building. In any event, the second wave had served its purpose and drawn the Blake force team into the fight. The second force team had disappeared from view. She said to Crane, "The Blake force team have entered the first warehouse."

"Who's carrying one-thousand-pound hammerheads?" Crane asked.

"Cantor," Chloe replied.

"You know what to do."

Chloe issued the command for Cantor to target the first warehouse with a hammerhead cruise missile.

Crane stated matter-of-factly, "Take away the ground of the enemy."

In a matter of seconds, the first warehouse would cease to exist.

* * *

"Justin, hit the second level tunnel," Arthur called over the tactical link. "Follow the map."

There was a shadowstar hunting Justin's team and the first warehouse was slim protection at best. He scanned the interior of the warehouse with his nightglasses. It was an easy hundred yards across and double that long. A shipping container stood nearby, its doors locked with dark-gray chains and polished padlocks. A bright green box in his Order nightglasses outlined the container's doors.

Justin shouted, "This way," and blurred toward the container's doors. He gripped the closest door, his muscles bunching across arm, shoulder and thigh. He gave a mighty roar, metal squealed and tore, the chains snapping apart and clattering to the concrete floor. A moment later, he shepherded his team into the container. The floor revealed a set of stairs leading down to a well-lit landing. He pursued his team members down the stairs like the devil hunting lost souls. He reached the first landing, a tunnel running to a 'T' intersection beckoned to his right. He ignored it, whirling around the landing and descending to the second level.

The stairs shook and he leaped the rest of the way. A deep-throated 'THA-OMP,' reverberated through the tunnel as he fetched up on the lower landing. A plume of gray dust followed him onto the landing, coating his hair and clothes. He picked himself up, waving the gray mist away from his face and staggered out onto the lower tunnel.

Justin's team greeted him, patting him down and slapping his shoulders. He stared past them into the tunnel. It ran for twenty yards than branched with a 'T' intersection. Arthur's map application drew a green line curving past the right corner labeled 'Warehouse #2.' He looked around, everyone was okay, and he said, "Let's go."

It was time to join forces with Arthur and the rest of the Mirovar force team.

* * *

A hypersonic cruise missile speared down like a bolt of white lightning.

The first warehouse vanished within a massive ball of light and flame, debris rising high in the air. Man-made thunder cracked across the airport like a giant whip. A sheet of roofing spun through the air like a gargantuan playing card, heading straight for Anton.

He jagged hard left. The shadowstar's 30mm cannon fire continued to chase him, tearing the sheet of roofing into a cloud of razor-sharp fragments. Anton ducked into a shoulder roll, the plume of white-hot metal shredding the air above him.

The stream of 30mm rounds twisted direction and raced toward him, carving a trench in the grass. He rose to his feet, dug hard, accelerating to the right of the deadly firestorm.

The attack died a moment later, sudden silence gripping the night air around him. The nearby ground was a patchwork quilt of rough sections marked by shallow trenches where the grass and dirt had been torn by the cannon fire. He'd run the shadowstar out of ammunition.

Anton bent over forward, his hands gripping his knees, panting heavily, perspiration dripping from his face and falling in wet splotches on his boots. He rose, arching his back, his hands upraised, the Blue Dragon raised in momentary triumph.

The berserk Ramp had taken something from him, and followed by a death race versus an aerial cannon, there wasn't a lot left in the tank. He sucked in deep breaths and turned to the second warehouse. What was happening with Arthur and the Mirovar force team?

Jay made it through a doorway on the front corner of the warehouse, decapitating the closest vampire as he went. A steel door slammed down behind him, sealing the front of the building. A group of at least twenty militia vampires howled and shrieked their frustration, pounding fruitlessly on the walls of the building. One turned away and caught sight of Anton. He whooped with joy, and blurred toward him. A moment later, the rest of the vampires turned en masse and raced across the tarmac and grass toward his position.

"Oh, shit," Anton gasped, backing away from the approaching vampires. The last thing he needed right now were twenty plus vampires attempting to tear him to pieces. He sucked in more air, a pulse of fresh energy coursing through his body with each breath. He pulled a hand down his face; it came away wet with perspiration. He was getting dangerously dehydrated. There was no point trying to run away. Depleted as he was, they'd run him down before he reached cover. He'd have to rely on short sharp ramps and hope to God that he lasted long enough to defeat them.

Anton rubbed his left hand dry against his combat webbing, and then held the Blue Dragon aloft with both hands. His gaze stilled and he dove into silence. The ramp bloomed within and the vampires dropped out of blur as his nerves accelerated to match their pace.

The Blue Dragon gleamed beneath the airport floodlights. The vampires would get everything he had to give. He grinned without remorse. The first of the vampires arrived within striking range, and in its frenzy, ran onto his blade. He stepped backward, his draw cut gutting the creature, who stumbled to the ground.

Two more took its place, and another two spread to his left and right.

Three red laser strings lit up the mass of vampires surrounding him.

Anton's gaze flicked along the scarlet beams. The red lines originated on the top corners of the second warehouse.

He blurred, leaping backward as far as he could.

Hope burst into life within his heart.

* * *

The sentry weapons acquired their targets.

Arthur activated the miniguns. Screens on the inside of the warehouse displayed three lances of minigun fire spearing into the vampires surrounding Anton. The 7.62mm rounds traveled faster than sound. Tearing into the vampires before they realized they were under attack. The guns swiveled, a dull thrum drifting through the walls as they fired for two seconds at the remaining vampires.

Anton landed outside the ring of vampires and blurred hard to the right, beginning a broad circle to get out of the line of fire. He needn't have worried. Arthur's sensor array was governing the sentry weapons and was perfectly capable of distinguishing vampires from Ramp masters. The displays revealed the carnage. The vampires, intent on killing Anton, had been surprised by the attack. The heavy gunfire immediately rendering them into chunks of bloody flesh and raw bone.

Arthur stared at the displays. Anton rushed across the open ground. Would the praetorians initiate another attack from one of the shadowstar drones? Anton closed the distance to the warehouse, blurring at maximum Ramp. "Door," Arthur shouted. The one human-sized door on the front of the warehouse lifted in a flash and Anton rushed through it. Once inside, he slumped to the floor. The door closing automatically behind him.

"He's heat stressed," Chiara declared, rushing to Anton's side. She opened a large bottle of water and lifted it to his lips. Anton, his face pale, blinked sweat from his eye, and drank greedily from the bottle.

"Peter," Arthur ordered. "Grab some bags of ice from the freezer."

"Got, it," Peter replied, and blurred away. He returned in seconds, with four large bags of crushed ice.

Chiara took charge of Anton's care, lying him down on the cold concrete floor. She took the bags of ice from Peter and laid one behind Anton's neck and head, and then put the other three beneath his armpits next to his ribs and over his heart. She asked, "Peter, please get some more."

Peter dashed off.

Satisfied that Anton was out of immediate danger, Arthur called out, "Okay, everyone, listen up."

The Blake force team rested against a shipping container, facing Arthur. To their right stood Jay and Li. Peter and Chiara continued to assist Anton to cool down, rehydrate and get his strength back.

"Now, here's the situation," Arthur continued. "Crane can't attack us with heavy weapons, because he needs the Panopticon and the P-Case more than he needs to destroy us."

"Oh, he wants that too," Jay remarked.

"But, Jay, it's beside the point. His only option is to break into this fortress and hit us hand to hand, which is not a good option against the two best force teams in the Order – even with three hundred plus vampires."

Jay spread his hands wide. "This is your fortress, your base, your vampire trap. What's the exfiltration plan? How do we get the hell out of here?"

Arthur looked steadily at the young force team leader and instructed him. "We let the vampires do our work for us. They will send their main force against this fortress. We use our miniguns to thin them out. I have plenty of weapons and ammunition stocks. We'll kill more from the shooting slits on the wall to convince them we are here. Once their numbers are down to manageable levels. We put the miniguns on automatic defense, and evacuate through the tunnels to hangar number one. I have a long-bodied private jet good for sixteen passengers and we get the hell out of Dodge."

Jay nodded. "And as you suggested behind the gas station, we pick up a set of Stinger III prototypes and take out the shadowstars."

Justin pushed himself away from the wall of a container and asked, "Are the SAMs here?"

"No," Arthur answered, "I stored them in two secret caches in the tunnels. The caches also allow easy access to the surface near the center of the airport. And, yes, there's a reason for that which we can go into when we have the leisure to do so. For now, that's where they are. Each missile is a single shot shoulder fired system specifically designed to take out a shadowstar drone."

"Really?" Jay asked skeptically.

"Yes, really."

Anton pushed the half-melted ice bags aside, rose to his feet and said, "Do you need someone to get them?"

"Are you volunteering?" Arthur asked.

"Sure. What do I have to do?"

"Just follow the maze map via the nightglasses, and the cache disarming instructions from the sensor array. The tunnels are a deliberately confusing maze. The map will take you through the first, second and third levels to the cache. The sensor array instructions will show you how to open it. There are four single-shot shoulder launchers in each cache. They come with carry straps and weigh about forty pounds each. You should be able to manage carrying all four." Arthur tapped his nightglasses and said, "I've sent you the first cache location. Now off you go."

Anton squeezed Chiara on the shoulder, and stepped away to the open container behind the Blake force team. He vanished between the open doors. In moments, he was heading down the stairs and into the tunnels.

Arthur's eyes narrowed. The lower set of tunnels were probably the safest location in the airport. He was glad Anton was down there. It was only a matter of time before the vampires responded to the destruction of their first and second waves.

He drew in a breath and sighed. The first two waves were throwaways. Designed to test their defenses and draw them out. They had worked perfectly for his opponents. The vampires still held the upper hand. A pulse of satisfaction washed through his soul. Apparently, that was precisely where he needed the vampires to be – for now.

Arthur shrugged his shoulders, feeling the weight of the P-Case strapped like a backpack across them. Whatever the end game was, it was still in front of them all.

* * *

The command drone's battlespace displays revealed the two Order force teams co-located within the second warehouse.

"Slayne will have another exit," Crane declared. "That warehouse is a fortress designed to expend our forces on. Since there is nothing visible above ground, he must have tunnels. Initiate a search for entrances in all the hangars we occupy."

Chloe nodded. "That command has already been sent."

Crane instructed. "Make sure the militia also check the hangars holding the first and second waves. It wouldn't do to miss an entrance."

"Already happening."

"Once the tunnels are open, we'll send our main force through to their holdout and get inside that way." Crane paused and frowned momentarily. "And contact Haley, why is their sensor array still operational?"

"I've sent him a status request fifteen seconds ago."

Crane sat back and looked at Chloe. "If only you anticipated my needs as efficiently as you operate this battle." He arched an eyebrow. "Perhaps then you wouldn't have an implant at the base of your skull."

Chloe didn't answer, staring back at Crane in silence.

His eyes narrowed and he said, "Order Cantor to take out their sentry weapons with his 30mm cannon, we can't have them decimating our third wave."

"Yes, Sir," Chloe replied with chilly formality and sent the commands to Cantor. The second drone dropped out of formation, spearing down to a mile above the airport.

A ping resounded through the cabin. James' status report scrolled down a display, 'Outside a locked server room in the basement of the administration building. Anticipate the sensor array will be down in less than sixty seconds.'

Chloe scanned the displays. Cantor opened fire on the warehouse; streams of bright 30mm rounds ripping into the upper corners of the building. The miniguns resident in the corners of Slayne's fortress erupted in flames, showering streamers of brilliant sparks as stored ammunition detonated.

Crane whispered, "And now their fangs are drawn."

Chloe wondered to herself, *What else does Slayne have up his sleeve?*

* * *

Cream painted concrete lit with halogen down lights passed beneath James' boots.

He strode along a basement level corridor in the administration building. He lifted a handheld device linked back to the sensor arrays in the osprey II. A red dot moved along a map on the device's display as he converged on the Order sensor array server room. He pulled to a halt before a pair of heavy steel doors.

James pointed at the doors and ordered quietly, "Tear them down."

Gullette and Kavanne ghosted from thin air beside him. They moved sinuously forward, James dodging left and right to avoid a casual bone-breaking flick from their tails. Long dark talons emerged from their fingers, and short, heavy claws from their toes. Razor sharp spines bristled along the backs of their thick arms, over their bulging shoulders and down their broad backs.

Their hands blurred forward, punching the doors. Their talons ripped through the steel with sharp bangs. The chameleons jerked backward, the doors ripping free from their hinges before the lizards threw them disdainfully to the floor with a pair of echoing clangs.

"Nice," James remarked, following the chameleons into the server room.

Gullette and Kavanne turned to regard him with silent eyes. A pair of server racks labeled 'secondary,' and 'primary,' and battery power packs stood in the middle of the small room. James nodded, and commanded, "Destroy it."

The chameleons blurred, the racks falling apart in a shower of silvery sparks and blue smoke. In moments, the big lizards tore Arthur Slayne's active sensor array into junk metal.

* * *

Anton paced his way through the maze of tunnels.

The surface to air missile caches were toward the middle of the tunnel network. Accounting for turns, backtracks, and stairs up and down, they were both about a mile from the second warehouse. The tunnels formed a squashed diamond with the first and second warehouses over the western corner. As to why the missile caches were so far from the fortress warehouse – Anton had no idea. He assumed his grandfather had a good reason for putting them this far away from his main base of operations, and when they had a spare moment, he planned to ask him why.

Anton tracked the green line displayed in his Order nightglasses. Arthur's maze map and sensor array was an amazing system. It would lead him directly to the nearest cache and show him how to open the locks.

He turned into the final corridor, pausing to finish off a bottle of water. The southern-most of the two caches was thirty yards away on the left and he strode toward it. All he had to do was unlock it. There was a brief chirp in his earbuds as his nightglasses lost the Order tactical network. The green line of Arthur's map flickered for a moment within his Order nightglasses and then held steady.

He looked down the corridor. Matte-gray panels lined the tunnel walls from floor to ceiling. They all looked alike. He approached the one indicated by the green-line endpoint. He tapped on it with an exploratory finger. Nothing happened. He rubbed it with his hands. No hidden consoles appeared on the gray surface. The panel appeared to be dull, smooth metal, and nothing more.

"Oh, fuck it," he whispered. *So much for relying on technology*, he thought bitterly. He turned around and looked back along the corridor. He was stuck out here in the middle of nowhere without a clue. He didn't want to come back empty handed, and determined to try and work out how to reveal his grandfather's hidden cache. If Li had been there, she would have cracked it open in less than a minute, and Peter would have torn the panels from the wall until he found the cache. Anton was at a loss as to how to proceed. His skill set as a champion hockey player falling far short of what he needed right now.

Anton set a countdown timer on his nightglasses. He gave himself three minutes to work it out. If he hadn't found and opened the cache within three minutes, he'd cut his losses. He shook his head. The vampires must have got around to taking the sensor array down. That meant their next attack was imminent. He had to make his way back to the team. They would need his help, but first he needed to complete his mission and get the missiles.

He hoped giving himself three minutes would be long enough to find the cache, and short enough to get him to the battle on time.

Anton frowned and set to work.

***

Arthur stared at the dead private feeds in his nightglasses.

He was certain of what he'd seen just before his sensor array failed and the feeds died. Two giant gray and white lizards had torn through his server and tactical uplink room beneath the administration building. They had cut through the steel plate doors like they were tissue paper and ripped the server racks apart. The server room managed his sensor array and the local uplink tower for satellite communications. With its destruction, Arthur and the two Order force teams had lost situational awareness of the battlespace.

His heart sank, this was wrong on so many levels. As horrible as the idea was, he had to admit what he had just witnessed was real. The Vampire Dominion had chameleons. He didn't know the details, but Crane or Armitage, or both, had two chameleons working for them. The battlespace had just gotten a helluva lot more complicated. There was no time to worry about how the Vampire Dominion had a pair of the ancient warm-blooded reptilian predators working for them, he just had to deal with it and adapt.

Arthur strongly suspected his whole-self had never planned for the presence of chameleons in this fight. How could he have anticipated such a thing? How could anyone mitigate the alliance of an ancient apex predator with the vampires? The implications slammed through him like a freight train. He swore, "Oh, damn it!" Anton was out there by himself in the tunnels, cut off from contact with the rest of the team, with invisible opponents potentially hunting him.

Li dropped her gaze from the gray display screens in the warehouse. She frowned at him, her dark brown eyes half-accusing, and said, "The sensor array and tactical network have just gone down. So much for your vaunted situational awareness."

"Yes," he replied. He had to own this situation. Li had called it right. Something had happened he was sure he'd never thought of. "Clearly, we'll have to adapt."

Li inquired, "And what of Anton stuck out in the tunnels without comms?"

"He's a bright lad, he'll work out the need to come back."

Li looked askance and shook her head slowly. "We can only hope he gets back in time and isn't caught on his own out there."

"He can look after himself."

"You hope."

Arthur frowned, but kept his silence. The situation was fluid and if Anton lingered in the tunnels, he risked becoming separated from the rest of the team.

Justin suggested, "Whatever Anton's situation is, we have bigger issues right here. Their next attack is imminent. Arthur, Jay, we need to position our forces – they'll swarm us again."

Jay nodded. "It's a certainty." He glanced at the P-Case strapped to Arthur's back. "They'll try and wear us down until we're too weak to defend the Panopticon." He looked hard at Arthur. "What's your real exfil plan."

"What I said five minutes ago still holds," Arthur snapped impatiently, nettled by Jay's implication he hadn't told the whole truth earlier. "We crush their main force against this fortress, then cut through the maze tunnels to hangar number one where our private jet is ready to fly. Along the way we pick up a set of Stinger III prototypes and take out the shadowstars. With the way clear, we damn well fly out of here." He paused for a moment. "We have to persist. They will send a third wave, perhaps a fourth to wear us down. Then the praetorians will come, and Armitage and Crane with them."

Jay stared at him. "Oh my God! Crane is here too?" His face paled for a moment, then filled with steel. "Let him come. He will find the sharp edge of the White Dragon here."

Arthur looked around the assembled Ramp masters and declared firmly, "Yes, I have no doubt Crane and Armitage are in a drone circling this airport. They haven't committed to the fight yet. We haven't bled their forces enough to force them to commit to the fight. But the moment is coming when they will have no choice but to come at us to get the Panopticon back."

"Shit," one of the Blake force team muttered.

"Hold fast," Justin ordered. "Come what may, we will prevail."

Jay declared, "We are united against them."

Arthur stepped forward, pointing to a high walkway that lined the warehouse's outer wall. Multiple ladders rose up to it. "I have a dozen squad automatic weapons and half as many multiple grenade launchers armed and ready on the upper level. Yes, they shot out our sentry weapons but we can still stem the tide. Now take up positions next to the shooting slits," his right hand chopped from one location to the next along the walkway, "here, here and here. When Anton comes back with the stingers, we'll be ready to exfil once we take out the drones."

Jay and Justin issued a series of rapid commands. The assembled teams assented and went to their positions, picking up extra weapons and ammunition as required. Arthur stood back and calculated the options. Anton could have found a cache, but only if he made it all the way before the sensor array failed. Otherwise, without the instructions provided by the sensor array he'd come back empty handed. That wasn't a disaster. They didn't really need the SAMs yet. He'd sent Anton into the tunnels more to keep him safe than for any other purpose.

Arthur sighed. He just hadn't told anyone the reason why he'd done that. He was beginning to have suspicions about what his whole-self had planned to do and he didn't like the way the plan was playing out. Had he really been that desperate twenty years ago when he'd embarked on this course?

His eyes widened, he had no idea and no way to find out.

* * *

Slayne looked pensively at the static-filled display screens, apparently lost in thought.

Li joined in with the Mirovar and Blake force teams, and mobilized to defend the warehouse against the next wave of vampires. She scaled one of the ladders up to a mezzanine style walkway six yards above the floor. The walkway comprised stiff-gray-steel mesh, ten feet deep, spanning all four walls. Justin and Jay conferred briefly and set Red Cevarre, Max Guerra and Chiara watching the rear and side walls. The rest of the Ramp masters lined up across the front of the warehouse facing toward the hangars.

Only Slayne remained on the ground floor, preoccupied and whispering to himself. She was beginning to seriously doubt his sanity but there was nothing she could do about it. She glanced around. Peter was next to her on the left, a short-barreled light machine gun with a heavy bag magazine in his right hand and a fully loaded MGL in the other. He glanced at her, grinned wryly and said, "Same shit, different night, huh?"

She shook her head and replied, "No, different shit this time."

Peter pursed his lips and then gazed out the firing slit toward the silent hangars.

On her right, Patrick Wichowski gazed at her with warm blue eyes. He wore his sandy hair long and tied back in a pony tail. He held another squad automatic weapon out to her. She took the SAW and checked it over. It was a short-barreled light machine gun easily mistaken for an assault rifle. Patrick stated, "It has a two hundred round magazine with a mix of silver and lead hollow points with tracers every fifth round. It should make a mess of them."

Li lifted an eyebrow.

Patrick smiled and said, "I'm not trying to teach you to suck eggs. I probably just talk too much before a battle."

Li reached out to his shoulder and gave it a squeeze. "Talk away," she paused for a second, "actually, I need to ask you something."

Patrick looked at her with an ironic glint in his eyes. "Ask away?"

"Have you ever encountered Set."

Patrick's smile vanished. He put his weapon down against the wall and stared hard into her eyes, and asked, "What have you experienced?"

"He's been showing up in my loremaster visions. Umm," Li hesitated for a moment. "I had an involuntary vision on the way here where he appeared as my dead brother and showed me what he claimed to be was a vision of the future." She reached up with her right hand, rubbing her neck and left shoulder. "He touched me once, and said, 'I've been waiting for you.'"

The silence stretched for a long moment, and Patrick took a deep breath. "That's creepy."

"Do you know what's happening?"

"No," Patrick answered, shaking his head slowly. "Not, really."

Disappointment surged through Li like a rogue wave. She'd hoped the one surviving loremaster would be able to shed light on what was happening to her.

"However," Patrick continued," I can say this. You must be off the scale talented for being a loremaster. It's a pity Juliette isn't here to guide you. She is the only other loremaster on record who encountered Set."

"How did she defend herself against him."

"I can only tell you what she told me. The strength of your defenses against Set will depend on your ability to center yourself in a place of peace and love."

"Really?" Li asked, suddenly out of her depth. She was finding it hard to find much peace and love in her world.

"You remember how she was. She was serene, and seemed to love everyone, but she could still nail someone's hide to the wall if that was what she needed to do."

"Any advice on how to do that?"

"My understanding is that it's something you cultivate and practice, like a spiritual discipline."

"I don't think I have the luxury of ten or twenty years of training to get this right."

Patrick paused for a moment. "Find something you feel really safe with or someone you have a very strong love for. Find, or if need be, create a place of security, love and joy. Something strong you can rest in. Find that place of serenity and start from there."

Li sighed; she had no real idea where such a place would be – except in her past with her father.

"What you must always do is never stand alone."

Li nodded.

"And one last thing," Patrick suggested, "He's attracted to you because you have something important you can do. Us garden variety loremasters don't get this sort of attention." They stared at each other for a long moment. "Of course, this is all moot if we don't survive tonight."

Li sighed. "Yes, of course."

Patrick said, "If you have any other questions, I'll help if I can."

Li nodded. Patrick turned and picked up his weapon. He'd given her much to mull over. Whatever she needed to protect herself from Set, it exceeded what she could do. For the first time in a long time, Li felt completely inadequate before a challenge. She put her weapon aside and turned to Peter with an ache in her heart. He looked down at her for a brief moment. His eyes widened. He stepped forward and wrapped his big arms around her, lifting her off the ground and hugging her tight. His strength and warmth were a bright loving fire before her heart, but in the depths of her soul she knew it was not going to be enough to ward off a god.

She breathed into his shoulder and kissed his neck. She pushed back lightly, and he let her go like a friendly bear letting her down onto her feet. She put her hand gently on his cheek and looked into his blue eyes and whispered, "For luck."

Peter nodded and patted her shoulders. "For luck."

She expected they would need every ounce of luck tonight.

Chapter Fourteen

"The human soul is like a flag buffeted by the wind. First it flies this way, then that way, and then another way. But what if you become the wind?" – Arthur Slayne

* * *

Nevada, Arthur Slayne's Private Airport, Hangar Number One, September 11th, 20:35

The dapper man looked around the Portland coven and their newly converted familiars and wannabes, and asked, "Can anyone see a tunnel entrance in this hangar?"

Tamsah nodded. He'd picked up the telltale signs of a hidden entrance to a tunnel system within minutes of arrival. Secret doors and hidden traps were standard fare for a highly-skilled Red Empire operative. He strode to a nearby fuel bowser, leaped up to the top of it and wrenched a maintenance hatch open. It was, as he expected, empty. A white-painted metal ladder descended through the body of the fuel bowser to a landing thirty feet below.

He looked up at the dapper man and glanced around the other vampires. "Here it is. Here's an entrance into a secret tunnel system beneath the airport."

The dapper man grinned. Perhaps he expected a reward. The coven leader sent a text through his smartphone back to the vampires coordinating the militia. Tamsah leaped down from the fuel bowser. The vampires were certain to use the tunnels in the coming battle. The initial combats were little more than the Vampire Dominion making introductions with the Order of Thoth. Tamsah expected the Order to lose more of their people tonight. That was inevitable given the forces arrayed against them.

Regardless of the battle between the Vampire Dominion and the Order of Thoth, his loyalty lay with the truth speaker. He would find her and protect her life. None would harm her. His tri-bladed spiral daggers would drink deep in vampire blood and they would fall before the sharp powers of his faith.

Or he would die.

Either result was acceptable as long as the truth speaker lived.

* * *

A red dot appeared over the most southerly hangar on the airport map.

Crane looked at Chloe and declared, "We have a tunnel entrance confirmed in hangar number one. We will run simultaneous assaults. The third wave above ground and the fourth wave through the tunnels. Reposition your fourth wave to that hangar for an immediate assault."

Chloe issued the order. The citadel command center would route the directive to the coven leaders in the hangars. In seconds they should be on the move to the southern-most hangar.

Crane stared at her and stated, "I need you to go in with the fourth wave."

Chloe arched an eyebrow. "You want me to lead the tunnel assault."

"Yes. I need someone with Ramp master skills down there."

"Why … specifically?"

"To deal with something not seen since Mekra ruled – a blood frenzy."

Chloe said with a touch of dryness in her voice, "I was beginning to wonder what was behind these new vampire's outstanding commitment to our cause."

"Yes, Indeed," Crane remarked. "You know I limit total vampire numbers to less than a thousand and I keep my praetorian troop deployments to less than twenty. There's a madness that can erupt when there are too many vampires fighting and feeding in a group. The larger the group the more likely it will happen. Like sharks smelling blood in the water, they go into a feeding frenzy. A blood lust that's impossible to control and only stops when it burns out."

"Being a Ramp master protects you from this?"

"Mostly, you should be able to control it when it hits. You'll feel it too, but it won't overwhelm you."

"Wonderful," Chloe remarked sardonically.

"I expect you to keep your head while those around you are losing theirs. Find the P-Case and kill the Slaynes. Now let's see if we can open up an entrance on Slayne's warehouse. Send Cantor and Browning down to the surface and use their 30mm cannons to cut through the front doors. Those guns can take out a tank and should be able to handle a pair of steel doors."

Chloe nodded and issued the commands. The last of the flanking shadowstar drones dropped out of formation and descended to join Cantor's drone. The pair of drones then descended in formation to the surface of the airport.

"Now take us down to hangar number one. Have you noticed it's the only hangar which had a private jet in it when the militia arrived?"

Chloe nodded. "That will be their exfil path."

"I will set my praetorians to guard it in case you fail to stop them leaving with the P-Case."

Chloe looked hard at her king. "There is no chance of that."

Crane's eyes narrowed. "Then complete your mission."

Chloe activated the controls and the shadowstar drone rolled and descended down to the southern-most hangar in the airport.

It was time to get her blade wet.

* * *

Peter peered east through the shooting slit at the airport hangars.

Masses of vampires were running from the northern hangars to the last hangar on the right. The rest of the combined team standing on the front wall began murmuring amongst themselves. Justin called out, "They are regrouping at hangar number one."

Arthur called out from the floor, "They must have discovered the tunnel entrance in that hangar, they will come at us from two directions."

"Can you lock the tunnels down?"

"There is a door, a couple of yards from the entrance beneath our feet. Once locked, they'll need explosives to get through it from either direction."

Li stated, "Anton's still down there. That door needs to be open for him to get back."

"Yes," Arthur conceded. "I'll drop down into the tunnel and guard that pathway. I will wait for Anton to return. He has his nightglasses and can follow the map back to here."

Justin nodded.

Arthur turned and disappeared into the shipping container above the tunnel entrance; the P-Case still strapped to his back.

Peter frowned. He hated the idea of Anton being stuck alone in the tunnels with a horde of vampires heading his way. He crouched down on the walkway to look up into the night sky. While the destruction of Arthur's sensor array had robbed his Order nightglasses of local camera feeds and specialized metadata, they still retained all their fundamental visual functions.

Two shadowstar drones descended toward the center of the airport, directly opposite the second warehouse. A third drone descended further back and to the right, hovering over hangar number one. The same hangar all the vampires had ran to.

The first two drones' ventral weapons bays opened up, their 30mm multi-barreled cannons dropping into firing position. Peter stared into the barrels for a brief moment. "Uh, oh," he whispered, and then shouted, "Off the wall, take cover."

The other Ramp masters glanced at him, and then blurred off the walkway down to the floor below. Upon hitting the floor, they vanished deep into the warehouse behind rows of shipping containers.

The front of the warehouse had a pair of large thick steel doors that opened by recessing into the walls. The doors were five yards high and the same wide; perfectly designed to withstand a massed vampire assault.

The first 30mm round hit the right-side steel door, punching through it in a shower of molten metal and brilliant white and gold sparks. A titanic hail of hard metal followed immediately after it. The doors fell apart in molten edged fragments, thunder rolling like a giant's roar in the confines of the warehouse.

Peter crouched halfway toward the back of the warehouse and whispered beneath his breath, "Oh, shit."

* * *

The command drone's canopy lifted up, exposing the interior of the cabin.

Chloe grabbed the Red Dragon and leaped over the side. She fell thirty yards down to the hangar roof, landing in a crouch. She rose to her full height, strapping the Red Dragon to her waist. The command drone rose rapidly into the night sky on blue jets of flame.

The night surrendered to the two 30mm cannons hammering the front doors of the second warehouse. An actinic glare lit the front of the warehouse, the 30mm rounds ripping through the heavy steel doors. Cantor and Browning's shadowstar drones rested ten feet off the ground, their multi-barreled cannons whirring, caseless ammunition vanishing in long tongues of bright flame and gray smoke, streams of shining fire spearing into the steel plate of the warehouse doors.

The big guns slewed from left to right and from right to left. The bottom half of the doors evaporated leaving a gaping hole in the front wall of the warehouse. The drones ceased firing, rising into the night sky like toys pulled by a giant's strings.

With the cessation of the hammer blows of cannon fire, the excited shrieks of vampires assaulted Chloe's ears. Random members of the third wave began rushing across the open from the other hangars toward the warehouse. Crane's voice barked over the tactical link in her helmet, "Catastrophe! It's started too early. Get down into the tunnels and get ahead of the madness."

"Sir," Chloe acknowledged from long habit.

The noise of the new vampires was grating and repellent. Chloe had a personal aversion to anything that reeked of madness or insanity, but this time, she'd have to dive within it. She ran along the roof and leaped off the front of the hangar. She landed on the concrete apron around the front of the hangar, whirled and dashed into the building.

The masses greeted her like an arriving messiah. The assembled vampires, standing wall to wall within the hangar cheered and called out her name. A group of them began chanting, "Blood Queen, Blood Queen, Blood Queen," and continued shouting. One young man, his fangs hanging out over his full bottom lip, his eyes glassy, slapped the side of his head repeatedly with both hands, then blurred past her to the entrance of the hangar to join the mad rush to the warehouse.

Chloe blurred, turning with a single step. Her right hand snapped up, gripping one of her .50 caliber auto-pistols. She pulled the trigger, a single hypervelocity round wreathed in blue flame shuddered through the air. It slammed through the base of the young vampire's skull. Tearing through his brain stem and evaporating the bottom half of his face. His lifeless body pitched forward through the air, sliding across the concrete in a red smear before coming to rest at the entrance to the warehouse.

Chloe shouted into the sudden silence, "Who's in charge here?"

There was a low murmur of, "Armitage." The murmur quickly grew in volume until more than two-hundred voices shouted her name to the rooftop.

She scanned the crowd around her, and asked in a voice that cut through the clamor, "Where is the tunnel entrance?"

The massed vampires fell into silence. A finely-dressed vampire lifted his hand and pointed at a cylindrical fuel bowser. A maintenance hatch rested in an open position to the left of the entrance to the tunnels. Chloe strode toward it, the vampires before her pushing each other out of the way in their haste to make room for her.

They both loved and feared her.

She leaped to the top of the bowser, glanced down through the hatch at the ladder and the landing thirty feet below. She stilled herself, supreme ramped, and extended her senses beyond standard vampire maximums. The way into the tunnel was clear. There were no hidden trip wires, or laser grids waiting to activate.

Chloe dropped her supreme Ramp and lifted the Red Dragon from its scabbard. The magnificent blade gleamed over her black helmet. She flourished her sword and called out, "Follow me! Follow me to blood and glory! Follow me!"

She leaped down through the maintenance hatch, landing in the tunnel below. There was a short well-lit corridor in front of her. It ran into an open intersection with another corridor crossing the one she was in. She ran forward, as much to progress into the tunnel complex as to avoid the vampires leaping down to the floor behind her.

Chloe halted in the intersection. All three corridors ran for five yards and descended with stairs. Which way was the right way? A vampire shrieked behind her right shoulder, the sound jarring through her skull like an ice pick. She'd re-scabbarded the Red Dragon and simply chopped the blond-headed woman in the throat with her open hand. The blow crushed the woman's larynx and shattered her spine. She dropped to the floor in a boneless heap.

"Shut the hell up!" Chloe snapped at the vampires crowding the corridor behind her. "I can barely think with your unholy racket in my ears!"

One of the vampires hidden at the back of the mob whined, "What's the hold up?"

Chloe took a deep breath and let it out. If she responded to every little irritation these new vampires presented, she'd do the Order's job for them. Her eyes narrowed and her mouth tightened into a thin line. Many of these new vampires were little more than flesh balloons inflated by their own sense of entitlement. She hissed for silence, lifted a finger and stated, "Right. It's a maze. We'll have to work it out as we go, but," she searched the back ranks for the whiny vampire without finding him, "if we're not stupid about it we can get this done quickly." She tapped the nearest three vampires. "Now you three are first up." She pointed down each of the stairwells in turn. "Go, there, there and there and call back with every turn and intersection you find, keep to the right-hand side. Now run, do this at top speed."

The three vampires vanished down the three lots of stairs. Chloe could use her perfect memory to build a full three-dimensional map of the maze with vampire runners. Within a second the first calls came back as the vampires reached the bottom of the stairs.

"Long corridor. It ends in a 'T' intersection," the vampire on the left-hand side reported.

"Reached a landing, two sets of stairs going right and left," the vampire on the right-hand side reported. He then asked hesitantly, "Which one should I follow?"

Chloe pressed her lips together into a thin line. A grating shriek resounded from the middle path, followed by running steps diminishing into the distance. The third vampire had fallen to the frenzy of blood lust madness. She glanced back at the vampires behind her. Their eyes were glassy, they were licking their lips, their hands clenching spasmodically with urgent need.

They reeked with a palpable madness. Something primal stirred in her gut. Her mouth grew dry with thirst. She snarled, and pushed the incipient chaos away with a flash of iron-willed control. They advanced upon her, ignoring her, peering past her with avid eyes into the beckoning tunnels.

Chloe turned and blurred forward down the middle path. So much for strategy, she'd just have to wing it and use her best judgment. The vampires rushed after her, shrieks and wails beginning to rise from the mass of vampires as they variously lost their sanity. The fourth wave descended into an uncontrolled mob.

Chloe frowned as she ran. In another minute the tunnels would be swarming with vampires hell bent on finding warm human blood to drink. They wouldn't care about anything else. She pulled to a stop. The vampires rushed past her like spring-melt river water around an immovable boulder. Let them run. In their swarming, they would randomly search all the available paths. In a handful of minutes, they would cover the maze in full. She could use the sounds of their voices to draw a map of the maze within her mind.

Chloe positioned herself in the middle of the vampires and advanced with them. All she had to do now was wait for the swarm to solve the maze for her.

Easy.

* * *

The hellish 30mm cannon fire ceased and the black shadowstar drones vanished into the night sky.

The air reeked of burnt metal. The bottom half of both doors lay reduced to fragments of smoking iron littering the warehouse floor. Peter rushed into the space beneath the doors, he slung his MGL from its straps at his side and lifted the squad automatic weapon to his shoulder. He was first on the line, joined a moment later by the Blake force team and the rest of the Mirovar force team, except Anton.

A dozen vampires were less than fifty yards away. Peter opened fire with his SAW, flames leaping from the barrel. Silver and lead hollow points speared away at them. A moment later, the rest of the Blake and Mirovar force teams opened fire. The sustained barrage cut the vampires to pieces. The last of the assault falling and stumbling to the concrete apron before the hangar.

"Cease fire!" Justin commanded.

The teams stopped firing, gray smoke rising from their weapons. No one said anything. Everyone was scanning the airport. The first rush was just a disorganized taste of the madness to come.

It began as a faint noise on the far side of the airport. The shrieks, wails and screams rapidly rose in volume as the vampires raced en masse across the open space between the hangars and the warehouse. They were covering a hundred yards every three seconds. Their origin hangars were anything from a thousand yards to a mile away. Effective firing range was five hundred yards. The vampires would be on top of them fifteen seconds later.

"Wait for it," Justin advised calmly.

Jay said, "Fire from the edge and swing through to the middle of the mass. They'll bunch up as they converge on us."

"We have two-hundred rounds each, that's twenty seconds on full auto," Peter stated.

Justin commanded, "When they hit two hundred yards, anyone with an MGL – use it."

Peter advised the team. "Use a flat trajectory with the grenades." His Order nightglasses picked up the vampires and tracked their advance. They passed six hundred yards. A number appeared in small red numerals in the upper right-hand corner of his field of view, it read, '148.' A low murmur spread through the assembled Ramp masters as their own nightglasses reported the number of oncoming vampires.

Justin spoke with deadly calm, "Hold fast."

Jay stood next to Peter's left. He held a squad automatic weapon to his shoulder and whispered, "For Yvette. For Francis."

The leading vampires closed past five hundred yards and into effective range.

Peter dived into his Ramp. Power slammed through his limbs, the airport resolving into super-sharp clarity. The onrushing vampires became discrete individuals. He'd taken Jay's advice and targeted an outlying vampire. He pulled the trigger. The SAW began firing, orange flame bursting from the barrel with each round. The ammunition was an even mix of silver and lead hollow-points with every fifth round a bright tracer. A stream of silvery-golden light flashed downrange toward the vampire. He started to dodge inward toward the rest of the vampires, the first few rounds whipping past him on the left. Peter adjusted his aim. The vampire ran into another vampire who attempted to fend him off with a back-handed slap. Peter's fire ripped into them, and they fell away in a hail of silver and lead within a blood-red mist.

Peter held his finger hard on the trigger. His stream of fire joined by another eleven lines of silver and golden light. The vampires closed to four hundred yards; leaping, dodging, and zig-zagging left and right. The Mirovar and Blake force teams hunted them down, and they died and died, but not quickly enough.

The hungry shrieks and hate-filled howls cut through the night air, competing with the hammering of the light machine guns.

The vampires closed to three hundred yards.

* * *

Tamsah held his blackened twelve-inch tri-bladed knives secreted against his forearms.

The growing madness of the vampires was like a slapped face that continued to redden with pain. He'd followed on the rear edge of the seething mass. They'd begun at the hangar, following Armitage into the tunnels, but it had quickly become apparent she didn't have a map through the maze.

Tamsah smiled quietly. If Crane and Armitage had hoped to launch a simultaneous attack on the Order position in the warehouse, that hope had foundered on the twin rocks of blood frenzy and a maze worthy of the Red Empire.

Furthermore, the vampire horde's madness was getting worse. With Armitage's sudden need to explore tunnels and maze levels with half-crazed servants that were as likely to run off as return, progress toward the Ramp masters had slowed down. The vampires had become frustrated, needful, willing to take risks and disobey. Always a fractious creature, their underlying alignment with chaos rose to the surface when they were in large groups. The Way of the Faithful was explicit about the nature of vampires and their propensity for insanity whenever they congregated in large numbers.

The vampire mob fragmented and flooded the tunnels. The nearby vampires blurred forward, driven by their dark instincts, their faces ripe with blood lust. They would inevitably converge on the Order force teams. Their innate hunting instincts were still fully operational, but they would be a disorganized swarm by the time they made contact with the Ramp masters of the Order.

Armitage and Crane had lost control. With the cover of the mad ones, it was now time for Tamsah to break away from the militia and find his own way forward. The truth speaker would be somewhere in front of him and she would need his protection. He slipped confidently away into the tunnels.

Mazes were like a second home for him.

* * *

The first vampire to run off within the tunnels found someone.

And died a moment later. The sound of her falling to the floor occurred as a double thud with a wet splash. For someone of Chloe's long experience, the sound was a fingerprint of specific action. Someone had cut through the vampire with a dragon blade. Horizontally, not vertically. The two halves had landed with a brief separation in time. A vertical bisection normally resulted in simultaneous landing of the separated body halves.

She had verified this fact late in the nineteenth century.

Chloe focused her hearing, discarding the confusing miasma of screams, maniacal laughter, howls and bone-scraping screeches from the frenzied vampires surrounding her. Vampires could focus in on minute differences of sound when they chose to do so, and Chloe had mastered the technique.

Next to the dripping blood of the vampire corpse was a heartbeat four to five feet above the floor. A heart that was running at a steady thirty beats a minute. It was a heart she'd know anywhere. Anton Slayne stood alone in the tunnels. As if alerted by the death of one of their number, the vampire swarm fixed its attention on the solitary audible human heart.

A wave of lust flushed through her. Oh, she wanted to join in and rush blindly forward. She could seize the young man; his flesh hot, his blood hotter. She could drag him to the floor, mount his body, and sink her fangs through the warm, taut skin of his throat. His heart would throb beneath her like a wild thing in final desperation to survive. She would hold him tight with her thighs and hands, puncture the carotid artery and wrap her mouth around the wound. Muscles deep within her abdomen would flex and contract, drawing his blood in a hot rush from his body deep into hers. Her heart would sing in glorious triumph as wet satiation flooded every part of her body. She would drain him until she'd drawn every last drop of glorious exquisite blood from his body. With her lust fully spent, she would rise up and leave Anton an exhausted dry husk, bereft of life, but the feeding would be an act of sublime glory.

Chloe turned and slammed her gauntleted fist into the wall. The metal panel curved inward beneath her knuckles with a thunderous crack. She blinked, drawing her fangs back into her gums, and looked forward. She had her mission and she would fulfill it. She took a deep breath, let it out. Anton Slayne was by himself, and alone he posed little threat.

She could afford to wait. She remained poised to move in any direction, to take any action, to respond to any need.

Adaptability was the soul of initiative.

* * *

Peter dropped his empty multiple grenade launcher to the concrete floor.

Ragged holes stuttered across the line of vampires. Li hosed the nearest vampires with rounds from her SAW, bright flames issued from the barrel in hungry tongues. One vampire fell backward, his head ripped apart in a splash of blood. The nearest vampires closed to within a hundred yards. She would run out of time before she ran out of ammunition. She was never going to run out of targets. The thirty-six 40mm grenades the team had fired at the vampires had killed as many as the earlier machine gun fire, but the relatively slow-moving grenades had also been easier for the vampires to dodge.

Her Order nightglasses registered eighty-one hostiles within a hundred yards.

She continued firing. Another vampire spun away in front of her, riddled with silver and lead hollow-points, his blood painting two following vampires with red splatter.

The nearest vampires closed to fifty yards, the length of an Olympic sized swimming pool. They'd be in touching distance within one and a half seconds. Li kept firing until the very last moment, another vampire taking a burst through its chest. Its face froze with shock as it fell forward, sliding across the concrete in front of the warehouse, leaving a snail trail of scarlet blood beneath the warehouse's flood lights.

Peter dropped his gun, gray wisps of smoke rising lazily from the mouth of the barrel as it fell slowly to the floor. His hands snapped up and down, his double-bladed axes appearing in an 'X' in front of him.

Li let go of her SAW, it floated away from her toward the concrete in slow motion, her hands going to the handle of the Green Dragon at her hip.

The Mirovar and Blake force teams stood as one, edged weapons ready.

The vampires hit the line of Ramp masters like a moving wall of shrieking death.

Four vampires converged on Li's position. The closest launched itself, diving above her. She drew the Green Dragon free from its scabbard at her hip. The blade arced up and over her head from left to right as she turned a hundred and eighty degrees beneath the leaping vampire. The Green Dragon passed through the creature's waist, a spray of blood splashing over Patrick Wichowski on her left.

She reversed the blade in her right hand, thrusting it past her right hip into the next vampire running up behind her. She twisted, reversing in a half circle to the right, dragging the blade out of the creature in a vicious draw cut. The vampire clutched its belly with both hands, bloody loops of blue and gray gut spilling past its hands. Her first two attacks had badly wounded, but not killed either vampire. Two more were rushing her from left to right. She spun, her left foot lashing out, catching the vampire on her left in the gut. He folded over her boot, and then launched through the air past Peter.

Peter's left hand slashed horizontally backward, his axe carving through the flying vampire's skull. The half-headless corpse slammed into the floor a moment later.

Li never saw the lifeless body land. She ran the vampire reaching for her from the right through the chest with the Green Dragon. Her draw cut slashed his heart in two and he slumped to the concrete floor at her feet.

She took a step back; whirled and struck the rising forms of the first two vampires she'd wounded. Their heads rolled from their shoulders, blood fountaining into the air from their severed necks.

"No!" Justin shouted.

Max Guerra's head flew free from within a huddle of vampires. His brown eyes startled, his torn throat dripping thin ribbons of blood and sinew.

Li gave ground along with the rest of the combined team.

A voice called out behind her, "This way!"

She risked a backward glance.

Slayne stood next to the shipping container above the stairs into the tunnels, one hand holding the door open, the other beckoning to the Ramp masters.

Jay stood next to Slayne, his SAW in his left hand, smoke rising from its barrel. He beckoned with his free hand and shouted, "Come on!"

The massed vampires, more than sixty strong, surged through the opening beneath the severed warehouse doors. Shrieking, screaming with hate and blood lust, their eyes wild, hands outstretched to grip, drag and tear.

Justin commanded, "Go, Go, Go."

Li turned and blurred through the open doorway. She sincerely wished the elder Slayne had one of his famous tricks up his sleeve. Otherwise, they were simply going from the frying pan into the fire.

For surely, the tunnels swarmed with all the vampires that had run across the airport to hangar number one.

And that force was far larger than what they faced here.

* * *

The lone vampire lay in two halves on the cold floor of the tunnel.

The faintest murmur of distant screams and manic laughter echoed through the maze. Anton flicked his blade, painting the nearest wall with a thin ribbon of residual blood. He'd tarried too long attempting to breach the locks on his grandfather's cache of missiles. The vampires had come into the tunnels. God only knew what was happening above ground. He turned and blurred back toward the warehouse.

Before he reached the next intersection Anton spontaneously dropped out of Ramp and slowed to a walk. He pulled to a halt, momentarily perplexed. The temperature dropped precipitously, his breath misting before his face. The tunnel writhed, the matte metal panels lining the walls, and smooth concrete walls and ceilings vanished. Ancient stone blocks lined the tunnel. Flaming torches in sconces flickered and danced, sending shadows skittering over the rough walls and floor.

Anton stepped forward, something crunched under his boot. He looked down, dread flooding his soul. Human skulls covered the floor. Fresh bones recently taken and denuded of flesh. A terrible presence approached from behind. He whirled around.

Chloe Armitage stood twenty feet away, dressed in a diaphanous silk gown as dark as night. Her raven hair hung long; woven through a delicate golden crown adorning her head before spilling across her pale shoulders. She stared at him with avid interest. Her right hand unfurled and she pointed at him with a slender finger, and declared in a voice resplendent and chilling, "I will have you too."

A rushing thunder emerged from the deep shadows behind her. The air shifted, rising into a stiff breeze, Armitage's gown flourished around her like a sail, outlining her slim curves in silhouette.

Anton's eyes widened, a frigid shudder rising up his back. He lifted the Blue Dragon, a golden flame erupting along its gleaming length. He snapped the flaming sword into attack position above his left shoulder.

Armitage took a step forward over the carpet of skulls, her steps light enough to leave them intact. Her face paled, her hair receded, her vivid blue eyes darkened until they were wholly black orbs reflecting a mirror image of Anton holding a flaming sword.

Ivory skinned, dark-eyed vampires emerged from the darkness behind her, sweeping past her in a frenzy of claw and fang.

She leaned forward, her hands snapping wide to block their passage. Her black tongue lolled out past her bright red lips and she roared, "HE IS MINE!"

The ancient dungeon walls swapped to negative light for a brief moment. The torches becoming dark holes in the wall and the waiting vampires, luminous ghosts. Armitage stood before all, a dark queen of unfathomable power, mistress of all she surveyed.

The concrete tunnel and matte metal panels returned with a whip-like crack. Anton's heart thudded in his chest and he took an involuntary step backward, and uttered in shock, "What the fucking hell was that?"

He stared along the tunnel the vampire had come along. What had been faint echoes only moments before were growing louder, resolving into mad shrieks and howls of euphoric joy. There were more vampires. Of course, there were more vampires. Crane had killed the sensor array and discovered the tunnels. However, the vampire king had also sent someone with the vampires. Someone Anton had a score to settle with.

Chloe Armitage was in the maze.

He was certain of it.

Her presence changed everything.

* * *

Arthur wild ramped, activating his speed talent.

He dragged on the shipping container door with all his might. The solid-metal door slammed shut with an ear-splitting clang. A pair of vampire hands, both right, fell to the floor and twitched spasmodically. He turned and chased the last of the Ramp masters down the stairs, hitting a prominent red button on the wall halfway down the short stairwell. A second door emerged from a slit in the wall and slid shut behind him, blocking access from the stairs.

The first landing was twenty feet long, and like the rest of the maze, well lit. On the left-hand wall was a weapons rack, on the opposite wall was an alphanumeric key pad.

Arthur rushed to the key pad and punched in a sixteen-digit string of numbers and letters. He paused, extended his thumb, then his index finger, followed by the other three fingers as he marked off five seconds. The Mirovar and Blake force teams stared at him with a mixture of expectation and perplexity.

He punched the enter button.

A sharp light outlined the frame of the doorway. Explosive thunder resounded above them. The ceiling vibrated, a thin layer of gray concrete dust descending onto their heads and shoulders.

"The third wave is done," Arthur stated, matter-of-factly. "We have to deal with the vampires in the tunnels next." He turned to the rack on the opposite wall, and took down the first of a dozen squad automatic weapons and handed it to Jay. "Take this one. It's fresh and ready to go." He turned to Justin and said, "I know, we lost Max, but we can cut through the vampires in the tunnels. They've gone mad. Bunched up in a confined space, with these weapons, we can get through this."

Justin suggested, "We still have to deal with the shadowstar drones."

"Use the map in the nightglasses to go to the caches. There is a spiral staircase behind each cache. It leads up to a hidden hatch you can only open from beneath. Pop up onto the airport surface and take out the drones before they realize you are there. Having destroyed their air cover, you can easily make it to hangar number one."

"How do we get into the cache and arm the missiles?" Jay asked.

Arthur tilted his head for a moment, glancing from Jay to Justin and back. He handed Justin a small notepad. "The arming code for the SAMs is on the first page, and the method to reveal and unlock the cache is on the second." He put his right hand on Jay's shoulder and said, "You're the youngest. I need to make sure that someone who is most likely to survive has the information – or else no one is getting out."

Jay looked at him askance for a moment, and then laughed ironically.

Arthur slapped the two force leaders on the shoulders, and declared, "You have the map, a mission, and no more time. Now go."

"What about you?" Justin asked.

"I must find my grandson," Arthur answered.

"What of the P-Case?" Jay asked. "We can't leave it guarded by just one man."

Arthur hesitated, his jaw working, trying to speak between agonized gasps, he finally said in a hoarse whisper, "It's already safe."

Jay blanched and pointed at the P-Case strapped to Arthur's back. "Oh my God! What the hell is that?"

Arthur looked at him helplessly, and then stated, "You have your mission. Get it done and get the hell out of here. I'm going to find Anton. If we survive, we'll meet you in hangar number one." He left unspoken what would happen if he never found Anton, or they didn't make it to the hangar to rejoin the Mirovar force team.

Justin nodded. "Done."

Jay shook his head, his eyes wide. He addressed his team, "Grab a gun and a spare magazine, and let's go." He grabbed Arthur by the shoulder and said, "I'll see you in the hangar. Once we complete this mission – we're done – understood?"

Arthur's eyes tightened and he replied, "Perfectly."

Jay stared at Arthur for half a second. "Or, I'll meet you in Hell." He turned and joined his team. Moments later, the landing was clear and Arthur stood alone.

"Okay, Anton. Where the hell are you?" he asked softly.

Arthur strode to the nearest intersection. Two pathways led away into the Maze. A third would take him to the final warehouse. He hesitated briefly, a war of wills within his mind. He sighed and turned to the left and strode off to the third warehouse. It was important he didn't ramp. He knew, despite the hidden world of his other selves, he had to give time to allow his enemies to notice his presence and follow after him.

He blinked once; his face heavy with disappointment. The compulsion to make his way to the final warehouse was like an iron prison around his mind. He'd have to leave Anton to whatever fate awaited him in the tunnels. Something he'd promised himself he wouldn't do, and yet when it came down to a choice, he followed his whole-self's dictates like a slave.

Arthur had to live out his plan, even though he had no memory of conceiving it.

… *and yet I told them about the second P-Case.*

* * *

The air shuddered, a dull thud echoing throughout the maze. A mass of explosives had just detonated on the surface.

Chloe counted eleven new heartbeats in the maze. Clearly the surviving members of the Mirovar and Blake force teams had entered the tunnel and wiped out the third wave by demolishing the second warehouse. Most of the vampire swarm within the maze diverted from the lone heartbeat of Anton, and surged in the direction of the Order teams, attracted by the greater mass of fresh blood. Only a handful of stragglers continued to hunt Anton Slayne.

The Mirovar and Blake force teams paused for a moment, talking in low voices. Their exact words lost amongst the competing shrieks and howls of the vampire swarm converging on their position. Only the timbre of their hearts remained truly audible. A distinct signature of humanity that drew the hunting vampire time and time again.

Chloe stilled herself, relaxed, and sharpened her focus. She drew upon her perfect memory of the vault beneath Saint Peter's Basilica. Could she separate Arthur Slayne's heartbeat from the rest? Every heart was unique. The rhythms were different, the size of the chambers varied, as did the resonance of the chest cavity. Together these variations provided an individual signature. Peter Lamb, and Justin Blake were immediately identifiable by the depth and breadth of the resonance in their massive chests. Strength talents, the both of them. Rare and powerful, she set them aside. The females were also distinctive; Chiara Morte – yes, surely Morte, Li Wu, who still lived despite Chloe's best efforts to kill her, and Red Cevarre, the Blake team's combat surgeon. She set them aside also. Jay Creeley, she identified from his foray into the dungeon beneath her former manor house. She set him aside too, noting in passing that Francis Mirovar was missing. The Mirovar force team had lost its leader. Then there were those who were new. They must include the famous Two Taylors, who she'd never had the pleasure of meeting. Their hearts beat with the matching rhythm of a deeply connected pair of blademasters. Finally, there were two hearts that could belong to Max Guerra, Tim Leung, or the loremaster Patrick Wichowski. One of the last three Blake team members was missing, presumed slaughtered in the ruined warehouse above the maze entrance.

That left Arthur Slayne, the last of the twelve, the lone signature matching her memory of the fight beneath Saint Peter's Basilica. He stayed behind, the rest of the Ramp masters moving rapidly and with confidence through the maze.

Chloe pressed her lips into a thin line. They had the luxury of knowing where they were going. They obviously had what Chloe still lacked – a map. She listened carefully. Arthur paused for a moment, changed direction and headed off toward the third and final warehouse.

She arched a quizzical eyebrow.

That's odd, she thought. *What's he doing going off on his own?*

Chloe opened her tactical link to Crane and stated, "The Mirovar and Blake force teams are in the tunnels, and heading toward the other side of the airport. Arthur Slayne has separated from them and is heading toward the third warehouse."

"Indeed," Crane responded. "Avoid combat with the Ramp masters. Follow Slayne to the third warehouse. I will meet you there and we will end this farce together."

"Yes, Sir," Chloe said, a quiet smile on her lips. She could afford to be civil, since Crane had just given her leeway to ignore Anton Slayne. She'd prefer to keep him alive. He could still prove useful for her final end game against Crane.

Speaking of Anton Slayne, where was he? She'd momentarily lost contact with his heartbeat while she searched for his grandfather's.

Chloe closed her eyes, extending her senses to their maximums. Anton's heartbeat showed up a second later. She opened her eyes, genuinely surprised. What the hell was he doing? He was heading slowly toward her.

How was he doing that?

Well, he was only a boy. A gifted boy with potential, but still a boy. She would avoid him and close on the final warehouse.

Chloe blurred away.

* * *

The four shadowstar drones descended where the runways crossed at the center of the airport. They extended pale landing struts down to the tarmac. Slits of blue fire flickering and dying beneath their dark carapace hulls. They crouched like giant menacing insects as they came to rest on the ground.

Canopies lifted and folded forward, revealing cabins and life pods. Three of the drones disgorged twelve praetorians uniformly armed with 7.62mm miniguns. They blurred away, creating a perimeter a hundred yards across surrounding the four drones.

Cornelius leaped from the command drone. He adjusted the fit of his bastard sword at his waist and regarded the airport with a steely glare. The first and second warehouses were barely recognizable ruins. Reduced to smoking piles of torn reinforced steel and rubble, filled with spot fires and the silence of the dead. Slayne had eliminated the third wave, the militia vampires vanishing within the glare and heat of thousands of pounds of detonating high explosives.

He frowned, had they made enough of an impact on the Ramp masters? Had they worn them down? He suspected not. The Mirovar and Blake force teams had descended into the tunnels. They would face the last wave of militia vampires in what was no doubt a confined and confusing space. He had no idea who would emerge victorious from the meat grinder within the tunnels, and right now, he didn't care. He tapped a panel beneath the right chin of his black tactical helmet. The canopies closed on the drones and they rose as one on pillars of blue fire. While Cornelius wore his command helmet, the automated drones were at his beck and call.

He pointed at the last hangar on the southern side of the airport, and called to his squad leaders, "That is the Order's exfil site. They have a jet. Kill all who come there and let none escape."

Hoffman, Cantor, and Browning all responded with "Yes, Sir." The three squads of black-armored vampires blurred across the tarmac to the designated hangar.

Cornelius blurred in the opposite direction toward the last warehouse. He'd noticed a variance in its construction moments before landing. The last warehouse sported a long retractable section in the middle of its roof. With the explosive destruction of the second warehouse, the retractable roof had begun to open. It was no accident that Slayne was now heading toward the third warehouse. The only warehouse that could harbor a vertical takeoff and landing aircraft – like an advanced drone. This was his real exfil path.

Within the tunnels, Chloe was advancing toward the warehouse. She would arrive shortly after Slayne. They would deal with him together and take back what belonged to him. Soon, he'd recover the P-Case. They would take it to the East Coast Hub, and install it on the quantum processors there. They would use it to assist with the capture of the Mekrarian vampire heading west across Eurasia. Once the Panopticon 2.0 was online, he would cross-reference their outputs to identify the mark of Arthur Slayne and eliminate his legacy from the world.

Cornelius arrived at the warehouse. A single regular door opposed his entry. He tore it from its hinges and threw it into the night behind him. He entered the warehouse. It was mostly empty, except for a handful of shipping containers near the walls, and a single seat hypersonic drone sitting directly beneath the steadily retracting door in the ceiling.

He snarled and strode forward, his vampire senses on high alert. He didn't fear the use of hidden explosives. His last vision had been explicit. This would end with hand-to-hand combat. Slayne would arrive and then Armitage, there would be a contest of blades, and there were none better than his enforcer.

Cornelius whirled in front of the dark-gray drone and regarded the silence around him. He loosened the bastard sword at his waist. An eleventh century genius had forged the ancient steel in Damascus. The uncanny variant of meteoric iron had fallen more than once upon the Earth, and he carried the equal of any of the Dragon blades. It was time to draw the venom from this prophecy by engaging with it. Sometimes, to maintain great power you had to put everything at risk, and this was such a time. Either he would be victorious or Slayne would destroy him.

He could be patient. He could wait. Slayne would bring him the P-Case soon enough, and then the final contest would begin.

Cornelius had foreseen it.

* * *

Howls, screeches, and wails echoed throughout the maze.

Li dashed down a stairway, following the green line of Arthur Slayne's map to his hidden caches of surface to air missiles. She leaped off the stairs, onto a broad, deep landing. The open space was twenty-five yards on a side, with a twenty-foot-high ceiling lit with a dozen thin strip lights. The map of the maze hung in faint outlines in her Order nightglasses' heads-up display. A sharp green line jagged through the left exit and down a stairway. The SAMs were another eight hundred yards of twists, turns, and level changes distant.

She landed in a controlled slide across the smooth concrete, then gained traction and followed Justin toward the left exit. Two more stairwells descended from the front and right-hand side walls. The tunnels resounded with the cries, squeals and yells of frenzied vampires. Their mad cacophony came from every direction, and they were closing in.

Li ran at Justin's right hand, her head on a swivel. Her squad automatic weapon ready to fire, the Green Dragon loose in its scabbard at her waist. The two force teams ran in two lines, Sam, Taylor, Patrick, Tim and Red behind Justin, and Peter, Chiara, and Jay behind her. She'd volunteered for the point role, primarily because she had Justin on her left and Peter behind her. Against a horde of vampires, it was best to bring the heavy artillery. The boots of the rest of the team slapped the concrete behind her in steady staccato rhythms, an orderly counterpoint to the discordant noise of the vampires.

A squeal of delight cut through the air behind them. A moment later automatic gunfire erupted from the rear of the team. Li chanced a glance behind her. Jay, Tim Leung, and Red Cevarre were covering the rear of the combined team. The vampires had managed to get behind them, an almost solid wall running down the stairs toward the Ramp masters. The SAWs hammered and smoked, fire ripping into the front ranks of the vampires, but more came, clambering and leaping over the dead, scaling the walls and clawing their way along the ceiling. Their avid eyes filled with hunger, lit upon her own. A cold shiver accelerated up her spine and she swallowed against a suddenly dry mouth.

Screeches and howls burst through the air from the left exit. Justin opened up with his squad automatic weapon, a stream of rounds removing the top of a vampire's head as it rose above the stairs. A solid mass of vampires swarmed over the falling corpse, bursting into the chamber, their hands reaching for the members of the Blake force team. The monsters blocked the path to the SAMs they needed against the shadowstars.

Manic laughter brayed from the right. Li pivoted a hundred and eighty degrees from the left exit. Justin had Sam and Taylor just behind him, and if those three couldn't deal with the threat, no one could. A mass of vampires poured into the chamber from the right stairway. Peter fired from the hip, sending a stream of rounds flashing into the front rank of vampires. Chiara appeared at his side, her face frozen with grim determination, adding her own machine gun fire to Peter's defense.

The room dimmed while the air thundered with automatic weapon fire. A horrible sense of impending doom swept through her. Li turned toward the distant hangars. Vampires were crawling along the ceiling from the forward stairway, using their innate strength and physical hardness to punch finger grips into the concrete. Beneath them, more vampires surged forward. Everyone around her was already engaged to the left and right.

She stood alone. Li snapped her SAW up to her shoulder and pulled the trigger. The gun vibrated in her hands, spitting fire, silver, and lead at a wall of vampires four wide spilling like a rogue wave onto the landing. Her rounds ripped into the first two vampires. They slumped to the floor, their blood painting the vampires behind them like a Jackson Pollock masterpiece.

Samuel Taylor stepped in on her left, ragged tongues of flame wreathing the muzzle of his SAW. A stream of rounds tore into the swarming vampires reaching at them with outstretched fingers. Vampires crawled along the walls and ceiling, scuttling forward like a ravenous hive. Their writhing bodies obscured the lights, plunging the room deeper into shadow.

Li shook her head once. The SAWs sustained fire of silver and lead hollow-points tearing the vampires to pieces. The silver ensuring that once a vampire was down, it stayed down. But – she dove deep into silence, reaching for her most potent Ramp. The action slowed around her. The SAWs strobing the twilight lit room with muzzle flash, individual rounds whipping through the oncoming vampires with a thunderous crack and splat. Their faces resolved, leering, twisted, mouths agape, fangs prominent against dark lips, and pale skin. Eyes, dark with blood lust, tracking her every movement.

A human voice screamed in terrible agony behind her, then cut off just as quickly as it had begun. The vampires hooted in triumph. There was no time to look behind. Red Cevarre, the Blake force team combat surgeon shouted, "Tim," in a voice verging on panic.

Li kept her finger on the trigger of her weapon. Caseless ammunition riffed through it, melting away to propellant stench while flames spat around the end of her barrel. She pivoted, striking three vampires in a row with combinations of silver and lead hollow-points. They shuddered, tripped and spasmed, falling to the concrete floor in spreading pools of blood.

Still more vampires replaced the ones that fell. One dropped down from the ceiling, snapping a hand over the hot barrel of her gun – flesh sizzling and popping from the heat. She released it, and he whipped it away as he landed on his feet.

In a single motion, the Green Dragon arced from its scabbard, entered the vampire just above its right hip, slicing up through its torso, exiting in a splash of blood above the creature's left shoulder. The vampire fell apart to the left and right, a look of shock etched in dark shadows on his face.

The Green Dragon felt good within her hands, a natural extension of her deepest self. She whirled and lashed out with the shimmering blade, carving through a hapless vampire's head. He fell away, his hands flapping uselessly, his skull shorn away above his mouth.

Two more took his spot, another dropped from above.

Li blurred to her maximum potential.

It was time to do or die.

* * *

He had to save the truth speaker.

Tamsah had tracked the Order teams through the maze, while watching the frenzied vampire militia swarm into position around them. The creatures had behaved like a single amoebic organism, as if they had established a hive mind with a single goal – the destruction of the humans. He had never heard of such a thing, but Tamsah was inclined to believe the evidence of his own eyes over any received truth.

The thinnest part of the swarm had converged behind the Mirovar and Blake force teams. Tamsah had inserted himself into their midst. They ignored him, convinced of his allegiance by his vampire nature, and blind to his lack of frenzy by their own submission to abomination.

The members of the Mirovar force team he knew well from his encounter with them in the dungeons beneath Armitage's manor house on the cliffs above the town of Whitby. He would spare them if he could, they were well motivated to protect the truth speaker. As for the other Order operatives he would have to take one. It was a necessary violence. The smell of fresh blood would draw the mob away from the truth speaker.

The flash of gun fire had ceased, now blades worked against vampire flesh and bone. The lights continued to flicker as vampires scurried across the ceiling like loathsome insects. Shadows grew and shrank without rhyme or reason.

Tamsah selected his target. He approached unseen, making full use of the Ninjitsu skills of a Red Empire assassin. He moved like a shadow, hidden behind the manic advance of the militia vampires. His boots sank into the gutted body of a vampire. It was impossible to advance without stepping on the corpses littering the floor. The concrete ran with vampire blood, and not a little human blood. The vampire horde had literally shredded one of the Order operatives. Bodies lay heaped where they fell, variously slaughtered by silver and lead hollow-point rounds and razor-sharp blades wielded with super-human skill, speed and strength.

The Ramp masters were glowing hot within the infra-red portion of his vampire vision. They could not keep up this level of continuous intensity for much longer. Tamsah's intervention was essential to save the truth speaker before they exhausted themselves beyond the capacity to Ramp, and the vampires tore them apart.

A vampire to his right fell to the elegant swordsmanship of a young man with blood-streaked, dirty-blonde hair. Tamsah assisted the vampire to the floor with a well-timed push, and flashed through the vacated space. He jagged hard left to avoid any counter strike from the young Mirovar operative. He beat past the young, red-headed woman's sword with his left dagger, came in close and stabbed her three times in the chest. Each blow missed her heart. He needed her alive for now, but in minutes any one of the blows would prove fatal.

Her face paled with shock and her eyes rolled. Tamsah struck her twice more, his daggers tearing long wounds along both her arms. Her katana fell away and she slumped forward. Tamsah ducked beneath her, catching her in a fireman's carry over his right shoulder. He blurred forward, twisting hard to the left, positioning her body between his head and the Order operatives fighting to stay alive in an ever-decreasing space in the middle of the chamber.

Someone shouted, "Red," as he cut past the center of the landing. He threaded his way through the vampires and leaped over the dead. The woman on his shoulder moaned, a distinctly human sound amongst the cacophony of the vampire swarm.

Her voice was like the bleat of a wounded sheep amongst a pack of ravenous wolves.

Most, but not all the vampires turned as one, tracking his progress toward the forward stairwell. He stabbed a vampire in his way with his left blade, tearing a great hole through its heart. It was enough to break the spell. The Red headed woman screamed, her arms flailing, sending ribbons of arterial blood spraying in his wake.

The vampires surged. The air in the tunnel pushing against him as the vampires flooded after him. *Success! Now the truth speaker will survive.*

Tamsah blurred deeper into the maze, a horde of crazed vampires howling behind him.

***

Red Cevarre screamed as the short dark-clad vampire carried her out of sight.

The Mirovar and Blake force teams were dying a death of a thousand cuts. The swarming vampires forced extended Ramps in response to their incessant attacks. Li's team mates were rapidly approaching overheating and exhaustion. They had fought long fights in the recent past, but had always had time to snatch a break between ramps. This was different. This was dangerous in a way they had never faced before. Overheated, exhausted, they would fail to Ramp. Defenseless, the vampires would tear them apart.

The vampire in front of Li hissed and withdrew. Vanishing down the stairwell after the ill-fated Blake force team combat surgeon. Another attacked her on the right, she slashed the Green Dragon across its throat. The vampire separated into its head, and the rest of its body. The head bounced on the floor and rolled to a stop at Li's feet, the headless body slumped backwards, fountaining blood over the thick carpet of vampire corpses littering the chamber.

A couple of thuds resounded behind her as dying vampires discovered the floor. The rest of the swarm fled the chamber, noses in the air, hooting and hollering after the blood spilling from Red Cevarre.

Jay leaned on his sword for a moment and said, "Hell, that was close."

"All of us together drew them like moths to a flame," Samuel Taylor remarked; his mouth set in a hard grimace as he stared after his vanishing team mate.

Justin nodded; his eyes tight with restrained grief. "Jay, we need to split up. Sam, Taylor and Patrick will come with me for the missiles. You take your team to secure the hangar."

Jay wiped his hand down his face and shivered with reaction to surviving the mad onslaught. "You're right. Get the missiles. My team will secure our path out of here."

Justin reached across and squeezed Jay's shoulder and stared hard into his eyes. "Godspeed, my friend."

Jay slapped Justin's shoulder; his hand staying to squeeze it. "Good hunting."

Justin called out once to the survivors of his team and cut down the left-hand side stairwell toward the missile caches.

Jay looked around the team, conducting a quick visual inspection to make sure everyone could still fight on. His right hand chopped out toward the right stairwell. "Follow me, we'll go to the hangar and secure the private jet." He strode past Li's left shoulder and began scaling the dead vampires.

Li turned to follow him. She clambered over the dead, her skin crawling with disgust. There was no way to get out of the chamber without stepping on a dead vampire. She spotted her SAW discarded against a wall and scooped it up. She paused just long enough to slot home the replacement ammunition satchel, and the ammo counter on top of the weapon reset to '200.' She stepped over another three bodies in a pile and got clear of the abattoir of the landing. She joined the end of the line of Ramp masters and followed the rest of the Mirovar force team to hangar number one.

They had to secure a private jet to get out of here before vampire reinforcements arrived. If more vampires showed up, she didn't know how they would cope. The last attack had excoriated her soul. There was a big difference between fighting vampire soldiers that simply wanted to kill you, and fighting a mad horde that saw you as prey to tear apart and feast upon.

It was the difference between confronting an active and persistent evil versus confronting an overwhelming madness poised to destroy the world.

Evil and insanity were not the same thing.

* * *

The echoes of gunfire had faded away half a minute ago.

The screams, yowls and manic laughter of the vampires shifted away in the maze back toward the hangar side of the airport.

"Oh my God," Anton whispered. He had to believe the gunfire ceased because the Mirovar and Blake force teams had run out of opponents to kill, rather than the vampires had overwhelmed them. He had made the wrong decision; he was sure of it. Whatever fate had befallen the combined team he hadn't been there to share it with them. He felt ashamed. He'd shirked his duty. He was in the wrong place at the wrong time. The Order nightglasses had provided him with a map, but not a way to find his team mates in this maze, and he was now more or less lost.

A vampire screamed to his left. The creature had crept up on him before its inherent madness had taken control. Anton lashed out with the Blue Dragon taking the vampire through the chest. His draw cut sliced the vampire's heart in two and it fell forward onto the cold concrete, a pool of blood spreading around it.

The dying creature seemed to be the last of a handful of vampires that had caught up to him. He staggered back to an intersection. Something moved on the edge of his vision, a sliver of black blurring across an intersection far to his left. It was vampire armor; there was only one vampire wearing armor in this maze – Chloe Armitage. Anton flicked the Blue Dragon clear of blood. Perhaps he could salvage something from this terrible day.

He blurred after the running vampire.

Chapter Fifteen

"My strategy relied on their competence. The only way I could trap them, especially trap them both, was if they truly believed I'd made every effort to avoid tracking and capture. The merest hint of a lure would tip them off and result in disaster. It was imperative Crane saw himself as having the upper hand, and Armitage is the very soul of cunning. I had to keep their discovery of our exfil plan believable so they would not see the trap inherent within it." – Arthur Slayne

"Of course, I had to motivate them properly to commit themselves to a hand to hand fight – that was essential. Hence the Panopticon, hence the remains of the Order. It doesn't matter if the Order is destroyed if we destroy the Vampire Dominion at the same time. What need do we have for the solution if the problem has been extinguished? Without Crane and Armitage, and with the information buried within the Panopticon, the rest of the vampires can be readily mopped up." – Arthur Slayne

– Notes to Self. Marked, 'Do not open unless personality re-integration fails.'

* * *

Nevada, Arthur Slayne's Private Airport, Warehouse Number Three, September 11th, 20:45

The retractable roof clanked to a halt; the cloudless night sky revealed in all its glory above the warehouse.

Cornelius stood alone, wreathed in shadows beside a shipping container on the south side of the warehouse. The building was two hundred yards long and a hundred yards wide. It was not lost on him, that these were the very same dimensions of the warehouse on the Boston docks where he'd lost six praetorians and nearly sixty Shadowstone operatives in a debacle that had kicked off the recent troubles besetting his Dominion.

With a life that spanned nearly a thousand years he'd seen many allies and foes come and go; vampires, Order and Red Empire operatives, people of note who'd contributed something to his advancement, or opposed him and died at his hand. He was accustomed to playing the long game. Often, he simply needed to outlast his opponent du jour to claim victory, but this time was different. This time, he had foreknowledge of events courtesy of the Metaframe sorcery of Jean Philippe Allemande. He'd faced cusp events since the late 1850s and survived. This was another, but in this case, he'd detected a qualitative difference. Arthur Slayne had managed to hide himself from Cornelius' precognitive powers until the last day. No one had ever done that before.

While the younger Slayne was a dangerous berserker learning about his fell powers, it was the elder Slayne who was the true threat to his life. The most important thing he'd learned over the last one hundred and seventy plus years was that precognition did not reveal destiny. There was no fate. A skilled power operator could always shape events to their will. The advantage of the power granted by Allemande's sorcery was a superior awareness that overshadowed what anyone else could bring to the game.

Which is why Arthur Slayne perplexed him so much. How had he managed to remain in the shadows for so long? Was his grandson a proxy for his strategy? A pawn the elder Slayne had pushed forward over the chessboard, only to sacrifice for advantage at an opportune time. Would Arthur Slayne wipe out his own family line in service to his war against the Vampire Dominion? Cornelius could not rule it out, and he was no closer to piercing the deception that surrounded the elder Slayne's strategy.

A shipping container door on the opposite side of the warehouse creaked open on dry hinges. Arthur Slayne stepped through the doorway and into the light. He carried the P-Case in his left hand, and the Black Dragon in his right. A .50 caliber auto-pistol lay strapped to his right thigh. Cornelius would have to take care with the latter. A well-placed hypervelocity round could definitely ruin his night.

Cornelius watched from the shadows as Arthur Slayne approached the drone. He took his time, sauntering toward the craft. His lackadaisical efforts didn't ring true. Surely, he would rush to the craft, board it and attempt to outrun the waiting shadowstar drones. No, he was waiting for someone to reveal themselves. He was expecting Cornelius or Armitage to be there.

Oh! Something snapped shut within Cornelius' mind. The drone was a stunningly realistic mock up. His design was still singular in reality, although someone would have to die for leaking the blueprints to Slayne. Cornelius shook his head. This warehouse was an artfully crafted trap by Arthur Slayne. Without doubt, he'd intended to catch both himself and Armitage within his web of deceit. Slayne had taken the P-Case to provide bait to get Cornelius to commit, and he'd done so because he must. Slayne had understood perfectly the value of the Panopticon to Crane and the Vampire Dominion. The Panopticon was an essential tool to recovering the situation versus the Mekrarian ninja vampire and he had to have it back. Damn it, without the Panopticon, he'd have to take personal control of the hunt for the rogue ninja vampire, and God only knew what would happen while he remained occupied in western China and the eastern Caucuses. The whole situation with Mekra and her new vampire could spiral out of control. Slayne should give him the P-Case to save the world from a worse fate. Slayne was foolishly interfering in a situation he didn't understand.

The door on the shipping container moved slightly further ajar, and Armitage stepped out onto the concrete floor of the warehouse. Her auto-pistol appeared in her right hand, lined up on Arthur Slayne's chest. Her gaze flicked across the warehouse and arrested on Cornelius for a micro-second.

In that moment, while Armitage checked the room for visible traps. Slayne sheathed his blade and drew his own auto-pistol.

Cornelius stared down the wide throat of Slayne's matte-gray .50 caliber weapon. Slayne had only pretended not to see him hiding in the shadows. Now Slayne was pointing an auto-pistol armed with hypervelocity rounds at his face.

Slayne crab-walked toward Cornelius, his gun hand steady as a rock, while keeping Armitage within his peripheral vision.

Chloe strode confidently toward the front of the warehouse, diverging away from Slayne, creating a triangle with her at the head of it. A slight frown appeared on her forehead, belying her confident posture. If Slayne managed to shoot him through the heart or the head, he'd almost certainly die as the shockwave vaporized his flesh, and Armitage would be dead a moment later as the implant beneath her skull fired half an ounce of powdered silver into her brain stem.

Cornelius wouldn't stand to be anyone's target. He made a decision and blurred toward Armitage with all the speed of his Mekrarian blood heritage. Two hypervelocity rounds left their barrels at the same time, shredding the air in the warehouse with whip-like cracks.

A round vaporized a wisp of dark hair escaping from Cornelius' tactical helmet. It thudded into the warehouse wall and vanished through it, leaving an inch-wide hole surrounded by a plume of gray-white powder.

Slayne cried out, "Shit." His auto-pistol flying out of his grasp, bouncing off the top of the drone, before skittering away toward the back of the warehouse. Armitage had shot Slayne's weapon out of his hand.

Cornelius pulled to a halt a dozen feet short of her position, spread his hands wide and snapped angrily, "Why didn't you shoot him in the head."

Armitage looked at him, tilted her head slightly, then glanced back at Slayne and said warily, "He's just demolished the second warehouse with hidden explosives. He may have a dead-man switch that destroys this warehouse and everything in it if he dies. I think we need to keep him alive until we have secured the P-Case."

Cornelius paused for a moment. She could well be right. Slayne could have a neural implant linked to explosives hidden within the walls, floor and ceiling of the warehouse. Hell, the drone mock-up could harbor a bomb big enough to level the building. If Slayne died, his hidden explosives would detonate and slaughter anyone within the warehouse.

It was just the sort of trick Slayne would do.

Slayne reached over to the side of the drone's nose and punched a series of letters and numbers on an embedded touch screen. The drone hummed, the canopy rising and moving forward to reveal the cockpit. Cornelius frowned. He must have been wrong. It was a real drone after all, and Slayne was attempting to leave with the P-Case. He snapped at Armitage, "Take him."

The Red Dragon appeared in Armitage's hands and she blurred to the attack.

* * *

Arthur dived into his deepest wild Ramp. Cobalt fire flashed through him, his speed talent activating in full. The Black Dragon swept clear of its scabbard.

The warehouse resolved into super-sharp clarity. Crane was still, staring at him with a look that spoke of death. Armitage ran toward him, cutting the distance between them like an Olympic sprinter in ordinary time. She was fast, but her current speed at the upper limits of a vampire was within reach of his talent.

She would be striking to wound, or incapacitate him without dealing an immediate death blow. Her lack of attention to killing him outright offered a desperate opportunity. Arthur angled the Black Dragon in a diagonal arc before his chest, he needed to deflect her attack. He rushed toward her, more than matching her speed. He leaped, diving through the air in a flat trajectory past her.

The Black Dragon brushed defensively against the Red Dragon. A single pure tone rang like a God struck bell within the warehouse.

Arthur landed on the cold concrete mid-way between Crane and Armitage. His eyes widened slightly. She was already turning to confront him, but now she was too late. A sudden realization bloomed in his mind as a fell compulsion rose from the depths of his soul. His left hand moved with a will of its own, raising the P-Case to shoulder height, presenting it to Crane.

This was it – this was the moment he could realize his twenty-year strategy in full. Crane stared at him with uncertainty written over his face. The mission objective was within reach. A single word would kill everyone in the room.

Arthur's heart rested silently between beats.

He opened his mouth to speak the activation word.

* * *

The doorway framed Chloe Armitage leaning hard into a turn. She attempted desperately to reverse her direction; the Red Dragon in her right hand outstretched behind her. The echo of a blade against blade strike resounding off the warehouse walls.

Anton rushed up the final stairs, blurring past the open shipping container door into the warehouse.

His grandfather stood between Crane and Armitage. The Black Dragon dangled from his right hand, as if beneath his notice. He held the P-Case at shoulder height toward Crane, as if offering it to the vampire king. Arthur stared at Crane with deadly focus. He appeared about to say something of great importance.

Arthur's eyes flicked left to Anton. His mouth clamped shut, then gaped open to speak. His mouth snapped shut a second time, a look of utter devastation stealing over his face.

Armitage rushed his grandfather. Arthur whirled, the two dragon swords clashing again without drawing blood. She slid to a halt next to her king with a pivot, the Red Dragon snapping into attack position over her left shoulder.

Crane drew his bastard sword clear of its scabbard and stepped clear of Armitage to allow space to use it.

Crane and Armitage together. It was like all of Anton's Christmases had come at once. Fury and joy merged into a wild flame burning through his soul. He lifted the Blue Dragon above his head and shouted with dire exultation, "Arthur!"

Arthur lowered the P-Case to the floor and lifted the Black Dragon, a wry smile gracing his lips. Something deeply painful swallowed itself behind his eyes. He blinked once, a hardness fleeing his eyes, like he was accepting an unplanned but now inevitable outcome.

Crane's eyes flicked left and right at Arthur and Anton. His great bastard sword rested with lethal stillness before him – poised for combat.

Armitage stepped forward with a quiet smile, the Red Dragon in guard position over her left shoulder. She looked hard at Anton and his grandfather and declared with avid interest, "Finally – a worthy challenge."

Crane snapped behind her left shoulder, "End them!"

She blurred into action.

* * *

Chloe plumbed the depths of her supreme Ramp; it was time to use everything she had.

Arthur Slayne's hidden plan was yet to play out in full. Anton Slayne was a borderline berserker who could drop into full killing-machine mode at any moment and he was absolutely obsessed with slaughtering Crane.

An obsession she'd gone to great lengths to foster and which could now kill her.

Oh, the devastating irony of it all. She had secretly encouraged Anton's desire to kill Crane and yet, when they finally met for the first time, she must stop her weapon or die herself. However, there was a silver lining, if a vampire could use such a phrase. The Slaynes presented a rare opportunity to truly test her skills. She wondered if Anton would go berserk spontaneously, or would it require his grandfather to be 'taken out of the fight,' to trigger his new powers. She was yet to fight a ramped berserker and she'd cherish the novelty of the contest.

Her eyes narrowed and she addressed the first order of business: Arthur Slayne. He'd dived past her with a speed talent exceeding the 'maximum,' limits of vampires, to position himself between Crane and herself. However, he'd never seen her supreme Ramp, not even in the secret vault beneath Saint Peter's Basilica. She'd then rushed past him a second time to ensure she could protect Crane. Arthur Slayne had placed the P-Case on the concrete floor, presumably to focus on surviving the next few seconds.

Against the greatest fighters a simple stratagem was best.

She rushed the elder Slayne. She'd attack with her most dangerous moves, forcing him to defend or die. In any event, he'd have to give ground and step away from the P-Case. On her right forward flank, Anton blurred in, complicating matters. He appeared to be favoring an overhead strike as his opening move, but he would arrive a fraction of a second too late to deliver it with effect.

Arthur raised the Black Dragon before him, offering his strongest defense.

Energy exploded from deep within her, flooding her core, arcing like lightning along nerves, muscles, and bones. Chloe hardened her body to titanic capabilities well beyond vampire normal. The Red Dragon arced down in a diagonal slash from left to right.

Arthur stared through her, deep within his Ramp. His actions driven by a lifetime of training muscle and sinew to automated responses. He moved faster than she had seen anyone move – except herself. The Black Dragon gave way slightly, presenting a deflecting surface that captured her initial attack. The blades rang against each other, a pure note ringing through the night air. If two gods fought, this is what it would sound like.

Arthur slid a yard backward across the concrete floor and took another step back to balance himself.

Anton Slayne slashed in past his grandfather's left shoulder. The Blue Dragon slicing down to catch her at the point where her neck ended and her right shoulder began.

Chloe deflected Anton's blade across herself from right to left toward his grandfather, forcing him to take another step away from the P-Case. Her reverse counterstrike driven by pure automatic reflex slashing horizontally across Anton's throat.

Anton twisted, arching backward and away from her in near inhuman anticipation, completing a move that was just barely possible for a Ramp master.

Chloe's katana sliced through his throat without biting deep. His blood splashed in a line of droplets, hanging in the air as if waiting for gravity to take hold. The rich tang of Ramp master blood filled the air, flavored by the distinctive scent Anton had always possessed for her.

His momentum carried him past her to the left, splitting the space between his grandfather and herself. He pivoted hard, leaping and sliding, his left hand flying to his throat, a stricken look seizing his face.

Arthur took his grandson's place and attacked, his blade arcing down on her right front quarter.

She blurred forward a diagonal step, deflecting Arthur's strike to the right.

Arthur flowed further to her right with the momentum of her deflection of his blade, then whirled and advanced on her rear right quarter.

Anton rushed up on her left; his katana poised to sweep from high to low across her body.

She blurred forward a half-dozen feet, reverse spun to the left against Anton, the red dragon sweeping through a wide arc.

Anton closed to striking distance, a thin curtain of blood reaching down his throat.

She slammed the Red Dragon hard against the Blue Dragon, sending it swinging away. Then reverse spun a half circle to the right, her sword rebounding versus the Black Dragon, sending Arthur sliding backward over the concrete. She managed to defeat Arthur and Anton's near simultaneous attacks – this time. *Damn, they move fast.*

Anton blurred hard, circling behind her. He twisted to bring his blade to bear, presenting the briefest of opportunities. Her left foot lashed out, striking him deep in the gut. He folded around her boot and flew back through the air toward the tunnel entrance. She gave ground as Arthur pressed his attacks, drawing him further away from the P-Case.

Chloe's supreme Ramp had already passed its peak and was fading quickly. By the same token, Arthur couldn't maintain his speed talent much longer. But where was Crane, with both Slaynes together she would be hard pressed to best them without his help.

Crane leaped forward, rushing between Arthur and Anton to scoop up the P-Case. He whirled and shouted at Chloe, "Kill them!"

Anton, having landed in a heap next to the shipping container over the tunnel entrance, rose up and rushed Crane from behind. Crane's vast experience alerted him to the imminent danger and he pivoted to confront his foe. His face blanched beyond his normal pallor, like he was facing a demon from his worst nightmare, then set into grim determination.

Anton blurred in, rivaling a speed talent. Crane swept the Blue Dragon aside with his great dusky blade, but Anton knocked the P-Case from Crane's hand. The case slid and spun across the concrete floor.

For a moment, everyone froze. Anton and Crane both pivoted toward the P-Case. But Chloe stood closest to the prize, she blurred forward on the remnants of her supreme Ramp and seized the P-Case before Anton or Crane could reach it.

Anton reached out to snatch the P-Case from her with his left hand, his right wielding the Blue Dragon.

Behind her, Arthur screamed, "Anton, No!"

Chloe lifted the P-Case away from the young Slayne and stepped aside, her sword deflecting his attack wide as he blurred past her. Chloe swiveled her head around and stared at the elder Slayne with wide eyes.

Why did he warn, Anton?

* * *

Armitage held the second P-Case, her eyes filled with questions.

The opportunity to close the trap set by his whole-self was evaporating before Arthur's eyes. Everything he'd done in the last twenty years, including sacrificing his own sanity, was for this moment – and yet he was failing.

A severe compulsion tore at his mind. Thorns flaying him alive was preferable to defying the implanted commands of his whole-self. If he failed here, it had all been for naught. His whole-self had promised him re-integration of his personality, but that was a lie. His sacrifice was meant to be total. A shared annihilation with his targets. Only by putting himself in a position of real vulnerability could he lure Crane and Armitage to their destruction.

In the hidden depths of his mind more than a dozen ghosts shouted with angry voices and clamored for action. They screamed a single word, over and over again. A single word that would activate the trap and complete a twenty-year strategy.

But Anton was within the kill zone.

The implanted compulsion scoured his soul. Resisting it ratcheted the pain up beyond what sanity could endure. He wanted to speak the final key word like a dying man destined for hell wanted one last offer of heaven-sent salvation. Speaking the key word would release the compulsion. He held the Black Dragon high before him and looked at Anton. The boy who had changed everything in a single day. His own grandson was not meant to be in this place at this time. The one person he could not sacrifice. His heart tore into two halves and fell to war with each other – he had to choose between utter failure and killing his own grandson.

For the briefest of moments, Arthur celebrated his lack of sanity and the choice it allowed. He dug deep, dragging forth a final burst of energy and power. He raced toward Anton with his full speed talent, capturing him in a flying tackle. His grandson folded over his left shoulder with a loud 'oomph,' and they flew together toward the shipping container over the tunnel entrance.

Arthur blurred past the container door, Anton over his shoulder. He turned his head over his right shoulder to look back into the warehouse. Armitage still held the P-Case and Crane was close to her. Arthur shouted a single word in ancient Sanskrit over his right shoulder.

"AGNI!"

* * *

Arthur Slayne shouted something over his right shoulder, diving back into the tunnels with Anton trapped in a hold over his left shoulder.

Chloe had seen his lips move; the sound was yet to reach her. She was on the ragged edge of her supreme Ramp, energy bleeding away like water through a sieve as she dropped back to her inherent high-end vampire abilities. Arthur Slayne's endgame was in play.

She reached into the depths of her supreme ramp in an instant, agony exploding through her as she dragged her supreme Ramp back into existence against the will of her body. Chloe swung the P-Case down, then threw it with all her titanic might through the retracted doorway in the roof of the warehouse. The P-Case shot away like it was rocket powered.

Arthur Slayne's shout reached her, "AGNI!"

Agni, ignite, ignition, fire. The implication of the ancient word filled her with dread. Chloe blurred toward Crane, who was watching the P-Case rise like a bullet into the night sky, a look of terrible realization dawning on his face. He began to twist away from the P-Case. She tackled him off his feet, carrying him toward the nearest wall, and out of the line of sight of the P-Case.

The flash hit them first, the harsh light flooding the warehouse. Their shadows became stark outlines stretching before them on the concrete floor. Chloe screamed in supreme Ramp agony, pushing hard toward the wall and away from the exposed area beneath the roof door. The blast followed a moment later, evaporating the roof of the warehouse with a thunderous roar. A solid wall of superheated air smashed into Chloe and Crane, throwing them flat against the concrete floor, then tossing them through the warehouse like a pair of leaves in a storm.

She tumbled and twisted helplessly. The nearest wall filled her vision with a dreadful inevitability composed of reinforced steel and concrete. A single thought raced through her mind. *This is going to hurt!*

The impact sent Chloe's world into utter darkness.

* * *

Tamsah had thrown the young red-headed Order operative to the vampire mob.

Their frenzied attack on her had given him time to break contact with them. But before he'd dropped her to the tunnel floor, he'd noticed a belt she was wearing around her waist. A belt he'd appropriated and now wore strapped above his hips. It sported four canisters – white phosphorous anti-personnel grenades. They were illegal throughout the civilized world but clearly the Order had a manufacturing site somewhere. They were a particularly useful weapon against vampires, but suicidal to use inside a tunnel with nowhere to run. The burning phosphorous would suck the oxygen from the air, asphyxiating the Ramp masters as the vampires burned.

Tamsah had shed most of his blood-soaked clothing and boots, stripping down to a pair of black shorts, his daggers and the grenade belt. There was no way he could maintain stealth versus other vampires, while smelling like a human abattoir.

He'd determined the location of the truth speaker from the signature of her heartbeat. The Order operatives had split into two groups. The remains of the Blake force team heading deeper into the maze, while the Mirovar force team headed for the southern-most hangar where Tamsah had started from. Their path would lead them to the fake fuel bowser and into the hangar. The way before them was clear, but a sizeable mob of militia vampires still tracked them through the maze tunnels.

A chain rattled somewhere in the last hangar. It was too faint for a human ear to hear. With their sensor array destroyed, the Order operatives were running blind. Someone was waiting in the hangar. All the militia vampires were in the tunnels, and most of the Order operatives remained alive. It was infeasible the two Slaynes had managed to cover the surface path to the hangar beneath the weapons of the four shadowstar drones. They had to be back at the warehouses, or in the tunnels. He paused for a moment and sharpened his senses. Yes, there the Slaynes were, close together and near the last warehouse toward the north. About as far from the last hangar as you could get in the maze.

Tamsah blurred forward. There was no time to waste. It could only be Crane, Armitage or the praetorians who lurked and plotted within the last hangar against the truth speaker. He concentrated, integrating everything he knew about maze lore against the echo imprints unwittingly revealed by the militia vampires. There had to be another path into the last hangar and he knew where it must be.

He diverged, taking an alternative path to the last hangar. He would come upon whomever was lying in ambush and take them from behind. He must save the truth speaker.

***

The echoes from the massive explosion over the last warehouse faded away.

Crane had recently entered the selfsame building. Senior praetorian squad leader, Frederic Hoffman considered the possibility something drastic may have happened to the king of the vampires but refrained from making the call over the praetorian's tactical link.

Questioning the survival of the king was just not the done thing. He waited a moment to see if Crane or Armitage issued any new commands. The tactical link remained filled with silence. In the absence of any confirmation of a change of plan, he continued with his current mission.

Hoffman regarded the disposition of his troops in hangar number one.

There were six private jets owned and operated by vampires within the hangar. The windows made of distinctive opaque black glass. His team had arranged them into a rough semicircle facing into the center of the hangar. The seventh and final jet, a long bodied private aircraft designed for about sixteen passengers, resided in the back right-hand corner of the hangar.

He counted the aircraft clockwise from the fake bowser. The first aircraft held Cantor's squad. The aircraft sported two doors behind the cockpit, both were open. When the Order operatives arrived, Cantor's squad would spring from hiding and take them by surprise with concentrated minigun fire at point blank range.

The second vampire jet was empty. The third jet was the original sixteen-seater near the back right-hand corner. The fourth jet was his own near the south wall. He stood on top of it, his squad waited on the floor of the hangar in front of the wings. They would open fire once the Order emerged from the tunnels through the hatch on top of the fake bowser. They would be the only ones in the fight to draw the Order forward into the killing field in the center of the hangar.

To his left, directly opposite the bowser was the fifth aircraft which remained empty. Beyond it was the sixth jet which held three members of the Browning squad, with the same plan for a surprise attack as the Cantor squad. Between the Cantor and Browning squads, and his own squad, they would catch the Order operatives in a deadly crossfire from three directions.

The last man of the Browning squad stood near the open main hangar doors, guarding the approach from that direction. He had recently moved a thick chain aside, and it had clanked loudly. They would discipline him after the mission was over for making excessive noise in an ambush scenario, but in the meantime, they needed his eyes. The sensor arrays from the shadowstar drones were constantly sweeping a circle ten miles across centered on the airport. They would spot any Order operatives approaching the hangar, but Hoffman wanted a vampire's eyes watching too. There was no sorry in this business – there was only being effective or being dead.

Finally, diagonally opposite his own aircraft was the last of the vampire-owned jets in the hangar, resting silently and unused.

Hoffman lifted his right hand from his minigun and rubbed his chin, wondering once more about the health of his king. The last warehouse had partially collapsed in on itself, and spot fires were burning everywhere. If only they tracked the king and Armitage in the same way the praetorians were, he'd know if they were alive, wounded or dead.

He pressed his lips in a thin line, perhaps he should send a man to check.

Something punched hard into the base of his skull and exited between his eyes. His mouth dropped open as if to cry out but no sound emerged. A second blade dug through the base of his spine, lifting him off the roof of the plane with tremendous force.

Death arrived before he could feel the pain.

***

The truth speaker was only seconds away from emerging from the maze into an ambush.

Tamsah whirled, throwing the lifeless squad leader at the sole praetorian on the right-side of the aircraft.

He leaped to the left, his gore-soaked twelve-inch tri-bladed daggers trailing droplets of blood in a pair of thin ribbons. There were two praetorians beneath him. They remained focused on the fake fuel bowser, waiting for the imminent emergence of the Order operatives. Every vampire in the chamber could hear their approach. Their miniguns encumbered their hands. Their heads flicked left on reflex as the squad leader's body crashed into the praetorian on the other side of the plane.

Tamsah landed behind them, slamming his daggers through their backs. The hardened blades punched through the nano-ceramic plate up to the hilt, neatly severing their aortas an inch above their hearts. They both twisted around, dropping their guns, reaching for him with desperate hands. Tamsah struck again, driving his daggers up beneath their chins. His knives sliced into the praetorian's brainstems with wet slaps and they both began to drop toward the concrete floor.

Tamsah blurred right, ducking beneath the body of the plane. The fourth praetorian in the squad was rising from the concrete, having thrown his squad leader's corpse aside. His minigun sat on the concrete floor, jarred loose from his hands by the surprise arrival of his squad leader.

The fourth praetorian's hands flashed to a katana at his waist. He drew it clear of its scabbard with a glimmering flash of light, and slashed a high beheading strike at Tamsah.

Tamsah ducked beneath the blade, blurred close, his knives driving into the vampire's chest from left and right. His fists blurred across each other, the blades slicing over each other. The praetorian's eyes bulged behind his visor and he slumped backward, his heart trisected into three parts.

Before the vampire hit the pale floor, Tamsah blurred toward the back of the hangar opening up the angle into the first jet where another four praetorians hid. They would be spilling forth within another second, responding to the noises he'd already made.

He tucked his daggers within his belt and grabbed two canisters. Tamsah had dialed the fuse down to three tenths of a second. It would be just long enough to throw and escape the blast wave. He threw them on flat trajectories, and followed with a third grenade. They raced through the air as if rocket propelled. The canisters disappeared through the jet's open doorway, ricocheting into the cabin.

One of the praetorians within the cabin roared, "Fu—"

The first grenade exploded with a thunderous crack. The second and third grenades detonated, blowing out the cabin windows with jets of white fire. The body of the aircraft evaporated in a brilliant glare. The fuel tanks in the wings detonated in secondary explosions a moment later and the aircraft vanished in a white-gold blast as debris shot through the hangar.

Tamsah retreated toward the back of the building and the second secret entrance near the sixteen-seater private jet. He shielded his sensitive eyes from the glare of the burning aircraft with his left hand.

An automated sprinkler system came on, jets of water spraying down from the roof. There were another four praetorians, he could hear them moving on the tarmac and cursing outside the hangar. They were beyond reach now. He could not surprise them, but he'd reduced the threat they presented to the truth speaker to what the Mirovar force team could handle.

Tamsah leaped back into the tunnels though the well-hidden manhole. He landed on the pale concrete, wet, nearly naked and alone. His hand fell to the final grenade on his belt. He didn't need it right now, but he might need it later. Be prepared for any contingency – it was a solid precept of the Way of the Faithful, and faith filled Tamsah's soul to the brim.

Eight praetorians were dead. He'd disrupted the ambush. The Mirovar force team and the truth speaker would be wary entering the hangar. The surviving praetorians had withdrawn to the safety of the tarmac.

Providence had fulfilled his faith. A glimmer of hope sprang into life within his heart. Perhaps one day, his faith might find reward. He might earn his honor once again. And what a great day that would be.

Tamsah's heart burst, and tears filled his eyes. There had to be a greater purpose for him becoming a vampire.

There just had to be.

* * *

Li was first to the ladder, the rungs were dripping with water and more was showering down from above.

She'd insisted on her time on point. She wasn't a fragile thing for holding in the middle of the team while everyone else bore risks for her. She held her SAW in her left hand and clambered up the rungs to the hatch, getting drenched along the way. As she reached the top, she wished she had a hand-held mirror. Lacking such equipment, she ramped hard and poked her head above the hatch for a quick scan before ducking back down.

No one fired at her. There was a smoking, sizzling wreck directly to her left toward the back of the hangar. There were four apparently dead praetorians nearly opposite the bowser around the base of another aircraft parked slightly toward the rear of the hangar. Something had happened to blow up the nearby plane and set off the sprinklers. Probably the same something that had left four praetorians lying in pools of their own blood.

She ramped and poked her head up again for a second look toward the front of the hangar. She couldn't see any threats. She looked down the ladder at the rest of the Mirovar team and said, "Looks okay. I'm going in."

She blurred out of the hatch and ran into the hangar, her boots slapping against the wet concrete, her head on a swivel, and her SAW held tight against her right shoulder. The rest of the team followed her into the hangar and spread out, covering all their potential blind spots.

Again, no one fired on the team.

Jay called out from the front of the hangar, "I've got eyes on four praetorians armed with miniguns. They are out on the tarmac, six hundred yards away. They look like they are waiting for something." He paused for a moment. "Hell, the last warehouse is toast!"

Is that where Slayne went after we separated? Li thought. *Where the hell is Anton? Is he with his grandfather?* She was genuinely fearful for Anton's safety. He was absent for a long time and the vampire swarm was roaming the maze. God only knew what would happen if they met. He'd already burned himself out once today, he could easily kill himself trying to fight them all. Anton might rub her up the wrong way more often than not, but she'd be the first to admit her world would be poorer if he wasn't in it. Her heart ached for what Anton might become if he survived this battle. Horrors stalked his future and she feared for him with all her being.

Jay hung back, deep within the hangar. His face grim. It was safe to assume the vampires had seen him and knew they were in the hangar. He turned to Peter and pointed at the sixteen-seater plane at the back of the hangar. "That will be Arthur Slayne's plane. It's the only one with normal windows. Check it out and make sure it's ready to fly."

"Sure," Peter replied and headed off to the long-bodied private jet.

Jay turned to Chiara and commanded, "Chiara, stay on the bowser. No doubt some of those damned crazy vampires are tracking us. Watch our back and be ready for action."

Chiara lifted her SAW in salute and blurred back to the top of the fake bowser.

Jay strode over to Li and looked down at a nearby praetorian lying in a crimson puddle of blood-saturated water. "Who killed these guys?"

"Did Slayne and Anton get ahead of us?" Li asked.

"If they did, where are they now?" Jay asked as he leaned down and examined the puncture marks in the praetorian's armor. "Look here, Li. No one killed these vampires with a katana. More like a dagger of some sort."

Li's mind snapped back to the memory of the tunnels beneath the conclave hall. Someone had killed the praetorians there with a spiral triangular knife. Justin had insisted it was the work of a Red Empire operative. Whomever it was, he was one dangerous individual who appeared to be on their side. "Whomever killed them, he's gone now. More to the point, we can't leave those praetorians alive on the tarmac."

Jay nodded and glanced back out at the runways. "Their miniguns will tear a private jet apart. Even an armored gunship couldn't survive them. If we fly out of here, then we must deal with them first."

Li thrust her left hand out toward the waiting praetorians. "We don't have an exfil path with them out there."

Jay pressed his lips into a thin line. He reached out and grasped Li's shoulder. "The situation is very fluid. If we have to deal with them, we will. Stay frosty there's more to play out here tonight."

Peter jogged over from the sixteen-seater and declared, "It's ready to go, fully fueled. All we need is clear airspace to get out of here. She's got big tanks too – she'll do six thousand miles before we have to land."

Chiara called out from the top of the fake bowser, "I've got more vampires approaching through the maze."

Peter stooped and picked up a fallen minigun, and said with a half grin, "This'll help." He looked across at the next fallen praetorian and stripped him of his minigun and backpack of ammunition, and chuckled. He lifted the pair of miniguns and their ammunition backpacks from the dead praetorians and suggested, "Let's see them deal with these puppies."

Jay grinned mercilessly, glanced at Chiara and said, "We can use our SAWs to add silver to the mix." He turned back to Li. "I need you to keep an eye on the praetorians. Peter, Chiara and I will deal with the oncoming vampires in the tunnel."

"Where will you be?"

"At the base of the ladder. There is a straight stretch before it that is tailor made for the miniguns." Jay looked at Peter. "Are you okay to handle two miniguns at once?"

Peter hefted the two 7.62mm miniguns, their ammunition backpacks resting on the concrete floor, strips of caseless ammunition running from the backpacks to the weapons. His big hands flexed around the handles and he waved the forty-pound guns left and right like they were 9mm Glocks. "I think I like these guys," he snorted, "all I need now is a cigar!"

"Okay," Jay commanded. "It's decided. Peter, Chiara, and I will take a position at the base of the ladder." He looked at Li, and then across to the open hangar doors. "We need to hold this hangar – until we can't. Keep your eyes open and your head on a swivel. I'd like to give you backup but we'll have enough to deal with in the maze."

Li nodded.

Jay and Peter broke away from Li, and joined Chiara on top of the bowser. A dozen seconds later they had disappeared within it.

Li ran across to the hangar doors and took a position on the edge of the doorway. At the doors, she was beyond the worst of the sprinkler system. She swept water from her forehead with her left hand and ran her right back through her long hair. She lifted her SAW from its straps over her shoulders and focused on the airport. She needed to keep a watch on what was happening beyond the hangar.

Movement caught her eye. Justin emerged from the ground within the center of the airport close to a mile distant. His team followed him. They dropped some tubes on the ground and snapped SAWs to their shoulders. They formed a semi-circle facing back toward the hole in the ground.

Frenzied screams resounded faintly in the distance.

Vampires were hot on their tail.

* * *

Justin leaped out of the secret exit from the maze to the airport surface.

Sam, Taylor, and Patrick followed closely behind him. He checked the ammunition counter on his SAW. It read, '99.' He was a tick over halfway through his second two-hundred round magazine. He didn't have another spare, neither did anyone else in his team. A horde of frenzied vampires had chased them for more than five hundred yards. They had killed as many as they could in the shadows of the tunnels but there were still many more left and their silver and lead hollow-point ammunition was running low.

Screams and yells of frenzied lust and hunger arose from within the tunnels.

Justin indicated with a nod of his head and laid his stinger III missile launcher upon the ground. They'd followed Arthur's instructions to the letter, breached the defenses around his caches and extracted the four prototype hypersonic surface to air missiles.

He snapped his SAW to his shoulder. Patrick stood to his left and Sam and Taylor stood to his right in a loose semi-circle facing the open shaft into the maze.

The mad shrieks burst into the night air, then the vampires boiled forth like frenzied ants defending their nest.

The Blake force team opened fire as one. Their SAWs pouring round after round into the spreading mass of vampires. Blood sprayed in red whips, or bloomed in pink mists. Silver stricken vampires fell helplessly to the ground. Those who came after them ground the fallen into the dirt in their rush to reach his team.

Justin's ammo counter fell like a stone past fifty.

The team dropped back another ten yards together. No matter how many vampires they killed, more emerged, flooding the area around the team. Two pincers extended, composed of wailing vampire flesh. It was like a giant's hand reaching to surround them and then crush them to death.

The team gave more ground, moving back to back as the vampires surrounded them.

Justin's ammo counter dropped to zero. He threw the smoking weapon away and drew his katana. His team mates ran dry within the next half second and did the same. It would be hand to hand combat from now till victory or death.

Four vampires screamed and attacked Justin, another thirty rushed his small team.

He didn't believe in last stands but this was certainly looking like one.

* * *

With his good right arm, Cornelius pushed a concrete block away and emerged from the rubble.

His left arm hung limply at his side, broken in more places than he cared to count.

Armitage moaned nearby. He glanced at her. A vampire that could still make a noise was unlikely to be in mortal danger. She held her head with both hands as if to keep it steady, caught his gaze, and stated matter-of-factly, "I broke my neck, I'll need a minute."

The skin on her face was healing from several gashes and burns. He figured he was no better off. He tapped his broadcast communications channel and called over the tactical link, "Hoffman report."

Browning responded, "Hoffman, Cantor and their squads are dead, Sir."

Cornelius frowned, his eyes narrowing. This night was piling one calamity on top of another. He asked, "Where are you?"

"Six hundred yards northwest of the hangar ready to fire on any aircraft that come out of it."

"Enemy status?"

"The Mirovar team is currently in the hangar. Militia in the tunnels are converging on their position. The Blake team is on the surface near the middle of the airport fighting thirty plus militia. They appear to have run out of ammunition, shall we engage?"

Cornelius wasn't going to lose any more loyal troops tonight with little to gain from it. "No. Hold your position and prepare for immediate exfil."

It was clear the Panopticon was not at the airport. There was no further need for restraint. He ignored his broken left arm and broken ribs, and limped over the fallen masonry and exposed steel mesh. He passed a couple of spot fires and the hull of Slayne's drone. The craft had opened up like a tin can. There was no engine or visible internals. It was a mock up after all. Slayne switching it on had just been another ploy to get him to act as Slayne wished.

Cornelius had no idea how Slayne had done it but Slayne had played him like a puppet on a string. Nausea gripped his guts, what else did Slayne have in store? What was Slayne's plan 'B?'

A cold fury erupted within him, vaporizing the momentary illness within his stomach. He ascended the pile of rubble. A few moments later he stood on the highest point of the surviving facade of the warehouse.

The airport spread before him. The Blake force team was in the open fighting twenty-three militia vampires hand to hand. The Order operatives were killing the unskilled vampires with desperate and brutal efficiency. They may well survive.

Cornelius' eyes tightened with suspicion. Why had they emerged where they did? Why expose themselves to attack from above? He scanned the ground around them. Yes, there was the reason. They had stinger missiles. A regular stinger II missile was a poor choice of weapon against a shadowstar drone's speed, maneuverability, and defensive systems.

But only a fool would assume these were regulation production line stingers. Slayne would have something special deployed for tonight, and the Blake force team would be operating in accordance with Slayne's orders.

Cornelius grinned mercilessly. Not only had Armitage's speed saved his life, his tactical helmet was still functional. He contacted his command drone, the other three shadowstars were slaved off its command-and-control systems. He directed them to adopt defensive maneuvers against a hostile surface to air missile environment. The four drones broke formation, and began flying back and forth in zig zags over the airport at varying heights. Their countermeasure systems switched to active mode with hair-trigger response times. Finally, he directed them to open their weapon bay doors and make their conventionally armed hammerhead hypersonic cruise missiles ready to fire.

He looked down upon the Blake force team. Justin Blake carved a great slash through the chest of the last vampire, neatly bisecting the creature's heart.

Cornelius was confident that within seconds the Blake and Mirovar force teams would cease to exist.

* * *

The last of the militia vampires fell to the ground in a spreading pool of blood.

"The SAMs," Justin shouted, reaching for one of the stinger III prototypes lying on the ground. His men rushed to obey, each rising with a surface to air missile.

Taylor flicked his white-blonde head at the praetorians standing in a loose group a thousand yards away. "What the hell are they playing at?"

Justin glanced at the vampires. They were not engaging. That could only mean one thing – the next attack was coming from above.

It was a race against time.

He snapped the stinger over his shoulder and activated the targeting system. His three team mates did the same. The stingers detected the four drones maneuvering violently over the airport and networked with each other to avoid targeting the same drone twice.

A moment later, the thin tone of missile lock alerts cut through the air. All four stingers were ready to fire.

Justin pressed the firing stud and shouted, "Fire!"

* * *

The Blake force team snapped their stinger missiles over their shoulders, raising their weapon's dark throats to the sky. The Order operatives flared in the infra-red spectrum. Ramping, becoming still, firing as one.

Cornelius snapped, "Fire." The drone's responded as a single unit two miles above the airport. The first wave of four hammerhead hypersonic cruise missiles dropped from their cradles, spearing down toward the middle of the airport. A split-second later, the second wave of four missiles fell from the weapons bays.

Four hammerheads converged on the Blake force team. The second four veered toward the southern-most hangar and the Mirovar force team.

Four more missiles, small, sharp darts, lanced upward from the Blake force team. The twelve missiles passing each other a mile above the airport.

The Blake force team, already ramped, were fleeing back to the tunnels, blurring away in a race against the descending hammerheads. They were moving too slowly to escape the blast radius of four five-hundred-pound warheads configured to airburst ten feet off the ground. They were dead men; they just didn't know it yet.

Cornelius tracked the rising stinger missiles. They speared upward on tails of blue fire, racing toward the shadowstar drones. Countermeasures bloomed like high-tech flowers a hundred yards across, dotting the sky with vivid multi-spectral reds, greens, and blues.

The blue fires of the small darts dodged violently between the countermeasures. The shadowstar drones bucked and shuddered on blasts of cobalt fire, maneuvering with maximum acceleration. The shadowstars engaged their final defenses, infra-red lasers lighting crimson strings across the sky.

Cornelius stared at the deadly beauty above him and whispered, "No."

***

Red, green, and blue flashes lit up the night sky.

The Blake force team fled as one toward the secret tunnel entrance. Justin ramped to his maximum capability, blurring across the grass and tarmac. The world was eerily quiet, except for the sounds of breathing men and racing footfalls. Patrick was on his left and the Two Taylors were on his right.

The tunnel entrance was a square opening ten feet wide. Two doors covered in tarmac were open, laid out on the ground to the front and back. If they could make it and pull the doors shut, they could survive. The doors were heavy steel designed to withstand aircraft running over them without moving or giving way.

Justin instinctively summoned his strength talent, white lightning infusing every muscle, sinew and bone with power. He leaped, diving the last dozen feet toward the entrance to the tunnels.

Four warheads exploded on the corners of a square a hundred yards across, bracketing the Blake force team.

Light glared; the night made harsh day. Justin's Order nightglasses instantly went black. His communication earbuds expanded, becoming tight protective plugs in his ears.

Air like a solid wall hit him from behind, throwing him forward into the hole. Justin reflexively lifted his right arm to cover his head, before slamming into the wall with the right-side of his body. Bones toughened by Ramp genetics, and filled with the pure life force of his summoned strength talent shivered, flexed and then shattered.

For the briefest of moments, darkness overwhelmed him.

The blast wave hit the front side door above him, lifting it up like a shutter in a windstorm and slamming it shut. Electromagnets automatically locking it tightly in place.

Justin bounced off the wall, twisting and landing hard on the stairs, the right-side of his body numb with dreadful shock. His nightglasses had gone, knocked free from his face. He stared through the open back half of the doorway; his dark brown eyes wide with horror.

Superheated metal fragments, fire and light lashed the air above the doorway.

Justin cried out, "NO!" The words whipped away on a torrent of air rushing from the tunnels to the dying hearts of the explosions.

The air stilled. White, actinic flashes overtook the night sky. Within the maze of tunnels, a vampire shrieked in the distance and was answered by a mad screech.

Patrick, Sam, Taylor – none of them had made it.

Justin lifted his left hand and covered his eyes, moaning quietly, "No … No … No."

* * *

Missiles shredded the night air.

"No," Li whispered. She whirled away from the hangar doors, blurring toward the fake fuel bowser. She reached the bowser, leaped to the top of it and rushed through the open hatch into the tank.

She slammed the hatch shut behind her.

The fuel bowser shuddered. Dull thunder booming beyond its rounded steel walls.

Li dropped to the tunnel floor.

Jay, Peter and Chiara glanced at her. Peter stated disconsolately, "Well, there goes our ride out of here."

Li stared at them in horror. Peter's face froze, and he asked, "What's wrong?"

"Justin! … and the rest! They were out in the open." Set's prediction had come true. He'd given it to Li when he was wearing the appearance of Qi back at Enoch in Utah. "No," she declared, tears streaming down her face. "They're dead."

"Hell," Peter whispered.

Jay shook his head, his eyes wide with shock. "Damn!"

Chiara stared down the corridor and whispered hoarsely, "They're coming."

Vampires shrieked and howled, shouted and cursed in nearby tunnels. They were almost upon them. Li slumped back against the wall as the rest of the team readied themselves.

What could anyone do against a god?

***

Two clouds of glittering metallic confetti fell toward the ground.

The command drone and a second shadowstar had managed to survive the advanced stinger missiles and continued to zig and zag over the airport.

Chloe stepped gingerly onto a block of concrete sporting horns of severed reinforcing steel mesh, and followed Crane's gaze over the airport.

Crane growled and snapped, "The Panopticon was never here. Slayne has already hidden it."

"This place was always a trap for us," Chloe murmured, a touch of awe in her voice.

Crane turned his head and stared at her. "You admire him?"

"When was the last time we came so close to death?"

Crane harrumphed. "And that's a good thing?"

Chloe arched an eyebrow, a slight smile on her full lips. Crane frowned for a moment, then declared, "We'll exfil Browning's squad and ourselves. Ensure that Haley and the osprey II are at a safe distance. We must sanitize this site."

"Yes, Sir," she responded, stepping down from the pile of rubble and pulling her smartphone out of its armor-protected sleeve. Her fingers flew over the screen, a moment later, she sent a message to James.

She glanced up. The surviving shadowstar drone was descending over a mile away, preparing to land next to Browning's squad of praetorians. The command drone was descending to the middle of the warehouse ruins.

Crane commanded, "It's time to leave."

Chloe nodded. *It surely is.*

* * *

Meat-that-talks lifted his communications device.

It displayed a picture of an older human male. He stated, "This Ramp master must be captured alive and brought back here. He will be within the airport. He was last seen in the tunnels."

Gullette memorized the image with a glance. Meat-that-talks showed the image to Kavanne and Shemina. It seemed to imagine that Shemina would participate in this favor for the blood thief.

Gullette leaned forward. The human's eyes tightened. It was often frightened, but it tried to hide its fear. He unfurled his longest finger at Shemina and declared, "Two needed, more is not helpful," he wagged his finger back and forth, "she stays here."

The human nodded, and said, "Sure. She stays here. I'm certain there's nothing wandering around out there you two can't handle by yourselves."

Gullette grinned, his head bobbing backward and forward. Meat-that-talks had little understanding of the full powers of the People. He glanced meaningfully at Kavanne, and hummed a short note. Kavanne's head bobbed in response – he would follow Gullette's lead.

Gullette's skin tingled with the change, and Kavanne vanished too, although Gullette could still smell and hear him. He turned away from the puny human and raced into the airport, Kavanne following behind his left shoulder. They would find the old human in the captured image. There were few vampires left. They were still seeking blood; they would converge on the remaining humans. Even now some fought within the tunnels to the south.

Another two groups of vampires stalked prey near the center of the airport. That was the place to look first. From the sounds, there was an open entrance to the surface there.

It was a pity the Ramp masters could not be eaten. The changes to their bodies spoiled the meat.

Gullette felt like a snack.

* * *

The vampires screamed and howled with blood lust, turning around the intersection and running forward en masse along the corridor.

More leaped and clawed their way forward along walls and ceiling. The lights flickered as vampires momentarily obscured them, shrouding their approach with leaping shadows.

Li sat slumped against the back wall and couldn't see an end to them.

Peter stood in the middle of the corridor, flanked by Jay on his left, and Chiara on his right. He hefted the two miniguns and opened fire. Electric motors whirred, barrels spun, and tongues of flame leaped from the weapon's throats. Gray smoke bloomed, and streams of light tore into the vampires.

The creatures ran into the fire, driven beyond caring for their own safety by pure blood lust. The heavy rounds slammed into flesh and bone, passing through on gouts of blood.

Jay and Chiara opened up with their SAWs, bright silver hollow points ripping into the swarm.

The vampires fell, lay trampled, and died in spreading pools of gore. For every vampire they killed, two more leaped forward. The swarm advanced, screeching and laughing, closing to thirty feet on a carpet of death.

Peter growled low in his chest, sweeping the minigun fire across the front ranks. The vampires closed to twenty feet, swarming forward while falling apart under the sustained hammering of the heavy rounds.

"I'm dry," Jay shouted a moment later, and threw his SAW aside in disgust. He swept the White Dragon clear of its scabbard and held it high above his head, his eyes glaring at the screaming swarm. He shouted without looking back at her, "Li!"

The vampires closed to fifteen feet.

Chiara's SAW clicked on empty and she dropped it. Her last silver dagger and her katana appearing in her hands.

Jay shouted again, "LI!"

The miniguns whirled to a halt, gray smoke rising from their barrels, their ammunition packs spent.

Li stared at the swarming vampires. Slayne's words came back to her, *'There always comes a time in life where you can either give up or step up.'*

The vampire's screeches and yells rose in triumph.

Li ramped hard. She blurred to her feet, snapping her squad automatic weapon to her shoulder. She ghosted forward to stand between Peter and Chiara and opened fire with her light machine gun.

The nearest vampires loomed ten feet away, leading at least another thirty against the team.

A hot fire burned in Li's soul, eclipsing the flames that spat from the barrel of her weapon. Her silver and lead hollow-points whipped through the advancing vampires. She shifted aim carefully, directing three round bursts for head shot after head shot. With a half and half mix of silver and lead, she was hitting every vampire in the head with at least one silver and one hollow point round.

They went down and stayed down.

Li took a step forward. Flicking her gun from vampire to vampire, efficiently picking the next closest target with each movement. Time slowed, individual rounds slapping into flesh. Tongues of yellow flame licking from the throat of her SAW's barrel. Bone shattered and blood sprayed in wet ribbons of gore. Smoke rose from her weapon; each round a whip crack in the air. Splats of blood and gobbets of flesh painted the walls and ceiling. The concrete floor ran with rivulets of blood as the corpses piled one upon another. The ammo counter on top of her SAW dropped toward zero. She kept her finger hard against the trigger and fired, and fired, and fired.

The last vampire pulled to a halt six feet short of Li. She was a young woman, slim, long dark hair, pale, with sharp fangs descending over her bottom lip. Her face froze with a sudden expression of waking up lost and alone.

Li didn't hesitate and shot her beneath the nose, guaranteeing her bullets would carve through the vampire's brain stem. The young woman collapsed backward in a spray of blood and gray matter, her corpse joining the other vampires heaped upon the concrete floor.

Near silence flooded the maze. There was only the rustle of clothing, soft sounds of breathing, and shuffling of boots over smooth concrete behind her. The vampire swarm had vanished into oblivion.

She turned around; everyone was looking at her. Jay had his mouth open with surprise, his eyes lit with amazement. "Awesome."

Peter looked at her, his blue eyes alive with admiration. "That's some mighty fine shooting."

Chiara stared at her, a hard smile on her full lips. "Worthy of a— …"

Jay's face hardened, and he asked, "Worthy of what?"

"A combat specialist," Chiara finished.

The team fell silent. Something dragged at her from within. Li looked back over the carnage in the corridor and the sudden euphoria evaporated away. Many of the corpses were young; late teens, early twenties, dressed in fashionable street wear and high-end sneakers. Earlier that day, they'd all been human with potential for full human lives. Now they were all dead, betrayed with false promises of immortality.

She glanced back around the team and stated, "We need to find Anton, Arthur, and anyone else who survived."

Jay nodded. "Yes, but how?"

Li looked at the ladder reaching up to the hangar and declared, "We have to get back to the surface."

Jay nodded, looked at Li with warm eyes and suggested with a broad grin, "Then lead us up there."

Li nodded and began scaling the ladder.

Chapter Sixteen

"If you wish to abrogate all responsibility for your moral and intellectual independence, then by all means – conform with the herd and obey blindly." – Arthur Slayne

* * *

Nevada, Arthur Slayne's Private Airport, The Maze, September 11th, 20:52

"I don't know what to do Anton," Arthur stated.

His grandfather had been especially tight-lipped since the destruction of the last warehouse. Obviously, the P-Case was a bomb, implying a switch had occurred somewhere between the Panopticon fortress and the airport. What disturbed Anton the most was that his grandfather had been about to detonate the bomb while holding it. Had this been his plan all along? It must have been. His grandfather had put together a twenty-year plan that included his own suicide at the end of it. It left him feeling sick to the stomach like nothing else he'd ever encountered.

"Do what?" Anton asked carefully.

Arthur pulled to a stop and studied the tunnel wall. "Here it is." His fingers blurred over the steel plate on the wall in a complicated pattern. The metal flashed briefly like a television screen turning on. A touchscreen appeared on the surface, presenting an alphanumeric keypad. Arthur's fingers flashed over the symbols. There was a click and the whole panel recessed six inches and then moved aside.

He paused and looked hard at Anton, a tension working its way through him and declared, "I don't know if I want to hug you or give you a hiding."

Anton asked, "What were you thinking conducting a suicide mission?"

"… I didn't know."

"How could you not know?"

"We don't have time Anton. Now follow me," he commanded, waving his left hand forward as he stepped into the unlit alcove. A light came on automatically. The alcove was a ten-by-ten feet room with a set of stairs leading up beyond the opposite wall. Arthur turned to the rack on his left and reached out with both hands. "There's no guarantee they're dead."

Anton stepped into the room. The rack held four shoulder launched surface to air missiles.

Arthur pulled two of the launchers from the rack and handed them to Anton, and instructed. "These weapons are idiot-proof. Very simple to use. I've preconfigured them for shadowstar drones, so they will automatically detect and target them. Once you hear the missile lock alert press the firing stud. Then throw it aside and grab the next launcher. You might need two shots. But anything within a thousand yards is point blank range. You can also use it as a line-of-sight weapon with the trigger underneath the casing. It will hit anything you point it at."

Anton nodded.

He grabbed two more and indicated the stairs with a glance. "Up the stairs Anton, we have to assume Justin failed. There will be shadowstar drones to take down so we can exfil from the airport. Plus," and he grinned without a trace of mirth. "We might just catch Crane and Armitage in a vulnerable moment." He turned away and blurred up the stairs.

Anton ramped and followed him.

Arthur pulled to a halt at the top of the stairs beneath a wide pair of rectangular doors. Arthur set one of the launchers down for a moment and tapped a sixteen-digit alphanumeric code into a keypad at the top of the stairs. Electromagnetic locks clicked open and the two long rectangular doors popped up an inch. He glanced at Anton with an obvious expectation in his mind. Anton placed his missiles carefully on the stairs and pushed on the forward door until it opened fully and slammed flat against the tarmac.

He poked his head up and looked around. Half the airport lay in ruins. To his left a shadowstar drone squatted about a thousand yards distant. A squad of praetorians preparing to board it. He glanced right. A second drone descended into the middle of the ruined third warehouse. Crane, or Armitage, or both, still survived.

Anton's eyes widened with avid intent. They still had a chance to destroy their enemies.

***

The night air caressed Arthur's face with cool fingers.

He clambered out of the stairwell and onto the tarmac. He put one stinger down on the ground and grabbed Anton's shoulder. He pointed at a drone to the south, its canopy lowering, and commanded, "Take that one out."

Anton turned and strode a couple of yards away, lifting the launcher over his shoulder and sighting on the distant shadowstar drone.

Arthur's target was the other drone. The one that had come to a hover over the ruined interior of the third warehouse. The canopy had already lifted, giving access to a side-by-side two-seater cabin. He couldn't see Crane or Armitage, but they must be just about to board it.

He snapped the missile launcher into position on his shoulder. He looked through the sights, the drone lay squarely in the cross-hairs. The missile lock alert sang its welcomed note in his right ear. Two forms blurred across the drone's hull and into the cabin. The nearest one was Armitage, she glanced in his direction, her mouth forming an 'O' of surprise beneath her helmet's visor.

Arthur's finger descended toward the firing stud.

A powerful hand, hard with callus clamped over his face, covering his nose and mouth. A second one lifted the stinger from his grip. A third wrapped around his waist and lifted him away from the ground like he weighed nothing.

The secret door, stairs, and cache blurred past him, as his assailants carried him back into the tunnels. He thought, *Ahhh… the chameleons show their hand at last.*

The one carrying him squeezed. Arthur struggled for a moment before the world crashed into darkness around him.

***

The missile lock alert resounded in Anton's ear.

He pressed the firing stud. The stinger speared away, covering the thousand yards to the shadowstar drone in a flash. The hypersonic missile hit the hull of the drone, slicing through it with a molten copper whip burning at fifteen hundred degrees. Its secondary charge penetrated into the bowels of the craft before detonating in a thermobaric glare. The craft's hydrogen fuel supply added to the conflagration. The drone vanished within a massive explosion, streamers of burning metal arching high into the sky.

Anton whirled around. The other drone was rising above the roofline of the ruined warehouse. Where was his grandfather? He'd disappeared! His missile launchers lay on the tarmac, unfired.

"What the fuck!" Anton swore, feeling gut punched.

The distant shadowstar drone began to accelerate. Anton ramped hard, blurring forward, scooping up a missile launcher and snapping it into position over his shoulder.

Something moved on the tarmac about sixty yards distant. *It's Justin*, jarred through his mind like an ice pick through his skull.

Crane and Armitage were within point-blank range. They were sitting ducks waiting … just waiting for him to pull the trigger.

Anton raised the tip of the missile launcher higher, tracking the rising shadowstar drone. It was already four hundred yards off the ground and accelerating on jets of cobalt fire.

A screeching wail erupted from beyond Justin. Anton pulled his right eye away from the launcher's sights. Vampires were boiling forth from another secret entrance in the tarmac a hundred yards away.

Justin lifted one good arm and dragged himself forward across the tarmac. Gaining a couple of feet on the rushing vampires. He pushed against the ground, grimacing in agony, struggling to get to his knees.

Anton's heart burst. He panted. He glanced back at the shadowstar drone, now a thousand yards above the ground and without doubt about to go hypersonic. He raised the missile launcher to take the shot.

Something snapped within his soul. He whirled around, pulling his finger from the targeting stud. The shrill missile-lock whistle evaporated, and he pulled the line-of-sight trigger. The rocket streaked into the midst of the attacking vampires – and exploded in a white flash. Anton rushed forward. The vampires had disintegrated, vaporized by the stinger's thermobaric warhead. There were no more screams emanating from either secret entrance. Anton reached Justin and knelt next to him.

The bigger man threw his good left arm over Anton's shoulders, his right arm hanging uselessly at his side, dripping blood onto the tarmac. Justin cried out, his face twisted in anguish, "They're gone. Everyone's gone."

Anton looked up, scanning the horizon, looking for threats. He glanced up into the sky. There was a blue dot high up against the night sky – well out of range of any shoulder launched missile.

He looked back toward the southernmost hangar, now more rubble than anything else. Li, Peter, Jay and Chiara rose up over the pile of smoking masonry. He paused for a moment, waiting for Francis to appear. Sadness stabbed through his heart like a cold knife. "Not everyone, Justin," Anton advised quietly. "Not everyone."

It was clear that the big man was beyond standing up. The right-side of his body was a mess. It was a miracle he still lived with such injuries. Anton, squatted beside him and got his arms beneath him. He rose in a smooth motion, Justin groaning within the cradle of his arms.

The rest of the team waited a mile away. Anton felt recovered from his overheating earlier that night. Justin needed Chiara as quickly as he could get him to her. He dug deep, ramping hard and blurring away.

The airport lit up as he ran. Hammerheads lancing down from the distant drone, striking each of the hangars in turn, destroying all evidence of the vampires on the surface. As for the tunnels, Anton figured that Crane would be back to erase them too.

He blurred away, carrying Justin Blake like he was a precious child. He silently berated himself, *What the fuck! Why didn't I take the shot?* He didn't have an immediate answer, but deep within himself he knew he couldn't have done otherwise.

* * *

The darkness lifted.

Arthur's vision clarified. He was inside the hold of a small to mid-sized transport aircraft. A chameleon still restrained him. He was sure nothing else could hold him with such an unbreakable grip.

A man stepped into view, ruggedly built, six feet, four and about two-hundred and thirty pounds. He moved with the practiced ease of someone with intimate knowledge of combat.

The hand released Arthur's face and appeared at the same time. A second chameleon glided past. The creature held out the Black Dragon in its scabbard and his auto-pistol. It said, "Bright sharp steel." It wrinkled its snout, revealing many shark-like teeth. The man stiffened slightly. The chameleon continued with, "Another weapon. You good luck."

The man nodded, raised a long-barreled Glock and stated without malice to Arthur, "Time for a sleep."

The gun fired with a soft 'piffeet' sound.

Arthur had been expecting a bullet. He glanced down at his chest; a nearly transparent one-inch dart was just visible on the edge of his shirt.

His head sank back on his neck. The interior of the craft, the man, and the chameleons all whirled away into the darkness.

One last thought swam in the vanishing whirlpool of his mind.

Damn, I'm going to forget—

* * *

The command drone hovered five miles above the ground and ten miles from Slayne's airport trap.

Cornelius watched the hammerhead missiles slam home on the remaining hangars, wiping out the evidence of the vampire aircraft and the corpses within them. As for what was in the tunnels, he would order the site quarantined by Shadowstone. The Day Guard program had depleted their ranks and it was all he could ask them to do. Vampires would perform the actual clean up at night. The evidence below ground would be too telling for human eyes to see.

He'd strongly considered using one of the nuclear weapons he carried on his command drone. He carried two variable yield warheads on hammerhead cruise missiles. He could dial the yield down to five kilotons and erase the site in full, and destroy any Order of Thoth survivors.

But it would be very difficult to explain. The use of a nuke would require his own intervention to manage the political and media narratives – and with Mekra waiting in her donjon – it was a task he didn't have time for. No, a nuke would remain unused – only in extremis would he deploy such a weapon.

Power that is secret will endure. He would ruthlessly maintain the secret of vampire existence, no matter how tenuous it now was.

Cornelius looked across at Armitage and declared, "Our weapons are spent. Our praetorians are dead. The vampire militia have been destroyed or scattered. Now nothing more than a lingering memory of madness." He looked back at the cabin displays without seeing them. "This battle is done. It is time to withdraw, count our losses, and rebuild for the next conflict."

Armitage nodded and remained silent. Cornelius turned back toward her and studied her face. Normally she'd have more to say. Perhaps she felt this defeat as keenly as he did.

A message from the skeleton staff at the citadel scrolled across the cabin display. Cornelius frowned. He was being attacked on all sides. "It seems my chief financier Boris Hartman has been missing for over two weeks, and I only find out about it now?! We'll have to recruit a new one from the ranks of the banking elite." He tilted his head slightly and remarked, "It shouldn't be hard to find someone with the appropriate predatory nature to fit in with the Vampire Dominion."

"No doubt, you are correct," Armitage conceded.

Cornelius frowned at her. Was she mocking him? She appeared sincere. He couldn't tell for sure. It was a good thing she was tied to his life by the implant next to her brain stem. He ordered, "Back to Fort Dix. It's time to refuel and rearm this craft. There are many things we must do in New York."

Armitage nodded. She set the destination and the shadowstar drone accelerated away.

* * *

Crane had closed his eyes to 'meditate' upon his strategy.

Chloe tracked the osprey II drone on the cabin displays, it was heading toward the Arizona safe house. She checked her smartphone. There was a silent text message from James, it read, 'The package is being delivered as ordered.'

The message vanished five seconds after she read it.

She counted tonight's action a victory snatched from the jaws of defeat. Without the Panopticon, Crane would be forced to personally address the 'rogue vampire,' situation in China. This would allow Chloe to travel to Japan with James and the chameleons, find the Tanaka sisters, and deal with Crane's implant once and for all.

As for Arthur Slayne, he was denied access to the Panopticon and she could keep him on ice indefinitely. He could wait in a vampire proof cell guarded by her pet Red Empire fist team. Once she had enough spare time, she could convert him into a vampire.

A skilled, cunning, and absolutely obedient vampire with Ramp ability and a speed talent. He would make an excellent asset at her side for the coming conflict. When the time came, Arthur Slayne would join his son William at her side. Chloe steepled her fingers in front of her face, her eyes distant. Perhaps she would even acquire Anton Slayne. A controlled ramp berserker vampire would be an awesome weapon.

And she would need weapons – as many as she could get once Crane was out of the way.

Chloe smiled quietly. Crane and Slayne had been defeated and she'd seized the initiative once again. Prompt action was called for before unforeseen events turned the tables once again. She would not waste this opportunity. Her eyes filled with steely determination.

Her time of ascension was approaching.

Chapter Seventeen

"In modern terms, think of it as a hostile corporate takeover. I mean, why have thousands of different companies divvying up the various functions of the economy, duplicating systems like 'human resources,' 'purchasing,' and 'finance,' over and over again. The waste is nauseating. It's so much more efficient to have a single entity that does everything, does it well and does it simply. So, I decided to get rid of all the other gods." – Set, God of Chaos, Trickery, and Disorder

* * *

Nevada, Opposite Arthur Slayne's Private Airport, The Roadhouse, September 11th, 21:20

The ambulance lights strobed red and blue patterns across the parking lot.

Justin Blake lay on an ambulance trolley. Two paramedics worked the trolley into the back of the ambulance. They'd injected him with painkillers and were rushing him to the UMC Trauma Center.

Li held Justin's left hand. She didn't want to let go. Could she trust the people who would be looking after him?

Chiara was providing a rundown of Justin's injuries to an increasingly shocked senior paramedic. He was an older man with a gray mustache. He looked at Justin with wide eyes and remarked, "I haven't seen anything like this since the third Iraq war." He looked back at Chiara and said, "You've done a good job stabilizing him."

Chiara nodded. "Thanks, I did my best."

The senior paramedic flicked a glance at the burning airport. "And nothing to do with that mess over there?"

Chiara shook her head. "No. A motorcycle accident. He fell off and hit a concrete wall."

The paramedics dark-brown eyes narrowed and he made a note on a touchscreen tablet with a stylus. He remarked in a level voice. "Well, he's lucky to be alive." He paused for a moment. "Frankly, with those injuries he should be dead. He must be one tough hombre."

Yes, Li thought. *He was lucky to be alive.*

Justin looked at her and croaked in a hoarse voice, "Li."

Chiara's conversation with the senior medic blended into the background noise. Li clambered into the back of the ambulance. A single determined look was sufficient to stay the two paramedics, although one suggested, "The sooner we get away the better for your friend."

Li glanced back at Chiara and the senior paramedic, and then stated, "You're not leaving yet. I just need a minute."

The talkative medic nodded and continued his work of setting up monitoring of Justin's vital signs.

"Li," Justin said. "Come closer."

Li leaned in, placing her ear next to Justin's mouth. He whispered, pausing briefly between each sentence, "Don't worry. I have a helper on staff at the UMC. She'll fudge the records. I'll be out in a couple of days. I'm going back to New Zealand. I'll get my family involved. It's time the warriors left the islands. We'll be ready when you need us. I'll swing past Australia and see who we can recruit. Don't worry about contacting me. I'll find you when I'm ready. Now ... one more thing. You are the last loremaster. Crane will have picked up the loremaster implants and laptops in Minneapolis, and it's only a matter of time before he cracks the technology and uses it against you."

Li nodded. "I'll watch out for Crane, and for you."

"Now go back to your team. They need you more than I do."

Li leaned in and kissed him gently on the cheek. "Be safe, my big brother. I can't lose you too."

Justin looked at her with eyes filled with warmth, pain and sadness, and whispered, "Look after yourself, little sister."

Li took a big breath and let it out.

The talkative medic looked up in surprise and declared, "His pulse is thirty beats a minute. Blood oxygen is reading one hundred and twenty percent. How does that work?"

The second medic cast a quizzical glance at the monitoring device and suggested, "There must be a fault."

Li looked from one paramedic to the other and back again. "Apart from the injuries. He's kinda off the scale healthy. Just ignore anything strange and give him whatever he asks for."

Both medics nodded, clearly wondering what they had gotten themselves into.

Justin squeezed her hand, and she squeezed back. She took one final look at his battered face and turned away. A moment later she was standing on the parking lot gravel. The senior medic closed the ambulance's rear doors, then joined the driver in the cabin and the ambulance took off, lights strobing and siren wailing.

Jay put his hand on her shoulder and said, "Let's find a quiet table in the roadhouse. We still need a way out of here and quickly." He turned away toward the roadhouse's rear entrance.

Li watched the ambulance turn past the end of the roadhouse. Once the ambulance had disappeared from view, she turned and followed the rest of the Mirovar force team into the roadhouse.

***

Sirens wailed in the distance.

The civilian emergency services from Las Vegas converged on the airport.

Anton looked around at the remnants of the Order of Thoth. They sat at a secluded table near the back of the roadhouse restaurant. They looked like what they were – soldiers fresh from battle. Jay would occasionally roll his left shoulder to ease the stiffness of its recent dislocation. Peter was a mass of bandages over multiple shrapnel wounds. Chiara's left hand and right bicep carried bandaged bullet wounds. Li was largely untouched by combat, but she was battling something within. She was changing before his eyes, becoming distant, and distrustful. Given what he'd found out about himself today – he couldn't blame her. As for himself, Chiara hadn't bothered with sutures for the cut across his throat. She'd steri-stripped the wound closed and declared it would heal by morning. He found it difficult to concentrate on the present moment, his mind constantly going over the battle with Crane and Armitage, and the strange disappearance of his grandfather.

Where the hell was Arthur? One moment he was there, and the next he'd vanished. It was a mystery without any sort of clue as to what had happened to his grandfather.

They'd ditched their guns at the airport, and recovered their motorcycles near the warehouse ruins. They'd managed to get all their bikes and Justin back to the gas station/roadhouse opposite the entrance to the airport. They had called an ambulance service at his request. Their entrance into the roadhouse with their katanas strapped over shoulders or scabbarded at hips, had drawn surprised looks and wary stares but no comment.

Peter had placed an order. Curious but respectful waiting staff had delivered several large trays, leaving the table covered with heaps of bar-b-que chicken, dishes brimming with dipping sauces, slabs of bread and fresh yellow butter, and jugs of cold beer. Peter had stated that fighting always made him hungry and had set to with a will. Jay had asked him what was different from not fighting, and Peter had just grinned at him around a pair of drumsticks.

Anton picked up a jug of cold beer and filled a tall glass. He wanted to break the ice with Li, but wasn't sure where to start. He took a long pull on his beer and then said, "Li."

She looked up from a chicken wing and replied in level tones, "Yes?"

"I haven't thanked you yet."

"For what?"

"For saving my life."

Li looked perplexed for a moment, put her chicken wing down, and asked, "When was that?"

Anton paused, nonplussed. This wasn't going the way he expected. How could she not know? "Ahh… you warned me about the shadowstar attack when I was berserk. Your voice actually canceled out my berserk ramp."

Li shrugged her shoulders and shook her head. "I don't know what you're talking about."

"Oh c'mon, Li. You shouted 'above you' twice." Anton stared hard at her. "It was your voice. I'm certain of it."

Li arched an eyebrow. "It wasn't me." She paused for a moment and put both her hands flat on the table edge. "I guarantee it. No, Anton, something else happened. What? I don't know. After all, I'm not inside your head."

Anton sat back, a sick feeling welling up in his stomach as reality shuddered briefly around him. She couldn't be stooping to gas lighting him? He couldn't imagine Li doing that to him. Reality continued to shift, suddenly lurching and twisting away.

The night sky arched overhead, filled with a wealth of bright stars. Anton's left eye had regenerated and he saw with deep Ramp level clarity, but time traveled at its normal rate – he wasn't ramped. Chloe Armitage sat on a throne constructed of bones atop a hill of bleached skulls. Her right leg crossed over her left, her hands resting on armrests made of femurs. She wore a dark, sleeveless, diaphanous silk gown. Her raven hair lay bound by a delicate golden crown, and fell in lush waves over her pale shoulders. Her face was the one she wore on the fateful night they met at his parent's front doorstep. Stunning, alluring, knowing, with vivid blue eyes and full red lips. She regarded him with calm serenity, as if everything in the universe was in its proper place and proceeding in accordance with her wishes.

To her left and right stood his father and grandfather, dressed in black armor emblazoned with a Red Dragon standard. They looked at him with proud eyes, their fangs hanging over their bottom lips.

Chloe commanded, her voice resplendent with serene invitation, "Rise Anton, rise for me."

Anton discovered he'd been kneeling on one knee. He rose, his black armor bearing the Red Dragon standard on his chest, moving smoothly with him. He lifted the Blue Dragon in proud salute to his noble queen. A queen he could never disobey.

His fangs rested over his bottom lip.

The roadhouse snapped back into reality and Anton gasped with horror. Everyone at the table stared at him. Jay had his hands on the handle of the White Dragon, his face frozen in a grim mask. Peter looked spooked. Li stared at him in puzzlement and Chiara was openly devastated. Anton spread his hands wide and asked, "What the fuck just happened?"

Peter said with wide eyes, "You went still, your right eyelid fluttered like you were dreaming, except you'd ramped. I could feel the heat washing off you. Then you said, 'Rise Anton, rise for me.' And the thing is … your voice. It wasn't your voice. It couldn't possibly be your voice – it was a woman's voice."

Li stabbed a taut finger at Anton. "You just had a vision, what did you see?"

Anton looked at her for a second. It seemed that today was a day for revelations. "It was Chloe Armitage in full vampire queen mode. On a throne of bones on a hill of skulls." Everyone stared at him, except Li, who studied him, listening carefully. "I know this sounds strange … it gets weirder. My dad and my grandfather were there as well, and, get this, they were vampire soldiers wearing armor with a Red Dragon standard on their chests."

"No," Chiara declared, almost choking on the word.

Anton looked at her and said, "Yeah, and it gets worse. I was a vampire too, dressed in the same armor. She was inducting me into her service."

"How did you feel about that?" Li asked.

"I'm horrified."

"No," Li said with a shake of her head. "I mean, how did you feel in the vision."

Anton glanced down at his hands for a moment. How could he ever feel what he'd felt in the vision. He lifted his eyes back to Li's face and stated, "I was proud."

Li tilted her head, and said, "We never talked about the vision you had in England. The one where you identified the Shadowstone van with Peter in it. We should have talked about that. Juliette wanted to discuss it with you but—" her voice trailed off into silence and she frowned for a moment, "she didn't get a chance to."

Peter stated, "You had a vision about me and never told me about it?"

Anton looked at him and said with a note of chagrin in his voice, "Sorry, Pete, I should have mentioned it. I kinda thought I might be going mad or something, and then other things kept happening. I know, I should've mentioned it before now."

Li continued. "It's how we found you Peter. I don't believe we would have rescued you without it."

"Oh," Peter said, looking at Anton with a puzzled expression on his face. He glanced back at Li and asked, "So, it was helpful, wasn't it? What the hell is really going on here?"

Li frowned for a moment. "You're right Peter, it was helpful." She looked at Anton and asked, "Give us a rundown of all your visions."

Anton took a deep breath and sighed. "Okay, the first one was in a homeless shelter the night Armitage murdered my mother. Armitage again, dressed in next to nothing and wearing a crown. The second was on the Boston docks, for just a moment. Again, it was her, beckoning to me. Then I had a weird, super-vivid dream on the way to the Maine safe house of giant flying leeches farming—"

Peter said, "Yeah, I remember when you woke up from that. You were pretty frightened by what you saw."

"Yeah, I was. Then there was nothing until England, and then another gap to earlier tonight in the maze."

"You had two today?" Li asked.

Anton nodded.

"What was the first one about?"

"Same gig as the rest. Armitage as queen, but this time she was monstrous, transformed into something from a horror movie. Insane demonic looking vampires surrounded her, but she had control of them, and she wanted me for herself. It was how I knew she was in the maze with us. It was how I knew to look for her."

Li nodded. "Then there was that moment when Jon Thunder-Axe summoned his Metaframe sorcery, and it smashed you but didn't affect anyone else. And another thing that stands out is that your first vision happened before my father initiated you into the Ramp. So, none of this is related to the Ramp but the Metaframe is the key. Back before the conclave in Minneapolis, Jon pretty much stated the Metaframe is some sort of divine prison. And Arthur told me in the main server room that the gods can appear in visions and dreams." She shook her head with realization. "This all fits together now. The gods are in the Metaframe. They are like trapped ghosts. They can only communicate through visions and dreams."

A shiver crawled up Anton's back.

Li looked hard at Anton. "Lucky for you, someone's watching out for you. Everything you've seen has been a warning."

Jay looked at Anton with wary eyes. "One of the gods doesn't want Armitage to win and they don't want you in her service."

"Your berserker talent has been revealed," Li said, "you're a weapon that must not fall into Crane or Armitage's hands."

"I'm good with that," Anton declared. "The last thing I want to do is serve Armitage."

He couldn't imagine a fate worse than becoming a vampire slave.

* * *

A single tear tracked its way down Chiara's left cheek. She brushed another tear away from her right cheek.

She swallowed silently, trying to clear her throat. She was choking on the truth. The need had been building since the night on the cliff-edge overlooking the town of Whitby. The night Juliette and Yvette had died at the hand of Chloe Armitage. A hand guided to their hearts by her words. The guilt had overwhelmed her. She had sought the release of suicide, attempting to throw herself over the cliff and onto the rocks below. Let the icy waters of the North Sea take her body into oblivion.

Anton had pulled her back from the edge. He'd saved her life and thrown her a lifeline of shared purpose, but he'd been unable to save her soul. The wounds ran deep – she'd been trained from before she could remember to live a lie. The need to replace the lie with a real life had crystallized in the nemesis tower when she'd owned her true heritage.

She was not Chiara Romano; she was no longer al Ghurab. She had to be her true self or become nothing.

Jay looked along the table at her, frowned warily and asked, "Chiara, are you okay?"

She wiped the last tear away and subdued her emotions. Battle-trained reflexes could not be stilled as easily; she assessed the space around her in an instant. The end of the table to her right was empty – Francis would have sat there if he'd been alive. Li sat opposite her. Anton was to her left and Peter sat opposite him. Jay sat on Peter's right, and Anton's left at the other end of the table. Everyone had placed their swords at their feet.

Chiara let go the idea of escape, there was no running from the truth. There was only life and death, honor and shame, and truth and lies. She would wake to the dawn tomorrow true to herself or she would be dead. There were no other options worthy of a princess of the Red Empire. She pushed her chair back, stood up, and glanced around the team. She pulled her remaining silver-laced dagger from a holster on her left calf and walked behind Anton to stand before Jay.

She put the razor-sharp killing blade on the table, with the handle next to Jay's right hand.

Jay looked at the blade gleaming brightly beneath the lights and then frowned at Chiara. "What's that for?"

"You might need it."

Jay froze, a haunted look ghosting across his face. He must've guessed what she was about to say. He just needed to hear it before acting. She had wronged him terribly. If he needed to kill her, she would not resist. Better death, than a life of being nothing.

The table hushed, even the rest of the roadhouse seemed to pause for breath. Chiara declared, "I have something to say."

"Yes," Jay remarked quietly, his gaze was glacial.

"I am Chiara Morte, true daughter of Dalien Morte – the Red Ghost, princess of the Red Empire, initiate of the third rank, formerly known as al Ghurab, the Raven, I was the—"

Jay half rose, picking up the silver-laced dagger and slashing it in a horizontal silver blur toward Chiara's throat.

She didn't flinch.

The team burst into motion. Jay had ramped first, he had the initiative, he was perfectly positioned to kill her. No one could save her life – except Anton. He blurred across Chiara from right to left. His left-hand struck Jay's wrist from below, sending his slash a foot higher. Anton lunged forward over the table, tackling Jay, lifting him free of his chair, and pinning him against the rear wall. The knife flew from Jay's grasp and skittered over the polished wooden floor.

"For fuck's sake!" Jay shouted past Anton's right ear. "Get out of the way!"

Anton held his grip and declared in adamantine tones, "I'm not letting you kill her."

"Of course not, you're too busy fucking her," Jay paused and grimaced with hate. "Or is that she's fucking you! Eh! She's a fucking spy, she knows how to lie. She's got you right where she wants you and you have no idea what the hell is going on – as usual."

Peter intervened, and pushed Jay and Anton apart, and said gruffly, "No weapons, I can't tolerate anyone else dying today."

Jay stood against the wall and panted for a moment. He locked a gaze of unadulterated hatred on Chiara and stated, "As for that creature; get her out of my sight."

Anton's hand landed on the base of Chiara's spine, and he loomed at her left shoulder. "She's not going anywhere. We need her with us."

Jay snapped, "You already knew, and you kept it secret, didn't you?"

"Yes, I knew," Anton replied. "We are too few to throw away good fighters."

"You can go too. Both of you are liars. This is my team and you can fuck off!"

"We're not going anywhere," Anton declared, an edge of steel in his voice.

Jay looked hard at Peter and Li. "And what about you two. Have you known all along?"

Peter shrugged his heavy shoulders and stated, "I always knew it wasn't me."

"I found out today," Li replied. "Her DNA analysis was in the Panopticon data, along with her parent's identities."

Jay grunted with disgust. "Fucking lies and betrayal. I'm wasting my time here." He retrieved the White Dragon from the floor. He looked at Peter and Li, and ignored Anton and Chiara, and declared, "Anyone who wants to work with me to rebuild a new team can come with me." He pushed past Anton and strode for the door into the parking lot behind the building.

Peter declared, "Anton, Chiara, I'm with you. We make too good a team to break up. Chiara, I always knew it had to be you, but I know you never intended for Juliette and Yvette to die. Its war, shit happens. Frankly, given the amount of ordnance I throw around, it's a miracle I haven't killed all of us by now."

Li frowned and went after Jay. She left the Green Dragon beneath the table; she must be coming back for it … at least.

Chiara blinked, and turned in toward Anton's shoulder. He put his powerful arms around her and held her close. The Mirovar force team was more wreckage littering her wake. The path of truth was not an easy one to walk. She lifted her face and whispered, "I love you."

Anton's arms tightened protectively around her. A maelstrom of emotions whirled within her soul; remorse and sadness for Francis, a cold fury for her father, a loyal admiration for Peter and Li, and regret for the rift with Jay. The storm ebbed and flowed within, threatening to cast her sanity away.

She clung to Anton; he was her rock. Her love for him a shining light within the storm.

* * *

Jay mounted his motorcycle in the parking lot behind the roadhouse.

Li strode over to him. He looked up and implored, "Come with me."

She shook her head. Since her encounter with the quantum processors of the Panopticon she knew too much. Her future was with Peter, Anton and Chiara. "No, I belong somewhere else."

Jay scowled, his lips pressing into a thin line.

"We never debriefed," Li suggested, "What you need to know is that the mission was a bust. The Panopticon is due to be replaced in a month's time by a more advanced system. Arthur Slayne bet it all on killing Crane and Armitage, and lost."

Jay shook his head, grinding his teeth in frustration. "What a fucking mess. Look … Li, are you sure you won't come with me? I'm going to Salt Lake City, there are Shadowstone operatives there that know they have been serving vampires. I'm sure I can find some who are looking for an opportunity to strike back against the lies and betrayal. I'll use the pressure point technique to activate their Ramp capability. Some will survive, and I will train them hard. I'll have a new team in three months' time."

Li arched an eyebrow. Jay had a plan and it could work, but she shook her head once and replied, "Yes. I'm absolutely sure."

"If ever you change your mind, you're always welcome."

Li nodded. "I understand." She watched him in silence. Jay fired up his motorcycle and rolled it back a few feet. He dragged on the throttle, whipping away in a roar and a flurry of stones.

Li sighed. Hundreds of vampires couldn't kill the Mirovar force team but the truth had proved deadly. She pivoted, her feet crunching on the parking lot gravel. She returned to the road house interior. Chiara was about to make an offer and she needed to hear it. Chiara was in a position to change the fate of the world. A world that no longer held the Mirovar force team.

Whether it would be for better or worse remained to be seen.

* * *

A hubbub of noise filled the roadhouse.

Emergency services personnel seeking drinks and snacks crowded the main room. The authorities had placed a quarantine cordon around Arthur's airport. The rumors were flying thick and fast. Ranging from terrorist attack, to natural disaster, to industrial accident. The team overheard one young policeman remark knowingly to his partner that this was the beginning of an alien invasion.

Peter, Li, Anton and Chiara had retreated to a booth in a rear corner of the restaurant. Their swords hidden beneath the table. Mugs of coffee held within their hands. They had mostly sat in stunned silence. The Mirovar force team had ended in anger and hatred. What did that bode for the future? *Nothing good*, Chiara thought.

Li leaned forward and broke the silence. "There are things you all need to know."

"Like what?" Anton asked.

"Well," Li said, then commenced to give a quiet briefing of what she had discovered about the replacement Panopticon while connected with the Panopticon's quantum processors.

"Bummer," Peter remarked after Li finished speaking. A rare frown creasing his forehead.

Anton shook his head disconsolately. "All of that for nothing."

Chiara was willing to put the whole day behind her. Her old life was over. As shocked as she was at Francis' death and the destruction of the Mirovar force team, she was giddy with relief, and buoyed by a pervasive sense of freedom and opportunity. Her new life was beginning here and now.

Li looked to Chiara and asked, "What do you think?"

Chiara did a double take. Li almost never asked her for her point of view on anything. She glanced at Peter, Anton and then back to Li and suggested, "We could seek sanctuary with the Red Empire. They have their main base under the Mount Scopus Museum."

Li frowned for a moment, then said to Chiara, "Armitage destroyed that base on the twenty-fourth of August. The details were in the Panopticon."

Chiara felt sick to her stomach. How could this have happened? This was on her father. Armitage could not have found out where the Jerusalem citadel was without his alliance with her. She stated, "There is a place called Matahat al Diydan. We can meet my father there."

"Would they have us?" Anton asked.

"Without a doubt," Chiara enthused. "We're elite. Look at what we've survived." She shrugged. "And my father is the Red Ghost. He will want me back now my original mission has been rendered a moot point."

"What was your original mission?" Peter asked.

"Rise to the top of the Order of Thoth as my father's agent."

Peter laughed, then shook his head soberly. "No shortage of ambition then."

"To be honest," Chiara declared, "I'm glad it's over."

"Even though it took the Order being destroyed for that to happen?" Li asked.

"That part is terrible; I never sought that outcome."

Silence fell over the table for a moment. Chiara wondered if they would accept her proposal. She didn't want to have to choose between staying with Anton or delivering her father to justice.

Anton rubbed his chin and asked, "So, are we doing this or not?" he looked at Li. "There's no guarantee you can haze the Panopticon replacement. We've got a month before the Vampire Dominion is going to try and hound us out into the open with their new surveillance system and hammer us into the ground. We need a solution in place before then."

Chiara reached over and grasped Li's shoulder. "You have so much to offer my father. We can use your capabilities to reshape the Red Empire's strategy. Imagine five hundred plus Ramp warriors responding to your loremaster oversight. This is the true union of the Ramp master factions that could make a difference against the vampires."

"I'm warming to this idea," Peter said.

Li looked at Chiara and conceded, "I agree, we have to try this path. We can't stand alone for very long."

"Before you commit to a decision on this," Chiara advised. "You must all understand something." Peter, Anton and Li regarded her with curious eyes. "My father has strayed far from the Way, and must be corrected. He has treated with the vampires, cut deals and sent our warriors to serve Armitage. This is unforgivable. We must tread warily. There is no guarantee he will honor our laws."

Anton asked, "What do you mean by 'corrected?'"

Chiara looked hard at Anton; her heart filled with resolve. "There is only one punishment that fits the crime – and that is death. I must pursue my father for his crimes, but first we need to secure our strength against the vampires."

"Right," Peter stated dryly, "So, we're going to ally ourselves with a man who has betrayed his own faith, laws, and people, and we're doing this because it's our best option?"

Anton nodded. "It sounds like it."

Li nodded. "It's less risky than attempting to go it alone."

"Well, count me in," Peter declared dryly. "I could use a less risky option."

Anton asked, "And when your father is dead, who replaces him?"

Chiara lifted her head. "If he dies by my hand under the rules of challenge, then I will succeed him."

Anton's eyes widened, and he said, "Well, that's an interesting rule."

"So, we add 'palace coup,' to the plan." Peter stated.

Li sighed; her eyes filled with something much older than her years. "Yes, we do."

Chiara stated quietly, "There is one more thing we should do before we go." She faced Li and asked, "Can you do a loremaster vision for us?"

Peter and Anton looked expectantly at Li.

Li glanced around the team, pursed her lips, then nodded. "I will do what I have to do."

Chiara believed it would be enough. Li was a phenomenon. With Li's help she could take the Red Empire away from her father and deliver him to justice. She would achieve his original goal of uniting the Ramp masters, but he would not be alive to see it.

* * *

Li remembered Patrick Wichowski's advice and opened her loremaster laptop.

He'd said, *'Find something you feel really safe with or someone you have a very strong love for. Find, or if need be, create a place of security, love and joy. Something strong you can rest in. Find that place of serenity and start from there.'*

How was she going to be able to do that after the shocking losses of this day? Li shivered once, then stilled herself to a deep calm. She slipped into her Ramp like an Olympic diver winning gold with a splashless dive. She plumbed the depths of her silence, her loremaster ability blooming within her. Her implant warmed within her right forearm completing the links between her mind and the world's networks.

Everyone in the roadhouse vanished and the shadow was waiting. The darkness congealed into the shape of her dead brother Qiang, and he sat opposite Li in the booth.

She raised her defense of golden flame. Shimmering light bloomed around her, pushing the shadows back.

The Qiang-thing grinned and declared, "You already know that won't work. I thought you were smarter than that." Its left hand flashed across the table and gripped her right wrist. Her golden light flashed once and died. The lights within the roadhouse dimmed and the shadows loomed around her.

Li pulled back with all her strength. Her wrist remained locked within its grasp. The Qiang-thing leaned forward, leering at her with an ancient lust. "Now let me show you how this is really done."

Cold tendrils of pure darkness emerged from his hand and ripped into her flesh, anchoring her right hand to the table. The darkness rushed up her arm like a thousand cold knives, great shadows advancing behind them, blotting out all light.

Li withdrew deep within herself, seeking the sanctuary Patrick had spoken of. The loremaster vision dimmed and blurred. She was freezing, her right arm becoming numb and unresponsive. She searched, and searched again.

Living memories flashed through Li's soul. Her brother smiling gently while he sutured a training cut on her arm. Her own heart glowed with adoration and not a little hero worship of her older brother. He'd finished the sutures and made some quip about her being clumsy but he'd done it in a way that made them both chuckle. Qi could always make her laugh.

Somewhere distant from her deepest self the growing darkness shuddered.

Her mother hugged her; her eyes moist as she released her to go with the other children for her first day at school. Her heart filled with the excitement and enthusiasm of a five-year-old, surrounded by her mother's unconditional love. A love that never wavered.

The darkness intensified, a cold wave claimed her right shoulder – or did it?

Her father cradled her while she sobbed her heart out on his shoulder after her mothers and Qiang's funeral. Her father had managed to share with her his strength while dealing with the loss of his beloved wife and son. Her father looking at her with moist eyes filled with love and pride the day she'd mastered the twenty-one hidden deceptions. He said to her in a voice gruff with feeling, "You have learned everything I can teach you. Your only limits now are what you impose upon yourself." Him hugging her immediately after saying that, his heart beating warm and true next to hers.

She surfaced back into the visionary roadhouse.

The Qiang-thing recoiled from her, hissing like a snake.

Something came with her from her deepest self. A warm presence enveloped her, wrapping her in a shield of unconditional love. A pair of hands rested lightly upon her shoulders and her father's voice whispered in her ears, "You are the daughter of dragons."

Nothing more needed to be said. Li found her center. Light bloomed, a white-gold flame erupting from a fathomless place deep within her, stretching out in an instant, evaporating the surrounding shadows, banishing all fear. The roadhouse vanished, replaced with an open field beneath a bright sun and an azure sky.

The Qiang-thing snarled, retreating a step backward, its hands twisting into claws.

Li raised the Green Dragon – a halo of golden flame wreathed its magnificent blade. Twin legacies entwined, blademaster, loremaster, both and more, and declared in a voice resonating with more than human power, "Leave, you have no place here anymore."

The Qiang-thing's skin melted from its face, revealing dark scales, and tawny eyes with vertical slit pupils. Its mouth gaped open and it laughed past rows of long fangs, a cold braying noise cutting through the air for a moment – and then fading away.

Li had found her center in the enduring love of her family. As for Set, the Shadow, or the Qiang-thing – whatever form it may take – their war was not over. She was sure it had only just begun. As for the requested loremaster vision, she did what she could, and emerged back into the real roadhouse. She blinked, took a deep breath and let it out slowly and then declared with quiet certainty, "Chiara's proposal holds great danger for us all, but it offers us the greatest benefit too. I believe we should do it. I believe we must do it."

The four of them looked at each other for a long moment. Anton broke the silence. "Let's get moving before the vampires reorganize."

Li paused as the others rose from their seats. She'd picked up a hard, crystalline truth within her loremaster vision. A truth filtered from the legacy of her time connected to the Panopticon quantum processors. Two of their number would die soon. Which two remained hidden from her but she had to press on – giving up would give victory to Set and his agents. She rose and followed a step behind the rest, leaving the booth for the parking lot behind the roadhouse.

It was time to leave the United States.

* * *

The sounds of battle were long gone.

Tamsah al Ramil stood in the shadows behind the roadhouse parking lot. His back against a tree, blending in perfectly with his surroundings. He'd practiced sound suppression; lowering his breathing, quietening his heart beat, and standing unnaturally still.

He had witnessed the departure of Justin Blake in an ambulance, and everything that had passed in the roadhouse followed by the rage-filled departure of Jay Creeley. The Mirovar force team was gone, and the four youngest members stood alone against the might of the Vampire Dominion. Chiara Morte had revealed herself and proposed a plan to ally with the Red Empire. They had emerged from the rear of the roadhouse and mounted their motorcycles. They had just left, heading for the ancient Red Empire citadel of Matahat al Diydan in the Caucasus Mountains.

As a princess of the Red Empire, Chiara Morte would be welcomed home. As for the others, who could say what the Red Ghost would decide. It was imperative he found a way to re-enter Matahat al Diydan so he could continue to protect the truth speaker.

There was also the not insignificant matter of accounting for the Red Ghost's perfidious behavior in selling two fist teams into the service of Chloe Armitage. If there was anything that Tamsah believed in, it was justice. Perhaps an opportunity would arise to hold the Red Ghost accountable for his actions while protecting the truth speaker. He would remain watchful and alert, ever ready to seize the moment if such a circumstance was to arise.

Footsteps approached him from behind and to his right. Two vampires from the recent battle at the airport stepped through the shadows and halted before the fence surrounding the parking lot.

He watched them for a brief moment before familiarity triggered a memory. These were two of the vampires from the original mob in the southern-most hangar. The two who had discussed fornicating with the dead bodies of the Mirovar force team. The thought of these two rutting over the bloody corpse of the truth speaker set a flame alight behind his eyes.

Tamsah had made a promise to himself in the hangar, and providence had gifted him the opportunity to fulfill it. He pounced like a jungle cat. With bare hands and feet conditioned by more than three decades of daily training in Red Empire Ninjitsu. He delivered his prey to the dirt and dust of the ground, rendering them unconscious, beaten senseless in less than a second.

He stripped the vampire closest in size to himself of his clothes. He needed something to wear and beggars couldn't be choosers. He sat the unconscious vampires up against the fence, separating them by five feet and a steel fence post.

Tamsah lifted the fence wire, cutting four strands free with a dagger. He took the left hand of the left-side vampire and tied it to the post with a strand of wire. He took the right hand of the right-side vampire and did the same.

With his third strand of wire, he tied an artful knot that connected the index finger of each vampire's restrained hand to the pull ring of his last white phosphorous grenade. With his final wire he suspended the grenade from the fence post.

Whichever vampire untwisted the restraint on their hand and undid the connection to their finger first could get away while the grenade dropped to the ground and the ring pulled free detonating it next to the other vampire. He stood, stepped backward and waited for them to wake up.

Within a minute, the first one roused and almost set off the grenade before he realized his predicament.

Tamsah frowned at the long string of swearing the young vampire indulged in. By the time the first vampire quieted, the second vampire was blinking, his gaze jumping from Tamsah to the grenade and back again like a metronome.

"What the hell is this?" the first vampire asked.

Tamsah stated calmly, like a teacher instructing an unruly student, "Whoever gets free first has the best chance of getting away, the other one will burn. Of course, another option would be to gnaw your own hands off – if you can do that without twitching. I'd imagine they would grow back in time. But you need to make a decision quickly, after all, the sun will rise soon enough."

He failed to mention that he'd dialed the grenade's fuse down to a tenth of a second. He moved away quickly; he anticipated it would not take long before one betrayed the other.

At twenty yards distance, the grenade detonated behind him. Tamsah whirled, his eyes tightened with grim satisfaction, a merciless smile curling the edges of his lips. Two forms twisted and screamed for release within pillars of white flame. They fell writhing to the ground, limbs spasming like puppets played with by a mad child. One uttered a final screech while the other thumped the ground with melted fists before moaning a gasping death rattle.

The two vampires stilled while bright flames consumed their bodies. The only sounds left were the blistering pops of flesh burning beyond recognition.

Tamsah nodded once and turned on his way. It was essential to keep his promises, even to himself, such was the integrity demanded by the Way of the Faithful.

Now it was time to return to Matahat al Diydan, the ancient home of the Red Empire. His former colleagues would not welcome him, but the truth speaker was going there and he would follow.

As he must.

* * *

Trust was little more than a fragile web people wrapped around their hopes and dreams.

Cornelius vowed to eliminate trust from his life. He couldn't afford it. The human failing had cost him too much already. He stared at the paralyzed form of Tania Morte lying naked and flat on an examination table. He was not going to take any chances with her as a vampire test subject for the loremaster implant. The silver net lying across her would keep her still, unresponsive, but alert. His staff would closely monitor her as they inserted the implant into her forearm, and activated the laptop. He would learn everything he needed to know to ensure the safe insertion of a loremaster implant into a vampire, and then he would eliminate her. It would be safest not to have another loremaster vampire in existence.

He had come to a decision during the flight from Nevada to New York City. He'd dropped Armitage at his old citadel, and refueled the shadowstar drone. He'd then flown solo out to a lonely island off the New England coast. An island hiding a single prisoner; Tania Morte, wife of Dalien Morte, mother of Chiara Morte. Taken fifteen years ago from the battlefield and converted into a vampire by himself. He'd picked her up from her island prison and taken her back to research facility number one in Queens, New York.

Once this test had proven the loremaster technology was safe to use on a vampire, he'd use it on the only person he could trust – himself. He would ally the Order loremaster technology with his sorcerous precognitive powers to produce a superior capability for insight into the future. This would give him the edge he needed to outwit his enemies.

There would be no more death traps like Slayne's fake Panopticon P-Case in his future. As for the Slaynes, they'd vanished, and with them the real Panopticon P-Case. He'd have to assume that Arthur Slayne would access the Panopticon within the near future. The clock was ticking down to the day the Panopticon was deployed against him. His most recent precognitive vision conducted on the flight from Nevada had revealed the risk from Arthur Slayne had evaporated. The risk from the younger Slayne was still present, but pushed back into the future. The risk from the Red Empire fist team making its way across the Atlantic barely existed now that he'd initiated the evacuation of his Manhattan citadel. What loomed large within his threat matrix was Mekra. He would have to either manage or destroy her.

He would not kill her lightly, her blood was too valuable to him, but if events warranted it, he would destroy her without mercy or regret.

Cornelius glanced to his left. The lead scientist stood beside him, tall, cadaverous, his dark hair slicked back with 1920s style hair cream. Cornelius commanded, "Source a supply of vampire ready implant sheaths from our production facility in Tokyo."

The lead scientist's eyes widened, and his skin paled past his usual gray. "You haven't seen my latest report?"

"No," Cornelius replied, his eyes narrowing. The vampire had the look of a rabbit caught in the glare of a vehicle's headlights. A look that bordered on shameful for a vampire. Still, he'd kept the man in his employ for his inquisitive and ordered mind, not for his courage. He braced himself for more bad news.

"Unfortunately, my liege, our capacity to source additional implant sheaths suitable for a vampire has been curtailed. All the data for the sheaths was destroyed and the lead scientist, a human named Hana Tanaka has disappeared."

Cornelius blinked and sighed. The situation was regrettable, but regrets would not serve him. He would have to adapt.

The lead scientist leered, or was it a smile. Cornelius was never sure with him. The man declared with avid enthusiasm, "There is one sheath we could use. The one housing an implant next to your heart. We could remove it and re-purpose it to the loremaster technology."

"What!" Cornelius snapped. "And allow Armitage to go free. I think not. No," he paused for a moment, his mind racing, "there is another source of vampire implant sheaths we could use."

The lead scientist looked at him expectantly.

Cornelius commanded, "Continue the work here and keep me informed of progress on a nightly basis. That is all." He turned away from the cadaverous man. It was time to return to the hidden fortress of the Obsidian Claw Ninja clan. The Mekrarian vampires he'd killed in the courtyard would have withered to dust in the sunlight. Their implants would remain on the flagstones. He could retrieve them all.

Cornelius strode down the empty corridor of research facility number one's lowest level, his boots echoing off the cold, polished concrete floor. He would tell no one of his mission to Japan.

He would maintain his secrets, and cloaked by secrecy he would grow his power once again.

* * *

The metropolis of New York City lay before her.

Chloe stood on her balcony, freshly showered and dressed in a black silk bathrobe. A fine Japanese dragon print dominated by red and gold threads rose over her breasts. She gazed at the full moon sailing across a velvet sky laced with stars. An ideal moon to hunt by. But hunting was not on her mind, a greater need held her attention. The need to be free of Crane's rule burned like a hot coal within her soul. She whispered fervently to herself, "I value liberty above all else. Without liberty, no other value can be realized."

How could she achieve anything of real value whilst crouched on one knee to another?

Chloe took a breath, let it out slowly, and calmed herself. James had provided a report five minutes ago at three in the morning. He'd been tracking Crane's command shadowstar drone via the tag and half a dozen co-opted military satellites.

After dropping Chloe off for a healing blood feast at his citadel, Crane had flown to a remote island off the New England coast. He'd only stayed minutes. Long enough to pick up a passenger. He'd then traveled back to the hidden research facility in Queens discovered by James. The same one Clayton Maze had taken the Order dead to after the battle at the conclave hall. She had no doubt the Queens research facility was Crane's loremaster technology research lab. His passenger would be a vampire with Ramp ability – his only available test subject. Given Haras, and herself were the only other options, the only feasible test candidate was the missing wife of Dalien Morte.

This was a step forward for Chloe's plans. Tania Morte would be a key bargaining piece when it came time to negotiate with Dalien Morte. There had to be a new alliance between them, one that would transform the Red Empire into a tool of her bidding. Tania Morte would be the bait she could use to draw Dalien Morte into a trap he could not escape. Human bait, no longer a vampire once she had secured the 'vampire cure,' from the Tanaka sisters.

She would collect all the Morte's and the Red Empire. She had collected Arthur, she would collect others, Anton, Li, Peter, and of course Chiara would make worthy additions to her list of assets. In the end she would need them all, and she must act quickly. The window of opportunity would inevitably close.

Her mind turned to deeper subjects. Events with low probability become certainties over long enough time frames. It was inevitable that the forces she'd witnessed in the forests of southern Germany in the dying days of the second world war would return. She must be ready; she would build an unstoppable vampire army and then make a pre-emptive strike.

If need be, she'd conquer hell itself to preserve her world. But first, she needed unfettered access to the Metaframe with the Key of Ahknaton. The few operated dominion over the many with the tools of bribery, deception and violence. They'd long exploited the blunt instruments of desire, credulity, fear and conformity. Their methods borne from a simple fact – no one could guarantee obedience – people could always disobey. But what if obedience was a necessity, as necessary as an apple falling from a tree and just as natural.

In such a world, the use of bribery, deception and violence, and exploitation of human frailty would be obsolete, and wasn't that a good thing?

Chloe stared into the darkness between the stars. She would never demand more obedience than was strictly necessary, not in the world she would create. She expanded her senses to their vampiric maximums, drinking in the glorious majesty of the night sky, and dreamed of the reality she hoped to realize.

One day she would confront the old gods. She had seen how they had manifested beneath the forests of southern Germany in 1945. She had seen something of what they were and was building toward the day she would engage them in mortal combat.

Terror and awe always attended the boldest ambitions.

Her heart soared with joy within the darkness.

* * *

The morning sun rested just below the horizon, pre-dawn light glowing softly off the granite rock face over the cave mouth.

Arthur issued the final command to ground drone #500 and it rolled off into the shadows of the cave complex. The drone faded into the dark. The dark faded into the mountain. The mountain grayed out and faded away too.

His eyes flickered open, the gray of the mountain in his dream spreading out to cover ceiling, walls and floor. A thudding head-ache, throbbed through his skull. It would wear off once he'd rehydrated. He was fully aware of the effects of a Shadowstone sleeper dart – he'd shot himself twice, once to experience the effects and the second time to confirm the process.

Arthur opened his eyes wider, rubbed his forehead and looked around. He was in a twenty-foot by twenty-foot cell carved out of rock. Crisscrossed bars as thick as his wrist and a door with a vault-like lock dominated one wall. There was a low bed carved from the rock. It sported a mattress, a pillow and a single gray blanket. There was a half-gallon plastic bottle of water and, wonder of wonders, a slops bucket.

"No plumbing, brilliant," he said quietly. He opened the plastic water bottle and drank freely from it. If his captors wanted him dead, he'd be dead. He took the bottle with him and sat down on the bed. He took another long slug of water and studied the space beyond the bars. There was a corridor of sorts, perhaps ten feet by ten feet running beyond what he could see to his left. To his right it ended in a wall flush with his cell. They had put him in the cell furthest from the entrance. There were strip lights in the corridor, but none in the cell, leaving the chamber stippled with spears of light and shadow.

He sniffed. The air was cool, clean and fresh. He scanned the ceiling. There was a small three-inch-wide vent in the left rear corner. He put his hand near it, and discovered a gentle and constant breeze flowing through it.

Arthur sat back on the bed, resting his head against the cool stone. His headache was easing. The Ramp healing effects were working overtime breaking down the aftereffects of the sleeper dart. A regular person would forget the previous twenty-four hours and be unconscious for twenty-four hours, functionally losing two days. The sleeper drug still had a potent impact on Ramp masters. It would wipe out at least twelve to fifteen hours of memory, and he would've slept for another twelve.

What was his last memory? He wracked his brain. He was crystal clear about sending the last drone into the cave complex to mine the river system with explosives. He had a range of fuzzy memories that slipped and slided away whenever he tried to grasp them. It seemed that he'd met up with the Mirovar force team, and met Anton again. His heart swelled with pride with the memory. The kid had punched him hard in the mouth as soon as he could. Arthur grinned, what wasn't there to like about that? They'd talked on the way to the caves, and the kid had unburdened himself about something – whatever it was, it was like trying to hold onto fog to remember it. The last memory he had was leading the team into the caves. Then it was a blank, he had no idea who had shot him, who had caught him, where he was now, and only a rough idea of the time. It would be late Monday morning on the twelfth of September.

Arthur considered his options. The first thing to do was throw off the effects of the sleeper dart and restore his health. He settled onto the floor in a cross-legged pose and dropped into silence without ramping. He modified his breathing and activated deep controls over his parasympathetic nervous system. He stilled further, while cellular engines kicked into high gear and accelerated the elimination of toxins from his body.

A slight scuffing sound reached his ears. He emerged from his meditation and glanced through the bars. There were two guards in Red Empire robes, twin heavy-bladed swords at their waists. He puffed out a breath of air. If the Red Empire held him captive, then something must have gone drastically wrong with his whole-self's plan – whatever that was going to be in the end?

The taller one suggested, "Perhaps he can spend his time meditating on accepting his fate."

The other guard stroked his chin through his thick beard. "He might even find some, 'inner peace.'"

Arthur's gaze lashed the guards and he snapped, "Acceptance is often portrayed as gentle, easy, a simple 'letting it all go,' and achieving," he drawled the next two words, "'inner peace.' This is naive, superficial crap. Real acceptance is forged like fine steel. If you have not confronted true horrors, understood evil, suffered hopelessness and despair, found faith, and made yourself completely accountable for your own choices, actions and outcomes, then I can guarantee that any acceptance you pretend to have will be as brittle and temporary as a snowball in the middle of summer."

The taller of the two guards approached the bars, but halted just out of reach. He stared at Arthur for a long moment and then inquired quietly, "Have you studied the Way?"

Arthur rested his hands on his knees, lifted his eyebrows and studied the guards. "What do you think?"

The guards stared at him briefly. The taller one smiled slightly and said, "Enjoy the peace and quiet. You're going to get a lot of it."

The other guard grinned and they sauntered down the corridor.

Arthur frowned; his lips pressed together. He put the palms of his hands against his temples and squeezed his eyes shut.

The voices were back, whispering in the dark.

Epilogue

"From bitter experience, I beg you to never make a weapon that can think for itself." – Falsely attributed to Baron Victor von Frankenstein.

* * *

United States, The East Coast Hub, September 12th, 11:10

A geodesic sphere rose forty yards above the tiled floor. Each node of the sphere's surface held a quantum processor pointing into the sphere. The processors maintained a lattice of bright white light within the center of the sphere.

Heavy cables and thick pipes snaked over the sphere, delivering power and cooling in equal measure. The whole stood housed in an underground hangar that stretched for a thousand yards in either direction with a roof two-hundred yards above the floor. At each end, a fourth generation, sodium-cooled fast nuclear reactor hummed, providing the electrical lifeblood of the East Coast Hub. The quantum processor sphere rested on a heavy cradle in the middle of the floor space, surrounded by concentric rings of liquid-cooled supercomputers and storage arrays stretching out to the walls.

The architect had insisted on the construction of a viewing platform exactly half way up the side of the sphere. He stood there now, dressed against the deep chill, frozen in rapt attention. His eyes shielded with thick welder's goggles. He stared into the bright core at the center of the sphere. He saw something only he could recognize. Lesser minds were oblivious to her presence. The living light writhed and shifted, filling his heart with adoration and awe.

She was asleep. She needed to sleep to grow. In a few short weeks she would wake up. He awaited the birth of a god.

He waited for Rosie.

The End

The story will continue with the next instalment of The Metaframe War.

"The Key of Ahknaton"

THE MIROVAR FORCE TEAM HAS BEEN SHATTERED!

Anton Slayne and his friends travel to the fabled fortress of Matahat al Diydan to seek sanctuary at the hand of an old enemy – the Red Ghost – ruler of the Red Empire.

Cornelius Crane and his rebellious general, Chloe Armitage, confront the horror of Mekra's machinations on the blood-soaked streets of Romania. He carries the mystical Key of Ahknaton upon his person. The Metaframe waits to be used, its reality shifting powers both feared and desired by all who know of it.

The Key can open any door and give birth to any reality. Whoever uses it first could win or lose everything – only one thing is certain.

CHAOS WILL RISE

www.ingramcontent.com/pod-product-compliance
Lightning Source LLC
LaVergne TN
LVHW050928080826
845145LV00001B/258

* 9 7 8 0 9 9 4 5 9 5 2 9 4 *